"I've waited so long for you, my love," Clay said.

The words were what made Nicole awaken. They were intimate words of love meant for another woman. She could believe the caresses that made her mind go blank were hers, but those words belonged to another.

"Clay," she said quietly.

"Yes, love," he answered as he kissed the soft skin at the side of her throat. It seemed so natural to pull him closer to her. It flashed through her mind that she should let him find out the truth in the morning . . .

"Clay, I'm not Bianca. I'm Nicole . . ."

She felt his body stiffen. He stared at her in the darkness. Suddenly he was out of the low bunkbed. His mouth, which she knew to be soft, was drawn in a tight, angry line. His jaw was strong, hard, and the muscles were working now.

"All right," he demanded. "Just who the hell are you, and where is my wife?"

JUDE DEVERAUX . . . AMERICA'S QUEEN OF HISTORICAL ROMANCE

Books by Jude Deveraux

The Velvet Promise
Highland Velvet
Velvet Song
Velvet Angel
Sweetbriar
Counterfeit Lady
Lost Lady
River Lady
Twin of Ice
Twin of Fire
The Temptress
The Raider
The Princess
The Awakening
The Maiden
The Taming
A Knight in Shining Armor
Wishes

Published by POCKET BOOKS

COUNTERFEIT LADY

JUDE DEVERAUX

POCKET BOOKS

New York   London   Toronto   Sydney   Tokyo   Singapore

An *Original* Publication of POCKET BOOKS

POCKET BOOKS, a division of Simon & Schuster Inc.
1230 Avenue of the Americas, New York, NY 10020

ISBN: 0-671-70674-8

First Pocket Books printing December 1984

18 17 16 15 14 13 12 11 10

POCKET and colophon are registered trademarks of Simon & Schuster Inc.

Printed in the U.S.A.

Dear Readers,

Years ago, long before it was fashionable, I researched the family tree of both my parents back to the time when our ancestors arrived in this country, some during the American Revolution, some years before. Always a romantic, I was hoping to find a dashing highwayman or a disowned duke. Instead, what I found were generations, hundreds of years, of American farmers. There were no fascinating criminals that I could find, but only an embarrassing number of illegitimate children.

When I was older, I realized that passion that resulted in out-of-wedlock children was far more romantic than robbers, dashing or not. And when I started writing I began to think of all my farmer ancestors and their uncontrollable passions and wondered if a series of romances could be written about men who didn't control armies or fight with kings, but written, instead, about plain men and women whose lives revolved around spring crops.

I hope you like my stories about ordinary people with ordinary problems and the ordinary needs for love that we all have.

Jude Deveraux
Santa Fe, New Mexico
September 1983

Counterfeit Lady

Chapter 1

IN JUNE OF 1794, THE ROSES WERE IN FULL FLOWER and the lawns were of a green lushness that is known only in England. In the county of Sussex stood a small, square, two-story house, a plain house surrounded by a short iron fence. The house once had been part of a greater estate, an outbuilding for a gardener's or gamekeeper's family, but the rest of the estate had been subdivided long ago and sold to pay off the Maleson family's debts. All that was left of this once great family was this small, neglected house, Jacob Maleson, and his daughter Bianca.

Jacob Maleson now sat before the empty fireplace in the parlor on the ground floor—a short, corpulent man, the lower buttons of his vest unbuttoned over the expanse of his large stomach, his coat carelessly tossed over another chair. His plump legs were encased in broadcloth breeches, reaching to just past his knees where they were fastened with brass buckles, his calves were covered with cotton stockings, his feet were bulging from thin leather pumps. A large, sleepy Irish setter leaned against one arm of the old wing chair, and Jacob idly fondled the dog's ears.

Jacob had grown used to his simple country life. Truthfully, he rather liked having a smaller house, fewer servants, and less responsibility. He remembered the big house of his childhood as a place of wasted space, a place that took up too much of his parents' time and energy. Now he had his dogs, a good joint of meat for dinner, enough income to keep his stables going, and he was content.

His daughter was not.

Bianca stood before the tall mirror in her second-floor bedroom and smoothed the long muslin dress over her tall, plump body. Every time she looked at herself in the new French fashions, she felt a touch of disgust. The French peasants had revolted against the aristocracy, and now, because those weak Frenchmen could not control their underlings, all the world had to pay. Every country looked at France and worried that the same thing could happen to them. In France, everyone wanted to look as if they were part of the commoners; therefore, satins and silks were practically banned. The new fashions were of muslins, calicos, lawns, and percale.

Bianca studied herself in the mirror. Of course, the new gowns suited her perfectly. She was just worried about other women less fortunately endowed than herself. The gown was cut very low, with a deep scoop across her large breasts, hiding very little of their shape and whiteness. The pale blue India gauze was tied with a wide ribbon of blue satin just under her breasts, the gown falling straight down from the ribbon to the floor where a row of fringe ran along the hem. Her dark blond hair was pulled back from her face and held with a ribbon, and fat sausage curls hung over her bare shoulder. Her face was fashionably round, with pale blue eyes like her dress, light brows and lashes, her little pink mouth forming a perfect rosebud, and when she smiled there was a tiny dimple in her left cheek.

Bianca moved away from the tall mirror to her dressing table. It, like nearly everything else in the room, was decorated with pale pink tulle. She liked pastels around her. She liked anything that was gentle, delicate, and romantic.

There was a large box of chocolates on the dressing table, the top layer almost empty. Peering into the box, she wrinkled her nose prettily. The horrible French war had stopped the manufacture of the best chocolates, and now she had to make do with second-rate English chocolate. She chose one piece of candy, then another. When she was on her fourth piece and licking her dimpled fingers, she saw Nicole Courtalain enter the room.

The inferior chocolates, the thin fabric of the dress, and Nicole's presence were all a result of the Revolution in France. Bianca chose another chocolate and watched the young Frenchwoman as she moved quietly about the room, putting away the gowns Bianca had strewn across the floor. Nicole made Bianca realize how very generous she and all the English were. When the French had been thrown out of their own country, the English had taken them in. Of course, most of the French had supported themselves economically; in fact, they had even introduced a new thing called a restaurant to England. But then there were people like Nicole—no money, no relatives, no occupation. That's when the English had shown their true generosity. One by one, they'd taken these waifs into their homes.

Bianca had gone to a port on the eastern coast of England and met a shipload of the refugees. She had not been in a good mood. Her father had just informed her that he could no longer afford to pay for her personal maid. There'd been an awful row between the two until Bianca had remembered the émigrés. She had dutifully gone to help the poor, homeless Frenchmen and to see if she could extend her charity to one of them.

When she saw Nicole, she knew she'd found what she wanted. She was small, her black hair hidden under a straw bonnet, her face heart-shaped with enormous brown eyes shaded by short, thick, dark lashes. And in those eyes was a great deal of sadness. She looked as if she didn't care whether she lived or died. Bianca knew that a woman who looked like that would be very grateful for Bianca's generosity.

Now, three months later, Bianca almost regretted all that she had given Nicole. It wasn't that the girl was incompetent; actually, she was almost too competent. But sometimes her graceful, easy movements made Bianca feel almost clumsy.

Bianca looked back at the mirror. What an absurd thought! Her figure was majestic, stately—everyone said so. She gave Nicole a nasty look in the mirror and pulled the ribbon out of her hair.

"I don't like the way you did my hair this morning," Bianca said, leaning back in the chair and helping herself to two more pieces of candy.

Silently, Nicole went to the dressing table and took a comb to Bianca's rather thin hair. "You haven't yet opened the letter from Mr. Armstrong." Her voice was quiet, with no accent, except that each word was pronounced carefully.

Bianca gave a little wave of her hand. "I know what he has to say. He wants to know when I'll be coming to America, when I'll marry him."

Nicole combed one of the curls over her finger. "I would think you'd want to set a date. I know you'd like to marry."

Bianca looked up in the mirror. "How little you know! But, of course, I couldn't expect a Frenchwoman to understand the pride and sensibilities of the English. Clayton Armstrong is an American! How could I, a descendant of the peers of England, marry an American?"

Carefully, Nicole tied the ribbon around Bianca's head. "But I do not understand. I thought your engagement was announced."

Bianca tossed the empty first layer of the candy box onto the floor and took a large piece from the second layer. Caramel was her favorite. With her mouth full, she began to explain. "Men! Who can understand them? I must marry if I am to escape this." Waving her hand, she indicated the small room. "But the man I marry will be far removed from Clayton. I've heard that some of the Colonials are close to being gentlemen, like that Mr. Jefferson. But Clayton is far from being a gentleman. Do you know that he wore his boots in the parlor? When I suggested that he purchase some silk stockings, he laughed at me—said he couldn't deal with a cotton field in silk hose." Bianca shuddered. "Cotton! He is a farmer, a boorish, overbearing, American farmer!"

Nicole straightened the last curl. "And yet you accepted his proposal?"

"Of course! A girl cannot have too many proposals; that only makes the bait more enticing. When I am at a party and I see a man I do not like, I say I am engaged. When I see a man I know is suitable for a woman of my class, I tell him I am considering breaking my engagement."

Nicole turned away from Bianca and picked up the empty candy papers. She knew she shouldn't say anything, but she couldn't help herself. "But what of Mr. Armstrong? Is this fair to him?"

Bianca walked across the room to a chest of drawers and tossed three shawls to the floor before she chose a paisley one from Scotland. "What does an American know of fairness? They're an ungrateful lot to declare themselves independent of us after we'd done so much for them. Besides, it was insulting to me that he thought I'd ever marry a man like him. He was a bit frightening in his tall boots with his arrogant ways. He looked more at home on a horse than in a drawing room. How could I marry someone like that? And he asked me after I'd known him only two days. He received a letter that his brother and sister-in-law had been killed, and suddenly he asked me to marry him. What an insensitive man! He wanted me to return right then to America with him. Of course I declined.''

Not allowing Bianca to see her face, Nicole began folding the discarded shawls. She knew that what she felt too often showed in her face, that her eyes mirrored her thoughts and feelings. When she'd first come to the Maleson household, she'd been too numb to listen to Bianca's tirades about the ignorant, weak French or the crude, ungrateful Americans. Then, all that occupied her thoughts was the red horror of the Revolution—her parents dragged away, her grandfather . . . No! She wasn't ready to remember that stormy night yet. Maybe Bianca had explained before about her fiancé, and Nicole hadn't heard. It was highly likely. Only in the last few weeks had she seemed to awaken from her sleepwalking.

Three weeks ago, she'd met a cousin of hers in a shop while she waited for Bianca to have a dress fitted. Nicole's cousin was opening a little dress shop in two months, and she'd offered to let Nicole buy into it. For the first time, Nicole had seen a way to become independent, a way to become something more than an object of charity.

When she'd left France, she'd escaped with a gold locket and three emeralds sewn into the hem of her dress. After seeing her cousin, she sold the emeralds. The price she'd received was very low, for the English market was flooded with French jewels and the hungry refugees were often too desperate to quibble about price. At night, Nicole stayed up late in her little attic room in Bianca's house and sewed pieces for her cousin, trying to earn more money. Now she almost had enough, carefully hidden inside a chest in her room.

"Can't you hurry?" Bianca said impatiently. "You're always daydreaming. No wonder your country is at war with itself, when it's populated by people as lazy as you are!"

Nicole straightened her back and lifted her chin. Just a few more weeks, she told herself. Then she'd be free.

Even in her numb state, Nicole had learned one thing about Bianca—her dislike of the physical presence of men. She would allow no man to touch her in any way if she could help it. She said she found them crude, loud, insensitive beings. Only once had Nicole seen her smile with genuine warmth at a man, and he was a delicately boned young man with abundant lace at his cuffs and a jeweled snuff box in his hand. For once, Bianca had not seemed afraid of a man, and she had even allowed him to kiss her hand. Nicole was awed by Bianca, who was willing to overlook her aversion to the male touch and to marry in order to better her social status. Or maybe Bianca had no idea what went on between a husband and a wife.

The two women left the small house, walking down the narrow central stairs with its worn carpet. Behind the house was a small stable and carriage house, which Jacob Maleson kept in much better repair than the house. Every day at half past one, Nicole and Bianca rode together through the park in an elegant little two-seat, one-horse carriage. The parkland had once belonged to the Maleson family but was now owned by people Bianca considered upstarts and commoners. She'd never asked if she could ride through the wooded park, yet no one had challenged her. During this time of day, she could imagine herself the lady of the manor as her grandmother once was.

Her father refused to hire a driver for her, and Bianca would not ride in the same carriage as the smelly stablemen, nor would she drive her own carriage. The only thing left to do was have Nicole drive the thing. She certainly didn't seem afraid of the horse.

Nicole liked driving the little carriage. Sometimes in

the early morning, after a few hours of sewing and before Bianca awoke, she'd go to the stables and pet the beautiful chestnut gelding. In France, before the Revolution had destroyed her home and her family's way of life, she'd often ridden for hours before breakfast. These quiet early mornings almost made her forget the death and the fire she'd seen since then.

The park was especially beautiful in June, the trees hanging over the graveled paths, shading them, making lovely little dappled patches of sunlight across the women's dresses. Bianca held a ruffled parasol at an angle over her head, working hard at keeping her pale skin that way. Glancing at Nicole, she snorted. The silly girl had put her straw bonnet on the seat between them, and the air was blowing through her glossy black hair. The sunlight made her eyes sparkle, and her arms holding the reins were slim and curved in places. Bianca looked away in disgust. Her own arms were exceptionally white and softly plump, as a woman's should be.

"Nicole!" Bianca snapped. "Could you for once act like a lady? Or at least remember that I am one? It is bad enough that I must be seen with a half-undressed woman, but now you have us nearly flying in this thing."

Nicole gathered the thin cotton shawl over her bare arms, but she did not put on her bonnet. Dutifully, she clucked to the horse and slowed it down. Just a little more time, she thought, and she would no longer be at Bianca's beck and call.

Suddenly, the quiet afternoon tranquility was shattered by four men on horseback. They rode large, big-footed horses, more suited for pulling a wagon than for riding. It was unusual to see anyone else on the path, especially men who were obviously not gentlemen. Their clothes were tattered, their corduroy trousers stained. One of the men wore a long-sleeved cotton shirt with large red and white stripes.

For a solid year in France, Nicole had lived in terror. When the furious mob had stormed her parents' chateau, she and her grandfather had hidden inside a clothes chest and later escaped under the cover of the black smoke that came from their burning home. Now, her reactions were swift. Recognizing the menace of the men, she used her long whip to flick the gelding's rump and urge the horse to a trot.

Bianca slammed against the horsehair carriage cushion, giving a soft grunt before screaming at Nicole. "Just what do you think you're doing? I will not be treated like this!"

Nicole ignored her as she glanced over her shoulder at the four men who had reached the path where the carriage had been. She realized they were quite far from any house, dead center in the park, and she doubted if anyone would even hear a scream.

Bianca, holding tightly onto her parasol handle, managed to twist around and look at what Nicole kept glancing at, but the four men did not frighten her. Her first thought was how dare such a rabble enter a gentleman's park. One of the men waved his arm, motioning for the others to follow him as he pursued the fleeing carriage. The men were awkward on their horses, holding onto the saddles as well as the reins, and they did not lift themselves in the posting manner but hit the saddle again and again with teeth-jarring hardness.

Looking back at Nicole, Bianca began to be frightened, too, finally realizing the men were after them. "Can't you make that nag go any faster?" she screamed, holding onto the sides of the carriage. But it wasn't made for speed.

The men, hanging on for dear life atop their slow,

clumsy horses, realized the women were getting away. The one in the striped shirt drew a pistol from his wide belt and fired a shot that sailed over the carriage and went right past the horse's left ear.

The gelding reared, and the carriage rammed into its legs as it stopped abruptly, with Nicole pulling back hard on the reins. Bianca screamed once again and cowered in the corner of the carriage with her arm thrown over her face, as Nicole stood up in the carriage, her legs wide apart as she steadied herself, one hand on each rein. "Quiet, boy!" she commanded, and the horse gradually calmed, but its eyes were wild. Tying the reins to the front rail of the carriage, Nicole stepped down and went to the horse, running her hands along its neck, speaking softly in French as she placed her cheek against its nose.

"Look at that, mate. She ain't scared of the bleedin' animal at all."

Nicole looked up at the four men surrounding the carriage.

"You sure can handle a horse, little lady," said one of the other men. "I ain't never seen nothin' like it."

"And her just a little thing, too. It's gonna be a real pleasure to take you with us."

"Wait a minute," commanded the man in the striped shirt, obviously the leader. "How do we know it's her? What about that one?" He pointed to Bianca, who still cowered in a corner of the carriage, making an unsuccessful attempt to disappear into the cushion. Her face was white, terror draining the blood away.

Nicole stood quietly, holding the horse's head in her hands. To her, this was all a repeat of the horror she had known in France, and she knew enough to be quiet and look for a way to escape.

"That's her," said one of the men, pointing at Nicole. "I can tell a lady when I see one."

"Which one of you is Bianca Maleson?" demanded

the man in the striped shirt. He had a strong jaw covered with several days' growth of beard.

So it was a kidnapping, Nicole thought. All the women had to do was prove that Bianca's father was not wealthy enough to pay a ransom.

"She is," Bianca said and sat up straight, her plump arm pointing rigidly at Nicole. "She's the bleedin' lady. I just works for her."

"What'd I tell you?" said one of the men. "She don't talk like no lady. I told you this one here's the lady."

Nicole stood very still, her back straight, her chin high, watching Bianca, whose eyes danced with triumph. She knew there was nothing she could do or say now; the men would take her away. Of course, when they learned she was a penniless French refugee, they would release her, since they would have no hope of obtaining a ransom.

"That's it, then, little lady," one of the men said. "You're to come with us. And I hope you got more sense than to give us any trouble."

Nicole could only shake her head mutely.

The man extended his hand down to her, and she took it, slipped her foot into the stirrup beside his, and was quickly in the saddle in front of him, with both of her feet hanging down one side of the horse.

"She's a looker, ain't she?" the man said. "No wonder he wants her brought to him. You know, I knew she was a lady as soon as I seen her. You can always tell a lady by the way she moves." He smiled in satisfaction at his knowledge. He held one hairy arm around Nicole's waist and awkwardly reined the horse away from the still carriage.

Bianca sat perfectly still for several minutes, staring after them. She was glad, of course, that her sharp wit had let her escape from the men, but it made her angry that the stupid men couldn't see that *she* was the lady. When the park was silent again, she began to look about her. She was stranded, alone. She could not drive the carriage, so how was she to get home? The only way was to walk. As her heel touched the gravel and the rocks bit into her flesh through the thin leather slippers, she cursed Nicole for causing her such pain. On the long, painful walk home, she cursed Nicole repeatedly and was so angry when she finally arrived home that she completely forgot about the kidnapping. Only later, after she and her father had shared a seven-course supper, did she mention the abduction to him. Jacob Maleson, half asleep, said they'd release the girl, but he'd talk to the authorities in the morning. Bianca made her way up to her bedroom, dreading having to find another maid. They were such an ungrateful lot.

The ground floor of the inn was one long room with stone walls that made it cool and dark inside. There were several long trestle tables set about the room. The four kidnappers sat on the benches at one table. Before them were thick stoneware bowls filled with a coarsely chopped beef stew and tall mugs of cool ale. The men sat gingerly on the hard benches. A day spent on horseback was a new experience, and they were paying for it now with their soreness.

"I don't trust her, that's all I'm sayin'," said one of the men. "She's too bleedin' quiet. She looks all innocence with them big eyes, but I say she's plannin' somethin'. And that somethin' is gonna get us in trouble."

The other three men listened to him, frowns on their faces.

The first man continued. "You know what he's like. I ain't gonna risk losin' her. All I want is to get her to America, to him, just like he ordered, and I don't want nothin' goin' wrong."

The man in the striped shirt took a long drink of ale. "Joe's right. Any lady can handle a horse like she did

12

ain't gonna be afraid of tryin' to escape. Anybody want to volunteer to watch her all night?"

The men groaned, feeling their sore muscles. They would have considered tying up their prisoner, but their orders about that had been very strict. They were not to harm her in any way.

"Joe, you remember that time the doc took them stitches in your chest?"

Joe nodded, puzzled.

"Remember that white stuff he gave you to make you sleep? Think you could get some?"

Joe looked around at the other patrons of the inn. They ranged from a couple of gutter rats to a well-heeled gentleman alone in a corner. Joe knew he could buy anything from such a group. "I think I can get some," he said.

Sitting quietly on the edge of the bed in the dirty little upstairs room, Nicole looked at her surroundings. She'd already been to the window and had discovered there was a drainpipe outside and a storage shed roof just below the window. Later, when it was darker and the yard was quieter, maybe she could risk trying to escape. Of course, she could tell the men her true identity, but it was a little early yet as they were only a few hours away from Bianca's home. She wondered how Bianca had gotten home, how many hours it had taken her if she'd had to walk. Then it would take Mr. Maleson some time to get to the county sheriff and send out alarms and searches for her. No, it was too soon yet to reveal herself to the men. Tonight she would try to escape, and if that failed she would tell them in the morning of their mistake. Then they would release her. Please, God, she prayed, let them not be angry.

As the door opened, she looked up at the four men entering the little room.

"We brought you somethin' to drink. Real chocolate

from South America. You know, one of us could of been on the voyage what brought this here."

Sailors! she thought as she took the mug. Why hadn't she realized it before? That's why they were so awkward on the horses, why their clothes smelled so strange.

As she drank the delicious chocolate, she began to relax, the warmth and creaminess seeping through her and making her realize how tired she was. Trying to concentrate on her plan of escape, her thoughts kept drifting, floating away. She looked up at the men as they hovered over her, watching her anxiously like giant, grizzled babysitters, and she wanted to reassure them for some reason. Smiling, she closed her eyes and let herself drift away into sleep.

The next twenty-four hours were lost to Nicole. She was vaguely aware of being carried about, handled as if she were a baby. Sometimes, she sensed someone was worried about her, and she tried to smile and say she was fine, but the words just wouldn't seem to surface. She dreamed constantly, remembering her parents' chateau, her swing under the willow tree in the garden, smiling at some of the happy times spent at the miller's house with her grandfather. She lay quietly in a hammock, gently swaying on a hot, close day.

When she slowly opened her eyes, the swaying hammock of the dream did not go away. But instead of the trees above her was a row of slats. Odd, she thought, someone must have built a platform above the hammock, and she idly wondered what it was for.

"So, you're awake! I told those sailors they gave you too much of the opium. It's a wonder you ever woke up at all. Trust a man to do everything wrong. Here, I've made you some coffee. It's good and hot."

Turning, Nicole looked up as a woman placed a large hand behind her back and practically lifted her from the bed. She wasn't in a garden at all but in a bare little room. Perhaps the drug made it seem to sway. No wonder she had dreamed she was in a hammock. "Where are we? Who are you?" she managed to ask as she gulped the hot, strong coffee.

"You're still groggy, aren't you? I'm Janie, and I was hired by Mr. Armstrong to take care of you."

Nicole looked up sharply. The name Armstrong meant something to her, but she couldn't remember what. As the black coffee began to clear her senses, she looked at Janie. She was a tall, big-boned woman with a broad face, her cheeks looking to be permanently pink, reminding Nicole of a nursemaid she'd once had. Janie exuded an air of confidence and common sense, a feeling of safety and serenity.

"Who is Mr. Armstrong?"

Janie took the empty cup away and refilled it. "They surely did give you too much of that sleeping stuff. Mr. Armstrong. Clayton Armstrong. Remember now? The man you're supposed to marry."

Nicole blinked rapidly, drank more coffee from the pot set on a little brass charcoal brazier, and began to remember everything. "I'm afraid there's been a mistake. I'm not Bianca Maleson, nor am I engaged to Mr. Armstrong."

"You're not—" Janie began, sitting down on the lower bed of the bunk beds. "Honey, I think you'd better tell me the whole story."

When Nicole had finished, she laughed. "So, you see, I'm sure the men will release me once they hear the whole story."

Janie was silent.

"Won't they?"

"There's more to this than you know," Janie said. "For one thing, we're twelve hours out to sea, on our way to America."

Chapter 2

STUNNED, NICOLE LOOKED AT THE ROOM AROUND HER. A ship! It was bare, with oak walls, floor, and ceiling, and against one wall were two bunk beds. There was very little space from the bed to the other wall, which was bare except for a round porthole. A door was at one end of the room, and the other end was piled high with boxes and trunks held securely with ropes fastened to the wall. A low cabinet was in one corner, the brazier on top of it. Suddenly, Nicole realized that the rocking was the motion of a ship on a calm sea. "I don't understand," she said. "Why would anyone want to kidnap me—or Bianca, rather—to America?"

Janie went to one of the trunks and opened the lid, withdrawing a little leather portfolio tied with ribbon. "I think you'd better read this."

Puzzled, Nicole opened the packet. There were two sheets of paper inside, covered with a bold, strong handwriting. She began to read.

My dearest Bianca,

I hope by now Janie has explained everything to you. I also hope you will not be too angry at my unorthodox methods of bringing you to me. I know what a kind and dutiful daughter you are and I know how much you worry about your father's health. I was willing to wait for you while he was so very ill, but now I can wait no longer.

I have chosen a packet boat for your passage to America since they are faster than any other. Janie

16

and Amos have been instructed to purchase all the food you need for the journey as well as the makings of a new wardrobe since this haste has deprived you of your own. She is an excellent seamstress.

Even though I have you on your way to me, I do not trust that nothing will go awry. Therefore, I have instructed the captain to marry us by proxy. Then, even if your father did find you before you reached me, you would still be mine. I know I am being high-handed about this but you must forgive me and remember that I do it because I love you and am so lonely without you.

When next I see you, you will be my wife. I count the hours.

All my love,
Clay

Nicole held the letter for several moments, feeling that she was prying into something very personal and private that she should not see. She smiled slightly. She'd always heard that Americans were quite unromantic, but this man had gone through an elaborate kidnapping scheme to bring the woman he loved to him.

She looked up at Janie. "He seems like a very nice man, one who is obviously very much in love. I envy Bianca. Who is Amos?"

"Clay sent him with me to help protect you, but there was an illness on the passage over." She looked away, not wanting to remember the time when five people had died. "Amos didn't make it."

"I'm sorry," Nicole said as she stood. "I must find the captain and straighten this out." Catching sight of herself in the mirror over the corner cabinet, she paused. Her hair was a mess, tumbling about her face in short, fat, corkscrew curls. "Do you know where I could find a comb?"

"Sit down and I'll fix it."

Gladly, Nicole sat down. "Is he always so . . . so impetuous?"

"Who? Oh, you mean Clay." Janie smiled fondly. "I don't know if he's impetuous as much as arrogant. He's used to getting what he wants. I told him when he concocted this whole scheme that it would go wrong, but he just laughed at me. Now here we are in the middle of the ocean together. It's going to be me laughin' when Clay sees you."

She turned Nicole's head and tilted her face to the light. "On second thought, I don't think any man'd laugh at you," she said, taking her first good look at Nicole. The big eyes were striking, but Janie thought that what would intrigue a man most was her mouth. It wasn't very wide, but the lips were full and deep pink. What was so unusual was that her upper lip was larger than her lower. It was an extraordinary combination, one that Janie guessed would fascinate men.

Blushing lightly, Nicole turned away. "But of course I won't meet Mr. Armstrong. I need to return to England. I have a cousin who has asked me to be a partner with her in a dress shop. I have saved nearly all the money I need."

"I hope we can go back for your sake. But I don't like those men up there." Janie nodded her head toward the ceiling. "I told Clay I didn't like them, but he wouldn't listen. He is the stubbornnest man ever created."

Nicole glanced at the letter on the bed. "A man in love surely can be forgiven for some things."

"Humph!" Janie snorted. "You can say that, but you've never had to deal with him."

Leaving the cabin and climbing the narrow stairs to the main deck, Nicole felt the soft sea air blow through her hair, and she smiled into the breeze. Pausing, she was aware of several men staring at her. The sailors watched her avidly, and she pulled her shawl close about her. She knew her thin linen dress must be clinging to her, and she suddenly had the feeling that she was standing nude before the men.

"What is it ye be wantin', little lady?" one of the men asked, his eyes going up and down her body.

Concentrating on not letting her feet take a step backward, she answered, "I'd like to see the captain."

"And I'm sure he'd like to see you."

She ignored the laughter of the men around her as she followed the sailor to a door at the front of the ship, where he gave a curt knock. When the captain bellowed for them to come in, the sailor opened the door and half shoved Nicole inside, closing the door behind her.

After her eyes took a moment to adjust, she saw that the cabin was twice as big as the one she and Janie shared. There was a large window on one side, but the glass was so filthy that little sunlight came through. A dirty, rumpled bed was under the window, and in the middle of the room was a big, heavy table bolted to the floor, covered with rolled and flat maps and charts.

As a rat ran across the floor, she gasped. A low rumble of laughter made her look toward a dark corner to the man sitting there, his face dark with unshaved whiskers, his clothes rumpled, and one hand holding a bottle of rum.

"I was told you were a bleedin' lady. You better get used to the rats on this ship, the two-legged as well as the four-legged kind."

"Are you the captain?" she asked, stepping forward.

"I am. If you can call a mail packet a ship, then I'm her captain."

"May I sit down? I'd like to talk to you."

He pointed the rum bottle at a chair.

Nicole told her story quickly and succinctly. When she finished, the captain was silent. "When do you think we will be able to get back to England?"

"I ain't goin' back to England."

"But how will I get back? You don't understand. This is all a terrible mix-up. Mr. Armstrong—"

He cut her off. "All I know, girl, is Clayton Armstrong hired me to kidnap some lady and bring her to him in America." He squinted his eyes at her. "Now that I look at you, you ain't much like he described."

"That's because I'm not his fiancée."

Waving his hand in dismissal, he took a deep drink of the rum. "What do I care who you are? He said you might give me some trouble about the marriage, but I was to do it anyway."

Nicole stood up. "Marriage! You cannot think—!" she began but calmed herself. "Mr. Armstrong is in love with and wants to marry Bianca Maleson. I am Nicole Courtalain. I have never even met Mr. Armstrong."

"That's what you say. Why didn't you tell my men right off who you were? How come you waited this long?"

"I thought they would release me when they found out who I was, but I wanted to be far enough away from Bianca so I knew she would be safe."

"Is this Bianca the fat one the men said told 'em who you were?"

"Bianca did identify me, yes. But she knew I would be safe."

"Like hell she did! Are you expectin' me to believe that you kept your mouth shut to protect a bitch who would happily turn you over to kidnappers? I can't believe that. You must think I'm stupid."

There was nothing Nicole could say.

20

"Go on. Get out of here while I think about this. And on your way out, tell that man you came with I want to see him."

When Nicole was gone and the captain and the first mate were alone, the captain spoke. "I guess you heard, since you spend most of the time listenin' at doors."

Smiling, the first mate sat down. He and the captain had been together a long time, and he'd learned how useful it was to know what the old man was up to. "So what do you plan to do? Armstrong said he'd see we were locked up because of that shipload of tobacco that disappeared last year if we failed to bring his wife to him."

The captain took a drink of rum. "His wife. That's what the man wants, and that's what he's gonna get."

The mate thought about this. "And what if she's tellin' the truth and she ain't the one he wants to marry?"

"I figure there's two ways to look at it. If she ain't this Maleson woman and the other one is, then Armstrong is askin' to marry a bitch that's a liar and who'd betray her best friend. On the other hand, that pretty little dark-haired lady could be this Bianca and she's lyin' just to get out of marryin' Armstrong. Either way, I think there ought to be a weddin' in the mornin'."

"And what about Armstrong?" the mate asked. "If he finds himself married to the wrong woman, I don't think I'd like to be around."

"That's what I thought, too. I plan to collect my money before he sees her and then be out of Virginia immediately. I don't think I'll even wait to see whether she is or isn't who he wants."

"I think I agree with you. Now, how do we go about persuadin' the little lady? She didn't seem taken with the idea of marriage!"

The captain passed the rum bottle to his mate. "I can think of several persuasions that might work on that little doll."

"I take it you couldn't talk the captain into returning to England?" Janie asked when Nicole returned to the little cabin.

"No," Nicole said, setting down on the bed. "Actually, he didn't seem to believe me when I told him who I was. For some reason, he seemed to think I was lying."

Janie grunted. "A man like him's probably never told the truth in his life so he doesn't believe anyone else has. Oh well, at least we can enjoy the voyage together. I hope you aren't too upset."

Hiding her feelings, Nicole smiled at the large woman. Yes, she was very disappointed. By the time she sailed to America and back again, her cousin would have found another partner. And also, she thought of the money she'd saved, hidden in an attic room in Bianca's house. Rubbing her fingertips together and feeling the many little sore places where the needle had pricked her fingers because she'd worked by the light of one very small, very cheap candle, she thought of how hard she'd worked for that money.

But she wouldn't let Janie see her disappointment. "I've always wanted to see America," she said. "Maybe I can stay a few days before returning to England. Oh dear!"

"What is it?"

"How will I pay for my return passage?" she asked, her eyes wide at the thought of this new problem.

"Pay!" Janie exploded. "Clayton Armstrong will pay for your return, I assure you of that. I told him again and again not to do this but it was like talkin' to a brick wall. Maybe after you see America, you won't want to return to England. We've got lots of dress shops there, you know."

Nicole told her about the money she'd saved and hidden.

For a few minutes, Janie didn't say anything. In Nicole's version of the kidnapping, Bianca was innocent, doing what should have been done, but Janie heard more than the words, and she wondered if Nicole's money would be there when she returned. "Are you hungry?" Janie asked, opening a trunk on the top of the pile against the wall.

"Why, yes, I am. Quite hungry, actually," Nicole said, and she went to look into the trunk. In those days, before ships catered to passengers, each traveler had to bring his or her own food for the long voyage. Depending on the skill of the navigator, the swiftness of the ship, the winds, the storms, and the pirates, a trip could take from thirty days to ninety, if it arrived at all.

The trunk held dried peas and beans, and as Janie opened another one Nicole saw salted beef and fish. Another trunk held oatmeal, potatoes, packets of herbs, flour, hardtack biscuits, and a box of lemons and limes. "Clayton also had the captain buy some turtles, so we'll have fresh turtle soup."

Nicole looked at the foodstuffs. "Mr. Armstrong seems to be an especially considerate man. I almost wish I *were* marrying him."

Janie was beginning to think that, too, as she turned and opened the doors of the corner cabinet and pulled out a tall, narrow hip bath. A bather could sit in it, knees drawn up, and the water would cover her shoulders.

Nicole's eyes sparkled. "Now, that is a luxury! Who would have thought a ship voyage could be so comfortable?"

Cheeks pink with pleasure, Janie grinned. She'd dreaded an ocean voyage in a tiny cabin with an English lady, thinking the English were terrible snobs and king-worshippers. But, then, of course, Nicole was

French and the French understood revolutions. "I'm afraid we'll have to use sea water, and it'll take a long while to heat the water on that little stove, but it beats a sponge bath."

Hours later, after a delicious bath, Nicole lay in the bottom bunk bed, clean, fed, and tired. It had taken a long time to heat enough water for the two baths. Janie had protested that she was supposed to wait on Nicole, but Nicole had insisted that she wasn't Clayton's fiancée and therefore could only be Janie's friend. Later, Nicole had washed her only dress and hung it up to dry, and now the gentle rocking of the ship was lulling her to sleep.

Early the next morning, Janie pulled her hair back into a tight little bun before she began to arrange Nicole's hair into a fashionable chignon. Producing an iron, she pressed Nicole's dress while Nicole laughed and said Mr. Armstrong had thought of everything.

Suddenly, the door burst open to admit one of Nicole's kidnappers. "The captain wants to see you—now."

Nicole's first thought was that he had decided to return to England after all, and she gladly started to follow the sailor, with Janie right behind her.

With one sharp shove, the sailor sent Janie back into the room. "He don't want you. Just her."

Janie started to protest, but Nicole stopped her. "I'll be all right, I'm sure. Maybe he's realized I was telling the truth."

As soon as Nicole entered the captain's cabin, she knew something was wrong. The captain, the first mate, and another man she'd never seen before were there. All of them seemed to be waiting for something.

"Maybe I should introduce everyone," the captain said. "I want to be sure everything's proper. This is the doc. He can sew you up or whatever you need. And this is Frank, my first mate. I guess you already met him."

The sixth sense Nicole had acquired during the terror in France made her aware now of a feeling of danger. As always, her eyes reflected her emotions.

"Don't back away," Frank said. "We want to talk to you. And, besides, this is your weddin' day. You wouldn't want it said you were a reluctant bride, would you?"

Nicole was beginning to understand. "I am not Bianca Maleson. I know Mr. Armstrong instructed you to perform a proxy marriage, but I am not the woman he wants."

Frank gave her a lascivious look. "I think you're about exactly what any man would want."

The doctor spoke. "Young lady, do you have any proof of your identity?"

Taking a step backward toward the door, she shook her head briefly. Her grandfather had destroyed the few documents he had managed to save in their wild flight from the terrorists, saying their lives could some-day depend on people not finding out who they were. "My name is Nicole Courtalain. I am from France, a refugee, and I was staying with Miss Maleson. It is all a mistake."

The captain spoke. "We were talking, and we decided that it doesn't matter who you are. My contract says I'm to bring Mrs. Clayton Armstrong to America, and I plan to do just that."

Nicole straightened her back. "I will not marry against my will!"

After a crisp nod from the captain, Frank was across the room in seconds, grabbing Nicole roughly to him, one arm around her waist, the other about her shoulders, pinning her arms to her side.

"That upside-down mouth of yours has been drivin' me crazy ever since I seen it," he murmured, crushing her to him as he brought his mouth down on hers.

Nicole was so bewildered that she could not react

quickly. Never had anyone treated her like this. Even when she had lived with the miller and his family, the people around her had been aware of who she was and had treated her with great respect. This man smelled of fish and sweat, a filthy, overpowering stench. His arms cut her breath off; his mouth touched hers in a way that made her want to gag. She moved her head away, gasping, "No!"

"There'll be more of that," Frank said, and he bit her neck quite hard, running his dirty hand over her shoulder. With one violent jerk, he tore her dress, the chemise tearing away along with it, and her breast lay bare to his touch and to the sight of the other men. His big hand cupped her flesh, his thumb roughly bruising her nipple.

"No, please," Nicole whispered, struggling against him, feeling sick.

"That's enough," the captain ordered.

Frank did not release her immediately. "I hope you don't marry Armstrong," he whispered, his breath hot and foul on her face, but he moved away from her, and Nicole clutched at her dress. With weak knees, she collapsed into a chair, running the back of her hand across her mouth, sure she'd never be clean again.

"Looks like she don't like you much," the captain laughed before turning serious and sitting down in a chair opposite Nicole. "You just got a taste of what's gonna happen to you if you don't go through with this marriage. If you ain't Armstrong's wife, then you're a stowaway and mine to use however I want. First, I'll throw that big woman Armstrong sent over the side."

Nicole stared at him. "Janie? She's done nothing to you. That would be murder."

"What do I care? You think I could ever go near the Virginia coast again if I don't do what Armstrong says? And the last thing I want is a witness to what I'm gonna let the men do to you."

Seeming to grow smaller in the chair, Nicole caught her lower lip between her teeth, and her eyes almost swallowed her face.

"See, lady," Frank said, "we're givin' you a choice, real kind of us." His eyes never left her dress, which gapped at her breast. "Either you marry Armstrong or you come to my bed. That is, after the captain here gets through with you. Then, when I'm done with you—" he stopped and grinned. "I doubt if there'll be much left after I'm done with you." Leaning over, he put a dirty finger on her upper lip. "I never had me a woman with an upside-down mouth. Makes me think of all the things I could make that mouth do."

Nicole turned her head away and felt her stomach turn over.

The captain watched her. "Which is it gonna be? Armstrong or me and Frank?"

Concentrating on breathing deeply and evenly, she tried to think. She knew it was important to keep her mind clear and working properly. "I will marry Mr. Armstrong," she said evenly.

"I knew she was smart," the captain said. "Come, then, my dear, let's get it over with. I'm sure you want to return to the—ah—safety of your cabin."

Nicole nodded and stood up, her hand holding her dress together.

"Frank here will stand in for Armstrong. It's all done legal-like. Armstrong had a lawyer draw up papers sayin' I could choose a man to act as his proxy."

Numbly, Nicole stood beside Frank in front of the captain, who would perform the ceremony, and the doctor, who would act as a witness.

Frank readily answered the captain's questions in the traditional ceremony, but when the captain said, "Bianca, will you take this man to be your lawfully wedded husband?" Nicole refused to speak. It was all so unfair! She'd been abducted, taken away from a country she was just becoming accustomed to, and now she was being married against her will. She'd always dreamed of her wedding, a blue satin' gown, roses everywhere. Now she stood in a filthy cabin, her dress torn half off, her mouth bruised and tasting of a disgusting foulness. The last three days, she'd been thrown about like a leaf in a turbulent stream. But she would not give up her own name! At least she could hold on to that, even if everything else was out of her control.

"My name is Nicole Courtalain," she said firmly.

The captain started to speak, but the doctor nudged him.

"What do I care?" he grumbled, rereading the sentence and inserting Nicole's name for Bianca's.

At the end of the ceremony, he produced five gold bands of different sizes, pushing the smallest one on Nicole's finger.

The ceremony was finally over.

"Do I get to kiss the bride?" Frank leered.

The doctor firmly took Nicole's arm and led her away from the man to the table in the middle of the room. Taking a pen, he wrote something, then turned and handed the quill to Nicole. "You must sign it," he said, thrusting the marriage certificate at her.

Her eyes were filled with tears, and she had to wipe them away before she could see. The doctor had put her real name on the marriage certificate. She, Nicole Courtalain, was now Mrs. Clayton Armstrong. Quickly, she signed her name at the bottom.

She watched impassively, feeling numb, as Frank made his mark on the bottom of the document. It was legal now.

The doctor held her arm and escorted her from the captain's cabin. She was so numb that she was back at her own cabin before she realized it.

"Listen, my dear," the doctor was saying. "I'm very

sorry about all of this, because I do believe you are not Miss Maleson. But, believe me, it was better for you to proceed with the ceremony. I don't know Mr. Armstrong, but I'm sure that an annulment can be arranged easily when you reach America. The alternatives were . . . much worse. Now, let me give you some advice. I know the voyage will be a long one, but stay in your cabin as much as possible. Don't let the men see you on deck. The captain isn't worth much, but he does control his men—to an extent. But you need to help him by making the men forget your presence, at least as far as that is possible. Do you understand?"

Nicole nodded.

"And smile. It's not as bad as it seems. America is beautiful. You may not even want to return to England."

Nicole did manage to smile. "That's what Janie says."

"There, that's better. Now, remember what I said, and try to look forward to your arrival."

"I will. And thank you," she said as she turned and entered the cabin.

For a moment, the doctor stood still. Personally, he thought Armstrong would be a fool to let a woman like that get away from him.

"You were gone so long!" Janie said when Nicole entered the cabin, her voice rising sharply. "What happened to your dress? What did they do to you?"

Collapsing on the bed, Nicole lay back, her arm across her eyes.

Suddenly, Janie grabbed her left hand and studied the shiny gold wedding band. "I was with Clay when he bought these. He got five sizes so he'd be sure one of them fit. I bet the captain kept the others, didn't he?"

Nicole didn't answer as she held her hand out and studied the ring along with Janie. What exactly did it really mean? Did this bit of gold hold her to the promise she'd just made to love and honor a man she'd never met?

"What made you agree to the ceremony?" Janie asked, touching Nicole's neck where an angry red mark was forming.

Nicole grimaced. It was the place where Frank had bitten her.

Janie straightened. "You don't have to tell me. I can guess what happened. The captain made sure he got Clay's money," she said, tightening her lips. "Damn that Clay Armstrong! Pardon me, but this whole thing is his fault. If he weren't so pig-headed stubborn, none of this would have happened. Nobody could talk any sense into his head. No, he wanted his Bianca, and he meant to have her. Do you know he went to four ship captains before he found one low enough to do the kidnapping? And now look at everything! Here you are, an innocent little thing rough handled by a bunch of filthy men, threatened in disgusting ways, forced to marry someone you don't even know and, after this, probably don't want to know."

"Please, Janie, it isn't so bad, really. The doctor said we wouldn't be bothered by the men since I'm married to Mr. Armstrong, and I know they won't hurt you. I'm sure it can be annulled once we get to America."

"Me!" Janie said angrily. "I should have known those scum would threaten you with me. And you don't even know me!" She put her hand on Nicole's shoulder. "Whatever you want from Clay—an annulment, whatever—I'll see that you get it. I am going to give him a piece of my mind like he's never heard before. I swear that he's going to make everything up to you—all the wasted time you've spent going back and forth across the ocean, the money you saved for the dress shop, and—" Suddenly, she stopped in midsentence and gazed amusedly at the trunks along the wall.

Nicole started to sit up. "What is it? Is something wrong?"

Janie's broad face broke into a grin of pure devilment. "'Buy the best, Janie,' he said to me. There he was, standing on the dock, looking at it like he does everything, as if he owned it, and he was telling me to buy the very best."

"What are you talking about?"

Janie looked as if she were in a trance, staring at the trunks as if mesmerized. She took a step toward them. "He said nothing was too good for his wife," Janie said as the smile on her face deepened. "Oh, Clayton Armstrong, you are going to pay dearly for this."

Nicole swung her legs over the side of the bed and stared at Janie in puzzlement. Whatever was she talking about?

As Janie began to unfasten the ropes that held the trunks to the wall, she kept talking. "Clay gave me a bag of gold and told me to buy the very best fabrics available, the most expensive trims. He said that I could help his wife make dresses on the long journey," she chuckled. "The furs could be worked by a furrier in America."

"Furs?" Nicole remembered the letter. "Janie, those fabrics are for Bianca, not me. We couldn't make them up for me; they would never fit her."

"I have no intention of making clothes for some woman I've never seen," she said, struggling with a knot. "Clay said the clothes were for his wife, and as far as I know, you're the only one he has."

"No! It isn't right. I couldn't take something meant for someone else."

Janie reached under the pillow of the top bunk and withdrew a large ring of keys. "This is for me, not you. Just once, I'd like to see something Clayton couldn't buy or have just for the asking. He has every girl and woman in Virginia making fools of themselves over him, yet he has to pick some woman in England who I ain't sure even wants him." As she unlocked a trunk and carefully raised the flat lid, she smiled down at the contents.

Nicole couldn't help being curious. She walked beside Janie and looked down into the trunk, gasping at the loveliness there. It had been years since she'd seen silk and she'd never seen silk of such quality.

"The English are afraid of what they call the lower classes, so they pretend they're part of them. In America, everybody's equal. If you can afford to have pretty things, you don't have to be afraid to wear them." She withdrew a shimmering, delicate length of sapphire blue silk, twisted it around one of Nicole's shoulders, drew it down her back, and tied it loosely about her waist. "What do you think of that?"

Holding it to the light for a moment, Nicole rubbed it against her cheek and moved her body so she could feel it on her bare arms. It was a sensual, sinful pleasure.

Janie was opening another trunk. "And how about this for a sash?" She withdrew a wide satin ribbon of midnight blue and wrapped it around Nicole's waist. The whole trunk seemed to be full of ribbons and sashes.

Another trunk was opened. "A shawl, my lady?" she laughed, and before Nicole could speak she withdrew at least a dozen shawls—paisley from Scotland, cashmere from England, cotton from India, lace from Chantilly.

Nicole was gasping at the abundance and the beauty while Janie unlocked trunk after trunk. There were velvets, lawns, percales, soft wools, mohair, swansdown, shalloon, prunella, tammy, tulle, organdy, crepe, the delicate French laces.

Somewhere in the midst of all the lush wealth Janie was flinging about, Nicole started laughing. It was all too much. As she sat down on the bed and Janie started tossing the fabrics on top of her, both women started laughing, wrapping scarlets and turquoises, greens and pinks, around themselves. It was a silly, hilarious time.

"But you haven't seen the best yet," Janie laughed as she pulled long pieces of pink tulle and black Normandy lace off her head. Almost reverently, she opened a large trunk at the back of the pile and lifted an enormous fur muff from the trunk. "Know what fur that is?" she asked as she placed it in Nicole's lap.

Nicole buried her face in the long, deep fur, ignoring the six colors of silk wrapped around her arm and the transparent India gauze across her throat. There was only one fur that rich, that dark—so deep, so thick you could almost drown in it. "Sable," she said quietly, reverently.

"Yes," Janie agreed. "Sable."

Holding the muff, Nicole looked about her. The little room was full of colors that flashed or cried, shouted or lay still in sulky sexuality, all seeming to be alive and breathing. Nicole wanted to roll in them and hug them to her. There had been no beauty in her life since she had left her parents' chateau.

"Well, where do you want to start?"

Nicole looked at Janie and burst out laughing. "With *all* of it!" she laughed, hugging the muff to her and kicking six ostrich feathers into the air.

While she removed a chiffon shawl from around her legs, Janie lifted some magazines from a trunk. *"Heidledoff's Gallery of Fashion,"* she said. "Just choose your weapon, dear Mrs. Armstrong, and I shall show you my trunk of steel—pins and needles, that is."

"Oh, Janie, really, I can't." Her voice held no

conviction as she rubbed the sable muff along her arm, thinking she just might sleep with it.

"I'm not listening to another word. Now, if you think you can spare one arm out of that thing, let's put these back and get started. After all, we only have a month or so."

Chapter 3

IT WAS EARLY AUGUST OF 1794 WHEN THE SLEEK LITTLE packet arrived in the Virginia harbor. Both Janie and Nicole hung over the starboard rail, looking with awe toward the dock that pressed against the dense forest's edge, feeling as if they'd been freed from prison. For the last week of the voyage, they'd talked of nothing but food—fresh food. They spoke of vegetables and fruit, all the many plants that would be ripening soon, and how they planned to eat some of everything, all of it topped with fresh cream and butter. Blackberries were what Janie wanted most, while Nicole just wanted to see green living things growing from the sweet-smelling earth.

They'd spent the long days of confinement sewing, and there were very few of the luscious fabrics that hadn't been made into a garment for either Janie or Nicole. Now, Nicole wore a frock of muslin embroidered with tiny violets, with a row of violet ribbon around the hem. Entwined in her hair was more violet ribbon. Her arms were bare, and she thoroughly enjoyed the warmth of the setting sun on her arms.

The women had talked while they sewed. Nicole had been the listener, refusing to tell anyone about the time when her parents had been taken and, worse, when her grandfather had been torn from her. She told Janie about her childhood in her family's chateau, making the palace seem like an ordinary country house, and she told of the year she and her grandfather had spent with the miller's family. Janie laughed when Nicole spoke quite technically about the quality of stone-ground grain.

But most of the talking had been done by Janie. She told of her own childhood on a poor little farm a few miles from Arundel Hall, as Clayton's house was called. She was ten when Clay was born, and she talked of giving the boy piggyback rides. Janie had been in her late teens during the American Revolution. Her father, like so many Virginia farmers, had planted all his fields in tobacco. When the English market was closed, he went bankrupt. For several years, he and Janie had lived in Philadelphia, a place Janie hated. When her father had died, she returned to the place she'd always considered home—Virginia.

She said that on her return she had found Arundel Hall greatly changed. Clay's mother and father had died of cholera several years before. Clay's older brother James had married Elizabeth Stratton, the daughter of the overseer of the Armstrong plantation. Then, while Clay was in England, James and Elizabeth had both been killed in a tragic accident.

The little boy Janie had known was gone. In his place was an arrogant, demanding young man who was a demon for work. While one plantation after another in Virginia went bankrupt, Arundel Hall thrived and grew.

"Look," Nicole said and pointed out at the water. "Isn't that the captain?" The heavyset man sat in a little rowboat with one of the sailors working the oars.

"I think he's going to that other ship."

Several yards away from the packet was an enormous frigate, its sides bulging with two rows of cannons. There were many men carrying bundles up and down a wide gangplank. As the women watched, the captain stepped out onto the dock, several minutes ahead of the packet, which was still slowly maneuvering itself into the harbor. The captain climbed the steep gangplank and stepped onto the frigate's deck, walking toward the aft end of the ship.

The women were quite a distance away, and the men on deck looked small. "That's Clay!" Janie suddenly yelled.

Nicole looked in wonder at the man the captain was speaking to, but he looked like all the other men from this distance. "How can you tell?"

Janie laughed. She was so glad to be home. "Once you know Clay, you'll understand," she said, turning away abruptly and leaving Nicole alone.

Straining her eyes to see the man who was her husband, Nicole nervously twisted the wedding band on her left hand.

"Here," Janie said and thrust a spyglass into her hand. "Take a good look."

Even through the glass, the men were small, but she could feel the presence of the man talking to the captain. He had one foot on a bale of cotton, the other on the deck. He leaned forward, his forearms on his bent knee. Even bending, he was taller than the captain. He wore snug trousers of light brown and black leather boots to his knees. His waist was circled by a three-inch-wide black leather belt. His shirt was gathered just past the shoulders, open at the throat, and the sleeves were rolled to his elbows, revealing brown forearms. She couldn't tell much about his face at that distance, but his brown hair was loosely pulled back and tied behind his neck.

Putting the glass down, she turned to Janie.

"Oh no you don't," Janie said. "I've seen that expression too many times. Just because a man is big and handsome is no reason for you to give in to him. He's gonna be awful mad when he finds out what happened, and if you don't stand up to him, he'll blame all of it on you."

Nicole smiled at her friend, her eyes dancing. "You

certainly never mentioned that he was big and hand-some," she teased.

"I never said he was ugly either. Now, I want you to go back to the cabin and wait because, if I know Clay, he'll be here in minutes. I want to get to him first and explain just what that scoundrel of a captain did. Now scoot!"

Obeying her friend, Nicole returned to the dark little cabin, feeling almost nostalgic about leaving it. She and Janie had become quite close in the last forty days.

Her eyes had just adjusted to the dim light when suddenly the cabin door swung open. A man who was unmistakably Clayton Armstrong burst into the room, his broad shoulders filling the space until Nicole felt as if she were standing in a closet with him.

Clay didn't wait long enough to give his eyes time to adjust. He saw only the outline of his wife. One long arm shot out and pulled her to him.

Nicole started to protest, but then his mouth found hers and she couldn't protest. His mouth was clean-tasting, strong, demanding yet gentle, but she made a weak attempt to push away from him. His arms about her tightened, and he lifted her so that her toes were barely touching the floor, his chest hard against her womanly softness. She could feel her heart beginning to pound.

The only time she'd been kissed like this was by Frank, the first mate, but there was no comparison! He turned his head, moved his hand to hold the back of her head, making her feel as if she were fainting, drowning. Her arms went about his neck and pulled him closer to her. His breath was on her cheek.

As he moved from her mouth to her cheek, she felt his teeth on her earlobe, and her knees turned to water. His tongue touched the cord in her neck.

Quickly, his arm swept under her knees, lifting her off the floor and wrapping her body around his. Dazed,

Nicole was aware only that she wanted more and more of him as she turned her head back, offering her lips to him again.

He kissed her hungrily, and she returned his passion. When he moved to the bed, holding her body next to him, it seemed natural. She wanted only to touch him, to keep him near her. He pulled her down on the bed with him, his lips never leaving hers, throwing one strong, heavy leg across hers, his hand running up and down her bare arm. When he touched her breast through her clothes, she moaned and arched her body toward his.

"Bianca," he whispered in her ear. "Sweet, sweet Bianca."

Nicole did not come to her senses suddenly; her passion was too strong for that. Only slowly did she become aware of where she was, who she was—and who she was not.

"Please," she said, one hand pushing against his chest, but her voice was weak and strained.

"It's all right, love," he said, his voice deep and clear, his breath warm against her cheek. His hair was against her face, smelling of the earth she so longed to touch again. Momentarily, she closed her eyes.

"I've waited so long for you, my love," he said. "Months, years, centuries. Now we will be together always."

The words were what made Nicole awaken. They were intimate words of love meant for another woman. She could believe that the caresses that had made her mind go blank were hers, but those words belonged to another.

"Clay," she said quietly.

"Yes, love," he answered as he kissed the soft skin around her ear. His big, strong body was beside her, half on top of her. Somehow, she felt as if she'd been waiting for this all her life. It seemed so natural to pull him closer to her, and it flashed through her mind that she should let him find out the truth in the morning. Instantly, she discarded the idea as selfish.

"Clay, I am not Bianca. I am Nicole." She hesitated about telling him she was his wife.

For a moment he kept kissing her, but his head jerked up, and she felt his body stiffen as he stared at her in the darkness. In one movement, he was out of the low bunk bed. One minute he was in Nicole's arms, and the next they were empty. She dreaded the next few minutes.

He seemed to be familiar with the cabin, or one like it, because he knew where he would find a candle, and the little room quickly blazed with light.

Blinking rapidly as she sat up, Nicole had her first good look at her husband. Janie had been right about his arrogance. She could see it in his face. His hair was lighter than she'd thought, the rich brown of it streaked with sunlight. Heavy brows shaded dark eyes above a large, chiseled nose that thrust over his mouth, which she knew to be soft but was now drawn into a tight, angry line. His jaw was strong and hard, the muscles working.

"All right, just who the hell are you, and where is my wife?" he demanded.

Nicole's head was still foggy. He seemed to be able to turn their passion off rather quickly, but not so Nicole. "There has been a terrible mistake. You see—"

"I see someone else in my wife's cabin, that's what." He held the candle aloft and looked at the trunks along the wall. "Those are Armstrong property, I believe."

"Yes, they are. If you would let me, I can explain. Bianca and I were together when—"

"Is she here? You're saying you traveled with her?"

It was difficult to explain when he would not let her finish even a sentence. "Bianca is not here. She did not come with me. If you would listen, I—"

Setting the candle down on the cabinet, he moved closer, towering over her, legs wide apart, hands on his hips. "She didn't come with *you!* What the hell is that supposed to mean? I just paid the captain of this ship for performing a proxy marriage and for transporting my wife to America. Now I want to know where she is!"

Nicole also stood up. It didn't daunt her that her head reached only to the top of his shoulder or that the tiny cabin pressed them close together, but now they were more like enemies than lovers. "I have been trying to explain, but your complete lack of manners prevents any communication; therefore—"

"I want an explanation, not a school teacher's lecture!"

Nicole was becoming angry. "You rude, boorish—! All right, I'll explain. *I* am your wife. That is, if you are Clayton Armstrong. I have no idea, since your rudeness precludes any form of conversation."

Clay took a step toward her. "You are not my Bianca."

"I am happy to say I am not. How in the world she could agree to marry an insufferable—" She stopped, not wanting to get angry. She'd had more than a month to adjust to being Mrs. Clayton Armstrong, but he'd boarded the ship expecting Bianca and had gotten a stranger instead.

"Mr. Armstrong, I'm sorry about all this. I really can explain."

He backed away from her, sitting down on a trunk. "How did you find out that the captain hadn't seen Bianca?" he asked quietly.

"I'm afraid I don't understand."

"I'm quite sure you do. You must have heard somehow that he didn't know her, so you decided to substitute yourself for Bianca. What did you think, that one woman was as good as another? I'll say one thing, you certainly know how to greet a man. Did you think you'd make me forget my Bianca by substituting your lovely little body for hers?"

Nicole backed away, her eyes wide, her stomach turning over at his words.

Clay looked her up and down critically. "I guess I could have done worse. I do take it you persuaded the captain to marry us."

Nicole nodded silently, a lump forming in her throat and tears blurring her eyes.

"Is that a new dress? Did you make Janie believe you? Did you by some chance create yourself a new wardrobe at my expense?" He stood up again. "All right, consider the wardrobe yours. The lost money will keep me from being so naive and trusting next time. But you'll not get another cent from me. You'll return to my plantation with me, and this marriage, if it is such, will be annulled. And as soon as it's ended, you'll be put on the first ship back to England. Is that clear?"

Nicole swallowed hard. "I would rather sleep in the streets than spend another moment near you," she said quietly.

Moving to stand in front of her, watching the candlelight make her features golden, he ran one finger firmly over her upper lip. "And where else have you been sleeping?" he asked, but he left the cabin before she could reply.

Nicole leaned against the door, her heart pounding, and more tears came to her eyes. When Frank had run his filthy hands over her she'd kept her pride, but when Clay touched her she'd acted like a woman of the streets. Her grandfather had always reminded her of who she was, that the blood of kings flowed in her veins. She'd learned to walk erect, her head held high, and even when her mother had been carried away by the mob, she'd kept her head high.

What the horror of the French Revolution could not

do to a member of the ancient Courtalain family, one rude and overbearing American had done. With shame, she remembered her complete surrender to his touch, how she'd even wanted to remain in bed with him.

Even though she'd nearly lost herself to him, she would do her best to regain her pride. Looking at the trunks with pain, she knew they were full of clothing cut especially for her. If she couldn't bring the whole fabric back, maybe she could someday repay Mr. Armstrong.

Quickly, she removed the thin muslin dress she wore and donned a heavier, more practical one of light blue calico. She folded the delicate muslin and put it inside one of the top trunks. The dress she'd worn onto the ship had been discarded by Janie after Frank had torn it.

Taking a piece of writing paper from a trunk, she leaned over the corner cabinet and wrote a letter.

Dear Mr. Armstrong,
    I hope that by now Janie will have found you and explained some of the circumstances leading to our mistaken marriage.
    You are, of course, right about the clothes. It was only my vanity that allowed me, in effect, to steal from you. I will do my best to repay you for the worth of the materials. It may take me a while, but I will try to get it all to you as soon as possible. For the first payment, I will leave a locket that has some monetary value. It is the only thing of worth that I possess. Please forgive me that it is worth so little.
    As for our marriage, I will have it annulled as soon as possible and will send you notification.
                 Sincerely,
                 Nicole Courtalain Armstrong

Nicole reread the letter and placed it on the cabinet. With shaking hands, she removed the locket. Even in England, when she'd wanted money so badly, she'd refused to part with the gold filigree locket containing oval porcelain disks with portraits of her parents on them. Always, she'd worn it.

Kissing the little portraits, the only thing she had left from her parents, she placed it on top of the letter. Maybe it was better to break completely with the past, for now she must make her way in a new land—alone.

It was completely dark outside, but the big wharf was lighted with blazing torches. Calmly, Nicole walked across the deck and down the gangplank, the sailors too busy, still unloading the frigate, to notice her. The other side of the wharf looked black and frightening, but she knew she had to get to it. Just as she reached the edge of the woods, she saw Clayton and Janie together under a torch. Janie was speaking rather angrily to Clay while the tall man seemed to be listening silently.

There was no time to linger. She had so much to do. She needed to get to the nearest town, find a job and shelter. Once she was away from the bright lights of the wharf, the woods seemed to engulf her, the trees looking especially black, especially tall and formidable. All the stories she'd heard about America came back to her. It was a place of wild, murderous Indians, a place of strange beasts that destroyed people as well as property.

Her footsteps were the only sound on the forest floor, but there seemed to be many others—slithering movements, squeaks and groans, stealthy, heavy footsteps.

She walked for hours. After a while, she began to hum to herself, a little French song her grandfather had taught her, but it wasn't long before she realized that her legs wouldn't be able to carry her any farther if she didn't rest. But where? She followed a narrow little path, and both ends of it were nothing but black emptiness.

"Nicole," she whispered to herself, "there is nothing to be afraid of. The forest is the same during the night as it is in the day."

Her brave words didn't help much, but she used what courage she had and sat down by a tree. Instantly, she felt damp moss stain her dress. But she was too tired to care. Curling her body, pulling her knees into her chest, her cheek resting on her arm, she went to sleep.

When she woke in the morning, she was aware of eyes staring into hers, enormous eyes. Gasping, she sat up quickly, scaring off the curious little rabbit that had been watching her. Laughing at her silly fears, she looked around her. With the early morning sunlight coming through the trees, the forest looked friendly and inviting. But as she rubbed her stiff neck, and then when she tried to stand, she found her whole body was sore and aching, and her dress was damp, her arms cold. She hadn't even noticed yesterday how her hair had come unpinned and now hung about her neck in messy tangles. Hastily, she tried to put what pins were left back into her hair.

The few hours of sleep had invigorated her, and she set out on the narrow path with new energy. Last night she hadn't been so sure of herself, but this morning she knew she'd done the right thing. Mr. Armstrong's accusations were something she couldn't have lived with, and now she would be able to repay him and regain her pride.

By midmorning she was very hungry. Both she and Janie had eaten very little the two days before they reached America, and her growling stomach reminded her of this.

At noon, she reached a fence that protected an orchard of hundreds of apple trees, some barely ripe, and a few in the middle of the orchard laden with fat, ripe food. Nicole was halfway over the fence before Clayton Armstrong's voice accusing her of stealing made her pause in midair. What was happening to her since she had reached America? She was turning into a thief, a generally dishonorable person.

Reluctantly, she backed down from the fence. Although her mind felt good, her stomach gnawed at itself.

At midafternoon, she came to a steep-sided creek, painfully aware of the ache in her legs and feet. It seemed that she'd walked for days and she wasn't anywhere near civilization. The fence had been the only sign that a human had ever set foot on this land before.

Carefully, she walked down the side of the creek, sat down on a rock, unbuckled her shoes, removed them, and put her feet into the cool water. Her feet were blistered, and the water felt good.

An animal ran out of the bushes behind her and toward the stream. Startled, Nicole jumped and turned around quickly. The little raccoon was as shocked to see her as she was to see it. Immediately, it turned and ran back into the forest as Nicole laughed at herself and her fears. Turning back to get her shoes, she was just in time to see them floating downstream. With her skirts over her arm, she went after them, but the stream was deeper than it looked and much swifter. She'd barely gone ten steps when she slipped and fell, her skirts wrapped around her, tangling her feet, and something sharp bit into her inner thigh.

It took several minutes for her to right herself and unwrap her skirts, and when she tried to stand her leg gave way under her. Grabbing at an overhanging branch, she used it to help pull herself to shore. On the bank at last, she lifted her skirts to survey the damage.

There was a long, jagged cut on the inside of her left thigh, and it was bleeding profusely. She tore off the bottom of her chemise and gingerly daubed at the wound, gritting her teeth against the pain. With another piece of her chemise, she pressed harder on the cut, and after several minutes the bleeding stopped. Finally, she bandaged her leg with more linen.

The pain of her leg, her exhaustion, and the light-headedness from her hunger were all too much for her. She lay back against the sand and gravel of the creek bank and slept.

The rain woke her. The sun was nearly down, and the woods were growing dark again. With a jolt, Nicole sat up, then put her hands to her head until her dizziness passed. Her leg ached, and she felt weak, her whole body aching. It was difficult to stand, but the cold rain made her realize that she had to find shelter. Her blistered feet smarted when she stood on them, but she knew it was no use looking for her shoes in the dark and rain.

She walked for a long time, and she was beginning to feel as if she were out of her body and the misery did not affect her. Her feet were cut and bleeding, but she kept walking. The rain had never gone beyond a cold drizzle, and now it looked as if it might stop. Long ago, she'd lost the pins from her hair, and it hung coldly and wetly to her waist.

Two large animals approached her, their lips curled back into snarls, their eyes firelight bright. Backing away from them, she pressed her back against a tree and looked at them in terror. "Wolves," she whispered.

The animals advanced on her, and she pressed closer to the tree, knowing these were her last moments of life, feeling that she was dying very young and there was so much she'd never done.

Suddenly, a large shape—a man—appeared on

horseback. She tried to see if he were real or a figment of her imagination, but her head was spinning so badly she couldn't tell.

The man, or the apparition—whichever it was— dismounted and picked up some stones from the ground. "Get out of here!" he yelled, and threw the stones at the dogs. The dogs turned quickly and ran away.

The man walked to Nicole. "Why the hell didn't you just tell them to go away?"

Nicole looked at him. Even in the darkness, Clayton Armstrong's demanding tones were unmistakable. "I thought they were wolves," she whispered.

"Wolves!" he snorted. "Far from it. Just mongrels looking for a handout. All right, I've had enough of your nonsense. You're coming home with me."

He turned away as if he assumed she would follow him. Nicole didn't have the strength to argue. In fact, she had no strength whatsoever. She moved a foot away from the tree; then her legs gave out from under her and she collapsed.

Chapter 4

CLAY BARELY HAD TIME TO CATCH HER BEFORE SHE HIT the ground. He refrained from a tirade on the stupidity of females when he saw that she was nearly unconscious. Her bare arms were cold, wet, and clammy. Kneeling, he leaned her against his chest and removed his coat, which he wrapped around her. When he picked her up in his arms, he was amazed at how light she was. He set her on his horse, holding her while he mounted behind her.

It was a long ride to his plantation.

Nicole tried to sit up straight to avoid contact with him. Even in her exhausted state, she could feel his hatred for her.

"Here, lean back, relax. I promise I won't bite you."

"No," she whispered. "You hate me. You should have let the wolves have me. Better for everyone."

"I told you they weren't wolves, and I don't hate you. Do you think I'd have spent so much time looking for you if I hated you? Now, lean back."

His arms around her were strong, and when she put her head on his chest she was glad to be near any human again. The events of the last few days whirled in her head. She seemed to be swimming in a river, and there were red shoes all around her. The shoes had eyes and were snarling at her.

"Hush. You're safe now. The shoes or the wolves can't get you. I'm with you, and you're safe."

Even in her sleep, she heard him and relaxed as she felt his hand rubbing her arm, the motion good and warm.

When he stopped the horse, she opened her eyes and looked up at the tall house that loomed over them. Dismounting behind her, he held up his arms for her. Nicole, somewhat refreshed by her sleep, tried to regain her dignity. "Thank you, but I need no help," she said, then started to dismount. The weakness of her exhausted, starved body betrayed her, and she fell against him quite hard, nearly losing her breath, but Clay merely bent and swept her into his arms.

"You are more trouble than any six females combined," he said as he walked toward the door.

Closing her eyes and leaning against him, she could hear the strong, steady beat of his heart.

Inside the house, he set her down in a large leather chair and pulled his coat closer around her before handing her a large glass of brandy. "I want you to sit there and drink that. Do you understand? I'll be back in a few minutes. I've got to take care of my horse. If you've moved while I'm gone, I'll turn you over my knee. Is that clear to you?"

She nodded her head, and he was gone. She couldn't see the room she was in—it was too dark—but she guessed it was a library since it smelled of leather, tobacco, and linseed oil. She inhaled deeply. It was definitely a man's room. Looking at the brandy glass in her hand, she saw he'd nearly filled it. She sipped it slowly. Delicious! It had been so long since she'd tasted anything. As the first sip of the brandy began to warm her, she took a deeper drink. The two days of fasting had emptied her completely, and now the brandy went straight to her head. When Clay returned, she was smiling devilishly, the crystal brandy snifter dangling at the ends of her fingers.

"All gone," she said. "Every drop gone." Her words were not slurred like those of an ordinary drunk but were heavily accented.

Clay took the glass from her. "How long has it been since you've eaten?"

"Days," she said, "weeks, years, never, always."

"That's all I need," he grumbled. "Two o'clock in the morning, and I've got a drunken woman on my hands. Come on, get up, and let's get something to eat." He took her hand and pulled her up.

Nicole smiled at him, but her injured leg would not support her. When she collapsed against him, she smiled apologetically. "I hurt my leg," she said.

He bent and picked her up. "Did the red shoes do it or the wolves?" he asked sarcastically.

Rubbing her cheek against his neck, she giggled. "Were they really dogs? Were the red shoes really chasing me?"

"They were really dogs, and the shoes were a dream, but you talk in your sleep. Now be quiet or you'll wake the whole house."

She felt so deliciously light-headed as she leaned closer to him and put her arms around his neck. Her lips were close to his ear as she tried to whisper. "Are you really the awful Mr. Armstrong? You don't seem at all like him. You're my rescuing knight, so you can't be that horrid man."

"You think he's that awful?"

"Oh, yes," she said firmly. "He said I was a thief. He said I stole clothes meant for someone else. And he was right! I did. But I showed him."

"How did you do that?" Clay asked quietly.

"I was very hungry, and I saw some apples in an orchard, but I didn't take them. No, I wouldn't steal them. I'm not a thief."

"So, you starved yourself just to prove to him that you weren't a thief."

"And for me. I count, too."

Clay didn't answer as he came to a door at the end of

a hallway. He opened it and carried Nicole outside toward the kitchen, which was separate from the house.

Nicole lifted her head from Clay's shoulder and sniffed. "What is that smell?"

"Honeysuckle," he said succinctly.

"I want some," she demanded. "Would you please carry me to it so I may cut a piece?"

Closing his mouth on a retort, he obeyed her.

There was a six-foot brick wall covered with the fragrant honeysuckle, and Nicole tore off six branches before Clay said she had enough and carried her to the kitchen. Inside the large room, he set her on the big table in the center of the room as if she were a child and started the fire that had been banked for the night.

Lazily, Nicole toyed with the honeysuckle in her lap.

Turning from the fire to look at her, Clay saw that her dress was muddy and torn, her feet bare, cut, and bleeding in places. Her long hair hung down her back, the blackness of it playing with the firelight, and she didn't look more than twelve years old. As he looked at her, he noticed a darker stain on the light-colored fabric.

"What did you do to yourself?" he asked harshly. "That looks like blood."

Startled, she looked up at him as if she'd forgotten he was there. "I fell," she said simply, watching him. "You *are* Mr. Armstrong. I'd recognize that frown anywhere. Tell me, do you ever smile?"

"Only when there's something to smile about, which is not at the moment," he answered, lifting her left leg and propping her heel on top of his belt. Then he rolled her skirt back to expose her thigh.

"Am I really such a burden, Mr. Armstrong?"

"You haven't exactly added any peace and quiet to my life," he said as he gently pulled the bloody piece of linen from the cut. "Sorry," he said when she winced and grabbed his shoulder. It was an ugly, dirty cut but not deep. He thought it would heal properly if it were washed well. He swung her around so her leg was stretched out on the table and went to heat some water.

"Janie said you had half the women in Virginia after you. Is that true?"

"Janie talks too much. I think we'd better get some food in you. You know you're drunk, don't you?"

"I've never been drunk in my life," she said with all the dignity she could muster.

"Here, eat this," he commanded, thrusting a thick slice of bread at her, the top liberally coated with fresh butter.

She gave her concentration to eating.

After filling a basin with warm water, Clay took a cloth and began washing the cut on her thigh. He was bending over her when the door opened.

"Mr. Clay, where have you been all night, and what are you doin' in my kitchen? You know I don't like things like that goin' on."

The last thing Clay needed was another lecture from a woman who worked for him. His ears were still ringing from Janie's tirade. She'd screamed at him for a solid hour because he'd been writing a letter of explanation to Bianca to be sent on the frigate that was just leaving while Nicole was lost in the woods.

"Maggie, this is my . . . wife." It was the first time he'd said the words.

"Oh," Maggie grinned. "Is this the one Janie said you lost?"

"Go back to bed, Maggie," Clay said with great patience.

Nicole turned around and looked at the large woman. *"Bonjour, madame,"* she said, and raised her piece of bread in salute.

"Don't she speak English?" Maggie asked in a stage whisper.

"No, I doesn't," Nicole said, her back to Maggie but her big brown eyes flashing.

Clay stood up and gave a look of warning to Nicole before taking Maggie's arm and leading her to the door. "Go back to bed. I'll take care of her. I assure you I am quite capable of doing so."

"You sure are! Whatever language she talks, she looks about as happy as any woman can get."

A glare from Clay made Maggie leave the kitchen, and he went back to Nicole.

"I guess we are married, aren't we?" she said as she licked the last of the butter from her fingers. "Do you think I look happy?"

He stood up, emptied the dirty water into a wooden bucket, and refilled the basin. "Most drunks are happy." He began again on her thigh.

Nicole touched his hair, and he lifted his head to look at her for a moment before bending again to his work. "I'm sorry you didn't get who you wanted," she said quietly. "I didn't really do it on purpose. I tried to get the captain to turn around, but he wouldn't."

"I know. You don't have to explain. Janie told me everything. Don't worry about it. I'll talk to a judge, and you'll be able to go home again very soon."

"Home," she whispered. "Those men burned my home." She stopped and looked around her. "Is this your home?"

He straightened. "Part of it."

"Are you rich?"

"No. Are you?"

"No." She smiled at him, but he turned away to get a skillet from the side wall of the enormous fireplace. Quietly, she watched as he melted butter in the skillet and fried half a dozen eggs, putting another skillet into the fire and adding several slices of ham. Buttered bread went onto a griddle.

Within minutes, he set a long platter of hot, steaming food beside her on the table.

"I don't believe I can eat all that," she said solemnly.

"Then maybe I can help you. I missed supper." Lifting her, he set her in a chair before the table.

"Did you miss it because of me?"

"No, because of me and my temper," he said as he dished out a plate of ham and eggs for her.

"You do have a terrible temper, don't you? You said some very unkind things to me."

"Eat!" he commanded.

The eggs were delicious. "You did say one nice thing," she smiled dreamily. "You said I know how to greet a man. That was a compliment, wasn't it?"

He stared at her across the table, and the way he looked at her mouth made her blush. The food was clearing her head somewhat, but something about being alone with him, the warmth of the brandy through her body, made the memory of the first time she'd met him very vivid. "Tell me, Mr. Armstrong, do you exist in the daylight, or are you only a nighttime ghost, something I've created?"

No answer came from him as he ate his food and watched her. When they were finished, he took the plates away and poured more water into the basin. Without a word, he put his hands under her arms and lifted her back onto the table.

She was very tired, very sleepy. "You make me feel like a doll, like I don't have any arms or legs."

"You have them both, and they're all dirty." He took one of her arms and began soaping it.

She ran her finger along a crescent-shaped scar at the side of his eye. "How did you do that?"

"I fell when I was a kid. Give me your other arm."

She sighed. "I was hoping it was something romantic, like you got it in your Revolutionary War."

"Sorry to disappoint you, but I was only a boy during the war."

She ran one soapy finger along his jaw line and then his chin. "Why haven't you ever married?"

"I did. I married you, didn't I?"

"But it's not real. It wasn't a real marriage. You weren't even there. That man Frank was. He kissed me, did you know that? He said he hoped I didn't marry you, because then he could kiss me some more. He said I had an upside-down mouth. You don't think my mouth is upside-down, do you?"

With his eyes on her mouth, he paused as he was washing her, and when he started soaping her face he still didn't speak.

"No one ever told me it was ugly before. I didn't know." Tears began to gather in her eyes. "I bet you hated kissing me. I know it felt funny, not at all like it was supposed to feel."

"Will you stop talking?" Clay commanded as he finished rinsing the soap off her face. Then he saw that more tears were gathering in her eyes and realized the food hadn't sobered her up much after all, or at least he hoped it was the brandy and that she wasn't so silly all the time. "No, your mouth is not ugly," he finally said.

"It isn't upside-down?"

He dried her arms and face. "It is unique. Now, be quiet, and I'll take you to your room where you can sleep," he said, swinging her into his arms.

"My flowers!"

Sighing, he shook his head and bent so she could get the flowers from the table.

He carried her outside, into the main house, then up the stairs as she snuggled against him quietly. "I hope you stay like this and don't become that other man again. I'm going to stop stealing, I promise."

He didn't answer as he opened a bedroom door on

the second floor, and as he put her on the bed he realized that her dress was still quite damp. When he saw her eyes close in weariness, he knew she'd never be able to undress herself. Cursing under his breath, he began to undress her, aware that there wasn't much of the dress or the delicate chemise left. When the buttons gave him trouble, he tore the fabric away.

Her body was beautiful. She was slim-hipped and small-waisted, and her breasts lifted impudently. He went to the dresser to get a towel, all the while cursing the situation. What the hell did she think he was made of? First her thigh, and now he was supposed to treat her like a child and dry her. But she certainly didn't look like a child!

Clay's vigorous rubbing woke Nicole from her sleep. As she smiled at the pleasant sensation, he roughly pulled the light quilt back and put her under it, letting out his breath when she was out of view. He turned to leave the room, but she caught his hand.

"Mr. Armstrong," she said sleepily. "Thank you for finding me."

Bending over her, he smoothed her hair from her face. "I should apologize for causing you to run away. Now, go to sleep and we'll talk tomorrow."

She didn't release his hand. "Did you hate kissing me? Was it like kissing an upside-down mouth?"

There was a little light coming into the room, and Clay guessed it was nearly morning. Her hair was spread out over the pillow, and his memory of kissing her was far from unpleasant. He bent toward her, meaning to kiss her only lightly, but her mouth did entice him and he took her upper lip between his teeth and caressed it, running his tongue along its contours. Nicole's arms went round his neck and pulled him to her as she opened her mouth under his.

Clay nearly lost himself before he pulled away and

firmly put her arms under the covers. Nicole smiled at him dreamily, her eyes closed. "No, you don't think it's ugly," she murmured.

He stood and left the room, closing the door behind him. He started to go to his own room, but he knew it would be no use to try to sleep. What he needed was a plunge in a cold stream and then a long, hard day of work, he thought as he left the house to go to the stables.

When Nicole woke in the morning, her first impression was of sunshine and light. Her second was of a headache. She sat up slowly, her hand to her forehead, and as the bedcovers fell away she hastily pulled them up again, wondering why she'd slept in the nude. Looking over the side of the bed, she saw that her clothes lay in a torn heap.

As her mind became alert, she remembered seeing Clayton throwing rocks at the dogs and putting her on his horse. The ride was a vague memory, and the time after they reached his house was a blank.

She looked about her, realizing that this must be a bedroom in Arundel Hall. It was a beautiful room, large and bright. The floors were oak, and the ceilings and walls were painted white. Around the two doorways and three windows were carved pediments, simple and elegant. One wall contained a fireplace, another a deep window seat. The four-poster bed hangings, the curtains, and the window seat upholstery were all of the same fabric—white linen with blue figures. There was a blue wing chair before the fireplace and a white chippendale chair in front of a window, facing an empty rosewood embroidery frame. Another chair and a tall, three-legged tea table were at the foot of the bed. A matching wardrobe and bow-front cabinet of walnut inlaid with curly maple took up the rest of the room.

Stretching, Nicole could feel her headache leaving

her, and she threw back the covers and went to the wardrobe. All the clothes she and Janie had made hung there. She smiled, feeling welcome; it was almost as if this beautiful room were meant to be hers.

She slipped into a thin cotton chemise, the top of the bodice embroidered with tiny pink rosebuds, and over it went a dress of India muslin, a wide velvet ribbon around the high waist. The low neckline was filled with transparent gauze. Hastily, she swept her hair back, curls falling forward to frame her face, and she tied it with a green velvet ribbon to match the one on her dress.

Pausing as she turned to leave the room, she saw that two of the windows faced south toward the garden and the river. When she looked out the window, she expected to see a garden like the English had, but what she saw made her gasp. It was closer to a village!

To her left were six buildings, one attached to the corner of the house by a curved brick wall. Smoke curled from the chimneys of two of the buildings. To her right were more buildings, including another one connected to the main house. Most of these buildings were hidden by enormous walnut trees.

Directly in front of her was a beautiful garden. There were paths bordered by high walls of English box. In the middle of the paths was a tile pool, and just to the right could be seen the corner of a little white pavilion, hidden under two great magnolias. There was a long bed of flowers and herbs, a kitchen garden walled by a brick fence covered in honeysuckle.

Past the garden, the land dropped away sharply to form low, flat fields, and she could see cotton, golden wheat, barley, and what she suspected was tobacco. Past the fields was the river. And everywhere there seemed to be barns and sheds and people going about their work.

Breathing deeply of the sweet summer air, catching

the scent of the hundreds of different plants, she lost her headache completely and was impatient with a need to see the outside herself.

"Nicole!" someone called.

Nicole smiled and waved down at Janie.

"Come down and get something to eat."

Nicole suddenly realized she was ravenous as she opened one of the doors and went down the stairs. The hallway held several portraits, a few chairs, and two little tables. Everywhere she looked, she saw beauty. On the ground floor, the stairs ended in a wide central hallway, capped by a lovely, carved double arch over the stairs. She was standing there trying to decide which way to go when Janie appeared.

"Did you sleep well? Where did Clay find you? Why did you run off in the first place? Clay wouldn't tell me what he'd said to make you run away, but I can guess it was somethin' terrible. You look a little thin."

Laughing, Nicole held up her hand in surrender. "I'm starving. I'll answer what I can if you'll show me where I can get something to eat."

"Of course! I should have guessed and not kept you standing around."

Nicole followed her to the garden door, which was covered by an octagonal porch with steps leading off in three directions. The right-hand steps, Janie explained, led to Clay's office and the stables; the center steps led into the shady, secret paths of the garden. Janie took the left stairs, which led to the cook houses.

The cook was named Maggie, a large woman with frizzled red hair. Janie explained that Maggie had once been an indentured servant, but, like a lot of Clay's employees, she'd decided to stay on even after her time of indenture.

"And how's your leg this mornin'?" Maggie asked, her blue eyes twinkling. "Not that I think it'd be anything but healed after the sweet tendin' it got last night."

Nicole looked at the cook blankly and started to ask her what she meant.

"Be quiet, Maggie!" Janie said, but there was an air of conspiracy between the two women as she pushed Nicole toward the table and wouldn't let her speak.

Maggie piled food on Nicole's plate—eggs, ham, batter cakes, tansy pudding, fried apples, hot biscuits. Nicole could not eat half of it and apologized for the waste. Maggie laughed and said that with sixty people to feed three times a day, nothing went to waste.

After breakfast, Janie showed Nicole some of the dependencies, as the outbuildings were called, of a Virginia plantation. Off the kitchen was a milk room where the butter and cheese were made, and next to the kitchen was the long, narrow loom house where three weavers were at work. Beside the loom house was the wash house that stored enormous wash tubs and barrels of soap. There were quarters above these buildings for the plantation workers, who were a mixture of slaves from Haiti, indentured servants, and employees working for wages. The malt house and smoke house stood near the kitchen.

Across a path from the kitchen was the produce garden, where a man and three children were weeding the vegetables. Janie introduced Nicole as Mrs. Armstrong to everyone. Nicole tried twice to protest, saying that her visit was actually temporary and should be treated as so.

Janie put her nose in the air and acted as if she were deaf, mumbling something about Clay being as sensible as any man could be and she had great hopes for him.

Across the family garden, which Janie said she'd let Nicole discover on her own, was Clay's office, a large brick building shaded by maple trees. Janie did not offer to show this to Nicole, but she smiled when Nicole strained to see inside the windows. Near the office, under cedar trees, were more buildings: workers' quarters, ice house, storage shed, gardener's house, estate manager's house, stables and carriage house, tannery, carpenter's shop, cooperage.

Finally, when they were standing on the edge of the hill where the land fell away to the fields, Nicole stopped, her hands to her head. "It *is* a village," she said, her ears ringing with all the information Janie had given her.

Janie smiled smugly. "It has to be. Nearly all the travel is by water." She pointed ahead, across acres of fields to the wharf on the river. "Clay has a twenty-foot sloop down there. In the north, they have towns like in England, but down here each planter is almost self-sufficient. You still haven't seen all of it. Over there is the dairy barn and the dove cote. A little farther past that is the poultry house, and you haven't met half the workers. They're down there."

Nicole could see about fifty men in the fields, including a few on horseback.

"There's Clay." Janie pointed to a man in a large straw hat astride a big black horse. "He was out there before sunup this morning." She gave Nicole a sidelong look, obviously hinting she wanted to know more of what happened last night.

Nicole could give her no information since she remembered so little. "What's your job in this place?"

"I take care of the loom house mostly. Maggie oversees the kitchen buildings, and I take care of the dye pots, the weavers, and the spinners. It takes a lot of cloth to run a place like this. We have to make saddle blankets, cheesecloth, and canvas, as well as the workers' clothes and blankets."

Nicole turned back to look at the house. The beauty of the house was in its simplicity and classic proportions. It wasn't large, only about sixty feet long, but the brickwork and the pediments over the windows and doors were what gave the house elegance. It was two stories high, with a pitched roof with several dormer windows. The simplicity was broken only by the lovely little octagonal porch.

"Are you ready to see some more?" Janie asked.

"I'd like to see the house. I really only saw one room this morning. Is the rest of it as lovely as that bedroom?"

"Clay's mother had all the furniture made for the house. That was before the war, of course." She started walking through the tall hedges to the house. "I'd better warn you, though, that Clay's let the house go in the last year. He keeps the outside in perfect shape, but he says he can't spare the help to look after the house. He's a man who doesn't care what he eats or where he sleeps. Half the time he'll sleep under a tree out in the fields rather than ride back to the house."

Once inside the house, Janie excused herself, saying she had to get back to the loom house since she was very far behind in her work.

Nicole was glad to take her time studying the house. The bottom floor consisted of four large rooms and two hallways. The center hall contained the wide, carpeted staircase and served as a reception area. A narrow hallway ran between the dining room and the morning room, the outside doorway leading a path to the separate kitchen.

Facing the garden was a drawing room and the morning room. The library and dining room faced away from the river, toward the north.

Making a quick survey of each of the rooms, she decided that whoever had decorated them was a person of taste. They were simple, quiet rooms, each piece of furniture an example of the cabinetmaker's art. The library was obviously a man's room, the dark walnut shelves filled with leather-bound books, an enormous walnut desk filling a large part of the room. Two red leather wing chairs sat before the fireplace.

The dining room was done in the Chinese chippendale style, the walls covered in hand-painted textured paper, a delicate design of greenery and gently tinted birds. All the furniture was mahogany.

The drawing room was exquisite. The south windows made the room bright and cheerful. The drapes were dusty rose velvet with the seats of three chairs upholstered in the same fabric. A couch sat perpendicular to the marble fireplace, its fabric of green and rose striped sateen. The walls were covered with paper of the palest rose, a border of darker rose at the top, and a little rosewood desk sat in one corner.

But the morning room was Nicole's favorite. It was yellow and white. The curtains were of heavy white cotton sprigged with tiny embroidered yellow rosebuds. The walls were painted white. A couch and three chairs were covered in gold and white striped cotton, and against one wall stood a thin-legged cherry spinet, a music stand beside it. A mirror and two gilt candle holders hung above the spinet.

But everything was dirty! The beautiful rooms looked as if no one had entered them in years. The polished surfaces of the wood were dull and dusty, the spinet badly out of tune. The curtains and rugs were choked with dust. It was a shame to see such beauty hidden and neglected.

Standing in the hallway and glancing up the stairs, she meant to explore the whole house but right now couldn't bear to see more rooms covered in dust and dirt.

With a glance down at the muslin of her dress, she turned toward the narrow hall leading to the kitchen. Perhaps Maggie would have an apron she could borrow and the wash house would have cleaning supplies. She remembered Janie saying Clay didn't care what he ate. In the milk house she'd seen something that looked as if it hadn't been used in years, or maybe never—an ice cream freezer. Maybe Maggie could spare her some cream and eggs and a child who could turn the crank.

It was quite late when Nicole began to dress for dinner. She slipped on a dress of sapphire blue silk with long, tight sleeves, the bodice cut very low—almost too low, she thought as she looked in the mirror. With one more hopeless attempt to pull the fabric up, she smiled. At least Mr. Armstrong would see her in something that wasn't torn and dirty.

At a knock on the door, she jumped. A male voice, unmistakably Clay's, spoke through the closed door. "Could I see you in the library, please?" Instantly, she heard his boots on the hardwood floors, then muffled as he went down the stairs.

Nicole felt strangely nervous at what would be their first real meeting. Straightening her shoulders, remembering her mother's words that a woman must always stand upright and look whatever fears she had in the face, that courage is as important to a woman as it is to a man, she went downstairs.

The library door was open, the room faintly lighted by the setting sun. Clayton stood behind the desk, a book open in front of him. He was silent, but there was no doubt of his presence.

"Good evening, sir," Nicole said quietly.

He studied her for a long while before he set the book on the desk. "Please have a seat. I thought we should have a talk about this . . . situation. Could I offer you something to drink before supper? Dry sherry, maybe?"

"No, thank you. I'm afraid I have very little head for

alcohol of any sort," Nicole said as she took one of the red leather seats across from the desk. For some reason, one of Clay's eyebrows raised slightly at her words. In the light, she could see him more clearly. He was a solemn man, his mouth drawn too tightly into a straight line, a furrow between his brows making his dark brown eyes look almost unhappy.

Clay poured himself some sherry. "You speak with very little accent."

"Thank you. I admit, I must sometimes work hard at it. Too often, I still think in French and translate into English."

"And sometimes you forget to do this?"

She was startled. "Yes, that's true. When I'm very tired or . . . angry, I do revert to my native tongue."

He took a seat behind the desk, opened a leather folder, and removed some papers. "I think we should clear up some business matters. As soon as Janie told me the truth of what happened, I sent a messenger to a family friend—a judge—telling him of the unusual circumstances and asking for his advice."

Nicole nodded. He hadn't even waited until he had returned home to start annulment proceedings.

"Today the reply came from the judge. Before I tell you what he said, I'd like to ask you some questions. During the ceremony itself, how many people were present?"

"The captain who performed the ceremony, the first mate who was your stand-in, and the doctor who acted as a witness. Three."

"What about the second witness? There was another signature besides the doctor's for a witness."

"There were only the four of us in the room."

Clay nodded. No doubt, the name was forged or added later. It was another in a long list of illegalities about this marriage.

He continued. "And this man, Frank, who threatened you. Did he do it in front of the doctor?"

Nicole wondered how he knew the first mate's name and that he was the one who had threatened her. "Yes, it all happened inside the captain's cabin in a matter of minutes."

Clay rose and walked across the room, taking the seat opposite her. He still wore his work clothes, heavy dark trousers, tall boots, a white linen shirt open at the throat. When he'd stretched his long legs out toward her, he spoke. "I was afraid you'd say that." Holding the glass of sherry up to the light, turning it in his hand, his eyes came back to hers, flickering briefly over the low neckline where her firm breasts rose above the blue silk.

Nicole reminded herself not to act like a child and cover herself with her hand.

"The judge sent me a book on English marriage laws, which I'm afraid hold true in America also. There are several grounds for annulment, such as insanity or failure to be able to bear children. I assume you are healthy in mind as well as body?" Again his eyes flickered.

Nicole smiled slightly. "I believe so."

"Then the only other reason that would suffice is to prove that you were forced into the marriage." He wouldn't let Nicole interrupt. "The key word is *prove*. We must produce a witness to the marriage who can testify that you were forced."

"My word isn't good enough? Or yours? Surely the fact that I am not Bianca Maleson would carry some weight."

"If you had used Bianca's name instead of your own, then that would be grounds. But I have seen the marriage certificate and it is in the name of Nicole Courtalain. Is that true?"

She thought of her moment of defiance in the captain's cabin. "What about the doctor? He was kind to me. Couldn't he be a witness?"

"I hope he can. The problem is that he is already on a ship back to England, on the frigate that was being loaded when your packet arrived. I've sent a man to England after him, but it will take months, at the least. Until there is a witness, the courts will not annul the marriage. They call it 'putting the marriage aside lightly.'" He finished the last of the sherry and set the glass on the edge of the desk, and as he'd said all he wanted, he was silent, watching her.

Bending her head, she studied her hands. "So, you are locked into this marriage for some time to come."

"*We* are locked into it. Janie told me how you wanted to become partners in a dress shop, how you worked nights to save the money. I know an apology is little to offer, but I can only ask you to accept it."

She stood, her hand on the back of the chair. "Of course I accept it. But I would like to ask something of you." Looking at him, she saw his eyes were shaded, guarded.

"Anything."

"Since I'm going to be in America for some time, I will need employment. I know no one here. Could you help me find a job? I am educated, I speak four languages, and I believe I would make an acceptable governess."

Clay stood suddenly and walked away from her. "Out of the question," he said flatly. "No matter what the circumstances of the marriage, legally you are my wife, and I will not allow you to hire out like an indentured servant to wipe snotty noses. No! You will remain here until the doctor can be located. After that, we will talk of future plans."

Astonishment registered in her voice and looks. "Are you trying to plan my life for me?"

There was a hint of amusement in his eyes. "I assume I am, since you are in my care."

She held her chin up. "It is not by choice that I am in your care. I would like for you to help me find employment. I have many bills to repay."

"Bills? What do you want that isn't here? I can send to Boston for anything imported." Looking at her as she fingered the silk of the dress, he lifted a piece of paper from the desk. It was the letter she'd written him before she left the ship. "I believe you mean the clothes. I am sorry I accused you of theft." Again he seemed amused about something. "The clothes are a gift to you. Accept them with my apologies."

"But I cannot do that. They are worth a fortune."

"And isn't your time and inconvenience worth something? I've taken you from your home, transported you to a strange land, and behaved abominably toward you. I was very angry the first night I met you, and I'm afraid my temper overshadowed my reasoning. A few dresses are a small price to pay for the . . . hurt I've caused you. Besides, what the hell would I do with them anyway? They look a damned sight better on you than hanging in some wardrobe."

Smiling at him, her eyes twinkling, she gave him a full curtsy. *"Merci beaucoup, M'sieur."*

He stood over her, watching her, and when she started to rise he held out his hand for her. His palm was warm and callused as it swallowed Nicole's. "I see your leg's healed all right."

Nicole looked at him, puzzled. The cut was high on her thigh, and she wondered how he knew of it. "Last night, did I say or do anything unusual? I believe I was very tired."

"You don't remember?"

"Only that you chased the dogs away and put me on your horse. From then until this morning is a blank."

He studied her for a long while, his eyes staying on

her mouth so long that Nicole could feel herself begin
to blush. "You were charming," he finally said. "Now,
I don't know about you, but I'm hungry." Still holding
her hand and seeming to have no intention of releasing
it, he pressed it to his arm. "It's been a long time since
I've had a beautiful woman at my table for dinner."

Chapter 5

WHILE NICOLE WAS DRESSING FOR DINNER, MAGGIE had filled the big mahogany dining table with food. There was crab bisque, roast squab stuffed with rice, deviled crab in scarlet shells, poached sturgeon, cider, and French wine. The sheer abundance was amazing to Nicole, but Clay seemed to consider it ordinary. Nearly all the food had been grown or caught on the plantation.

They had barely sat down when the garden door banged open and some loud, excited voices shouted, "Uncle Clay! Uncle Clay!"

Clay threw his napkin onto the table and took two loping strides toward the dining room door.

Nicole watched in amazement. Clay's face, usually so solemn, had changed instantly at the sound of the voices. He didn't exactly smile; Nicole had never seen him smile, but neither had she seen such a look of joy. As she watched, he knelt on one knee and opened his arms to two children who fairly flew into them, wrapped their arms around Clay's neck, and buried their faces against him.

Nicole, smiling at the scene, walked quietly behind them.

Standing and holding the children close to him, he questioned them. "Did you behave yourselves? Did you have a good time?"

"Oh, yes, Uncle Clay," the little girl said as she looked adoringly at him. "Miss Ellen let me ride her very own horse. When am I going to get my own horse?"

"When your legs are long enough to reach the stirrups." He turned to the boy. "And what about you, Alex? Did Miss Ellen let you ride her horse?"

Alex shrugged as if the horse didn't matter. "Roger showed me how to shoot a bow and arrow."

"Did he? Maybe we can make you one for your own. What about you, Mandy? Do you want a bow and arrow too?"

But Mandy wasn't listening to her uncle. She was staring over his shoulder at Nicole as she leaned forward and said in a juicy, loud whisper that could have been heard in the dairy barn, "Who's she?"

Clay turned with the children, and Nicole got her first good look at them. They were obviously twins and she guessed about seven years old, with identical dark blond curls and wide-set blue eyes.

"This is Miss Nicole," Clay said as the children stared at her curiously.

"She's pretty," Mandy said, and Alex solemnly nodded agreement.

Smiling, Nicole held her skirt as she curtsied. "Thank you very much, *M'sieur, Mademoiselle.*"

Clay set the twins down, and Alex came to stand in front of Nicole. "I am Alexander Clayton Armstrong," he said quietly, putting one hand behind him and one in front, and he bowed, blinking at her several times. "I would offer my hand, but it is . . . what is the word?"

"Presumptuous," Clayton supplied.

"Yes," Alex continued. "A gentleman should wait for a lady to offer her hand first."

"I am honored," Nicole said, and held out her hand to shake Alex's.

Mandy edged beside her brother. "I am Amanda Elizabeth Armstrong," she said, and curtsied.

"Well, I see you two made it. You could have at least waited until I was ready so you could show me the way."

The four of them turned to look at the tall, dark-haired woman, in her forties, a stunning, large breasted woman with dancing black eyes.

"Clay, I hadn't heard that you had company. I'm Ellen Backes," she said, extending her hand. "My husband Horace and I and our three boys live next door to Clay, about five miles down the river. The twins were staying with us for a few days."

"I am Nicole Courtalain—" She hesitated, and looked over her shoulder toward Clay.

"Armstrong," he said. "Nicole is my wife."

Ellen stood still for a moment, holding Nicole's hand. Then she dropped it and exuberantly hugged Nicole. "His wife! I am so very, very happy for you. You couldn't find a better man unless you married mine." She released Nicole and hugged Clay. "Why didn't you tell us? This whole county could have used a wedding! And this house especially. There hasn't been any company since James and Beth died."

Nicole was very sensitive to Clay's reaction to Ellen's words. Visibly, he didn't move, but she felt a current pass through him.

In the distance, a deep horn sounded.

"That's Horace," Ellen said as she turned back to Nicole. "We have to get together. I have so many things to tell you. Clay has a long list of bad habits, one of which is being too antisocial. Now I know all that'll change." She glanced about the wide hallway. "Beth would be so glad to see this house come alive again. Now you twins come and give me a hug."

As Ellen hugged the children, the horn sounded again, and she ran out the door and down the path to the sloop at the wharf where her husband waited for her.

When she was gone, it seemed suddenly quiet in the hall. Nicole looked at the three who looked at the open door where their friend had just left, and she burst out laughing. "Come on," she laughed, and held out her hands to the twins. "I may not be Ellen, but I think I can put some sunshine back into this day. Do either of you know what ice cream is?"

The children timidly took her hands and followed her into the dining room. Nicole hurried to the ice house and back. When she returned, she carried pewter bowls that were so cold she had to use potholders. As the twins put the first bite of ice cream into their mouths, they looked at her with love.

"I think you've won them," Clay said as the twins dug into the creamy stuff. For herself and Clay, she topped the ice cream with brandied fruit.

Hours later, when the twins were in bed, she remembered that neither she nor Clay had eaten much supper. As she went down the stairs, Clay stood there, a tray in his hand.

"Personally, I'd like a little more for supper. Join me?"

They went to the library, and Nicole enjoyed the hastily contrived meal even if it was a little odd. Clay had made sandwiches out of thick slices of bread and smoked oysters, slathering both in hot mustard from Dijon.

"Who are they?" Nicole asked between bites.

"I guess you mean the twins." He sat in one of the red leather chairs, his long legs propped on the edge of the desk. "They're my brother's children."

"Is that the James and Beth Mrs. Backes spoke of?"

"Yes." His answer was almost hard in its brevity.

"Would you tell me about them?"

"They're seven years old. You know their names, and—"

"No, I mean your brother and sister-in-law. I remember Bianca mentioning that they died while you were in England."

74

He took a very long drink of beer, and Nicole got the feeling he was struggling with something inside himself. When he spoke, his voice seemed far away. "My brother's sloop capsized. They drowned together."

Nicole understood what it was to lose part of your family. "I think I understand," she said quietly.

Clay stood suddenly, nearly knocking the chair over. "You can't understand. No one could." He left the room.

Nicole was stunned at his vehemence and remembered Bianca saying that Clay didn't seem to care that his brother had been killed, that he went ahead and proposed as if nothing had happened. Yet Nicole had seen what happened at the mere mention of their names.

Standing, she started to clear away the empty plates but stopped. It had been a long day, and she was very tired. Leaving the dusty library, she went upstairs to the room Clay had given her, and it took only moments to undress and climb into bed, where she was asleep almost instantly.

The next morning, the early sunlight and the bright prettiness of the room made her smile. Maybe this room had been Beth's. As she went to the wardrobe, she thought that soon it would most likely be Bianca's, but she did not like the thought and refused to linger on it.

As she was looking into the wardrobes, she heard noises through the door. Yesterday, she'd had no time to explore the upstairs. One door led into the hallway, and the second door must lead to the twins' room. Still smiling, she opened it, only to be confronted by a half-dressed Clay.

"Good morning," he said, ignoring her blush.

"I'm sorry, I didn't know . . . I thought the twins—"

He reached for his shirt. "Would you like some

75

coffee?" he asked, nodding toward a pot on a table. "I'd offer you tea, but we Americans aren't as partial to tea as we used to be."

Self-consciously, Nicole walked across the room to the coffeepot. It was obviously a man's room, paneled in walnut, the bed enormous, taking up most of the room. Clay's clothes were thrown about over chairs and tables so that she could hardly see the furniture. There were two cups by the coffeepot, and she knew without asking that Maggie had assumed they'd be sharing the drink. Pouring a cup of coffee, she took it to him where he sat on the edge of the bed, his shirt unbuttoned, as he pulled on his boot. She couldn't help a lingering look at his chest, deep tan and thickly muscled.

"Thank you," he said as he took the cup and watched her turn back to the coffeepot. "Still afraid of me?"

"Of course not," she said as she poured another cup of coffee, but she didn't look at him. "I've never been afraid of you."

"I was just thinking that maybe you should be. I like your hair like that. And what's that thing you have on? I like that, too."

Turning, she gave him a radiant smile. Her hair hung down her back to her waist. "It's a nightgown," she said, thinking that she was glad she hadn't covered it with a robe. The high-necked, sleeveless bodice was made of cream-colored Brussels lace, and the thin silk that fell away from the high waist was almost transparent.

"I'm late this morning. Here." He held out his cup and saucer to her in a commanding way.

She took it from him, still smiling, but she didn't move away as he pulled on the other boot. "How did you get that scar by your eye?"

He started to say something, but as he looked at her he stopped, his eyes twinkling, his mouth soft, unlike its

76

usual grimness. "A bayonet wound during the Revolution."

"For some reason, I get the feeling you're laughing at me."

He leaned closer to her. "Never in my life would I laugh at a beautiful woman standing by my bed wearing only her nightgown," he said, running one finger across her top lip. "Now put that down," he said, nodding to the cup and saucer she held, "and get out of here."

Smiling, she obeyed him, but stopped when she had her hand on the door that connected her bedroom to his.

"Nicole."

She froze.

"I have a couple of hours of work to do, then I eat at about nine in the kitchen."

A nod was her answer as, without turning, she went into her own room and closed the door behind her, leaning against it for a moment. He had said her name and said she was beautiful. Laughing at herself for being a silly schoolgirl, after hurriedly dressing in a simple, sturdy gown of brown calico, she left the bedroom to go downstairs.

All morning, Nicole searched for the twins. She'd expected to find them still asleep, but their beds were empty. She asked people on the plantation, but everywhere she got only shrugs, and no one seemed to know where the children were.

At seven-thirty, she went to the kitchen, made crêpe batter, and set it aside to allow the flour to absorb the milk. Afterward, she spent another hour searching before, quite frustrated, she returned to the kitchen. She made crêpes while Maggie peeled and sliced peaches that were so ripe and juicy they fell apart in her hands. Nicole generously splashed the peaches with almond liqueur that was made on the plantation and wrapped the peaches in the thin, delicate crêpes, drizzled them with honey, and added a dollop of whipped cream.

When Clay appeared in the kitchen, Maggie and her three helpers left, mysteriously finding other work they had to do. Nicole set the plate of peaches and crêpes before him, and he got one bite before she asked the question she'd repeated at least twenty times that morning.

"Where are the twins?" When she saw Clayton calmly continue chewing and his shoulders begin to lift in a shrug, she got angry. Pointing the fork she held at him, her voice raised. "Clayton Armstrong! If you dare tell me you don't know where they are, I'll . . . I'll—"

Looking up at her across the corner of the table, his mouth full, he took the fork out of her hand. "They're around somewhere. They usually come in when they're hungry."

"You mean they have no supervision? They're just allowed to run free? What if they were hurt? No one would even know where to look for them."

"I know most of their hiding places. What is this? I've never had anything like this. Did you make it?"

"Yes," she said impatiently. "But what about their schooling?"

Clay was giving his full attention to the plate of food in front of him and didn't bother answering her.

Snarling and muttering something in French under her breath, Nicole grabbed the plate of crêpes from under his nose and held it aloft—over the slop bucket kept for the pigs' food. "I want your attention and some answers. I'm tired of getting no answers."

Clay bounded over the edge of the table and threw his arm around her waist, her back to his chest. When his grip had forced all the air from her lungs and she was helpless, he grabbed the plate of crêpes and set it safely on the table. "You shouldn't interfere with a man's food." He was teasing, but he didn't release her. Only when he felt her body start to go limp did he allow her any air. "Nicole!" he demanded, and turned her around in his arms. "I didn't mean to hurt you." He held her close to him, but lightly, as he listened to the return of her normal breathing.

Nicole leaned against him, hoping he would never release her.

Turning her gently, he helped her sit down. "You're probably hungry. Here, eat some of this," he said, putting a second plate of peaches and crêpes in front of her before retrieving his own.

Nicole sighed heavily, and she caught a teasing look from Clay, as if he could read her thoughts.

After breakfast, Clay told Nicole to follow him. He stopped in the shade of a cedar tree by the servants' quarters where a very old man sat whittling slowly. "Jonathan, where are the twins?"

"In that old walnut tree by the overseer's house."

Clay nodded curtly and started to turn away, Nicole on his heels.

"That your new missus?" Jonathan asked.

"She is." There was little warmth in Clay's voice.

Jonathan grinned, showing toothless gums. "Somehow I thought you'd marry a blonde, one a little taller and plumper than that one."

Clamping his hand around Nicole's wrist, Clay turned away sharply as the old man's laugh rang in their ears. Nicole was burning with questions, but she didn't have the courage to ask them.

The twins were indeed scampering about in the old tree. Nicole smiled up at them and asked them to come down, saying she wanted to talk to them. The children giggled and climbed higher into the tree.

She turned to Clay. "Maybe if you asked them, they'd obey."

He shrugged. "It's not me who wants them. I have work to do."

With a look of disgust at him, she again asked the twins to come down. They merely looked down at her, their eyes bright and mischievous, and she knew that if she was ever to have any authority over them, she had to win this contest. She turned back to Clay. "What would you do if you wanted them down? Order them?"

"They don't mind me any better than they do you," he said, looking up at them in conspiracy. "If it were me, I'd go up after them."

The twins' giggle was a challenge, and she knew Clay's lies were, too. Not for a moment did she believe that the children didn't obey him. Lifting her dress, she kicked her shoes off. "If you would give me a boost," she said.

Clay's eyes lit up. "With pleasure," he said as he bent and cupped his hands for her.

She knew he could have lifted her to the first branch, but he was going to give her as little help as possible. What none of them knew was that Nicole was an excellent tree climber. There'd been an old apple tree on her parents' estate that she knew by heart. Pulling herself onto a low branch, she stood up and saw the ladder leaning against the other side of the tree. She looked down at Clay as he stared up at her, his hands on his hips, his legs wide apart. He was thoroughly enjoying himself.

Several minutes were spent scampering around the tree, her skirt held to her knees, showing her bare legs. She caught Alex first and lowered him to Clay, who, she was grateful to see, was willing to help her at least that much.

Mandy climbed out onto a thin little branch and grinned at Nicole. Nicole grinned back and started crawling toward her. As the branch began to crack,

Mandy yelled, "You're too heavy!" Looking down, she laughed. "Catch, Uncle Clay," she called as she gleefully jumped into her uncle's waiting arms.

Too late, Nicole realized she was too heavy for the thin branch. It began to break away more. "Jump!" a voice commanded. Without thinking, Nicole let go and landed in Clay's arms.

"You saved her, Uncle Clay! You saved her!" Alex chanted.

Nicole, more frightened than she wanted to admit, looked up at Clay. He was smiling! She'd never seen such a smile before, or maybe it was that lately whatever Clay did seemed right, and she smiled back at him brilliantly.

"Let's do it again," Mandy shouted, and started for the ladder.

"No, you don't!" Clay said. "She got you, and you're hers now. You do what Miss Nicole says. And if I get one bad report—" He narrowed his eyes at them, and they backed away.

"I guess you can let me down now," Nicole said quietly.

His smile faded, and he stared at her in a puzzled way. "I'm curious. Have you always gotten into trouble like you have since I've known you, or is this new?"

The smile she gave him had one slightly curled lip. "I kidnapped myself, and I forced myself into marriage with you all for your pleasure." Her voice dripped with sarcasm, but Clay didn't take it that way.

Looking down at her bare legs slung over his arm, her dress lifted to above her knees, twisted in such a way that she couldn't pull it down, he grinned again. "I don't know which I like better—this, or you standing in front of the light in your nightgown."

As Nicole realized what he meant, she blushed furiously.

He set her on the ground. "As much as I'd like to stay and see what else happens, I have to get back to work." Still smiling, he walked toward the fields.

That night, when Nicole couldn't sleep, she told herself it was because she was uncomfortably warm. After putting on a thin silk dressing gown over her nightdress and tiptoeing down the stairs and out into the garden, she walked along the dark path, the tall hedges towering over her to the tile pool where she sat on the edge and put her feet into the water.

The night was alive with frogs and crickets and the smell of honeysuckle, making it cool and pleasant in the night air. As she started to relax, she began to think. In the years of the terror, and the year she and her grandfather had hidden with the miller, she'd never lied to herself. She'd always known that someday it would all end, and it had.

Now she faced another disaster in her life, but this time she was lying to herself that there wouldn't be an ending. She was a Frenchwoman, and Frenchwomen were noted for their practicality, but she was behaving like some silly, romantic child.

She had to face the fact that she'd fallen in love with Clayton Armstrong. She didn't know when it had happened, maybe in that first meeting when he had kissed her. All she knew now was that her thoughts and emotions, her very life, had begun to pivot around the man. She knew she wanted to provoke his anger so he'd hold her in his arms, and she wanted to parade in front of him in a thin little nightgown.

Pulling her knees up and putting her forehead on them, she felt like a woman of the streets because of the way she acted, but she knew she would do anything to have him touch her, hold her.

But what did he think of her? She was not his Bianca, as he'd called her that night on the ship. In a short time he would rid himself of her, and when she walked away she might never see him again.

She had to prepare herself for the end. These past few days had been wonderful, but they had to stop. She'd loved her parents a great deal, but they'd been taken from her, and later she'd transferred her love to her grandfather, and again she'd been left alone. Each time she'd given her whole heart, and when it had been torn out of her she'd wanted to die. She couldn't let it happen again. She couldn't let herself love Clayton so completely that she couldn't bear seeing him finally with the woman he loved.

Glancing up at the dark windows of the house, she saw a red glow that could only be the tip of Clay's cigar. He knew she was down here, knew she was thinking of him. She knew she could get herself into his bed if she wanted, but she wanted more than a night with him, as sweet as it would be. She wanted his love, she wanted him to say her name the same way he had said Bianca's.

Standing, she walked back to the house. The upstairs landing was empty, but the smell of cigar smoke was strong.

Chapter 6

NICOLE LOOKED OVER THE TOP OF THE BOOK SHE WAS holding to watch Clayton walk toward the house. She saw that his shirt was torn, his trousers and boots muddy. When he glanced her way, she looked back at her book, as if she hadn't seen him.

She and the twins were sitting under one of the magnolia trees at the southwest corner of the family garden. In the three weeks since the night she'd sat alone by the pool, she'd spent a great deal of time with the children—and very little with Clay. Sometimes she could have cried when he had asked her to join him for dinner or breakfast and she had pleaded fatigue or someone who needed her help. After a while, he'd stopped asking. He began to eat more meals in the kitchen, with Maggie for company, and sometimes he didn't come back to the house at night but slept in the quarters with his men—or women, for all Nicole knew.

Janie was still very busy in the loom house getting ready for winter, and Nicole spent several afternoons with her friend, who never asked questions like Maggie did.

Inside the house, Clay stood for a long time at the upstairs hall window looking out at the garden and at Nicole sitting with the children. He didn't understand her sudden coldness to him, why she'd changed from a laughing, friendly woman to one who was always tired, always working.

Striding across the floor of his bedroom to a tall chest, he removed his torn, muddy shirt and carelessly tossed it across a chair. The drawer he opened was full of clean, ironed shirts, and as he went to grab one he paused and looked around him. For the first time since his brother had died, his room was clean. His dirty clothes were taken away and returned clean and mended.

As he thrust his arms into the shirt, he went to Nicole's room. It also sparkled with cleanliness and sunshine. An enormous bowl of flowers stood on top of the bow-front chest, and a small vase of three red roses was on the little table by her bed. The embroidery frame held a half-finished piece of work. He touched the bright silk threads.

She'd been in his house less than a month, but already the changes were enormous. Last night, Alex and Mandy had shown him proudly how they could write their names. The food served on the plantation had always been good, if plain, but under Nicole's supervision new dishes had been added daily.

Clay had always thought he didn't care one way or the other what his house was like—only the fields interested him—but now he suddenly realized he liked the smell of beeswax, and seeing the twins clean and cared for. The only piece missing was Nicole's company, the way she laughed and made him laugh.

On his way down the stairs, he stopped and wondered how she'd been able to get the help to clean the house. Everyone on the plantation had a job, and as far as he knew about it, no one had neglected his or hers. It dawned on him that Nicole had done the scrubbing herself. No wonder she was always tired!

Smiling, he took an apple from a bowl on a table in the hall. She probably thought she was repaying him for those damned dresses he had bought her. First he went to the kitchen and told Maggie to find a couple of girls to help Nicole in the house, and then he went out to the garden.

"School's out," he said as he took Nicole's book

away from her, and the twins were gone before either of the adults could blink an eye.

"Why did you do that? It isn't time to stop yet."

"They need a holiday. Or at least you do."

She backed away from him. "Please, I have a lot to do."

Clay frowned at her. "What's wrong with you? Why are you acting like you're afraid of me?"

"I'm not. It's just that there's so much to do on a place this size."

"Are you trying to tell me I should get back to work?"

"No, of course not. I just—"

"Since you don't seem capable of finishing a sentence, then let me. You work too hard. You act as if you're one of the slaves, except that I don't work them as hard as you work yourself." Grabbing her hand, he pulled her forward. "Maggie's packing us a picnic lunch, and you and I are going to spend the rest of the day in idle pursuits. Can you ride a horse?"

"Yes, but—"

"You aren't allowed to say no, so it's better to be quiet."

He didn't release her hand as they walked across the plantation to the stables, where Clay put a soft leather side-saddle on a palomino mare for her, lifted her into the saddle, and headed for the kitchen. Maggie smiled broadly as she handed Clay the bulging saddlebags.

They rode for an hour, leaving the higher ground where the house and dependencies were, and went to the lower fields. The flat, rich bottomland followed the river in an arch that half encircled the higher ground of fields planted with cotton, tobacco, flax, wheat, and barley. To the east of the house were pastures where cattle and sheep grazed separately, and everywhere there seemed to be barns and tool sheds. They stopped once to feed apples to a pair of enormous draft horses.

As Clay talked to her about the quality of cotton, the ways of curing tobacco, she watched him, saw the pride of ownership in his eyes, how he cared for his land and the people who worked for him.

The sun was high in the sky when Nicole looked across the river and saw something that was very familiar to her—a water wheel. Staring through the trees at the stone and brick structure, she was flooded with memories. She and her grandfather had always lived in luxury, their every need had been satisfied before they had thought to want it, but when the Revolution had sent them into hiding they'd learned to survive. They had dressed as the miller and his wife did, and they had worked as they did. Nicole had scrubbed the kitchen twice a week, and she had learned to run the mill when the men went away to deliver grain.

Smiling, she pointed across the river. "Is that a grain mill?"

"Yes," Clay answered without much interest.

"Whose is it? Why isn't it running? Could we see it?"

Clay looked at her in astonishment. "Which one should I answer first? It belongs to me, and it isn't running because I've never hired anyone to run it and because the Backes mill my grain. And, yes, we can go see it. There's a house farther up the hill. You can just see it through the trees. Would you like to go across?"

"Yes, I would."

There was a little rowboat moored at the edge of the river, and Clay threw the saddlebags in, helped Nicole inside, and rowed them across. Standing back, he watched as she tramped across the overgrown path and started walking around the mill.

"It looks to be in good condition. Could I see the stones inside?"

Clay took the key for the big lock on the double doors from its hiding place, watching as Nicole inspected the grooves in the stones and muttered things about bolting cloth and a good millstone dresser. When she finished her inspection, she started asking more questions, until Clay held up his hand in protest.

"Maybe it would be quicker if I explained," he said. "When my brother was alive, we could run a bigger place, but now, with just me, I decided the mill was too much. When the miller died last year, I didn't look for another one."

"But what about your grain? You said the Backes have a mill."

"A small one. It's just easier to send it over there than to worry about running this place."

"What about the other farmers? Surely people like Janie's father need a mill. Or do they go to the Backes' too? Isn't it far away?"

Clay took her hand and led her outside. "Let's eat lunch, and I'll answer all your questions. There's a pretty place on the top of that rise."

When the lunch of cold baked ham, pickled oysters, and apricot tarts was spread on a cloth, Clay was the one who asked questions. He wanted to know why Nicole was so interested in the mill.

Nicole was very aware of him, close to her, that they were alone together in the quiet, secluded woods. "My grandfather and I worked at a mill for a while. I learned a great deal about them then."

"Your grandfather," he said as he stretched out, his head on his hands. "We've been living in the same house for some time, yet I know so little about you. Did you always live with your grandfather?"

Looking down at her hands, she was silent. She didn't want to talk about her family. "Not long," she said quickly, and looked back at the mill. "Did you ever consider selling the mill?"

"No, never. What about your parents? Were they millers, too?"

It took Nicole a moment to understand what he meant, and the idea of her elegant mother—her hair elaborately dressed and powdered, three tiny star-shaped patches at the corner of her eye, in a gown of heavy brocaded satin—working in a mill made her want to laugh. Her mother believed bread originated in the kitchens.

"What's making you laugh?"

"The idea of my mother working in a mill. Didn't you say there was a house here? Could we see it?"

Quickly, they gathered the lunch things, and Clay showed her the house, which was completely boarded. It was a simple one-room house with an attic, old-fashioned but strong and sturdy.

"Let's go back across the river. There's something I want to talk to you about and a place I want to show you."

Clay did not row them straight across the river but went upstream, past the planted fields, stopping at a point in the bank that looked to be impassable. The shore was thickly covered with shrubs, and willow trees dripped into the water.

Clay stepped out of the boat and tied it to a stake hidden by the bushes. He offered Nicole his hand and helped her to stand on the approximately one foot of sand at the edge of the river. He grabbed an enormous myrtle bush and pulled it aside, revealing a fairly wide path. "After you," Clay said, following her. The myrtle bush slipped back into place, once again hiding the path.

The path opened into a grassy clearing that was completely surrounded by trees and shrubs, and it was like entering a large, roofless room. Along two sides were flowers, a riot of them. Nicole recognized some of the perennials. Though heavily choked by weeds now, they were surviving and producing.

"It's lovely," she said, twirling about, the sweet grass about her ankles. "Someone made this. Surely it didn't grow naturally."

Clay sat down on the grass and leaned against a rock that looked as if it had been chosen for its comfort. "We made it as kids. It took a long time, but we spent every moment we had on it. We wanted a private place."

"It certainly is that. You could walk within a foot of it and not see it. The brush is too thick."

Clay's eyes had a faraway look. "My mother thought the dogs were carrying her seedlings away. She'd visit someone and leave with five cuttings. When she got home, there'd only be four. I often wondered if she suspected us."

"By *us* do you mean you and your brother?"

"Yes," he answered quietly.

Nicole's eyes twinkled. "Surely the two of you didn't plant the flowers. I can't imagine two boys risking punishment to steal iris bulbs. Could there have been a young girl involved?"

Clay's face hardened, and he didn't speak for a moment. "Elizabeth planted the flowers."

The way he said it made Nicole know that this Elizabeth had meant a lot to him, but she couldn't tell if he loved her or hated her. "James and Beth," she said quietly, sitting beside him. "Is their death the cause of your sadness, the reason you rarely smile?"

He turned to her with a face full of anger. "Until you are prepared to confide in me, don't ask for confidences *from* me."

Nicole was stunned. She thought she'd cleverly avoided answering his questions about her family, but he had been sensitive enough to realize that she was hiding something. Just as her past was still too painful to speak of, so must his be. "Forgive me," she whispered. "I didn't mean to pry."

They sat in silence for several minutes. "You said you wanted to talk to me about something," Nicole said.

Clay stretched out and let his mind change from his dead brother and sister-in-law to a more pleasant subject. "I've been thinking about Bianca," he said, his eyes turning dark. "When I planned the kidnapping, I also sent a letter to be delivered to her father after the packet had been out to sea for a week. I didn't want him to worry about her, but at the same time I didn't want him to think he could prevent our marriage. That's why I arranged the proxy marriage, which of course didn't go as I planned."

Nicole was only half listening to him. She wouldn't have believed his words could hurt so much, and to cover the pain she let her mind wander to the mill. She could run that mill. Maybe she could find work in America, or maybe she could live and work in the mill—and be near Clay.

"Remember the frigate that came in just before your ship?" Clay was saying. "I sent a letter to Bianca on that ship. I explained everything to her. I told her that by mistake I'd been married to someone else but that the marriage would be annulled immediately. Of course that was before I had the letter from the judge."

"Of course," Nicole said flatly.

"I also sent her passage money to America. I told her that I still wanted her and asked her to please forgive me and come to America." He stood and began to walk around the open area. "Damn! I don't know why all this had to happen. I couldn't return to England, not when I'm the only one running the plantation. I wrote her several letters and begged her to come to me, but she always had excuses. First her father was very ill then she was afraid to leave him. I could see that she was afraid to leave England. Sometimes the English have odd ideas about Americans." He looked at Nicole as if he expected her to answer but she didn't.

He went on. "It will be some time before she receives my letter, then months before I know if she accepts me or not. "That's where you come in." He looked at Nicole with hope in his eyes but still she didn't speak.

"I don't know what you feel about me. At first I thought you liked my company, but lately . . . You see how little I know about you. In the past weeks I've come to . . . respect you a great deal. My house is pleasant again, the twins love you, the servants obey you. Your manners are excellent and I believe you could manage a few social functions. It would be nice to have people visit again."

"What are you trying to say?"

He took a deep breath. "If Bianca refuses me, I'd like to remain married to you."

Her eyes turned from brown to black. "A marriage that would produce children, I assume."

Clay's eyes crinkled, and he smiled slightly. "Of course. I must admit that I find you quite attractive."

Nicole didn't think she'd ever been so angry in her life. She could feel the anger from her toes to her hairline. She stood up slowly, and it was a strain to speak. "No, I don't think that would do at all."

He grabbed her arm as she turned away. "Why not?" he demanded. "Isn't Arundel Hall big enough for you? With your looks, maybe you could get something bigger."

The hard slap she planted on his cheek echoed through the woods.

He stood there, his cheek turning red, his fingers digging into her flesh. "I would like the courtesy of an explanation," he said coldly.

She jerked away from him. *"Cochon!* You ignorant, vain man! How dare you make such a proposition to me!"

"Proposition! I just proposed marriage to you, and I

think I've shown a damned lot of respect for you in the last few weeks. After all, you are legally my wife."

"Respect! You wouldn't know the meaning of the word. True, you've given me a separate bedroom, but why? Because you respect me, or so you could tell your beloved Bianca that you hadn't touched me?"

The expression on his face answered her. "Look at me," she fairly shouted, her accent thick. "I am Nicole Courtalain. I am a human being with feelings and emotions. I am more than a case of mistaken identity. I am more than the fact that I am not 'your' Bianca. You say you propose marriage to me, but look at what you offer. Now I am mistress of the plantation, called Mrs. Armstrong by everyone. But my whole future hangs by a thread. If Bianca accepts you, then I'm to be cast aside. If she refuses you, then you will make do with second choice. No! Not even second choice. I happened to be in the wrong place at the wrong time. There was no choice."

She took a deep breath. "No doubt, you thought I'd remain and be the twins' governess if Bianca did come to America."

"And what would be wrong with that?"

She was so angry she couldn't speak. She pulled back her foot and kicked him. Her toe hurt more than his shin through his heavy boots, but she didn't care. She spat several French curses at him, then turned toward the path.

He grabbed her arm again. He was angry, too. "I don't understand you. I could have any of half the women in the county if Bianca refuses me, but I've asked you. What's so horrible about that?"

"Should I be honored? Honored that you will allow poor little me to stay with you? Do you think I want to be an object of charity all my life? It may surprise you, Mr. Armstrong, that I want a little love in my life. I want a man who loves me, as you do Bianca. I don't want a marriage of convenience but one of love. Does that answer your question? I'd rather starve with a man I love than live regally in your fine house with you when I'd know every day how you were pining for your lost love."

He looked at her so strangely that she had no idea what he was thinking. It was almost as if for the first time he was thinking of her as being something besides a mistake.

"Whatever you think," he said quietly, "I didn't mean to insult you. You are an admirable woman. You have made an intolerable situation into one that is a pleasure for those around you, if not for yourself. All of us, myself most of all, have used you thoroughly. I wish you'd told me earlier of your unhappiness here."

"I'm not unhappy—" she began, but she had to stop because tears clogged her throat. Another moment and she would throw her arms around him and say she'd stay with him on any terms whatsoever.

"Let's return, shall we? Let me think about it a while, and maybe I can arrange a more suitable situation for you."

She followed him down the path numbly.

Chapter 7

CLAYTON LEFT HER AT THE STABLES. NICOLE COULDN'T understand how she managed to walk back to the house. She tried to keep her head up, and she focused on one thing—the house.

She had barely shut the door to her bedroom before the tears came. The year of hiding had taught her the art of crying without making a sound. She flung herself on the bed, and the sobs tore through her.

Everything she'd said had been wrong. He hadn't meant the marriage proposal as she took it. And now he spoke of a "suitable situation." How much longer would she have before he sent her away? If Bianca came, could she bear to see Clay touch her, kiss her? Would she cry herself to sleep every night when she saw them shut the door to the bedroom they shared?

Both Maggie and Janie tapped on her door and asked if she were all right. Nicole managed to answer that she'd caught a cold and didn't want to spread it. Her swollen sinuses did make her sound as if she were ill. Later in the day, she heard the twins whispering outside her door, but they didn't disturb her. Nicole stood up and decided she'd felt sorry for herself long enough. She washed her face and removed her dress. Clay's footsteps sounded in the hallway, and Nicole stopped, holding her breath. She could not possibly face him yet. She knew that her heart would be in her eyes. During dinner, she'd probably beg him to allow her to stay near him—as his shoe polisher if that was all that was available.

She removed her chemise and slipped into a night-gown, the lace and silk one Clay had admired. She didn't know what time it was, but she was very tired and meant to go to bed. A summer storm was gathering outside. At the first distant rumblings of thunder, she closed her eyes very tightly. She couldn't remember her grandfather now, she couldn't!

She was reliving that whole dreadful night. The rain slashed against the windows of the mill, and the lightning made the outdoors as bright as day. It was the lightning that showed her her grandfather.

She sat up screaming, her hands over her ears. She didn't hear the door open or Clay cross to her bed.

"Quiet. You're safe now. Be still. No one can harm you," he said as he pulled her into his arms.

He held her like a child, and she buried her face in his bare shoulder. He rocked her against him and stroked her hair. "Tell me about it. What was your dream about?"

She shook her head and clutched desperately at his arms. Awake, she knew that her dream had been real. She knew she would never awaken from the nightmare. A flash of lightning lit up the room, and Nicole jumped, trying to pull Clay closer.

"I think it's time we talked," he said as he lifted her in his arms, keeping a quilt twisted about her.

Nicole shook her head mutely.

He carried her into his bedroom and set her in a chair as he poured her a glassful of sweet sherry. He knew she hadn't eaten since lunch, and he knew the alcohol would go straight to her head.

It did.

When he saw her begin to relax, he took her empty glass from her, refilled it, and set it on the table by the chair. He poured another glass for himself. Then he lifted her and sat back in the chair, holding Nicole close

96

to him, the quilt across them both. The storm outside made them seem especially isolated in the dark room.

"Why did you leave France? What happened at the miller's house?"

She hid her face in his shoulder and shook her head. "No," she whispered.

"All right, then, tell me about a good day. Did you always live with your grandfather?"

The sherry made her feel warm and languid. She smiled in a lopsided way. "It was a beautiful house. It belonged to my grandfather, but someday it was to be my father's. It didn't matter; there was room for all of us. It was pink outside. My bedroom had cherubs painted on it. They were falling off a cloud. Sometimes I'd wake up and open my arms to catch them."

"You lived there with your parents?"

"Grandfather lived in the east wing, and I lived in the main house with my parents. Of course, we kept the west wing for the king's visits."

"Of course," Clay answered. "What happened to your parents?"

Silently, tears began to run down her face. Clay held the glass and gave her another sip of sherry.

"Tell me," he whispered.

"Grandfather was home from Court. He was away so often. He came home because so many people were unsafe in Paris. My father said we should all go to England until the people calmed down, but my grandfather said that Courtalains had lived in the chateau for centuries, and he was not going to leave it. He said the rabble wouldn't dare oppose him. We all believed him. He was so big and strong. His voice alone could scare anyone." She stopped.

"What happened that day?"

"Grandfather and I went riding in the park. It was a beautiful spring day. Then we saw smoke through the

97

trees, and my grandfather spurred his horse forward. I followed him. When we broke through the trees, we saw it. My beautiful, beautiful house was going up in flames. I just sat there and stared. I couldn't believe it. My grandfather led my horse to the stables and lifted me off it. He told me to stay there. I just stood there and stared and stared, watching the fire turn the pink bricks black."

"What about your parents?"

"They'd gone to a friend's house and didn't plan to get back until late. I didn't know my mother had torn her gown and they'd returned early." The sobs became stronger.

Clay cuddled her close to him. "Tell me. Get it out."

"Grandfather came back, running through the garden hedges to the stable. His clothes were dirty with smoke, and under his arm was a little wooden box. He grabbed my arm and pulled me into the stables. He threw all the hay out of a long box and pushed me into it. Then he climbed into it, too. We lay there for only a few minutes before we heard the people shouting. The horses were screaming from the smell of the fire. I wanted to go to them, but my grandfather held me still."

She stopped, and Clay gave her more of the sherry.

"What happened when the mob was gone?"

"Grandfather opened the hay box, and we got out. It was dark, or it should have been. Our home was blazing, and it was nearly as bright as day. Grandfather pulled me away when I looked back at it. 'Always look ahead, child, never look back,' he said. We walked all that night and most of the next day. At sundown, he stopped and opened the box he'd taken from the house. There were papers inside it and an emerald necklace that belonged to my mother." She sighed, remembering how they'd used the emeralds to help the miller.

Then she'd sold the remaining two to buy a partnership in her cousin's dress shop. "I still didn't understand what was happening then," she continued. "I was such a naive, sheltered child. My grandfather said that it was time I grew up and heard the truth. He said that people wanted to kill us because we lived in a beautiful, big house. He said that from now on we must hide who we are. He took the papers and buried them. He said that I must always remember who I am, that the Courtalains are descendants and relatives of kings."

"Did you go to the miller's house then?"

"Yes," she said flatly, as if she planned to say nothing more.

Clay handed her the glass of sherry. He didn't like getting her drunk, but he knew it was the only way to get her to talk. For a long time, he'd sensed she was hiding something. This afternoon, when he'd asked her about her family, there'd been a quick look of terror across her eyes.

He stroked her hair back from her forehead, the curls damp with perspiration. She was so small, yet she carried so many things inside her. Today, when she'd gotten so angry at him, he realized how right she was. Since she had arrived, he'd never looked at her without wishing to see Bianca's blond features. Yet now, when he thought of all the things she'd accomplished since she'd been in America, he knew she wasn't second-rate to anyone.

He took the empty sherry glass away from her. "Why did you leave France and the miller's house? You must have been safe there."

"They were very kind." Her accent was growing thicker. Some of her words seemed to be pronounced more inside her throat than in her mouth. Each syllable came out as if it had been covered in cream. "My grandfather said I should learn a trade and that milling was a good one. The miller said a girl could never understand stones and grain, but Grandfather only laughed at him."

She stopped and smiled. "I could run that mill of yours. I could make it pay."

"Nicole," he said in gentle, commanding tones. "Why does the storm bother you? Why did you leave the miller's house?"

She stared at the window as the rain began to beat against the glass. Her voice was very quiet. "We had plenty of warning. The miller had come back from town before he'd even sold the grain he had in the wagon. He said there were some troublemakers down from Paris. Many people knew about my grandfather and me. He had been an aristocrat all his life, and he said he was too old to change. What no one understood was that my grandfather did treat everyone equally. He treated the king the same way he treated the stable boy. He said that after Louis XIV died, there'd been no more men born."

"The miller came back in a hurry," Clay urged.

"He told us to hide, to escape, anything so we'd be safe. He'd grown to love my grandfather. Grandfather laughed at him. A storm came and with it the townspeople. I was in the top attic of the mill, counting feed sacks. I stared out the window, and when the lightning flashed I saw them coming. They carried pitchforks and scythes. Some of them I knew. I had helped them with their grain."

Clay felt her body shudder, and he held her closer. "Did your grandfather see them?"

"He bounded up the stairs to where I was. I told him I would face the angry people with him, that I was a Courtalain also. He said he wanted more Courtalains, and I was the only one left now. He spoke as if he were already dead. He grabbed an empty feed bag and put it over my head. I think I was too stunned to speak. He tied the top of it, then whispered that if I loved him I wouldn't move. He piled full bags of grain around me. I heard him go down the stairs. Minutes later, the mob entered the mill house. They searched the attic and several times came very close to finding me."

Clay kissed her forehead, held it against his cheek. "And your grandfather?" he whispered.

"I worked myself free when they were gone. I wanted to get out and make sure he was safe. As I looked out the window—" Her body contracted violently, and he wrapped her closer to him.

"What was outside the window?"

She jerked away from him, pushing at him. "My grandfather was there. He was there, smiling at me."

Clay stared in puzzlement.

"Don't you understand? I was in the attic. They'd cut his head off and stuck it on a pike. They'd carried it high over their heads like a trophy. The lightning flashed, and I saw him!"

"Oh, God," Clay moaned, and he pulled her back to him even though she fought him. As she began to cry, he held her, rocked her, caressed her hair.

"They killed the miller, too," she said after a while. "The miller's wife said I had to get away, that she could protect me no longer. She sewed three emeralds into my dress and put me on a ship to England. The emeralds and my locket were all that was left of my childhood."

"And then you stayed with Bianca and were kidnapped by me."

She sniffed. "You make it sound as if all my life were bad. I had a very happy childhood. I lived on a great estate, and I had hundreds of cousins for playmates."

He was glad to see she was recovering. He hoped that talking of the tragedy would have some lasting effect. "And how many hearts did you steal? Were they all in love with you?"

"None of them were. One cousin kissed me but I didn't like it. I wouldn't let any of them kiss me again. You're the only one—" She stopped and smiled, then ran her finger along his lips. He kissed it, and she held the finger up to look at it. "Stupid, stupid Nicole," she whispered.

"Why do you call yourself stupid?"

"The whole story is quite comical, really. One day, I'm riding in the park. The next, I wake up on a ship bound for America. Then I'm forced to marry a man who says I'm a thief." She didn't seem to feel Clay wince. "It would all make an excellent play. Beautiful heroine Bianca is engaged to handsome hero Clayton. But their plans are disrupted by the villainous Nicole. The audience would hang on to their seats until the end of the play, when the course of true love runs straight and Bianca and Clay are reunited."

"And what of Nicole?"

"Ah! A judge gives her some papers that say she never existed, that the time she spent with the hero never was."

"Isn't that what Nicole wants?" he asked quietly.

She held the finger Clay had kissed to her lips. "Poor, ignorant Nicole has fallen in love with the hero. Isn't that funny? He's never even looked at her in their ten-minute marriage, but she's in love with him. Do you know that he said she was an admirable woman? The poor, dumb thing is standing there, begging, wanting him to offer her passion, and he talks of all the things she can do, rather like buying a mare."

"Nicole—" he began.

She giggled and stretched in his arms. "Did you know that I'm twenty years old? Half my cousins were married by the time they were eighteen. But I was always different. They said I was cold and unfeeling, that no man would ever want me."

"They were wrong. The minute you're free of me, you'll have a hundred men asking you to marry them."

"You're anxious to get rid of me, aren't you? You'd rather have your dreams of Bianca than have me, wouldn't you? I am stupid. Sexless, motherly, virginal Nicole, in love with a man who doesn't even know she's alive."

She looked up at him. Somewhere there was a sober part of her brain that was listening to what she'd said to him. He was smiling at her. Laughing! Tears came to her eyes again. "Let me go! Leave me alone! Tomorrow you can laugh at me, but not now!" She struggled to get off his lap.

He held her tightly. "I'm not laughing at you. It's just what you said about being sexless." He ran his finger across her upper lip. "You really don't know, do you? I can almost understand why your cousins shied away from you. There's an intensity about you that's almost frightening."

"Please, let me go," she whispered.

"How can any woman as beautiful as you not be sure of her beauty?" She started to speak, but he put his fingers over her lips. "Listen to me. That first night on the ship, when I kissed you—" He smiled in memory. "No woman's ever kissed me like that. You asked nothing in return, only to give. Later, when I saw you terrified of the dogs, I think I would have walked through boiling oil to get to you. Don't you understand, can't you see how your presence affects me? You say I've never even looked at you. The truth is I've never stopped. Everyone on the plantation is laughing at the weak excuses I make to come to the house every day."

"I didn't know you even knew I was here. Do you really think I'm pretty? I mean, my mouth, and to me a beautiful woman is blonde and blue-eyed."

He bent and kissed her, lingeringly, caressingly. He

ran his lips along hers, then his tongue and his teeth. He touched the tip of his tongue to each corner of her mouth, then fiercely took her lower lip between his teeth, tasting the firm ripeness of it. "Does that answer your question? Several nights I've had to sleep in the fields in order to get some rest. With you in the next room, I've never been able to sleep more than a few hours."

"Maybe you should have come to my room," she said huskily. "I don't think I would have turned you away."

"That's good," he said as he kissed her ear, then her neck, "because I'm going to make love to you tonight even if it's a matter of rape."

Her arms slid around his neck. "Clay," she whispered, "I love you."

He put his arms under her and stood up, then carried her to the bed. He lit a candle beside the bed. The delicious bayberry scent floated through the room. "I want to see you," he said, and sat beside her on the bed. The lace bodice of the nightgown was fastened with seventeen tiny, satin-covered buttons. Slowly and carefully, Clay unbuttoned each one. His hands against her breasts made Nicole close her eyes.

"Did you know that I undressed you the night I took you from the dogs? Leaving you alone in that bed was the hardest thing I've ever done."

"That's how my dress got torn."

He didn't answer her as he took her arms out of the lace bodice, then lifted her to remove the rest of the gown. He ran his hand down the side of her body, pausing at the curve of her hip. She was small but perfectly proportioned. Her breasts were high and full, her waist tiny, her legs and hips slim. He bent his head and kissed her stomach, rubbed his cheek against it.

"Clay," she whispered, her hand in his hair, "I'm frightened."

He lifted his head and smiled at her. "The unknown is what's frightening. Have you ever seen a naked man?"

"One of my cousins when he was two," she answered honestly.

"There's a big difference," he said, and he stood to begin unfastening the side buttons of his pants, the only garment he wore.

She was shy when they dropped to the floor, and she kept her eyes on his face. He stood quietly, and she knew he expected more of her. His chest was tanned from the sun. It was wide and muscled. The deep curve of his muscles played with the candlelight. His waist was very slim, his stomach muscles forming separate ridges. Quickly, her eyes went to his feet, his strong calves, and his heavily muscled thighs. He was a man who spent a great deal of time on a horse, and his thighs showed the result. Her eyes went back to his face, and he still wore a look of waiting.

She looked downward. What she saw did not frighten her. He was Clayton, the man she loved, and she wasn't afraid of him. She gave a low, throaty laugh of relief and pleasure. She opened her arms to him. "Come to me," she whispered.

Clay smiled at her as he stretched out beside her on the bed.

"Such a beautiful smile," she said as she ran a finger along his lips. "Someday, maybe you'll explain to me why I see it so seldom."

"Maybe," he said impatiently as he caught her mouth under his.

To Nicole, Clay's skin was electric. The size and strength of him made her feel small and feminine. As he kissed her neck, she ran her hand over his arm, feeling the dips and curves of it. Suddenly, she realized that he was hers, that his body was hers to explore and taste. She leaned toward him and kissed that smile of

105

his, ran her tongue across those even white teeth she so seldom saw. She placed little nipping bites along his neck, pulled at his earlobe with her teeth. She moved her thigh between his.

Clay was startled by her actions. Then he laughed inside his throat. "Come here, my little French vixen." He pulled her close to him and rolled with her across the bed.

Nicole laughed joyously, delightfully. He held her on top of him, ran his hands through her hair, then up her body to her breasts.

Suddenly, his expression changed, darkened. "I want you," he whispered.

"Yes," she answered. "Yes."

Gently, he laid her on the bed and moved on top of her. The alcohol on an empty stomach, the catharsis of telling someone about her grandfather, all conspired to relax her. All she knew was that she was with the man she loved and wanted. She wasn't afraid when she first felt Clay enter her. There was a moment of pain, but she forgot it at the thought of being closer to Clay.

A moment later, her eyes widened in surprise. Always before, when she'd imagined lovemaking, she'd imagined a rather holy pleasure, a feeling of closeness and love. The feeling that was coursing through her veins had nothing to do with love—this was fire!

"Clay," she whispered, then tilted her head backward and arched her body.

He went slowly at first, restraining himself, knowing this was her first time. But her reactions inflamed him. He'd guessed that she was a woman who understood passion instinctively, but he had never guessed the depth of her. Her throat was exposed, and he could see the blood pounding there. She clutched at his hips, ran her hands down along his body. She made him feel as if she enjoyed him as much as he did her. The women he'd had in his lifetime usually were demanding or believed they were doing him a favor.

He fell on top of her as his thrusts became harder and faster. She pulled him closer, closer, wrapping her legs around his waist. When they exploded together, they still clung, their bodies united, their sweat mingled.

For Nicole, it had been a new, wondrous experience. She'd expected something heavenly and uplifting. The animal passion she'd experienced was so much more than she knew existed. She fell asleep in Clay's arms.

Clay would not release her even the slightest distance. For all the times he'd spent in bed with women, he felt that this had been his first. For the first time in years, he fell asleep with a smile on his face.

When Nicole woke the next morning, it was some minutes before she opened her eyes. She stretched luxuriously, knowing that when she did open them she'd see Clay's dark-paneled bedroom, the pillow his head had touched. She sensed he was gone, but her happiness was too great to be spoiled.

When at last she looked about her, she was startled to see the white walls of her own room. Her first thought was that Clay had not wanted her to remain in his bed. She tossed the light quilt aside and told herself that was absurd. More than likely, he was concerned that she should have a choice about someone finding her in his bed or her own.

She went to the wardrobe and chose a lovely dress of pale blue muslin, the high waist and the skirt trimmed in deep blue satin ribbon. There was a note on top of the dresser. "Breakfast at nine. Clay." She smiled, and her fingers trembled as she buttoned the dress.

The hall clock struck seven, and she wondered how on earth she was going to wait until nine before seeing him again. A quick check of the twins' rooms showed they were dressed and gone.

She left the house by the garden door, but as she stood there under the little octagonal porch, she paused a moment. She usually went to the left, to the kitchen. Suddenly, she turned on her heel and took the right-hand stairs that led to the path to Clay's office.

She'd never been in Clay's office before, and somehow she got the impression that very few people did go there. It was shaped like a miniature of the main house, rectangular with a high-pitched roof. Only the dormers and the porches were missing.

She knocked lightly at the door, and when no answer came she lifted the latch. She was curious about the place where the man she loved spent so much time.

The wall facing the door contained two windows, which were surrounded, floor to ceiling, with bookshelves. The overhanging maple trees made the room cool and dark. The end walls contained oak files and a cabinet for rolled documents. She stepped fully into the room. The bookshelves were filled with books on Virginia law, surveying, and the raising of different crops. She smiled and ran her finger along some of the leather bindings. They were clean, and she knew from Clay's habits that the cleanliness came from use instead of a dust rag.

Still smiling, she turned toward the opposite wall where the fireplace was. Instantly, her smile faded. Over the fireplace hung an enormous portrait—of Bianca. It was Bianca at her very loveliest, a little slimmer than Nicole remembered her. Her honey-blonde hair was drawn away from her oval face, fat sausage curls hanging over one bare shoulder. Her eyes were deep blue and sparkling, her little mouth was drawn into a slight smile. It was a mischievous, impish expression, one Nicole had never seen. It was a smile meant for someone she loved very much.

Still stunned, she looked at the mantel. Slowly, she

walked toward it. A little red velvet beret lay there. She'd seen Bianca wear an identical one several times. There was a gold bracelet beside it, one she'd also seen Bianca wear. The inscription read, "B, with all my love, C."

Nicole stepped back. The portrait, the pieces of clothing, all went together to form a shrine. If she didn't know better, she would have thought it was a memory set up to a dead woman.

How could she fight this? Last night he'd said no words of love to her. She remembered with horror all the things she'd said to him. Damn him! He knew how she reacted to the least little bit of alcohol. It had always been a family joke that if anyone wanted to know any of Nicole's secrets, all they had to do was give her two drops of wine.

But this morning she was different. This morning, she must try and salvage what was left of her pride. She walked across the garden to the kitchen and had breakfast. Maggie kept giving broad hints about Mr. Clay returning and that Nicole should eat with him. Nicole ignored her.

After breakfast, she went to the wash house and got cleaning supplies. Once inside the main house, she changed into a serviceable dress of midnight blue calico, then went downstairs again to start polishing the morning room. Maybe the work would help her make some decisions.

She was busy on the spinet when Clay's lips touched her neck. She jumped as if she'd been burned.

"I missed you at breakfast," he said lazily. "I would have stayed with you if it weren't so close to harvest time." His eyes were dark, hooded.

Nicole took a deep breath. If she stayed here with him, she'd spend every night with him, until he finally got the woman he loved. "I'd like to talk to you."

He reacted immediately to her cool tone. His back stiffened. The lazy, seductive look left his face. "What is it?" His tone matched hers.

"I can't stay here," she said flatly, trying not to let him see her pain. "Bianca—" It hurt her even to say the name. "Bianca will surely come to America soon. I'm sure when she receives your letter and the passage money, she will take the first ship here."

"There's nowhere for you to go. You must stay here." It was a command.

"And be your mistress?" she flared.

"You're my wife! How can you forget that when you constantly remind me that you were forced into the marriage?"

"Yes, I'm your wife. For the moment. But how long will it last? Would you still want me for your wife if your dear Bianca walked through that door right now?"

He didn't answer her.

"I want an answer! I think I deserve that much. Last night, you purposefully got me drunk. You knew what it did to me, that's why I don't remember the night you saved me from the dogs."

"Yes, I knew. But I also knew you needed to talk. I had no other purpose in mind."

She turned away for a moment. "I'm sure you didn't. But there I was, sprawled across your lap, begging you to make love to me."

"It wasn't like that. Surely, you must remember—" He stepped forward.

"I remember everything." She tried to calm herself. "Please listen to me. I have some pride, even if it doesn't seem so at times. You're asking too much of me. I can't stay here as your wife, truly your wife, knowing that any day it may all end." She covered her face with her hands. "I've had too many endings in my life!"

"Nicole—" He touched her hair.

110

She jumped away from him. "Don't touch me! You've played with my feelings too much. You know what I feel about you, and you've used it already. Please don't hurt me anymore. Please."

He stepped away from her. "Believe me, I never meant to hurt you. Tell me what you want. What is mine is yours."

I want your heart, Nicole wanted to scream. "The mill," she said firmly. "It's nearly harvest time, and I can have it running in a couple of weeks. The house looks sound, and I could live in it."

Clay opened his mouth to say no, then he closed it, took a step backward, picked up his hat, and turned toward the door. "It's yours. I'll see the deed is drawn up. I'll also sign over the indenture papers to two men and a woman. You'll need the help." He put his hat on and left the room.

Nicole felt like the wind had been knocked out of her. She sat down heavily in a chair. A night of love and a morning of horror.

Chapter 8

NICOLE LOST NO TIME LEAVING THE HOUSE. SHE KNEW THAT her resolve wouldn't be strong for very long. She rowed herself across the river to the mill. It sat on a hill with a long wooden trough leading from the fall of the river to the top of the water wheel. It was a tall, narrow building with a stone foundation and a brick body. The roof was of split wooden shakes. A porch ran along the entire front of the building. The water wheel itself was one and a half stories high.

Inside the building, Nicole climbed to the second story, where two doors opened onto a balcony over-looking the wheel. As far as she could tell, the buckets on the wheel were in good shape, though the ones resting at the bottom could possibly be rotten.

The enormous millstones inside the building were five feet in diameter and eight inches thick. She ran her hands along the stone and recognized the irregular network of quartz. The stones were of French burr, the finest in the world. They had been brought to America as ballast in the hold of a ship, then carried downriver to the Armstrong plantation. The stones were deeply grooved, with a series of radiating ridges. She was pleased to see that the stones were well balanced, coming very close together but not touching.

Outside in the sunlight, she walked along the hill to the little house. She could tell very little about it because of the lumber nailed over the windows and doors.

A commotion toward the river drew her attention.

"Nicole! Are you here?" Janie was yelling as she trudged up the hill.

The large, pink-cheeked woman was a joy to see, and they hugged as if they hadn't seen each other every day since they had left the ship.

"It didn't work out, huh?"

"No," Nicole said. "It didn't work out at all."

"I was hopin', what with the two of you already being married and all—"

"What are you doing here?" Nicole wanted to change the subject.

"Clay stopped by the loom house and said you were moving over here, that you were going to run the mill. He said to pick out two good men, take all the tools we needed and help you. He said that if I wanted to I could live here, and he'd pay me just the same."

Nicole looked away. Clay's generosity was almost too much.

"Come on, you two," Janie yelled. "We got work to do." Janie introduced two men to Nicole. Vernon was tall and red-haired, while Luke was shorter and dark. Under Janie's instructions, the men used crowbars to pry the boards off the front door of the house.

It was still dark inside, but Nicole could see it was a beautiful little house. The bottom floor was one large room, an eight-foot-long fireplace along one wall, a staircase with a hand-carved balustrade in the corner. Three recessed windows were in two walls, the door and a window in another. There was an old pine chest under one window, a long, wide table in the center of the floor.

As the men pried the boards off the windows, very little light came through. The noise sent hundreds of little feet scurrying.

"Phew!" Janie said, and wrinkled her nose. "It's going to take a lot to clean this place up."

"Then I guess we'd better get started."

By sundown, they'd made some progress. The upstairs was a low-ceilinged loft, the sides of the room dropping off sharply. Under the filth, they found some beautifully crafted woodwork. The interior walls were plastered, and a coat of whitewash would make them like new. The clean windows let a great deal of light through.

Vernon, who'd been nailing down loose roof shingles, suddenly called that a raft was coming across the river. They all went down to the edge of the river. One of Clay's men was poling the raft ashore. It was loaded with furniture.

"Wait, Janie, I can't accept that. He's done too much already."

"This is no time to be proud. We'll need that stuff, and besides, it's only out of Clay's attic. It's not like it was costing him anything. Now, come on and grab one end of that bench. Howard! I hope you brought some whitewash—and a couple of mattresses."

"This is only the first load. When I get through, you're gonna have all of Arundel Hall on this side of the river," Howard answered.

Janie, Nicole, and the two men worked for three days on the house. The men slept in the mill, while the women fell each night, exhausted, onto straw-filled mattresses in the attic of the house.

On the fourth day, a short, gnarled man appeared. "I hear there's a woman here who thinks she can run a mill."

Janie started to give the man a piece of her mind, but Nicole stepped forward. "I'm Nicole Armstrong, and I plan to run the mill. Can I help you?"

The man watched her closely, then held out his left hand to her, palm down.

Janie was just about to speak to the man about his manners when Nicole took the offered hand in both of hers and turned it over. Janie grimaced, for to her the palm of the man's hand was mutilated, with gray lumps all over it.

Nicole ran her hands over the man's, then smiled brilliantly at him. "You're hired," she said.

His eyes twinkled. "And you know what you're doin'. You'll run your mill just fine."

When he was gone, Nicole explained. The man was a millstone dresser. He used a chisel and sharpened the grooves in the millstones. To do this, he'd cover his right hand with leather and leave his left one bare. Over the years, his left hand would become embedded with bits of stone. The men showed their left hands with pride. It was a symbol of their experience. There was a saying, "to show one's mettle." Mettle was an old English word for crushed stone.

Janie went back to work, muttering about gloves being made for left hands, too.

When the trough to the river was cleared of debris and the water flowed over the top of the water wheel and made it turn, there was a shout that could be heard for miles.

Nicole wasn't surprised less than a day later, when their first customer arrived on a little barge loaded with grain to be ground. She knew Clay had sent a man upriver and another down with word of the reopening of the mill.

It had been nearly two weeks since she'd seen him, yet there wasn't a moment that she didn't think of him. Twice she'd caught a glimpse of him riding through his fields, but each time she'd turned away.

One morning after the mill had been running for three days, she woke very early. It wasn't light yet, and she heard Janie's deep breathing of sleep from across the room. She hurriedly dressed in the half-light, leaving her hair hanging freely down her back.

Somehow, she wasn't surprised to see Clay standing

in front of the water wheel. He wore trousers of light tan and high boots with a top cuff turned down. His back was to her, his hands clasped behind him. His shirt was especially white in the dim light, as was the broad-brimmed hat he wore.

"You've done a good job," he said without turning. "I wish I could get half as much work out of the servants as you do."

"I guess it comes of necessity."

He turned and looked at her, his eyes intense. "No, not necessity. You could come back to my house at any time."

"No," she breathed. "It's better this way."

"The twins keep asking for you. They want to see you."

She smiled. "I've missed them. Maybe you'd let them come across."

"I thought you could come to them. We could have dinner tonight. A ship docked yesterday and brought some things from France. There's brie, burgundy, and champagne. They're being brought downriver today."

"It sounds tempting, but—"

He stepped forward and grabbed her shoulders. "You can't mean to avoid me forever. What do you want from me? Do you want me to tell you how much I miss you? I think everyone on the plantation is angry at me for making you leave. Maggie serves my food either burned or raw, nothing in between. The twins cried last night because I didn't know some damned French fairy tale about a lady falling in love with a monster."

"'Beauty and the Beast.'" Nicole smiled. "So you want me to come back so you'll get a decent meal."

He lifted one eyebrow. "Don't twist my words. I never wanted you to leave. Will you come to supper?"

"Yes," she said.

He grabbed her and gave her a swift, hard kiss, then released her and left.

"I thought things weren't workin' out," Janie said from behind Nicole.

Nicole had no answer for her. She walked back to the house to start the day's work.

During the long day, Nicole could hardly contain her nervousness about having dinner with Clay. When Vernon weighed the bags of grain and called out the numbers to Nicole, she had to ask him to repeat the figures so she could record them correctly. However, she did remember to send Maggie a recipe for *Dindon à la Daube,* a boned turkey that was stuffed and served in a casserole. Maggie loved good food so much, and Nicole knew she'd probably make two of the turkeys, one for the main house and one for her and her staff.

At six o'clock, Clay's rowboat came to the shore with his estate manager, Anders. He was a tall blond man. He lived with his wife and two children in a house just south of Clay's office. His children often played with the twins. Nicole asked after his family.

"Everyone's fine except that we all miss you. Karen made some peach preserves yesterday, and she wants to send you some. Is the mill working? You seem to have quite a few customers."

"Mr. Armstrong has spread the word, and more and more people are bringing their grain."

He gave her an odd look. "Clay is a respected man."

They reached the shore, and Nicole noticed that Anders kept looking upriver. "Is something wrong?"

"The sloop should have been back by now. We heard last night that a ship was in, and Clay sent the sloop out early this morning."

"You aren't worried, are you?"

"No," he said as he helped her from the rowboat. "It could be anything. The men could be having some ale with the ship's passengers—anything. It's just Clay. Ever since James and Beth drowned, he's anxious if the sloop is an hour overdue."

They walked side by side toward the house. "Did you know James and Beth?"

"Very well."

"What were they like? Was Clay very close to his brother?"

Anders took a long time answering. "The three of them were very close. They practically grew up in each other's pockets. I'm afraid Clay took their deaths too hard. It changed him."

Nicole wanted to ask a hundred more questions. How had it changed him? What was he like before their deaths? But it was not fair to Clay or to Anders to ask now. If Clay wanted to talk to her, he would, just as she'd confided in him.

Anders left her on the garden porch. The house was as beautiful inside as she remembered. The twins seemed to appear out of nowhere and grabbed her hands to pull her upstairs. They had a long list of stories they wanted her to tell them before they went to sleep.

Clay was waiting for her at the foot of the stairs, his hand outstretched to her. "You're even prettier than I remembered," he said quietly, and looked at her hungrily.

She looked away from him and started toward the dining room, her hand still caught firmly in his. She wore a gown of raw silk, the weave slightly nubby in places, the sheen gentle and subdued. It was a warm apricot color trimmed in satin ribbons of a darker apricot. The neckline was very low. The tiny cap sleeves and the bodice were trimmed with a row of seed pearls. The pearls gained luster from Nicole's skin. Her hair was intertwined with pearls and apricot ribbon.

Clay did not once take his eyes off her as they walked into the dining room. Nicole saw immediately that Maggie had outdone herself. The table fairly bowed under the sheer quantity of food.

"I hope she doesn't expect us to eat all that," Nicole smiled.

"I think she's trying to let me know that if you're here the food will improve. It would have to improve over what it's been."

"Did the sloop arrive yet?" She saw the frown cross his face before he shook his head.

They had just sat down at the table when one of the plantation workers burst into the room. "Mr. Clay! I didn't know what to do," he said in an explosion of words. He held his hat in his hands and threatened to destroy it any minute. He was very nervous. "She said she'd come all this way to see you and that you'd string me up if I didn't bring her."

"Calm down, Roger. What are you talking about, and who are you talking about?" He threw his napkin onto his clean plate.

"I wasn't sure I believed her. I thought she might just be some English scum tryin' to pull the wool over my eyes. But then I got a good look at her, and she looked so much like Miss Beth I thought it was her."

Neither Nicole nor Clay heard the man, for standing just behind him was Bianca. Her dark blonde hair was limp and straight about her round face. Her little mouth was pursed into a pretty little pout. Nicole felt as if she'd forgotten what Bianca was really like. Her life had changed so drastically in the last few months that the time in England seemed as if it had never happened. Now she vividly remembered the way Bianca liked to control people.

Nicole turned to Clay and was astonished by his expression. He looked as if he were seeing a ghost. There was a look of incredulousness as well as rapture on his face. Suddenly, it seemed that her whole body was turning to water. She knew then that deep within her she'd always hoped that when he saw Bianca again he would know he no longer loved her. As sharp tears stung the corners of her eyes, Nicole knew she'd lost, that he'd never looked at her as he was now staring at Bianca.

Nicole drew her breath in slowly and deeply, then stood and walked across the room to Bianca. She held out her hand. "May I bid you welcome to Arundel Hall?"

Bianca gave Nicole a look of hate and ignored the hand offered to her. "You act as if you own the place," she said under her breath, then smiled demurely at Clay. "Aren't you glad to see me?" she said teasingly, the dimple appearing in her left cheek. "I have traveled a long way to be near you."

Clay's chair nearly fell as he dashed across the room to Bianca. He grabbed her shoulders with both his hands, then stared at her face with a burning intensity. "Welcome," he whispered, and kissed her cheek. He did not notice the way she recoiled from his touch. "Take the trunk upstairs, Roger."

Roger backed away from the group. He'd just spent six hours in a sloop with the blonde woman, and a couple of times he had to restrain himself from throwing her overboard. He wouldn't have believed it was possible for one woman to find so many things to complain about in so short a time. She railed against Roger and his men's lack of subservience toward her. She seemed to expect all the men to cater to her merest wish. The closer the sloop got to the Armstrong plantation, the more Roger was sure he'd made an error in delivering her to Clay.

Now, looking at the way Clay stared at the woman, Roger was astounded. How could he look at her like that when that pretty little Miss Nicole was standing there, her heart in her eyes? Roger shrugged, jammed his hat on his head, and carried the trunk up the stairs.

Boats were his business, and he was thankful women were not.

"Clayton!" Bianca said sharply, twisting out of his grip. "Aren't you going to ask me to sit down? After that long trip here, I'm afraid I'm exhausted."

Clay attempted to take her arm, but she eluded him. He held a chair for her, to the left of his at the head of the dining table. "You must be hungry," he said as he took another place setting from the chippendale cabinet.

Nicole stood in the doorway and watched them. Clay hovered over Bianca like a mother hen. Bianca swept the green gauze of her dress aside and sat down. Nicole was aware that Bianca had gained at least twenty pounds since she'd last seen her. She was tall enough to carry the weight, and as yet it hadn't distorted her face, but her hips and thighs had greatly increased in size. The high-waisted fashions concealed it to a degree, but the sleeveless style completely exposed her heavy upper arms.

"I want to know everything," Clay said, bending toward her. "How did you get here? What sort of passage did you get?"

"It was dreadful," Bianca said, lowering her pale lashes. "After your letter to my father arrived, I was desolate. I realized what an awful mistake had been made. Of course, I came on the next available ship." She smiled up at him. After her father had shown her the letter, she'd laughed heartily at the joke played on poor, stupid Nicole, but two days later she'd received another letter. Some distant cousins of hers lived in America, not too far from Clay, and they'd written Bianca to congratulate her on her catch. They seemed to think she knew of Clay's wealth and asked to borrow from her as soon as she married Clay. Bianca dismissed the cousins instantly, but she was furious to read of

Clay's wealth. Why hadn't the stupid man told her he was rich? Her anger quickly turned from Clay to Nicole. Somehow, the conniving little bitch knew about Clay and had arranged to go in Bianca's place. Immediately, Bianca told her father she planned to go to America. Mr. Maleson just laughed and said that as soon as she earned the money she could go; it didn't matter to him.

Bianca turned to Nicole, still standing in the doorway. She smiled like a gracious hostess. "Won't you join us?" she asked sweetly. "A cousin of yours came by the house to ask after you," she said when Nicole was seated. "She had some wild story about your going into business with her. I told her you worked for me and that you had no money. She said the most fantastic things about your selling some emeralds and working at night. It was really quite preposterous. To make sure, I searched your room myself." Her eyes sparkled. "A passage to America is so expensive, isn't it? But, then, you wouldn't know, would you? My ticket cost about what I'd guess a partnership in a dress shop would cost."

Nicole kept her chin up. She wouldn't let Bianca see that her words hurt. But she rubbed her fingertips in memory of the pain of sewing in the dim light.

"It's so good to see you," Clay said. "It's like a dream come true, having you here again beside me."

"Again?" Bianca asked, and both women looked at him. He was staring at Bianca strangely.

Clay recovered himself. "I meant that I'd imagined you here so often that it does seem as if you've returned." He picked up a bowl of candied yams. "You must be hungry."

"Not at all!" she said, but her eyes never left the food. "I know I couldn't eat a thing. In fact, I may give up eating altogether." She laughed delightedly at this statement. "Do you know where they put me in that

122

horrible frigate? In the lower deck! With the crew and the livestock! It was beyond belief! The porthole leaked, the roof leaked, and for days on end I lived in semidarkness."

Clay winced. "That's why I had arranged a cabin for you on board the packet."

Bianca turned to look across the table to Nicole. "But, of course, I didn't get such luxurious treatment. I imagine your food was better than mine, too."

Nicole bit her tongue to keep from commenting that whatever the quality was, the quantity seemed to have been more than sufficient.

"Then maybe Maggie's cooking will help make up for it." Clay held the bowl a little closer to her.

"Perhaps just a little, then."

Nicole watched quietly as Bianca helped herself to some of each of the twenty-some dishes on the table. Never did she pile her plate high or seem to eat very much of anything. A disinterested observer would have said she was a moderate eater. It was a way she'd learned over the years to conceal her gluttony.

"Where did you get that dress?" Bianca asked as she delicately poured honey over a bowl of spoon bread.

Nicole knew her face must be turning pink. She remembered too well Clay's accusations that she'd stolen the fabrics from Bianca.

"There are some things we must discuss," Clay said.

His words saved Nicole from having to respond.

Before he could continue, Maggie burst into the room. "I heard you got some company off the sloop. She a friend of yours, Mrs. Armstrong?"

"Mrs. Armstrong?" Bianca said, and looked at Nicole. "Is she referring to you?"

"Yes," Nicole said quietly.

"What is going on here?" Bianca demanded.

"Maggie, would you leave us?" Clay said.

Maggie was very curious about this woman Roger had railed about for the last hour. It had taken four tankards of beer to calm him. "I just wanted to know if you were ready for dessert. There's almond cheesecake, peach and apple tarts, and a custard pie."

"Not now, Maggie! There's something more important than food to be discussed."

"Clay," Bianca said quietly. "It's been so long since I've had anything fresh. Maybe we could have the peach tarts."

"Of course," Clay said instantly. "Bring it all." He turned back to Bianca. "Forgive me. I'm too used to giving commands."

Nicole wanted to leave. More than anything else in the world, she wanted to get away from this man she loved who had suddenly turned into a stranger. She stood up quickly. "I don't believe I want any dessert. If you'll excuse me, I think I'll go home."

Clay rose with her. "Nicole, please. I didn't mean—" He looked down, for Bianca had placed her hand on his. It was the first time she'd voluntarily touched him.

Nicole's stomach turned over when she saw the look in Clay's eyes. She hurried out of the room, out of the house, and into the cool night air.

"Clay," Bianca said. She removed her hand from his arm as soon as Nicole turned away, but she'd seen the power her touch had over him. He disgusted her as much as she remembered. His shirt was open at the throat, and he didn't bother to wear a coat. She hated touching him, hated even being near him, but she'd suffer a lot to own the plantation. All the way up from the wharf, she'd looked at the houses around her, and that odious man from the boat said Clay owned it all. The dining room was richly furnished. She knew the wallpaper had been painted to order for the room. The furniture was obviously expensive, even if there was so little of it. Oh, yes, if she had to touch him to get this place, she'd do it. After they were married, she'd tell him to stay away from her.

Maggie brought in an enormous tray loaded with hot, deep-fried tarts and cool cheesecake. The custard pie was topped with an apricot glaze. "Where did Mrs. Armstrong go?"

"Back to the mill," Clay said succinctly.

Maggie gave him a suspicious look and left.

Bianca looked up from a plate heaped with three desserts. She told herself that since she'd eaten so little supper she could now be generous with herself. "I'd like an explanation."

When Clay was done, Bianca was finishing a second piece of custard pie. "So now I'm to be discarded like so much refuse, is that correct? All my love for you, all the misery I've gone through to get to you, means nothing. Clayton, if you'd only let those kidnappers tell me they were from you, I would have gone with them gladly. You know I wouldn't have stayed away from you." She blotted her lips gently, and tears came to her eyes. They were genuine. The thought of losing all Clay's wealth made her want to rage. Damn that Nicole! The opportunist!

"No, please don't say that. You belong here. You've always belonged here."

His words seemed strange, but she didn't question them. "When this witness to the marriage returns to America, you'll get the annulment? You wouldn't let me stay here and then . . . then discard me, would you?"

He raised her hand to his lips. "No, of course not."

Bianca smiled at him, then stood. "I'm very tired. Do you think I could rest now?"

"Of course." He took her arm to lead her upstairs, but she jerked away from him.

"Where are the servants? Where's your housekeeper and butler?"

Clay followed her up the stairs. "There are some women who help Nicole, or did help her before she moved across the river, but they sleep over the loom house. I never felt I needed a butler or housekeeper."

She stopped at the top of the stairs, her heart pounding from the exertion. She smiled demurely. "But now you have me. Of course, things will change."

"Whatever you wish," he said quietly, and opened the door to the room that had once been Nicole's.

"Plain," she said, "but adequate."

Clay walked to the bow-front cabinet and touched a porcelain figurine. "It was Beth's room," he said, then turned back to her. His look was that of a desperate man.

"Clay!" she said, her hand at her throat. "You almost frighten me."

"Excuse me," he said quickly. "I'll leave you alone." He left the room abruptly.

"Of all the rude, boorish—" Bianca began under her breath, then shrugged. She was glad to be rid of him. She looked around the room. It was too austere for her. She touched the white and blue bed hangings. Pink, she thought. She'd redo the bed in pink tulle with layers of ruffles. The walls would be papered in pink also, and maybe she'd have flowers painted on the paper. The walnut and maple furniture would have to go, of course. She'd replace it with some gilt furniture.

She undressed slowly and slung her dress across a chair back. The memory of Nicole's apricot silk made her angry. Who was she to wear silk, when she, Bianca, had to make do with gauze and muslin? But just wait, she thought, she'd show these ignorant Colonists what real style was. She'd purchase a wardrobe that would make Nicole's look cheap.

She slipped on a nightgown from the trunk that Roger had placed in the room and climbed into the bed. The mattress was a little too firm for her taste. She drifted asleep thinking of all the changes she would make in the plantation. The house was obviously too small. She'd add a wing, her own private wing where she wouldn't have to be too near Clay when they were married. She'd buy a carriage. A carriage that would surpass the queen's! The roof would be supported by gilded cherubs. She fell asleep smiling.

Clay quickly left the house to go to the garden. The moonlight glistened on the water in the tile pool. He lit a long cigar and stood quietly in the shadow of the hedges. Seeing Bianca had been like seeing a ghost. It was almost like having Beth back again. This time, though, nothing would take her away—not his brother, not death. She would be his for all eternity.

He dropped the cigar and crushed it under his foot. He strained his ears to hear the mill's water wheel, but it was too far away. Nicole, he thought. Even now, when Bianca was so near him, he thought of Nicole. He remembered her smile, the way she had clung to him while she cried. Most of all, he remembered her love—for everyone. There wasn't a person on the plantation to whom Nicole hadn't extended her kindness. Even lazy, mean old Jonathan had said some good things about her.

Slowly, he turned to go back to the house.

Bianca woke slowly the next morning. The comfort of the bed and the good food were a luxury after her days aboard the ship. She had no problem remembering where she was or what she planned to do; she'd spent all night dreaming about it.

She threw the covers back and made a little face at them. It was really too much to ask her, as mistress of such an estate, to sleep under linen covers. The very least she could abide would be silk. She pulled a pink cotton dress from the trunk and thought it was disgusting that Clay should leave her without a maid.

127

Outside the room, she gave a quick look down the hallways, but she had no curiosity about the house. It was enough that it was hers. Now her main interest was the kitchen, which had been pointed out to her last night.

She cursed the distance from the house to the kitchen. From now on, she'd see that food was brought to her so she wouldn't have to walk for it.

She stepped inside the big kitchen regally. It was all like a dream come true. All her life, she'd known she was destined to command. That idiot father of hers had laughed at her when she'd said she wanted the estate that the Malesons had once owned. Of course, the Armstrong plantation could never come close to the estates in England; how could anything in America compare to England?

"Good mornin'," Maggie said pleasantly, her arms covered in flour to her elbows as she prepared biscuit dough for the noon dinner. "Anything I can help you with?"

The big room was alive with activity. One of Maggie's helpers watched after three pots set in the coals of the fireplace. A little boy lazily turned a haunch of meat on a rotisserie. Another woman pounded dough in a large wooden bowl, while two girls chopped pounds of vegetables.

"Yes," Bianca said firmly. She knew from experience that it was best to establish superiority over servants right away. "I would like for you and the other servants to line up and get ready to receive my instructions. From now on, I expect you all to stop what you are doing when I enter a room and pay me the proper respect."

The six people in the room stopped what they were doing and stared, open-mouthed.

"You heard me!" Bianca commanded.

Slowly, awkwardly, the people moved toward the

east wall. All except Maggie. "Who are you to be givin' orders?"

"I do not have to answer your questions. Servants should know their place. That is, servants who want to keep their employment," she threatened. Bianca tried to ignore Maggie's hostile stare and the fact that she didn't line up with the others. "I would like to talk about the food that comes from this kitchen. Judging by last night's supper, the food is a bit plain. It needs more sauces. For instance, the ham's glaze was quite delicious." She smiled smugly, knowing her praise would brighten their day. "But," she continued, "more of the sauce should have been served."

"Sauce?" Maggie asked. "That ham was glazed with pure sugar. Are you saying you want me to send in a bowl of melted sugar?"

Bianca gave her a withering look. "I am not asking for your comments. You are here to obey my wishes. Now, about breakfast. I expect it to be served in the dining room promptly at eleven. I want a pot of chocolate made with three parts cream and one part milk. I would also like some more of those tarts that were served last night. Dinner is to be served at twelve-thirty, and—"

"You think you can go that long on just a few dozen fried pies?" Maggie asked sarcastically as she removed her apron and slammed it down on the table. "I'm gonna talk to Clay and find out just who you are," she said as she shoved past Bianca.

"I am the mistress of this plantation," she said, her back straight. "I am your employer."

"I work for Clay and his wife, who, thank the Lord, is not you."

"You insolent woman! I'll see Clay fires you for this!"

"I may quit before he can," Maggie said, and started for the fields.

She found Clay inside a tobacco barn where the long leaves were being hung for drying. "I want to talk to you!" she demanded.

In all the years Maggie had worked for his family, she'd never given any of them any trouble. She was quite outspoken, and more than once her ideas were used when it came to improvements made in the plantation, but her complaints were always fair.

Clay made a futile attempt to wipe the black tobacco gum from his hands. "Has something upset you? The chimney blocked again?"

"It's more than the chimney this time. Who is that woman?"

Clay stopped and stared at her.

"She came into my kitchen this mornin' and started demanding we all obey her. She wants her breakfast served in the dining room. She thinks she's too good to come to the kitchen like anybody else."

Clay angrily threw the dirty cloth away. "You've lived in England. You know that the upper class doesn't eat in the kitchen. For that matter, neither do most of the other plantation owners. It doesn't seem like such an outrageous request. Maybe it would do us all some good to learn a few manners."

"Request!" Maggie sneered. "That woman wouldn't know the meaning of the word." She stopped suddenly, and her voice became quieter. "Clay, honey, I've known you since you were just a boy. What are you doin' now? You're married to one of the sweetest women ever created, but she runs off and lives across the river. Now you bring into your house some snotty girl who's the spittin' image of Beth." She put her hand on his arm. "I know you loved them both, but you can't bring them back."

Clay glared at her, his face becoming angrier by the moment. He turned away from her. "Mind your own business. And give Bianca whatever she wants." He walked away, his head high, the shadow of his broad-brimmed hat hiding the pain in his eyes.

In the late afternoon, Bianca slammed out of Arundel Hall. She'd spent hours on the plantation, talking to the workers, making suggestions, offering advice, yet nowhere had she been treated with respect. The estate manager, Anders, had laughed at her idea for a carriage. He said the roads in Virginia were so bad that half the people didn't even own carriages, and certainly not ones with gold cherubs holding up the roof. He said that nearly all the traveling done was through the river. At least he didn't laugh at Bianca's list of fabrics she wanted. He merely stared at it with his eyes wide and said, "You want monogrammed sheets of pink silk?" She informed him that all the best people in England had them. She ignored his remark that she wasn't in England.

And everywhere she heard Nicole's name. Miss Nicole had helped in the garden. Bianca sniffed. Why shouldn't she? She had once been Bianca's maid, not a lady with a baron for an ancestor, as Bianca had.

After a while, though, Bianca grew tired of hearing Nicole's name. She was also sick of hearing the little Frenchwoman referred to as the mistress of the plantation. She walked toward the wharf and the rowboat that would take her to the mill. She planned to give Nicole a piece of her mind.

Roger rowed her across the river, and Bianca was angered at his insolence. He told her right away that he didn't want to have anything more to do with her.

Bianca had to walk up wooden steps beside the dock that jutted into the water, then up a steep path to the little house. The top half of the Dutch door was open, and she saw a large woman bending over a small fire in the enormous fireplace. She let herself in. "Where's Nicole?" she asked loudly.

Janie stood and looked at the blonde woman. Nicole

had come back early from dinner with Clay the night before, and all Janie could get from her was that Bianca had arrived. She said no more, but her face told a great deal. Her eyes showed her sadness. Today, she'd gone about her work as usual, but Janie felt that much of the life was gone from her.

"Won't you come in?" Janie said. "You must be Bianca. I was just making some tea. Maybe you'd like to join us."

Bianca looked about the room with disgust. She saw nothing charming in the plaster walls, the beamed ceiling, or the spinning wheel by the fire. To her it was a hovel. She dusted a chair with her fingertips before she sat in it. "I would like for you to get Nicole. Tell her I am waiting and don't have all day."

Janie set the teapot on the table. So this was the beautiful Bianca that Clay was so crazy about. She saw a woman with a colorless face and a body that was rapidly turning to fat. "Nicole has work to do," Janie said. "She'll be here when she can."

"I have had about enough insolence from Clay's servants. I'm warning you that if—"

"If what, missy? I'll have you know that my duties lie with Nicole, not Clayton," she half lied. "And furthermore—"

"Janie!" Nicole said from the doorway. She walked across the room. "We have a guest, and we must be gracious. Would you care for some refreshment, Bianca? There are some warm crullers from breakfast."

When Bianca didn't answer, Janie muttered something about her looking as if she could eat all the grain in the mill.

Bianca sipped her tea and ate the soft, warm, sugary crullers with disdain, as if she were forcing herself. "So, this is where you live. It's some comedown, isn't it? Surely Clayton would have allowed you to stay on the plantation in some capacity. Maybe as assistant cook."

Nicole put her hand on Janie's arm to keep her quiet. "It was my choice to leave Arundel Hall. I wanted to have a means of supporting myself. Since I knew about running a mill, Mr. Armstrong kindly deeded this place to me."

"Deeded!" Bianca said. "You mean he owned this, and he just gave it to you? After all you'd done to him, and to me?"

"I'd like to know what she's done to you," Janie said. "It seems to me she's the innocent party."

"Innocent!" Bianca sneered. "How did you find out Clayton was rich?"

"I don't know what you mean."

"Why else would you have volunteered so readily to go with those kidnappers? You practically leaped on that man's horse. And how did you get the captain to marry you to my fiancé? Did you use that skinny little body of yours to entice him? You lower classes always do things like that."

"No, Janie!" Nicole said sharply, then turned back to Bianca. "I think you'd better go now."

Bianca stood, smiling slightly. "I just wanted to warn you. Arundel Hall is mine. The Armstrong plantation is mine, and I don't want any interference from you. You've taken quite enough of what belongs to me, and I don't plan to give you any more. So stay away from what I own."

"What about Clay?" Nicole said quietly. "Do you own him, too?"

Bianca curled her lip, then smiled. "So that's how it is, is it? My, my, what a small world. Yes, he's mine. If I could have the money without him, I would. But that's not possible. I'll tell you one thing, though, even if I could get rid of him, I'd see you never got him. You've caused me nothing but misery ever since I met you, and I'd die before I let you have what was mine." She smiled more broadly. "Does it hurt, seeing the way he looks at me? I have him right there." She held out her plump, white hand, then slowly curled it into a tight little fist. Still smiling, she turned and left the room, leaving the door open behind her.

Janie sat down at the table beside Nicole. She felt like she'd just been run between the grinding stones. "So that's the angel Clay sent me to England to fetch?" Janie shook her head slowly. "I wonder if any man's ever been born who had any sense about women. What in the world does he see in her?"

Nicole was staring at the open doorway. She wouldn't mind losing to a woman who loved Clay, but it hurt to see him with Bianca. Sooner or later, he'd find out what she was like, and when he did he'd be miserable.

The twins burst into the room. "Who was that fat lady?" Alex asked.

"Alex!" Nicole said. Then her reprimand lost its bite as Janie started laughing. Nicole tried to keep from smiling. "Alex, you shouldn't call people fat."

"Even if they are?"

Janie's laughter was too loud for Nicole to speak. She decided not to go into Bianca's weight. "She's a guest of your Uncle Clay," she said at last.

The twins exchanged looks of silent communication, then turned quickly and sped down the path.

"Where do you think they're going?" Janie asked.

"To introduce themselves, probably. Ever since Ellen Backes taught them how, they've not lost an opportunity to bow and curtsy." Janie and Nicole looked at each other, then silently left the house. They didn't trust Bianca with the twins.

The two women got there just in time to see Alex make his bow before Bianca. They stood on the edge of the wharf. Bianca seemed to be pleased by the twins' formal manners, even if their clothes and faces were somewhat dirty. Mandy stood quietly by her brother, smiling proudly.

Suddenly, Alex lost his balance, and to keep from stumbling and perhaps falling off the wharf, he grabbed the nearest thing to steady himself, which was Bianca's dress. The fabric tore away at the seam of the high waist, leaving a long, gaping hole.

"You nasty little beast!" Bianca said, and before anyone could speak, she slapped Alex hard across the face.

The little boy balanced on the edge of the wharf, his arms twirling for a moment before he fell backward into the river. Nicole was into the water past her ankles before Alex came up the first time. He grinned at her look of fright and swam ashore. "Uncle Clay says you shouldn't swim with your shoes on," he said as he sat on the bank and began to unbuckle his. He nodded at Nicole, still standing in the water, her shoes soaked.

Nicole smiled at him and stepped back onto the dry land. Her heart was still pounding from the fright of seeing the boy fall.

While Janie's and Nicole's attention was on Alex, Mandy looked at the big woman beside her. She didn't like anyone who'd strike her brother. She took a step closer to Bianca and dug her little heels into the dock. She gave one good, hard push at Bianca and then stepped back quickly.

Everyone turned at Bianca's little squeal of fear. She fell almost as if she were in slow motion. Her lack of strength and muscle tone made her especially helpless. Her fat little hands clawed at the air.

When she hit the water, the splash threatened to flood the wharf. Mandy was drenched. She turned, the front of her dress soaked, water dripping off her eyelashes and nose, and smiled in triumph at her brother. Janie started laughing again.

"Stop it, all of you," Nicole commanded, but her voice was shaky with suppressed laughter. Bianca had looked so funny when she fell. Nicole walked to the other side of the wharf, and the others followed her. Bianca rose slowly out of the water. It was barely knee deep, but she'd gone completely under when she fell. Her blonde hair was straggling in thin, straight bits about her face. The curls she'd so carefully created with a hot iron were gone. The water plastered the thin cotton of her dress to her, and she may as well have been nude. She'd gained more weight than Nicole had realized. Her thighs and hips were so fat they were lumpy. She had a roll of fat around her middle where her waist should have been.

"She *is* fat!" Alex said, his eyes wide in wonder.

"Don't just stand there, get me out of here!" Bianca demanded. "My feet are caught in mud."

"I think I'd better get the men," Janie said. "The two of us aren't strong enough to pull in a whale."

"Hush! All of you!" Nicole said, then went to the rowboat to pick up an oar. "She doesn't like men. Here, Bianca, grab this, and Janie and I will pull you out."

Janie dutifully grabbed one end of the oar. "If you ask me, that woman only likes herself, and she doesn't like her that much."

It took some doing on the women's part to get Bianca out of the mud. She wasn't very strong, in spite of her size. When she was standing on the shore, Roger appeared out of the trees, where he'd obviously been for some time. His eyes were twinkling in delight as he helped Bianca into the rowboat and rowed her back across the river.

Chapter 9

CLAY WAS BENT OVER THE OLD TREE STUMP, FAST-
ening chains around its long, deep roots when the lone
rider approached. In another hour, the sun would be
down. He'd been working since long before sunup. He
was tired and his body ached thoroughly, not just from
today's work but from several days of work without
stop.

When the chains were finally secured around the log,
he hooked them onto the big percheron's collar. The
massive feet of the horse dug into the ground, mud and
bits of grass flying as it obeyed Clay's commands to
pull. Slowly, the log began to come out of the ground.

Clay took a long axe and hacked at the thin tendons
that held the large stump in the ground. When it was
finally free, Clay led the horse and the dragging stump
to the edge of the newly cleared field. When he had the
chains detached and was rolling them on the ground,
the man spoke.

"Good work! I haven't enjoyed a show so much since
I saw some dancers in Philadelphia. Of course, they
had better legs than you."

Clay looked up sharply, then slowly he began to grin.
"Wesley! I haven't seen you in ages. Did you and Travis
get your tobacco in already?"

Wes Stanford stood up and stretched. He wasn't a
tall man like Clay, but he was powerfully built, with a
deep, thick chest and heavily muscled thighs. He had
thick brown hair and very dark eyes, which laughed
often. He shrugged. "You know Travis. He knows he

137

can run the world by himself. I just thought I'd let him manage a part of it alone."

"You two quarreling again?"

Wesley grinned. "Travis would tell the devil how to run Hell."

"And no doubt the devil would obey him."

The two men looked at each other and laughed. Their friendship had grown over the many years they'd been neighbors. They'd been drawn to each other because they were both younger brothers. Clay had always stood in the shadow of James, while Wesley had to deal with Travis. Many times, Clay had been thankful for James whenever he was around Travis. He didn't envy Wes for having such a brother.

"What are you doing out here clearing your own fields?" Wes asked. "Did all your men leave you?"

"Worse," he said, removed his handkerchief from his pocket and wiped the sweat from his face. "I've got problems with women."

"Ah," Wes smiled. "Now, that's a problem I could deal with. Anything you'd like to talk about? I brought a jug, and I've got all night."

Clay sat down on the ground, his back to a tree, and accepted the jug of corn liquor from Wes, who sat down beside him. "When I think of what's happened to my life in the last few months, I don't know how I've lived through it."

"Remember that summer that was so dry, and three of your tobacco barns burned and half your cows died?" Wes asked. "How does it compare to that?"

"That was an easy time. I got more rest then."

"Lord!" Wes said seriously. "Drink some more of this, and tell me what's been going on."

Wes loved Clay's idea about kidnapping Bianca and then having her married to him by proxy. "So what happened when she got here?"

"She didn't. Or at least she didn't come in with Janie on the packet."

"I thought you said you paid the captain for performing the service."

"I did. He married me to someone, all right, but not to Bianca. The kidnappers took the wrong woman."

Wes stared at his friend with wide eyes and an open mouth. It was a while before he could speak. "You mean you went to meet your bride only to find out you were married to some woman you'd never met before?" He took a deep drink when he saw Clay's glum nod. "What's she look like? A hag, right?"

Clay leaned his head against the tree and stared up at the sky. "She's a little thing, French. She has black hair and big brown eyes and the most desirable mouth ever created. She's got a figure that makes my hands sweat every time she walks across a room."

"Sounds to me like you should be rejoicing, unless she's stupid or mean."

"Neither. She's educated, intelligent, a hard worker, the twins love her, and everybody on the plantation adores her."

Wes took another drink. "She doesn't seem like much of a problem to me. I don't believe she's real. She must have some flaw."

"There's more to this," Clay said and reached for the jug. "As soon as I learned about the mistaken marriage, I wrote Bianca in England and explained everything."

"Bianca's the woman you originally were to marry? How did she take it? I don't guess she liked your marrying someone else."

"I didn't hear from her for a long time. Meanwhile, I spent a lot of time with Nicole, who was legally my wife."

139

"But not your wife in any other way?"

"No. We agreed to get an annulment, but there had to be a witness that the marriage had been forced, and the only one who'd testify was already on his way back to England."

"So you forced yourself to keep company with a beautiful, charming woman. Poor man. Your life has been hell."

Clay ignored Wes's jibes. "After a while, I began to see what a gem Nicole was, so I decided to have a talk with her. I said that if Bianca read my letter and decided she wanted nothing more to do with me, I'd like to remain married to Nicole. After all, my first obligation was to Bianca."

"That sounds fair enough."

"I agree, but Nicole didn't. She raged at me for half an hour. She said she wasn't going to be second choice to any man, and . . . I don't know what all else. It didn't make much sense to me. All I knew was she wasn't very happy. That night—" He stopped.

"Go on! This is the best story I've heard in years."

"That night," Clay continued, "she was sleeping in Beth's room, and I have James's, so when I heard her scream I went to her right away. She was scared to death of something, so I fed her a lot of liquor and got her to talk." He put his hand over his eyes. "She's had an awful life. The French mob carried her parents away to the guillotine and burned her house, then later they killed her grandfather and carried his head around on a pole in front of her."

Wes grimaced in disgust. "What happened after that night?"

It wasn't what happened after that night but during it that was so important, Clay thought. Every night, he lay awake remembering the night he'd held her in his arms and made love to her. "The next day she left me," he said quietly. "Not really left me, but moved across the river to the old mill. She's running the place now and doing a damn good job of it."

"But you want her back, is that it?" When Clay didn't answer, Wes shook his head. "You said women problems, not woman. What else has happened?"

"After Nicole got the mill going, Bianca showed up."

"What's she like?"

Clay didn't know what to answer. She'd been living in his house for two weeks, but he didn't know any more about her than when she arrived. She was asleep when he left in the morning, asleep when he returned. Once Anders had talked to him about her spending so much money, but Clay had dismissed the complaint. Surely he could afford a few garments for the woman he was to marry. "I don't know what she's like. I think I fell in love with her the moment I saw her in England, and nothing's changed since then. She's beautiful, lovely, gracious, kind."

"It sounds to me like you know quite a lot about her. Now, let me look at the situation. You are married to one gorgeous creature and engaged to and in love with another equally gorgeous woman."

"That's about it." Clay grinned. "You make it sound like something desirable."

"I could think of worse situations. Being a lonely bachelor like me, for instance."

Clay snorted. Wes was far from needing more women in his life.

"I'll tell you what I'll do," Wes grinned, and slapped Clay on the leg. "I'll meet both women and take one of them off your hands. You can have whichever one I don't want, and that way you won't have to choose between them." He was teasing, but Clay was serious, and Wes frowned. He didn't like to see his friend so troubled. "Come on, Clay, it's bound to work out for the best."

"I don't know," Clay said. "I don't seem to be sure of anything lately."

Wes stood up, rubbing his back where the bark had bitten into his skin. "Is this Nicole still at the mill? Do you think I could meet her?" He saw a sudden flash go across Clay's eyes.

"Sure. She's there with Janie. I'm sure she'd welcome you. She seems to keep open house for everyone." There was a trace of disgust in his voice.

Wes promised Clay he'd return to Arundel Hall later for some of Maggie's cooking. Then he mounted his horse and rode toward the wharf. He rode slowly over the familiar path so he could think. Seeing Clay again after so many months had been a shock. It was almost as if he'd been talking to a stranger. As boys, the two had spent a lot of time together. Then, suddenly, a cholera epidemic had killed Clay's parents and Wes's father. Wes's mother died a short time later. The two families of James and Clay, Travis and Wesley had been drawn closer together by their mutual tragedies. There were long periods of separation as the young men worked the two plantations, but they'd gotten together whenever possible.

Wes smiled as he remembered a party at Arundel Hall when both Clay and Wes were sixteen. The boys had bet each other they could each get one of the luscious Canton twins behind the hedges. They'd both succeeded easily, except that Travis found out about it and grabbed each boy by the scruff of the neck and pitched them into the tile pool.

What had happened to that Clayton? Wes wondered. The Clay he knew would have laughed at this absurd situation with the two women. He would have grabbed the one he wanted and carried her upstairs. He knew the man who arranged the kidnapping of an English lady, but the man who acted as if he were afraid to go home was a stranger.

He dismounted his horse under a tree by the wharf, then unsaddled him. His guess was that what was wrong with him was the Frenchwoman. He'd said she was working for Bianca—her maid, no doubt. Somehow, she'd arranged to substitute herself for Bianca and had gotten herself married to a rich American. No doubt, she was now somehow blackmailing Clay into keeping her as his wife. So far, she'd already managed to get the mill and some property out of him.

And what about Bianca? Wes felt a surge of pity for the woman. She'd come to America expecting to be married to the man she loved, only to find someone else in her place.

He tied his horse and then went to the rowboat and rowed himself across. He was quite familiar with the mill, as it had been one of his favorite places when he was a boy. He smiled as he saw the twins crouched by the bank of the river, intent upon the complete lack of movement of a bored bullfrog.

"What are you two doing?" he demanded sharply.

The twins jumped in unison, then turned and smiled up at him. "Uncle Wes!" they yelled, giving him the honorary title. They scrambled up the bank to where he waited with open arms.

Wes grabbed them both by the waists and swung them around while they giggled uproariously. "Did you miss me?"

"Oh, yes," Mandy laughed. "Uncle Clay is always gone now, but Nicole is here."

"Nicole?" Wes asked. "You like her, do you?"

"She's pretty," Alex said. "She used to be married to Uncle Clay, but I don't know if she is now."

"Of course she is," Mandy said. "She's always married to Uncle Clay."

Wes set the children down on the ground. "Is she at the house?"

"I think so. Sometimes she's at the mill."

Wes rubbed the heads of both children. "I'll see you later. Maybe you can go back across the river with me. I'm meeting your Uncle Clay for supper."

The twins backed away from him as if he were poisonous. "We stay here now," Alex said. "We don't have to go back there."

Before Wes could ask any questions, the children turned and ran into the woods. He walked up the hill to the little house. Janie was inside, alone, intent over the spinning wheel. Wes opened the door silently and tiptoed behind her. He planted a loud kiss on her neck.

Janie didn't move or act surprised in any way. "Nice to see you again, Wes," she said calmly. She turned to him with twinkling eyes. "It's a good thing you weren't born an Indian. You couldn't sneak up on a tornado. I heard you outside with the twins." She stood up and hugged him.

Wes hugged her hard, lifting her feet off the ground. "You certainly haven't been starving yourself," he laughed.

"But you have. You're getting downright skinny. Sit down, and I'll get you something to eat."

"Not much. I'm supposed to meet Clay for supper."

"Humph!" Janie said as she filled a bowl with split pea soup with chunks of ham. On a plate she put cold, cracked crab legs and beside that a little bowl of melted butter. "You'd better eat here, then. Maggie's on the warpath, and her cooking's not what it can be."

"I guess that has to do with Clay's women," he said, his mouth full of crab. He smiled at Janie's look of surprise. "I saw Clay before I came over here, and he told me the whole story."

"Clay doesn't know the whole story. He's blind to most of it."

"What's that supposed to mean? It seems to me it's simple. All he has to do is get the marriage annulled to this Nicole and he's free to marry Bianca, the woman he loves. Then he can be happy again."

Janie was so angered at Wes's statements that she couldn't speak. She had the iron ladle from the pea soup in her hand, so she just conked him on the head with it.

"Hey!" Wes yelled, and put his hand over the hot mess in his hair.

Janie was immediately contrite. She wouldn't hurt Wes for the world. She grabbed a rag and dipped it in cool water to clean his hair.

While Janie was leaning over Wes, blocking him from view, Nicole entered. Janie started to move aside so Nicole could see him but then decided not to. Wes peered curiously around Janie's substantial form.

"Janie," Nicole said. "Do you know where the twins are? I saw them a few minutes ago, but now they seem to have disappeared." She removed a straw bonnet from her head and hung it on a wooden peg by the door. "I wanted to give them a few lessons before supper."

"They'll come home, and besides, you're too tired to work with them."

Wes was aware that Janie was purposefully hiding him yet allowing him to watch Nicole. Of all his thoughts about her, he knew she'd never been anyone's maid. She walked with a quiet grace and elegance that showed she'd never been a servant to anyone. And what Clay had said about her beauty was an understatement. His first thought was to throw roses at her feet and beg her to leave Clay and take him.

"Clay sent a message over today," Janie said.

Nicole paused, her hand on the stair rail. "Clay?"

"You remember him?" Janie said, watching Wes's face. "He asked if you'd attend supper with him tonight."

"No," Nicole said quietly. "I can't, though maybe I should send something. Maggie hasn't been cooking much lately."

Janie snorted. "She's refusing to cook for that woman, and you know it."

Nicole turned and started to speak. Then she stopped. Janie seemed to have grown two new legs. She left the stairs to walk closer to Janie.

"Hello," Wes said, then brushed Janie's hands away and stood. "I'm Wesley Stanford."

"Mr. Stanford," she said politely, holding out her hand to him. She gave Janie a troubled look. Why had she hidden this man? "Won't you please sit down? Could I offer you some refreshment?"

"No, thank you. Janie's already taken care of that."

"I think I'll go look for the twins," Janie said, and was out of the house before anyone could speak.

"Are you a friend of Janie's?" Nicole asked as she poured a mug of cool cider for him.

"More a friend of Clay's." He watched her face, his eyes always going to her mouth. The upper lip intrigued him. "We grew up together, or at least we spent a lot of time together."

"Tell me about him," she said, her eyes wide and eager. "What was he like as a little boy?"

"Different," Wes said, watching her. She's in love with him, he thought. "I think this . . . situation upsets him."

She stood and walked toward the fireplace behind him. "I know it does. I assume he told you the story." She didn't wait for his nod. "I tried to make it easier for him by moving out. No, that's not true. I tried to make it easier for me. He'll be happy again when our marriage is annulled and he's free to marry Bianca."

"Bianca. You worked for her in England?"

"In a manner of speaking. Many of the English kindly took us in after we fled our own country."

"How did the kidnappers get you instead of Bianca?" he asked bluntly.

Nicole blushed, remembering the scene. "Please, Mr. Stanford, let's talk about you."

Wes knew that her blush told more than her words. What sort of a woman would be so generous as to offer to prepare food for the man she loved when she knew he'd be eating with another woman? He'd already made one wrong judgment, and he wasn't going to make any more. He'd wait until he saw Bianca before he developed another opinion.

An hour later, Wes reluctantly left the quiet orderliness of Nicole's little house to go to Arundel Hall. He hadn't wanted to leave, yet he was looking forward to meeting Bianca. If Nicole was Clay's second choice, then his first must be truly an angel.

"What did you think of her?" Clay asked as he greeted Wes at the end of the garden.

"I'm thinking of sending some kidnappers to England. If I do half as well as you, I'll die happy."

"You haven't seen Bianca yet. She's waiting inside and is anxious to meet you."

Wes's first look at Bianca was one of shock. It was like seeing James's wife Beth again. He was instantly taken back to the days when the house had been full of love and laughter. Beth had a talent for making everyone welcome. Her loud laugh could be heard throughout the house. There wasn't an itinerant peddler within miles who wasn't welcome at her table.

Beth was a large woman, tall and strong. Her energy affected everyone. She could work on the plantation all morning, ride in a hunt with James and Clay all afternoon, and Wes suspected from James's constant smile that she could make love all night. She used to gather children to her bosom and hug them exuberantly. She could bake cookies with one hand and hug three children with the other.

For a moment, Wes felt his eyes blur with tears. Beth had been so alive that it was almost possible to believe she'd come back to earth.

"Mr. Stanford," Bianca said quietly. "Won't you come in?"

Wes felt like a fool and knew he must look like one. He blinked a few times to clear his eyes, then looked at Clay. He knew and understood the turmoil inside Wes.

"We have so few visitors here," Bianca was saying as she led the men into the dining room. "Clayton promises me that quite soon we will be able to have visitors again. That is, as soon as all of this unfortunate situation is put to rights and I am truly mistress here. Won't you have a seat?"

Wes was still mesmerized by her, by the resemblance to Beth; but the voice was different, the movements were different, and there was a dimple in her left cheek that Beth didn't have. He took a chair across from hers with Clay between them. "How do you like our country? Is it a great deal different from England?"

"Oh, yes," Bianca said as she ladled a thick pile of sauce over three slices of ham. She handed the silver gravy boat to Wes. "America is so much more crude than England. There are no towns, no places to shop. And the lack of society—decent society, that is—is appalling."

Wes paused with his hand on the gravy ladle. She had just insulted his country and his countrymen, but she didn't seem at all aware of her rudeness. Her head was bent over her plate. Wes dipped some of the gravy onto his plate and then tasted it. "Good God, Clay! Since when has Maggie been serving bowls of sugar with her ham?"

Clay shrugged disinterestedly. He watched Bianca as he ate.

Wes was beginning to be suspicious of the whole relationship. "Tell me, Mrs. Armstrong," he began, then stopped. "I beg your pardon, but you're not Mrs. Armstrong—yet."

"No, I'm not!" Bianca said, casting a malevolent look at Clay. "My maid thrust herself at the men who were to take me to Clay. Then, while she was on board the ship, she persuaded the captain that she was Bianca Maleson and managed to get herself married to my fiancé."

Wes was beginning not to like the woman. It had taken a few minutes to get past her resemblance to Beth, but even now that was starting to fade. She was soft and fat where Beth had always been strong and firm with large bones. "Your maid, you say? Wasn't she an escapee from the French Revolution? I thought only the aristocracy had to flee the country."

Bianca waved her fork. "That is what Nicole tells everyone. She says her grandfather was the Duc de Levroux, or at least her cousin told me that."

"But you know better, don't you?"

"Of course. She did work for me for some months, and I should know. It is my guess that she was a cook somewhere, or a seamstress. But please, Mr. Stanford," she said and smiled, "do you really want to talk about my maid?"

"Of course not," Wes smiled back. "Let's talk about you. It's rare that I am in such charming company. Tell me about your family and more about your ideas of America."

Wes ate slowly as he listened to Bianca. It wasn't easy to keep eating and still listen. She told him of the pedigree of her own family, of the house her father once owned. Of course, everything in America was dreadfully inferior to what was in England, especially the people. She itemized the faults of all of Clay's servants, told how they mistreated her, refused to obey her. Wes made little sounds of sympathy, all the while amazed at the quantity of food she was eating.

Once in a while he stole looks at Clay. Clay remained passive, as if he didn't hear or understand Bianca's words. Once in a while, he looked at Bianca with a glazed expression as if he didn't really see her.

The dinner seemed to go on forever. Wes was amazed at Bianca's sense of security. She never seemed to doubt that she and Clay would be married quite soon and that she would own Arundel Hall. It was when she started talking of tearing the east wall out of the house and adding an ornate wing, "not so plain as this house," that Wes wanted to hear no more.

He turned to Clay. "Why are the twins staying across the river?"

Clay frowned at Wes. "Nicole could give them an education, and they wanted to go," he said flatly. "Would you care to join us in the library, my dear?"

"Heavens, no," Bianca said sweetly. "I wouldn't think of intruding on you gentlemen. If you would excuse me, I think I will retire. It's been an exhausting day."

"Of course," Clay said.

Wes muttered goodnight to her, then turned and left the room. When he was in the library, he poured himself a stiff shot of whiskey and downed it in one gulp. He was pouring a second one when Clay entered the room.

"Where's the portrait of Beth?" Wes asked through clenched teeth.

"I moved it to my office," Clay said as he poured himself a brandy.

"So you can be near her all the time? You have a copy of Beth walking around your house and a portrait of her in the office where you spend the rest of the day."

"I don't know what you're talking about," Clay said angrily.

"Like hell you don't! I mean that vain, overweight bitch you've taken in as a substitute for Beth."

Clay's eyes flashed. He was the taller of the two, a strong, hard man, but Wes was powerfully made. They'd never fought.

Suddenly, Wes calmed. "Look, Clay, I don't want to yell. I don't even want to argue with you. I think you need a friend right now. Can't you see what you're doing? That woman looks like Beth. When I first saw her, I thought she *was* Beth. But she's not!"

"I'm aware of that," Clay said flatly.

"Are you? You look at her as if she were a goddess, yet have you ever listened to her? She's about as far removed from Beth as humanly possible. She's a vain, arrogant hypocrite."

The next moment, Clay's fist came smashing into Wes's face. Wes reeled against the desk and spun backward where he landed on one of the red leather chairs. He rubbed his jaw and tasted the blood inside his mouth. For a moment he considered going after Clay. Maybe a good fight would knock some sense into his head. At least a fighting Clay was one he recognized.

"Beth is dead," Wes whispered. "She and James are dead, and no matter how much you try, nothing is going to bring them back."

Clay looked at his friend slumped on the chair, rubbing his jaw. He started to speak but couldn't. There were too many things to say and too few. He turned and walked out of the room, out of the house, and toward the tobacco fields. Maybe a few hours' work would help calm him, keep him from thinking of Beth and Nicole—no, of Bianca and Nicole.

Chapter 10

THE TREES WERE CHANGING TO THE GLORY OF AUTUMN colors. The reds and golds blazed. Nicole stood on top of a hill that looked down on the mill and her house. Through the trees she could see the sunlight sparkling on clear, rushing water.

It had been ten days since Wesley Stanford had visited her and more than a month since that horrible night when Bianca had returned to her life. She had thought the hard work of the mill would block him from her mind, but it hadn't.

"Enjoying the quiet?"

Nicole jumped when she heard Clay's voice. She hadn't seen him in all the time he'd been with Bianca.

"Janie told me where you were. I hope I'm not intruding."

She turned slowly and looked up at him. The sun was behind his head, making the curling ends of his dark hair golden. He looked tired and older. There were deep circles under his eyes, as if he hadn't been sleeping well. "No," she smiled. "You weren't intruding. Are you well? Is your tobacco harvested?"

His mouth changed from a hard line to a soft smile. He sat down on the ground, stretched out on it, and stared up at the sky through a brilliant tree of red-gold leaves. He seemed to relax instantly. Just being near Nicole made him feel better. "Your mill seems to be doing well. I came over to ask a favor of you. Ellen and Horace Backes are giving a party for us. It's a real Virginia party, lasting at least three days, and you and I are the guests of honor. Ellen wants to welcome my wife to the community."

When Clay stretched out at Nicole's feet, his long legs extended, his muscles straining against the open shirt, she felt as if she were going to melt. She wanted to sink to the ground beside him and put her cheek against that brown skin. He was sweaty from the fields, and she could almost taste the salt of him as she imagined kissing his throat. But when she saw him relax near her, her impulse changed—she wanted to kick him. Her body felt like it was on fire, but he acted as if he'd just entered the peace and quiet of his mother's house.

It took a moment for her to understand his words. "I guess it would be rather embarrassing for you to have to tell Ellen that I refuse to go, wouldn't it?"

He looked up at her with one eye open. "She has met you and knows we're married."

"But she doesn't know that we won't be married very long."

Nicole turned away to start down the hill, but Clay grabbed her ankle. She stumbled and fell forward onto her hands and knees. He sat up, put his hands under her arms, and lifted her.

"Why are you getting mad at me? I haven't seen you for weeks, and when I do I invite you to a party. It seems you should be pleased instead of angry."

She couldn't very well tell him that his calmness made her angry. She sat back on the grass, away from his hands. "It just doesn't seem right that we should appear publicly as husband and wife when in a few months the marriage will be annulled. It seems you'd want to go with Bianca and tell everyone about the silly error. I'm sure it would make a wonderful story."

"Ellen's met you," he said stubbornly. He had no answer for her questions. All he knew was that the prospect of spending three days—and nights—with her made him happy for the first time in months. He took her hand from his lap and studied it for a moment. It was so small, so neat and clean, and it could give such pleasure! He raised it to his lips and kissed the soft pads of her fingertips one by one. "Please go," he said quietly. "All my friends, people I've known all my life, will be there. You've worked hard the last few months, and you need a holiday."

She could feel her bones beginning to melt at the touch of his lips on her fingers, yet a part of her cried out in anger. He was living with another woman, one he said he loved, but he kissed her, touched her, invited her to parties. It made her feel like his mistress, someone kept hidden and used only for pleasure. Yet now he wanted to take her to meet his friends.

"Clay, please," she said weakly.

He nibbled the inside of her wrist. "Will you go?"

"Yes," she said faintly, her eyes half closed.

"Good!" Clay snapped, dropping her hand and standing up. "I'll pick you and the twins up at five tomorrow morning. And Janie, too. Oh, yes, you'd better bring some food. Maybe something French. If you don't have everything you need, tell Maggie to get it from the storehouse." He turned and walked down the hill, whistling.

"Of all the insufferable—" Nicole began, then smiled. Maybe if she understood him she wouldn't love him so much.

Clay was thinking about tomorrow night. He'd be alone with Nicole, sharing a bedroom with her in Horace's big, rambling house. With that in mind, he could forego a quick tumble on the hillside where anyone could see them.

As soon as Clay was out of sight, Nicole stood up suddenly. If she was going to have to prepare food for three days, she'd better get started. She started planning as she went down the hill. There'd be chicken baked in Dijon mustard, pâté wrapped in a pastry shell, a cold vegetable mold, cassoulet. And pies! There'd be pumpkin, mincemeat, apple, pear, blackberry. She was out of breath by the time she reached the house.

"Good morning," Clay called as he tied the sloop to the wharf on Nicole's side of the river. He grinned at Nicole and Janie and the twins standing amid several enormous baskets. "I'm not sure the sloop will sail with that much on board, especially after all the food Maggie sent."

"I thought she might decide to cook something for you when you told her you were taking Nicole," Janie said.

Clayton ignored her as he began handing the baskets to Roger, who stored them in the bottom of the boat. The twins laughed as he literally threw them into Roger's arms.

"You seem cheerful this morning," Janic said. "It makes me almost think you've come to your senses."

Clay grabbed Janie by the waist and kissed her cheek heartily. "Maybe I have, but if you don't hush, I'm going to throw you into the boat, too."

"Maybe you can throw her," Roger said loudly and quickly, "but I can guarantee that I'm not going to try to catch her."

Janie snorted in indignation and held Clay's hand as she stepped down to the boat.

He held out his hand for Nicole.

"I might try to catch that one," Roger laughed.

"This one's mine!" Clay said as he lifted Nicole from the dock and held her tightly as he stepped into the boat.

Nicole stared up at him with wide eyes. He suddenly seemed to be a stranger. The Clay she knew was solemn and quiet. Whoever this was, she liked him.

"Let's go, Uncle Clay!" Alex shouted. "The horse races will be over before we get there."

Clay slowly lowered Nicole, then held her lightly with one arm for a few moments. "You look especially lovely this morning," he said, and ran his finger along her ear.

She merely stared at him, her heart pounding wildly.

He released her abruptly. "Alex! Untie us. Mandy, see if you can help Roger steer us out of here."

"Aye, aye, Captain Clay!" the twins laughed.

Nicole sat down beside Janie.

"Now, that's the man I remember!" Janie said. "Something's happened. I don't know what, but I'd like to thank the person who did it."

They heard the noise of the party a half a mile before they reached the Backes's wharf. It wasn't even six in the morning, but half the county was already spread out across the lawn. Some people were on the far side of the river shooting at ducks.

"Did you send Golden Girl over to Mrs. Backes?" Alex asked.

Clay gave the boy a look of disdain. "Wouldn't be much of a party if I couldn't empty everyone's pockets, would it?"

"Think she'll beat Mr. Backes's Irish Lass?" Roger asked. "I heard she's a fast horse."

Clay grunted. "It'll be no race at all." As he spoke, he buttoned his shirt and reached for a cravat from a basket close to the front of the boat. He quickly tied it, then slipped on a vest of creamy brown satin. A double-breasted coat of chocolate cord came next. The buttons were of brass, the front of it cut away, the back hanging to just above his knees. His buckskin trousers fit like a second skin. He wore tall, Hessian boots, taller in front of the knee than in the back. He gave them a quick buff, showing their mirror-like shine. He put on a dark brown beaver hat, the brim softly curved.

He turned to Nicole and offered her his arm.

Nicole had never seen him in anything except work clothes. Now the man who cut tobacco was transformed into a gentleman worthy of Versailles.

He seemed to understand her hesitation, and he grinned broadly. "I certainly want to seem worthy of appearing with the world's most beautiful bride, don't I?"

Nicole smiled up at him, glad she'd taken such care with her dress. Her gown was made of white lingerie silk, very fine and heavenly to touch. It had been hand-embroidered in England with tiny gold-brown jonquils. The bodice was velvet of the same rich, deep gold as the flowers. The collar and cuffs were trimmed in white piping. Her dark curls were entwined with ribbons of gold and white.

As Roger tied the sloop to one of the wharfs at the end of the Backes's property, Clay said, "I almost forgot! I have something for you." He reached inside his pocket and produced the gold locket she'd left on the ship so long ago.

Nicole clutched it tightly in her hands, then smiled up at him. "Thank you."

"You can thank me properly later," he said, and kissed her forehead. Then he turned to toss baskets to Roger who stood on the edge of the wharf. He held her close for a moment when he lifted her to the wharf.

"Here they are!" someone yelled as they walked toward the house.

"Clay! We thought maybe she was deformed, the way you keep her hidden away."

"I keep her hidden for the same reason I hide my brandy. Too much exposure isn't good for brandy or wives," Clay shouted back.

Nicole looked down at her hands. She was puzzled by this new Clay, by his announcement to the world that she was his wife. It made her feel almost as if she were.

"Hello," Ellen Backes said. "Clay, let me have her for a while. You've had her for months."

Reluctantly, Clay released her hand. "You won't forget me, will you?" he said as he winked at her. Then he followed several men toward a race track. She saw him take a long, deep drink out of a stoneware jug.

"You certainly have done wonders with him," Ellen said. "I haven't seen Clay so happy since before James and Beth died. It's almost as if he'd been away for a long time but now he's come home."

Nicole could say nothing in reply. The laughing, teasing Clay of today was a stranger to her. Ellen never gave her a chance to speak before she started introducing her to people. Nicole was bombarded with questions about her clothes, her family, how she had met Clay, where they'd been married. She didn't lie actually, but neither did she tell of being kidnapped and forced into marriage.

The front of Ellen's enormous house faced the river. She'd seen so few American houses, and this one was a surprise. Clay's house was pure Georgian, but Ellen's and Horace's house was a mixture of every architectural style imaginable. It looked as if each generation had added a wing in its favorite style. The house rambled in several directions with long wings, short wings, passageways leading to separate buildings.

Ellen saw Nicole staring at the house. "Remarkable, isn't it? I think I lived here a year before I learned my way around the inside. It's much worse inside than out. It has hallways that lead nowhere and doorways that open into other people's bedrooms. It's really frightful."

"And you obviously love it," Nicole smiled.

"I wouldn't change a brick, except I'm thinking of adding another wing."

Nicole looked at her in astonishment, then laughed.

"Maybe another story? Not one wing has a fourth story."

Ellen grinned. "You are a clever child. I think you truly understand my house."

Someone called Ellen away, and two women began asking Nicole more questions as she helped set up the food. There were at least twenty trestle tables set about the lawn. Some were laden with food; some had benches set by them. Every family seemed to have brought as much food as Nicole and Janie. A pit had been dug, and hundreds of oysters were being roasted. Some slaves were turning a whole hog over a spit and coating it with a tangy sauce. Someone told Nicole it was a Haitian way of cooking called barbeque.

Suddenly, a horn sounded from far across the plantation.

"It's time!" Ellen yelled, and removed her apron. "The races are about to begin."

As a body, all the women pulled off aprons, lifted their skirts, and began to run.

"Now that the beauty is here, we can begin," a man greeted them.

Nicole stood a little aside from the other women, who were gathering at the edge of the carefully tended oval track. Her hair had fallen somewhat in the wild run. She pushed a glossy curl under a ribbon.

"Here, let me," Clay said from behind her. His hands did very little for the stray curls, but his fingertips on her neck sent little shivers down her spine. He turned her around. "Enjoying yourself?"

She nodded, staring up at him. His hands were on her shoulders, and his face was close to hers.

"My horse is about to run. Would you give me a kiss for luck?"

As always, the answer was in her eyes. His arms slid around her waist as he drew her close to him. He held her for a moment, his face buried in her neck. "I'm so glad you came with me," he whispered, then ran his lips along her cheek and finally captured her mouth. Nicole could feel herself weaken, her legs growing limp as she clung to him.

"Clay!" someone shouted. "You have all night for that. Come and tend to your horses now."

Clay lifted his head from Nicole's. "All night," he whispered, and ran his finger along her upper lip. He released her abruptly and walked toward a man who looked like a larger version of Wesley. The man slapped Clay on the back. "Can't blame you, though. You think there're any more beauties like her in England?"

"I got the last one, Travis," Clay laughed.

"Just the same, someday I think I'll go have a look for myself."

Nicole stood watching the men walk away. She'd probably been introduced to Wes's brother, but all the names and faces had run together.

"Nicole!" Ellen called. "I've saved you a place by me."

Nicole hurried forward to watch the horse races.

It was three hours later when the men and women walked together back to the food that waited for them. Nicole was flushed with laughter and sunlight. She had not enjoyed herself so much since before the French Revolution. Her French cousins used to complain that the English were so somber, that they lived only for work and church, that they had no idea how to have fun. She looked about at the Americans around her and knew her cousins would enjoy these people. All morning they'd laughed and shouted. The women had been quite raucous, loudly delivering their opinions about a horse's worth. And they weren't always for their husbands' steeds, either. Ellen had wagered against Horace several times, and now she was bragging that

Horace was going to have to dig her a new flowerbed himself and order fifty new tulip bulbs from Holland.

Nicole had stood silently, an outsider, a spectator, until Travis had seen her frowning at one of Clay's horses.

"Clay, I don't think your wife likes your horse."

Clay barely glanced at Nicole. "My women wager with me," he said, with a meaningful look at Horace.

Nicole stared at Clay's back as he adjusted the light saddle on the horse, while his jockey stood by. She knew about horses. The French loved racing as much as anyone on earth, and her grandfather's horses had regularly beaten the king's. She raised one eyebrow. So! His *women* bet with him, did they?

"He won't win," she said firmly. "His proportions aren't right. His legs are too long for his chest depth. Horses like that are never good runners."

Everyone within hearing distance stopped, mugs of beer and ale halfway to their lips.

"Come on, Clay, you going to let a challenge like that stand?" Travis laughed. "Sounds to me like she knows something."

Clay barely paused in tightening the girth. "Care to put a little money on that?"

She stared at him. He knew she had no money. Ellen nudged her. "Promise him breakfast in bed for a week. A man'll kill himself trying to win that." Ellen's voice carried across half the racetrack. She, like nearly everyone except Nicole, had had too much to drink.

"That sounds fair to me," Clay grinned, and winked at Travis in thanks for starting the whole idea. Clay seemed to think the wagering was ended.

"And what do I get when the horse loses?" Nicole asked loudly.

"Maybe I'll bring *you* breakfast in bed," Clay said with a leer, and the men around him laughed in appreciation.

"I'd prefer a new winter cape," Nicole said coolly, then turned away to go back to the track. "A red wool one," she threw over her shoulder.

The women around her laughed, and Ellen asked if she was sure she wasn't an American by birth.

When Clay's horse lost by three lengths, he had to take a lot of ribbing. They asked if Nicole shouldn't take care of the tobacco as well as the horses.

Now, as the women walked toward the house, they laughed together over their wins and losses. One pretty young woman had promised to shine her husband's boots personally for a whole month. "But he didn't say which side of them," she laughed. "He'll be the only man in Virginia whose socks can see themselves."

Nicole looked at the mounds of food and realized she was ravenous. The stoneware plates stacked on one table were enormous, more platters than plates. Nicole helped herself to a little of everything.

"Think you can eat all that?" Clay teased from behind her.

"I may have to refill it," she laughed. "Where do I sit?"

"With me if you can wait long enough." He grabbed a plate and piled it much higher than Nicole's, then took her arm and led her to a large oak tree. One of the Backes's servants smiled and set large tankards of rum punch on the ground by the tree. Clay sat down on the grass, his plate in his lap, and began to eat. He looked up at Nicole, who still stood, her plate in her hand. "What's wrong?"

"I don't want to get grass stain on my dress," she said.

"Hand me your plate," Clay said as he set his on the ground beside him. When her plate was beside his, Clay grabbed her hand and pulled her into his lap.

"Clay!" she said as she started to move away. He

162

held her where she was. "Clay, please. We're in a public place."

"They couldn't care less," he said as he nuzzled her ear. "They're more interested in food than in what we're doing."

She pulled back from him. "Are you drunk?" she asked suspiciously.

He laughed. "You do sound like a wife, and, yes, I'm a little drunk. You know what's wrong with you?" He didn't wait for her answer. "You are completely sober. Do you know that you are absolutely delightful when you're drunk?" He kissed the end of her nose, then grabbed the tankard of rum punch. "Here, drink this."

"No! I don't want to get drunk," she said stubbornly.

"I am going to hold this to your mouth, and you either swallow it or you'll ruin your dress."

She considered refusing to obey him, but he looked so endearing, like a naughty little boy, and she was so very thirsty. The rum punch was delicious. It was made from three different rums and four fruit juices. It was cold, with bits of ice floating in it. It went to her head immediately, and she took a deep breath, feeling her tensions leave her.

"Feel better now?"

She looked at him from under her thick lashes, then ran her finger across his cheek bone. "You're the most handsome man here," she said dreamily.

"Better than Steven Shaw?"

"You mean the blond man with the hole in his chin?"

Clay grimaced. "You could have said you had no idea who I was talking about. Here," he handed her plate to her. "Eat something. You'd think a Frenchwoman wouldn't get drunk as easily as you do."

She leaned her head against his shoulder and pressed her lips next to his warm skin.

"Here, sit up," he said sternly, and lifted a piece of

163

cornbread to her mouth. "I thought you were hungry." The look she gave him made him shift his legs uncomfortably. "Eat!" he commanded.

Nicole reluctantly turned her attention to the food, but she enjoyed sitting on his lap. "I like your friends," she said through a mouthful of potato salad. "Are there more horse races this afternoon?"

"No," Clay said. "We usually give the horses and jockeys a rest. Most of the people play cards or chess or backgammon. Some of the others find their rooms in that maze Ellen calls a house and take a nap."

Nicole went on eating calmly for a while. Then she lifted her eyes to look at him. "What are *we* going to do?"

Clay smiled in such a way that only one side of his mouth moved. "I thought I'd give you some more rum and then ask you."

Nicole stared at him, then reached for her mug of punch. After she'd taken a long drink, she set it on the ground. She suddenly gave a big yawn. "I do believe I need . . . a nap."

Clay quietly removed his coat and put it on the ground beside him. Then he picked her up and set her on it. He kissed the corner of her surprised mouth lightly. "If I'm to walk you across the yard to the house, I need to be in a decent condition to do so."

Nicole's eyes went downward to the bulge in Clay's buckskin trousers. Then she giggled.

"Eat, you little imp!" he commanded in a mock fierce tone.

A few minutes later, Clay took her half-finished plate from her and pulled her to stand beside him. He slung his coat over one shoulder. "Ellen," he called when they were closer to the house. "Which room did you put us in?"

"Northeast wing, second floor, third bedroom," she answered quickly.

"Tired, Clay?" someone laughed. "Funny how tired newlyweds get."

"You jealous, Henry?" Clay called over his shoulder.

"Clay!" Nicole said when they were inside the house. "You're embarrassing me."

Clay grunted. "The looks you're giving me are making *me* blush." He pulled her along behind him as he wound his way through the corridors. Nicole had only an impression of an odd mix of furniture and paintings. The furnishings ranged from English Elizabethan to French court to American primitives. She saw paintings worthy of Versailles and some so crude they must have been done by children.

Somehow, Clay found the room. He pulled her inside and grabbed her into his arms while he slammed the door shut with his foot. He kissed her hungrily, as if he couldn't get enough of her. He held her face in his hands and tilted it to slant across his.

She gave up to his control of her. Her mind was whirling with the nearness of him. She could feel his sun-warmed skin through his cotton shirt. His mouth was hard and soft at the same time, and his tongue was sweet. His thighs pressed against her, demanding yet asking.

"I've waited a long time for that," he whispered as he pressed his lips to her earlobe. He pulled at it with his teeth.

Nicole pushed away from him. As he watched with a puzzled expression, she walked to the other side of the room, then lifted her arms and swiftly began to remove the pins from her hair. Clay stood still and watched her. He didn't even move as she struggled with the buttons down the back of the dress. The sight of her, alone in a room with him, was what he'd dreamed of for a long time.

She moved her shoulders forward and slipped out of

the dress. Under it she wore a thin cotton gauze chemise. The low neckline was embroidered with tiny pink hearts. It was tied under her breasts with a thin pink satin ribbon. Her breasts swelled above the delicate, nearly transparent cloth.

Very, very slowly, she untied the bow of the ribbon and let the gauze slide to the floor.

Clayton's eyes followed the fabric, going over every inch of her from her high, firm breasts to her little waist to her delicate feet. When he looked back at her face, she raised her arms to him. He took one long step across the room, lifted her in his arms and laid her gently on the bed. He stood over her, looking at her. The sunlight through the curtained window showed her skin to be flawless.

He sat down on the bed beside her and ran his hand over her skin. It felt as good as it looked, smooth and warm.

"Clay," Nicole whispered, and he smiled at her.

He bent and kissed her neck, the pulse at the base of her throat, then moved slowly to her breasts, teasing them, savoring the rigid pink peaks.

She buried her fingers in his thick hair and arched her neck backward.

Clay stretched out on the bed beside her. He was fully clothed, and Nicole could feel the coolness of the brass buttons of his vest against her skin. The buckskin of his pants was warm and soft. The leather of his boots rubbed against her legs. The clothes against her bare skin, the leather and brass, were all male, all strong like Clay.

When he moved on top of her, she rubbed her leg against the side of his boot. The buckskin caressed her inner thigh. He moved to one side and began to unbutton his vest.

"No," she whispered.

He looked at her for a moment and then kissed her again, deeply, passionately.

She laughed throatily when he lifted his leg and ran the smooth leather of his boot along the length of her leg. He unfastened the buttons at the sides of his trousers, and Nicole moaned at the first touch of his manhood.

He lay on top of her, holding her tightly as if he were afraid she'd try to leave him.

Slowly, very slowly, Nicole began to come alive again. She stretched and breathed deeply. "I feel like I've just gotten rid of a lot of tension."

"Is that all?" Clay laughed, his face pressed into her neck. "I'm glad that I was able to be of some service. Perhaps I should wear my spurs next time."

"Are you laughing at me?"

Clay rose on one arm. "Never! I think I'm laughing at myself. You have certainly taught me some things."

"I have? Such as?" She ran her finger along the crescent scar by his eye.

He moved away from her and sat up. "Not now. Maybe I'll tell you later. I'm hungry. You wouldn't let me eat much an hour ago."

She smiled and closed her eyes. She felt deliciously happy. Clay stood up and watched her. Her black hair fanned out beneath her, making a splendid contrast with the curves of her body. He could see that she was already half asleep. He bent and kissed the tip of her nose. "Sleep, my little love," he whispered softly, then pulled the other half of the bedspread over her. He tiptoed from the room.

When Nicole awoke, she stretched lazily before she opened her eyes.

"Come on, get up," said a husky voice from across the room.

Nicole smiled and opened her eyes. Clay looked at

her in the mirror. His shirt was thrown across a chair, and he was shaving.

"You've slept most of the afternoon. Are you planning to miss the dancing?"

She smiled at him. "No." She started to get out of bed, then realized she was nude. She looked around for something to cover herself. When she saw Clay watching her with interest, she tossed the bedspread aside and walked toward the wardrobe where Janie had hung her clothes. Clay chuckled and resumed shaving.

When he finished, he went to stand behind her. She wore an apricot satin dressing gown, and she puzzled over her clothes for something to wear.

Clay suddenly grabbed a gown of cinnamon-colored velvet. "Janie said you should wear this." He held it up and eyed it critically. "There doesn't look like there's much to the top of it."

"I supply that," she said smugly, and took the dress from him.

"Then I guess you won't need these."

She turned and saw what he held. Pearls! There were four strands of them, held together by four long gold clasps. She held the necklace in her hands, felt the creamy texture of the pearls. But she didn't understand how it was to be worn. It looked more like a long belt than a necklace.

"Put the dress on and I'll show you," Clay said. "My mother designed it."

Quickly, Nicole slipped into her chemise, then the gown. The bodice was very low, the sleeves mere straps across her shoulders. Clay fastened the hooks and eyes up the back. He then pinned one of the clasps to the center back of the dress, the second one to her shoulder. The third clasp was fastened to the center of the deep décolletage, another one on the other shoulder, then making a full circle to the back. The four strands were threaded in such a way that they draped. Two strands went across the breasts, while the others hung gracefully across the velvet.

"It's beautiful," Nicole breathed as she looked in the mirror. "Thank you for allowing me to wear it."

He bent and kissed her bare shoulder. "My mother gave it to me to give to my wife. No one else has ever worn it."

She whirled to face him. "I don't understand. Our marriage isn't—"

He put a finger to her lips to stop her. "Let's just enjoy tonight. There's time to talk tomorrow."

Nicole stood back as he dressed. She could hear the musicians on the lawn below. She was quite content not to think of any time but the moment. Reality was Bianca and Clay together in his house. Reality was his love for another woman.

They left the room, and Clay led her again through the maze of a house out to the garden. The tables had been reset with more food, and the people lounged about, eating and drinking. Nicole had hardly found time for a bite of food before Clay pulled her onto the platform that had been laid for dancing. The energetic Virginia reel left her breathless.

After four dances, Nicole begged Clay to let her rest. He led her away from the group to a little octagonal pavilion set under three willow trees. It had become night while they were dancing.

"The stars are beautiful, aren't they?"

Clay put his arms around her and drew her close, her head resting on his shoulder. He didn't speak.

"I wish this moment could go on forever," she whispered. "I wish it would never end."

"Have the other moments been so horrible? Have you been so unhappy in America?"

She closed her eyes and moved her cheek against him. "I have spent my happiest moments here and my most miserable." She didn't want to speak of it. She lifted her head. "Why isn't Wesley here? Did he have to return to take care of his plantation so his brother could come? And who is that woman with Wesley's brother?"

Clay chuckled and pushed her head back down. "Wes didn't come because I guess he didn't want to. As for Travis, he's mean enough he could run his place from England if he wanted to. And the redhead is Margo Jenkins. As far as I can tell, she's determined to get Travis whether he wants her or not."

"I hope she doesn't get him," Nicole murmured. "Did you and Wesley quarrel?" She felt him stiffen against her.

"Why would you ask that?"

"I think your temper makes me ask that."

He relaxed and laughed. "We did have a scuffle."

"Serious?"

He pulled her away from him and looked into her eyes. "It may have been one of the most serious conversations of my life." He lifted his head. "I believe they're playing another reel. Are you ready?"

She smiled in answer as he grabbed her hand and led her back to the dancers.

Nicole was amazed at the stamina of the Virginians. It had been a long day, even though she'd slept in the afternoon. On her third yawn, Clay took her hand and led her upstairs. He helped her undress, but as she was climbing into bed he held a long bathrobe up for her. She looked at him in puzzlement.

"I thought you might like a bath by moonlight," he said as he undressed and slipped into a cotton banyan, a loose-sleeved robe.

Quietly, Nicole followed him through more passages in the house to the outside. To her amazement, they came out close to the edge of the woods. She could hear the river not far away.

They walked through the lush darkness of the trees to where a bend in the river made a lovely pool. Clay put the soap and towels on the bank, undressed, retrieved the soap, and walked into the river. Nicole watched as the moonlight played on the muscles of his back. He parted the water cleanly, his long legs making very little sound as he swam to the center of the pool. He turned onto his back and looked at her. "Are you going to stay there all night?"

She hastily untied her robe and dropped it to her feet, then hurried after him. She dove under the water.

"Nicole!" Clay called when she didn't resurface. His voice held fear in it.

She surfaced behind him, nipped him on the back before she went under again. He growled at her, then grabbed her about the waist. "Come here, you little imp," he said, kissing her forehead.

She put her arms around his neck and kissed him deeply. Her skin felt good against his. The water was warm and luxurious.

Clay set her away from him, then began to lather the soap in his hands. He rubbed his hands all over her, very slowly. When he finished, she took the soap and washed him. They laughed together, enjoying the water and each other. Before Nicole could rinse herself, Clay began washing her hair. She dipped under the water to rinse. Her hair flowed out behind her in a long mass of black silver.

Clay watched her, then slowly drew her close to him. He kissed her gently, pulling her body close. He pulled back from her and looked into her eyes. He seemed to be asking her a question, and whatever answer he wanted he saw there. He kissed her again, then lifted her in his arms and carried her ashore.

He laid her gently on the grass and began to kiss her body. He kissed her wherever his soapy hands had touched. Nicole smiled, her eyes closed. She bent her head and pulled his mouth to hers. She ran her hands over his body, liking the feel of it, the strength of it.

He moved on top of her, and she was ready for him. "Sweet Nicole," he whispered, but she didn't hear him. Her senses had changed from reality to the pure passion that Clay made her feel. She lifted her hips to meet him.

It was some time later when Clay lay beside her and pulled her close to him. He kept one thigh thrown across her. His mouth was close to her ear, and his breath was sweet and warm.

"Will you marry me?" he whispered.

She wasn't sure she heard him correctly.

"Don't I get an answer?"

Nicole could feel her body tense. "I am married to you."

He bent over her, his head propped on one arm. "I want you to marry me again, in front of the whole county. This time, I want to be there when we're married."

She was silent as he ran one finger over her upper lip. "One time you told me you loved me," he said. "Of course, you were drunk at the time, but you did say it. Did you mean it?"

She could scarcely breathe. "Yes," she whispered, staring into his eyes.

"Then why won't you marry me?"

"Are you laughing at me? Are you teasing me?"

He smiled and nuzzled her neck. "Do you find it so hard to believe that I could have any sense at all? How can you love a man you think is stupid?"

"Clay, talk to me. I don't understand what you're saying. I've never thought you were stupid."

He looked at her again. "You should have. Everyone on the plantation gave their love to you except me. Even my horses are smarter than I am. Remember when I first kissed you on the ship? I was so angry because of what I'd lost—you. I never wanted to let you go, yet there you stood telling me that you weren't really mine. I was furious when I saw that note and frantic when I couldn't find you. I think Janie knew then that I'd fallen in love with you."

"But Bianca—" Nicole began, but Clay put a finger to her lips.

"She's in the past now, and I'd like for us to go on from here. Ellen knows we were married by proxy on the ship, and she will understand if we ask to be remarried here."

"Remarried? Here?"

Clay kissed her nose and smiled, his eyes twinkling brightly in the moonlight. "Is it such an impossible idea? Then we'd have about a hundred witnesses who'd swear we weren't forced into a marriage. I don't want the idea of an annulment to come up later." He grinned. "Even if I beat you."

Her tenseness left her. "You would be sorry."

"Oh?" he laughed. "What would you do?"

"Get Maggie to stop cooking, tell the twins what you'd done so they could hate you, too, and—"

"Hate me?" He was suddenly serious, and he pulled her close to him. "We're alone, you and I. We have only each other. You must promise never to hate me."

"Clay," she gasped, trying to breathe. "I didn't mean it. How could I hate you when I love you so much?"

"I love you, too," he said, then released his hold on her slightly. "It'll probably take about three days to prepare everything for the wedding, but you do agree, don't you?"

She laughed against him. "You ask me if I agree to the thing I want most in life? Yes, I'll marry you. Every day, if you want."

He began kissing her neck hungrily.

Nicole's mind soared. She'd wanted this day to last forever. Maybe she'd never have to return to a life where she lived in one house and Clay in another. If they could only be married publicly before they returned, she felt she'd be safe. There would be witnesses to the fact that Clay loved *her* and wanted *her*.

The word *Bianca* flashed across her mind, but Clay's kisses sent all thoughts far away. Three days, he'd said. What could happen in three days?

Chapter 11

WHEN NICOLE AWOKE THE NEXT MORNING, SHE COULDN'T believe the things that had happened the night before. It all seemed too good to be true. She was alone in the bedroom, and the sun was streaming through the window. She smiled as she heard the excited voices beneath the window. The horse races were about to begin. She jumped out of bed and quickly dressed in a simple gown of butterscotch muslin.

It took her several minutes to find her way out of the house to the tables set up for breakfast. She was eating a plate of scrambled eggs when she felt a hush fall over the people around her. One by one, they all seemed to grow quiet.

She stood up and looked toward the wharf. What she saw threatened to stop her heart. Wesley walked beside Bianca. Nicole had felt safe in this place, away from Bianca, but now she saw her world starting to crumble about her.

Bianca walked toward the group confidently. She wore a gown of mauve satin with large black flowers embroidered around the hem. There was a row of wide lace at the high waist and neckline. Her large breasts were only barely concealed by the brilliantly colored dress. She carried a parasol of matching satin.

Even as Nicole watched them approach, she began to wonder at the silence of the others. She knew that Bianca's presence upset her, but why did it affect the people who did not know her? She looked at them and saw the looks of surprise on their faces.

"Beth," she heard repeatedly. "Beth."

"Wesley," Ellen called across the lawn. "You gave us such a fright!" She started walking across the grass toward them. "Welcome," she said, and held out her hand.

Even when they were close to the tables, Nicole still couldn't move. Wesley broke away from Bianca, who had already taken a plate. The women surrounded her.

"Hello," Wesley said to Nicole. "How do you like our Virginia parties so far?"

When Nicole looked at him, her eyes were full of tears. Why, she wondered. Why had he brought Bianca? Did he hate her for some reason and want her away from Clay?

"Nicole," Wesley said, and put his hand on her arm. "Trust me. Please?"

She could only nod. She had no other answer for him.

Ellen walked behind Wes. "Where did you find her? Has Clay seen her?"

Wesley smiled. "He's seen her." He held his arm out to Nicole. "Would you like to walk to the racetrack with me?"

Mutely, she took his arm.

"What do you know about Beth?" Wes asked when they were away from the others.

"Only that she was killed, along with Clay's brother," Nicole answered. She stopped suddenly. "Bianca looks like Beth, doesn't she?"

"It's a shock at first. Standing very still, she does look like Beth, but once she opens her mouth all resemblance disappears."

"Then Clay—" she began.

"I don't know. I can't speak for him. All I know is that at first I thought she *was* Beth. I know Clay's . . . concern for her is based on her resemblance to Beth. There couldn't be anything else, since she's not what

I'd call a pleasant woman." He grinned. "Clay and I had a few words about her." He flexed his jaw. "I just thought maybe it would do him some good to see the two of you together."

Nicole realized he meant well, but she'd seen the way Clay looked at Bianca, had seen the way he adored her. She didn't know if she could stand to see him look at another woman that way again.

"What happened in the races yesterday? Did Clay beat Travis? I hope so."

"I think they're tied," Nicole laughed, glad to change the subject. "But would you like to hear about my plans for a new red cloak?"

It was a rule of Virginia house parties that all of the guests took care of themselves. There was food constantly in view, every game imaginable, servants to help with every wish. So, when the horn sounded for the morning's races to begin, the women felt free to leave Bianca to herself when she refused their invitations to attend the races with them. But Bianca's eyes couldn't leave the food on the tables. That horrible Maggie had all but refused to cook for her after Clay had left.

"Are you the Maleson woman I been hearin' about?"

Bianca looked across the plate she was filling to the tall man. He was thin to the point of emaciation. His worn, dirty coat hung on him. His face was obscured by long, straggling black hair and a thin black beard. His nose was large, his lips almost nonexistent, but his eyes were like two black coals peering out of the brush of beard and hair. His eyes were small and so close together that the inner corners seemed to overlap.

Bianca grimaced and looked away from the man.

"I asked you a question, woman! Are you a Maleson?"

She glared at him. "I don't see that it's any concern of yours. Now let me pass."

"A glutton!" he said, eying her heaping platter. "Gluttony is a sin, and you'll pay for it."

"If you don't leave me alone, I'll call someone."

"Pa, let me talk to her. I think she's kinda pretty."

Bianca looked with interest at the man who now stepped from behind his father. He was a strong, healthy young man, no more than twenty-five years old, but unfortunately with his father's face. The little dark eyes went over Bianca's soft white body.

"Our mother's maiden name was Maleson. We heard you was gonna marry Clayton Armstrong, and we wrote you in England. I don't know if you ever got the letter or not."

Bianca remembered the letter quite well. So this was the riffraff that dared to claim to be related to her. "I received no letter."

"The wages of sin are death!" the old man said in a voice that would carry across the plantation.

"Pa, those people over there are gamblin' and bettin' on horses. You oughtta go talk to them while we get to know our cousin."

Bianca turned and walked away from the group. She had no intention of talking with any of them. She had no more than sat down when two young men came to sit by her. Across from her sat the man who'd spoken before, and beside her was another man, a shorter, younger boy, about sixteen. The boy's looks were softened by lighter-colored eyes, the shape of them rounder, farther apart.

"This here's Isaac," said the older son, "and I'm Abraham Simmons. That man was our pa." He nodded to the old man hurrying toward the racetrack with a large Bible under his arm. "Pa don't care nothin' about anythin' except preachin'. But Ike and me got other plans."

"Would you please go somewhere else? I would like to enjoy my breakfast."

"That's enough for three meals, lady," Ike said.

"You sure are uppity, ain't you?" Abe said. "You'd think you'd be glad to talk to us, bein' as we're related and all."

"I am not related to you!" Bianca said fiercely.

Abe leaned away from the table and stared at her. His little beady eyes narrowed until they were only slits of black light. "It don't look to me like you're over-flowin' with friends. We heard you was to marry Armstrong and own Arundel Hall."

"I am mistress of the Armstrong plantation," she said smugly between mouthfuls.

"Then who's that pretty little woman Clay says is his wife?"

Bianca set her jaw as she chewed steadily. She was still burning over the fact that Clay had left her to take Nicole with him. He'd behaved strangely toward her after the night that nice Mr. Wesley Stanford had joined them for supper. Clay had seemed to be watching her constantly since then, and Bianca had begun to feel ill at ease. She'd broached the idea of adding a wing to the house, and he'd merely sat and stared at her. Bianca had angrily left the room. She vowed she'd repay him for his rudeness.

Then suddenly he'd left the plantation. She was glad when he was gone; his constant presence made her nervous. She'd spent hours planning menus for her meals while he was gone. She was livid when that disgusting Maggie prepared less than half the dishes she'd ordered. While she was in the kitchen telling the cook that if she valued her job she'd better get busy, Wesley reappeared. He told her of the party and that Clay had taken Nicole.

Reluctantly, Bianca had readied herself to travel to the Backes's plantation early the next morning. How dare that horrible Nicole try to take what was hers! She'd show her! All she had to do was smile at Clay, and he'd act like he did the first night he saw her. Oh, yes, she knew what charms the women of her family had.

"The woman was once my maid," Bianca said loftily.

"Your maid!" Abe laughed. "It looks like she's Clay's maid now."

"Take your filthy mind elsewhere," she said as she rose to refill her plate.

"Listen," Abe said, following her. He was serious now. "I thought you was gonna marry Clay and then you could help us. Pa's never cared about anything but preachin'. We've got some land not too far from Clay's, but we don't have any stock. We was hopin' you could loan us your bull and, seein' as we're family, maybe give us a couple of your heifers."

"And some chickens," Ike said. "Ma'd like some more chickens. She's your third cousin."

Bianca whirled on them. "I am not related to you! How dare you presume on me and my prospects? How dare you speak to me of . . . animals!"

It took Abe a moment to reply. "There's somethin' wrong here, Miss High-and-Mighty. You ain't gonna get none of Clay's money, are you? You come all the way from England, and then he married your maid instead of you!" Abe began to laugh. "That's the best story I've heard in years. Just wait till I tell that one around here."

"It's not true!" Bianca said, her eyes beginning to tear. "Clayton is going to marry me! I am going to own the Armstrong plantation. It will just take time, that's all. He's going to annul his marriage to my maid."

Abe and Ike exchanged looks of suppressed laughter. "Annul, huh?" Abe smirked. "Yesterday, when she was sittin' on his lap and feedin' him, it didn't look like he was thinkin' of gettin' rid of her."

"And what about when he took her upstairs in the middle of the afternoon?" Ike said. He was at an age when he'd just discovered the opposite sex. He'd spent an hour under a tree imagining what Clay was doing with his pretty little wife. "When he come down, he had a grin from one ear to the other."

The dirty little harlot, Bianca thought. The bitch thought she could take the plantation away from her by using her body to entice Clay. She looked from the plate of food to the path to the raceway. As soon as she finished her breakfast, she'd straighten Nicole out. She put her chin into the air and walked past the young men.

"You may find you'll be wantin' a friend sometime," Abe called after her. "We don't forget family as quick as you, but our price is gonna be a lot higher from now on. Come on, Ike, let's go get Pa outta trouble."

It was an hour later when Bianca finally made her way to the racetrack. She found the entire day strenuous and wearing on her nerves. She'd be glad when she would no longer have to fight to get what she wanted. Someday, the Armstrong plantation would be hers and she'd be able to rest after meals to allow her food to digest properly. Now, all because of Nicole, she had to attend these disgusting parties with these loud, lower-class people.

She saw Nicole standing beside Ellen Backes at the edge of the racetrack. The other women were loudly yelling at the horses, but Nicole was quiet, a look of worry on her face. She kept looking toward one end of the track, where Clay stood in the midst of several men.

Bianca tapped Nicole on the shoulder with the point of her parasol. "Come here," she commanded when Nicole turned around.

With resignation, Nicole followed Bianca away from the others.

"What are you doing here?" Bianca demanded. "It's

not your place to be here, and you know it! If you won't think of me or of Clay, think of yourself. I've heard how you've acted like the lowest street trash around him. What are people going to say when he rids himself of you and marries me? Who will want to marry you when they know you're such used goods?"

Nicole stared at the taller woman. All she could think of was the horrible idea of being with any man except Clay.

"Shall we go together to see him?" Bianca asked smugly. "Do you remember how he ignored you when I first arrived from England?"

Nicole knew those few minutes were branded on her heart.

"You'll learn someday that a man must respect a woman before he can love her. When you act like a street woman, you'll be treated as one."

"Nicole," Ellen said from behind her, "are you all right? You look as if you're not feeling well."

"A little too much sun, perhaps."

Ellen smiled. "It couldn't be a little one, could it?"

Nicole's hand flew to her stomach. How she wished Ellen could be right.

"Maybe it's too much food," Bianca said. "One should never overeat and then stand in the sun. I think I'll walk back to the house. I think you should come with me, Nicole."

"Yes, do," Ellen urged.

The last thing Nicole wanted was more of Bianca's company, but she saw Clay and the men walking toward them. She couldn't bear to see Clay's eyes melt at the sight of his beloved.

There were at least three great rooms in Ellen's house, and now all of them were full of people. A sudden cold shower had sent them scurrying inside.

Fires had been lit all over the house, and as the massive masonry units of the fireplaces began to heat, the house grew warm.

Clay sat in a leather wing chair, sipping a mug of small beer and watching the twins pop corn over the fire. A few minutes before, he'd gone upstairs to find Nicole asleep in their bed. He was worried about her because all morning people had told him about the woman who looked just like Beth.

"Won't you sit down?" he heard a familiar voice say. He turned to see Wes standing rather close, facing him. A figure that was unmistakably Bianca's had her back to him.

Clay hadn't wanted to see her yet. First he wanted to talk to Nicole, reassure her, prevent her from worrying. He started to rise, but Wes gave him a look of warning. Clay shrugged and sat back down. Maybe Wes wanted to be alone with her.

"This must be a great shock to you," Wes said, his voice carrying easily across to Clay.

"I don't know what you mean," Bianca said.

"You can be honest with me. Clay told me the whole story. You came all the way from England, expecting to marry Clay, only to find he'd married someone else. Now he openly lives with her."

"You *do* understand!" Bianca cried gratefully. "Everyone seems to be against me, and I don't understand why. They should be against that awful woman, Nicole. I'm the one who's been wronged."

"Tell me, Bianca, why did you want to marry Clay in the first place?"

She was silent.

"I've been thinking," Wes continued. "It seems that we could help each other. You know, of course, that Clay is a man of some means." He smiled at Bianca's eager nod. "The last few years, my own plantation

183

hasn't been doing so well. If you were mistress of Arundel Hall, you could help me."

"How?"

"Now and then a piece of livestock could stray onto my land or maybe a few bushels of wheat could disappear. Clay wouldn't miss them."

"I don't know."

"But you'd be his wife. You'd own half the plantation."

Bianca smiled. "Of course. Could you help me get to be his wife? At first, I was sure I would be, but lately I'm not so sure."

"Of course you'll be his wife. If you'll help me, I'll help you."

"I will. But how will you get rid of that awful Nicole? She throws herself at him and, stupid man that he is, he enjoys her harlot's ways."

"I've heard enough," Clay said flatly from where he towered over Bianca.

She turned, her hand flying to her throat. "Clay! You gave me such a fright! I had no idea you were near."

Clay ignored her and turned to Wes. "There was really no need for this. It took me a while, but I finally saw what you meant. She's not Beth."

"No," Wes said quietly, "she's not." He stood up, his eyes going from Clay to Bianca. "I think you have some talking to do."

Clay nodded, then held out his hand. "I owe you a lot."

Wes grinned and shook his friend's hand. "I haven't forgotten that punch you gave me. But I'll pick my time to repay you."

Clay laughed. "It'll take you and Travis both."

Wesley snorted, then left Clay alone with Bianca.

She was beginning to understand that Clay had heard all of her conversation with Wes and that Wes had purposely planned it so he would. "How dare you eavesdrop on me?" she breathed as Clay sat opposite her.

"Your words didn't tell me anything I didn't already know. Tell me, why did you come to America?" He didn't wait for her answer. "I once thought I loved you, and I asked you to marry me. I was . . . haunted by you for a long time, but now I realize that I never loved you, that I never even knew you."

"What are you trying to say? I have letters where you say you'll marry me. It's against the law to go back on a proposal."

Clay looked at her in astonishment. "How could you consider a breach of promise when I'm already married? No court in the world would ask me to leave my wife to marry someone else."

"They would when I tell them the circumstances of the marriage."

Clay's jaw hardened. "What do you want? Money? I'll pay you for your time. You've already accumulated a sizable wardrobe."

Bianca fought back tears. How could this crude Colonial ruffian understand what she wanted? In England, she'd not been able to mingle with the crowd of people who had once been her family's peers because of her lack of wealth. Some of the people she knew in her reduced status laughed behind her back at her proposal from an American. They insinuated that she couldn't get anyone else. Bianca had hinted that she'd had several proposals, but it wasn't true.

So what did she really want? She wanted what her family had once had—security, position, freedom from bill collectors, the feeling that she was wanted and needed. "I want the Armstrong plantation," she said quietly.

Clay sat back in the chair. "You certainly don't ask

for much, do you? I can't, or won't, give it to you. I've grown to love Nicole, and I mean to keep her as my wife."

"But you can't! I came all the way from England. You have to marry me!"

Clay raised one eyebrow. "You will return to England in as much comfort as can be managed. I will try to compensate you for your time and for . . . the breach of promise. It is the best I can do."

Bianca glared at him. "Who do you think you are, you insufferable, uneducated boor? Do you think I ever wanted to marry you? I only came when I heard you had some money. Do you think you're going to discard me like so much baggage? Do you think I'm going to return to England as a jilted woman?"

Clay stood up. "I don't give a good goddamn what you do. You're going back as soon as possible, even if I have to personally throw you in the hold." He turned on his heel and left her. If he stood near her another minute, he just might hit her.

Bianca was seething. Never would she allow that disgusting man to jilt her. He thought he could demand that she marry him, then he could command her to go away just as easily, just as if she were a serving girl. Nicole! That's who was the scullery maid! Yet he tossed her, Bianca, aside for that lower-class scullion.

Her hands made fists at her side. She wouldn't allow him to do it! Once an ancestor of hers had known the nephew of the king of England. She was an important person, with power and influence.

Family, she thought. Those men this morning had said they were part of her family. Yes, she smiled. They'd help her. They'd get the plantation for her. Then no one would laugh at her!

Clay stood under the roof of one of Ellen's several porches. The cold shower beat down around him, isolating him. He took a cigar from his pocket and lit it, inhaling deeply on it. He'd had time in the last few days to curse himself for a fool, but today curses weren't enough.

In spite of what he'd said to Wes, seeing Bianca in a clear light had been a revelation. His mind had always been hindered by the vision of Beth.

He sat on the porch railing, one long leg on the floor as he watched the rain begin to slacken. Through the trees, he could see a faint glimmer of sunlight. Nicole had known what Bianca was, he thought. Yet Nicole had always been gracious and kind to the woman, had never been hostile or allowed her anger to vent itself on her.

He smiled and threw the cigar stub into the wet grass. The rain was dripping off the eaves of the house, but already the sun was making the drops sparkle on the lawn. He glanced up toward the window of the room where Nicole slept. Or did she? he wondered. How had she reacted when she saw Bianca at the party?

He went inside the house, through the corridors, and up the stairs to their room. Nicole was the most giving person he'd ever met. She'd love him, his children, his servants, even his animals, yet she'd never ask anything in return.

He knew she wasn't asleep as soon as he opened the door. He went straight to the wardrobe and grabbed a dress, a plain calico one of chocolate brown. "Get dressed," he said calmly. "I want to take you somewhere."

Chapter 12

SLOWLY, SHE THREW BACK THE COVERS AND SLIPPED her chemise over her head. Her body felt stiff with misery. At least he hadn't forgotten her, she thought. At least this time his beloved Bianca's presence hadn't completely blinded him. Or maybe he was taking her back to the mill, as far away from Bianca as possible.

She didn't ask where they were going. Her hands shook so badly as she buttoned the dress that Clay's hands pushed hers away. He looked at her face, watched her eyes, enormous and liquid, filled with fear and longing.

He bent and kissed her softly, and her mouth clung to his. "I don't guess I've given you much reason to trust me, have I?"

She could only stare at him, her throat too swollen to speak.

He smiled at her in a fatherly way, then took her hand and led her from the room and out of the house. She lifted her long skirt to keep it off the wet grass. Clay pulled her behind him quickly, paying little attention to the fact that she had to nearly run to keep up with his long strides.

He handed her into the sloop without saying a word, then untied the boat and unfurled the sail. The elegant little boat sliced through the water cleanly and swiftly. Nicole sat calmly, watching him at the helm of the ship. The sheer width of him looked like a mountain to Nicole—impenetrable, mysterious, something she loved but didn't understand.

Her chest began to tighten when she saw they were

heading back toward the Armstrong plantation. She'd been right! He was returning her to the mill. The iron band around her chest was too tight for her to cry. When they sailed past the wharf to the mill, she felt her breath release and a wave of joy flow through her.

At first, she didn't recognize the place where Clay stopped. It seemed an impenetrable mass of foliage. He stepped out of the boat, the water up to his ankles, tied the boat, and then held his arms out for her. Gratefully, she nearly fell into them. He stared at her a moment in amusement before he carried her through the hidden gate and into the beautiful clearing. The rain had made everything fresh and new. The sunlight glittered on the raindrops on the hundreds of flowers.

Clay put Nicole down, then sat down against the big rock by the flowers and pulled her into his lap. "I know how you hate to get grass stain on your dress," he teased.

She was serious as she looked up at him. Her eyes looked worried, frightened. She nibbled at her upper lip. "Why did you bring me here?" she whispered.

"I think it's time we talked."

"About Bianca?" Her voice was barely audible.

His eyes searched hers. "Why is there fear in your eyes? Do I frighten you?"

She blinked several times. "Not you, but what you have to say. That frightens me."

He pulled her against him, her head snuggled against his shoulder. "If you don't mind listening, I'd like to tell you about me, about my family, about Beth."

All she could do was nod silently. She wanted to know everything about him.

"I had one of those idyllic childhoods that was like the fairy tales you tell the twins," he began. "James and I were loved and disciplined by the two most wonderful parents ever created. My mother was a lovely, kind woman. She had a great sense of humor, which bewildered James and me when we were younger. If she'd pack a lunch for us to go fishing, sometimes we'd open a crock and find a frog inside. It used to embarrass us that she could catch more fish than any of us."

Nicole smiled against him, imagining his mother. "What about your father?"

"He adored her. Even when James and I were grown, they'd romp and play like children. It was a very happy household."

"Beth," Nicole whispered, and felt him stiffen for a moment.

"Beth was our overseer's daughter. Her mother died when Beth was born, and she had no brothers or sisters. My mother just naturally took the little girl under her wing. And James and I did, too. James was eight when Beth was born, and I was four. There was never any jealousy about the little baby my mother gave so much time to. I remember carrying her around myself. When she could walk, she followed us everywhere. James and I couldn't spend a day in the fields without little Beth right beside us. I learned to ride a horse with Beth behind me."

"And you fell in love with her."

"Not fell, exactly. Both James and I were always in love with her."

"Yet she married James."

Clay was quiet for a moment. "It wasn't like that. I don't think anyone ever mentioned it, but we always knew she would marry James. I don't guess he ever actually proposed. I remember we had a party for Beth's sixteenth birthday, and James said didn't she think it was time they set a date. The twins were born before she was seventeen."

"What was she like?"

"Happy," Clay said quietly. "She was the happiest person I ever knew. She loved so many people. She was a woman full of energy, always laughing. One year, the crops were so bad we thought we were going to have to sell Arundel Hall. Even Mother stopped smiling. But not Beth. She told us all to stop feeling sorry for ourselves and *do* something. By the end of the week, we were able to map out a plan of economy so we'd survive the winter. It wasn't an easy winter, but we were able to keep the plantation, all because of Beth."

"Yet they all died," Nicole whispered, thinking of her own family as much as his.

"Yes," he said quietly. "There was a cholera epidemic. There were many deaths throughout the county. First my father died, then my mother. I didn't think any of us would recover from the blow, but in a way I was glad they went together. They wouldn't have liked being separated."

"But you still had James and Beth and the twins."

"Yes," he smiled. "We were still a family."

"You didn't want your own home, your own wife and children?" she asked.

He shook his head. "It sounds odd now, but I was content. There were women when I wanted them. There was a pretty little weaver who—" He stopped and chuckled. "I don't guess you want to hear about that."

Nicole vigorously nodded her head in agreement.

"I don't guess I ever met anyone who fit in with the three of us. We'd spent our childhoods together, and we knew each other's thoughts and wishes as well as our own. James and I worked together, rarely speaking even, then we'd go home to Beth. She . . . I don't know how to say it, she made us welcome. I know she was James's wife, but she took care of me just as well. She was always cooking things for me, making me new shirts."

He stopped. He held Nicole close to him, buried his face in her sweet-smelling hair.

"Tell me about Bianca," she whispered.

His voice was very low when he spoke. "At one of the house parties Beth gave, a visitor, a man from England, kept staring at Beth. Finally, he told her that he'd recently met a young woman who could be Beth's twin. James and I laughed at him because we knew no one could be like our Beth. But Beth was very interested. She asked the man a hundred questions and carefully took down Bianca Maleson's address. She said that if she ever visited England, she'd see if she could find Miss Maleson."

"But you went to England first."

"Yes. We felt we weren't getting as good a price from our English markets for our cotton and tobacco as we should have gotten. At first, James and Beth planned to go and I'd stay here with the twins, but Beth discovered she was going to have another baby. She said nothing would make her risk losing the baby on an ocean voyage, so I'd have to go alone."

"And she asked you to go see Bianca."

Clay's body turned rigid as he gripped Nicole tightly. "James and Beth were drowned only days after I left, but it took months for the news to reach me in England. I had just finished my business and had traveled to Bianca's house. By then I was terribly homesick. I was tired of poorly cooked meals and having to arrange for my shirts to be washed. I only wanted to go home to my family. But I knew Beth would have my hair if I didn't make an effort to see this woman who was supposed to look like her. I'd been invited to stay with the Englishman who'd told Beth about Bianca. When Bianca walked into the room, all I did was stare. Right then, I wanted to grab her and hug her and ask her about James and the twins. It was hard for me to believe she wasn't Beth."

He stopped for a moment. "The next day, a man came to tell me about James and Beth. He'd been sent by Ellen and Horace, and it'd taken him a long time to find me."

"It was shock as much as grief, wasn't it?" Nicole said from experience.

"I was stunned. I couldn't believe it was true, but the man had seen both of them taken from the river. All I could think was that when I returned to Arundel Hall, it would be empty. My parents were gone, and now James and Beth were gone. I thought about remaining in England, having Horace sell the plantation."

"But Bianca was there."

"Yes, Bianca was there. I began to think that Beth wasn't really gone, that it was an omen that news of her death reached me while I was near a woman so like her. At least I thought Bianca was like her. All I could do was stare at her and tell myself that Beth was still alive, at least someone I loved was still with me. I asked Bianca to marry me. I wanted her to return to Virginia with me so I wouldn't have to enter an empty house, but she said she needed time. I had no time. I knew I needed to go home. Knowing that Bianca was going to join me soon, I felt I could face the plantation, and I hoped the work would help me forget."

"Nothing can make you forget."

He kissed her forehead. "I did the work of two men, three maybe, but nothing could even dull the pain. I stayed away from the house as much as possible. The emptiness of the place screamed at me. The neighbors tried to help, they even tried to find me a wife, but I only wanted things the way they were."

"You wanted Beth and James back."

"Every day, the idea of Beth once again sitting beside me grew stronger and stronger. I accepted James's death, but I was haunted by Bianca. I thought she could replace Beth."

"So you arranged for her to be kidnapped and brought to you."

"Yes. It was a desperate measure, but I felt desperate, like I was going crazy."

Nicole moved her cheek against his chest. "No wonder you were so angry when you found out I'd been married to you instead of Bianca. You were expecting a tall blonde, and you got—"

"A little dark beauty with a funny mouth," he laughed. "If you'd taken a pistol to me, I'd have deserved it. I put you through a lot then."

"But you were expecting Bianca!" she said in his defense, lifting her head to look at him.

He pushed her back to his shoulder. "Thank God I didn't get her! I was a fool to think any human could replace another."

His words sent a thrill through her. "Do you still love Bianca?"

"I never did. I know that now. All I saw was her resemblance to Beth. Even when she came here, I never listened to her or thought about her as anything except Beth. Yet even in that state of ignorance, I knew something was wrong. I thought that when Bianca was in my house everything would be all right again, that I would feel like I did when Beth was alive."

"But you didn't?" Nicole said with hope in her voice.

"I have you to thank for that. Even though I say I didn't hear Bianca, I think that some part of my small brain must have. All I knew was that I didn't want to return home at night, that I was working harder than I ever had in the last year. But when you were living in the house, I wanted to come home. When Bianca was at the house, I preferred the fields, especially the fields closest to the mill."

Nicole smiled and kissed his chest through his shirt. His words were the most wonderful she'd ever heard.

"It took Wes to knock some sense into me," he continued. "When Wes first saw Bianca, I could see how he was affected. I felt justified then for having her

194

in my house and not you. I knew Wes would understand."

"I don't think Wesley likes Bianca."

Clay chuckled and kissed the tip of her nose. "That's a polite way of putting it. When he told me he thought she was a vain, arrogant bitch, I hit him. It made me sick, and I didn't know if I was sick from hitting my friend or from hearing the truth. I left the house and didn't return for two days. I had a lot of thinking to do. It took me a while, but I began to see what I'd done. And I made myself face the fact that Beth was dead. I'd tried to bring her back through Bianca, but that couldn't work. What I had, but had ignored for the most part, was the twins. If James and Beth still lived, it was through their children and not some stranger. If I wanted to give Beth anything, it would be a good mother for the twins she loved so much, and not one who knocked Alex in the water because he tore her dress."

"How did you know about that?"

"Roger, Janie, Maggie, Luke," he said with disgust. "Everyone seemed to think it was his duty to tell me about Bianca. They'd all known Beth, and I guess they could sense that most of my attraction to her lay in that resemblance."

"Why did you ask me to the party?" she asked, holding her breath.

He laughed and hugged her tightly. "When it comes to brains, I think we have equally small ones. When I realized that I was trying to replace Beth with Bianca, I also knew why I spent so much time staring at the mill wharf—which needs repairing, I might add. There's a sawmill on the other side of the Backes's plantation."

"Clay!"

He laughed again. "I love you. Didn't you know that? Everyone else did."

"No," she whispered. "I wasn't sure."

"You nearly tore me apart the night of the storm when you told me about your grandfather and said you loved me." He paused for a moment. "You left me the next day. Why? We spent such a night together, then the next morning you were cold to me."

She remembered clearly the portrait in Clay's office. "The portrait in your office is Beth, isn't it?" She felt him nod against her. "I thought it was Bianca, and it looked like a shrine. How could I compete with a woman you worshipped?"

"It's gone now. I put the portrait back over the fireplace in the dining room. The pieces of garment I locked in a trunk to be stored with the others. Maybe Mandy will want them someday."

"Clay, what happens now?"

"I told you. I want you to marry me again, publicly, with lots of witnesses."

"What about Bianca?"

"I've already told her that she's to return to England."

"How did she take it?"

He frowned. "She wasn't what I'd call gracious, but she'll obey me. I'll see she is paid. It's a good thing I came to my senses as soon as I did. She's already run up enormous bills." He stopped suddenly and laughed at her. "You're the only woman I've ever met who is so considerate of her enemies."

Nicole moved away from him and looked up in a startled way. "Bianca isn't my enemy. Maybe I should love her since she was the one who gave you to me."

"I don't believe *gave* is the proper word."

Nicole giggled impishly. "I don't believe it is either."

He smiled down at her and caressed her temple. "You'll forgive me for being blind and stupid?"

"Yes," she whispered before his mouth closed on hers. The knowledge that he loved her made her especially passionate. She wrapped her arms about his neck and pulled him very close to her. Her body arched against his.

Neither of them noticed the first cold drops of rain. Only when the sky split with a slash of lightning and opened with a pure sheet of icy rain did they break apart.

"Come on!" Clay yelled as he stood up and pulled her with him.

She turned toward the path to the sloop, but Clay pulled her in another direction. They ran toward the side of the clearing opposite the river. While Nicole stood in the rain, rubbing her cold upper arms, Clay withdrew his knife and slashed at some hedges.

"Damn!" he cursed loudly when he couldn't seem to find what he wanted. Suddenly, the bushes broke away and revealed what looked to be a little cave. Clay threw his arm around Nicole and nearly pushed her inside.

She shivered. Her dress was soaked from the cold rain.

"Just a minute, and I'll have a fire going," Clay said as he knelt at one corner near the opening.

"What is this place?" she asked, kneeling beside him.

"We found this little cave—James, Beth, and I—and it's what caused us to plant the hedges and trees. James had one of the bricklayers show him how to build a fireplace." He nodded toward the rather crude structure where he was now working to build a fire. He sat back on his haunches as the fire took hold. "We always thought this was the world's most secret place, but when I was older I realized the smoke was as good as a flag. No wonder our parents never objected to our 'disappearances.' All they had to do was look out a window to see where we were."

Nicole stood up and looked around her. The cave was about twelve feet long and ten feet wide. Along the walls were set a couple of crude benches and a large pine chest, its hinges rusty and broken. Something glittered from a niche in the wall. She went to it. Her hand touched something cool and smooth. She withdrew it and held it up to the light from the fire. It was a large piece of greenish glass, and embedded inside was a tiny silver unicorn.

"What is this?"

Clay turned and smiled up at her. For a moment he was serious, then he reached out and took the piece of glass as Nicole sat beside him. He studied it as he spoke, turning it in his hands. "Beth's father bought the little unicorn for her in Boston. She thought it was so pretty. One day we were here in the cave, James had just finished the fireplace, and Beth said she hoped we would always be friends. Suddenly, she took the unicorn off the chain around her neck and said we were going to see the glassblower. James and I followed her, knowing she was up to something. She got old Sam to work up a ball of clear glass. Then the three of us touched the unicorn and swore always to be friends. Then Beth dropped it into the hot glass. She said that was so no one else could ever touch it." He looked at the glass one more time, then handed it back to Nicole. "It was a silly, childish act, but it seemed to mean a lot then."

"I don't think it's silly, and it certainly seemed to work," she smiled.

Clay wiped his hands together, then looked at her, his eyes dark. "Weren't we doing something interesting before the rain started?"

Nicole looked at him in wide-eyed innocence. "I have no idea what you mean."

Clay stood, went to the dilapidated old chest, and pulled out two of the dustiest, most moth-eaten blankets that had ever been seen. "Not exactly pink silk sheets," he said, laughing at some joke Nicole didn't share. "But better than the dirt." He turned and held out his arms for her.

Nicole ran to him, hugged him close to her. "I love you, Clay," she whispered. "I love you so much that it scares me."

He began pulling the pins from her hair, dropping them to the floor. He stroked the black, silky mass of her hair. "Why should you be frightened?" he said softly, his lips playing along her neck. "You're my wife, the only one I want or will ever have. Think about us and our children."

Nicole felt her knees begin to weaken as Clay's tongue touched her earlobe. "Children," she said under her breath. "I'd like children."

He pulled away from her and smiled. "Creating children isn't easy. It takes a lot of . . . ah, hard work."

Nicole laughed, her eyes dancing in delight. "Maybe we should practice," she said solemnly, "All work becomes easier with . . . experience."

"Come here, imp," he said, and picked her up into his arms. He carefully laid her down on the blankets. Somehow, the musty smell of them fit the atmosphere. It was a place of ghosts, ghosts Nicole felt smiling on them.

Clay unfastened the buttons of her wet dress, and as he revealed a piece of skin he kissed it. He pulled the dress out from under her, then off as if she were a child. Nicole removed her chemise herself. She was hungry to bare her skin to his touch. Clay moved her across his knee, his arm behind her back as he touched and teased her body. "You're so beautiful," he said, the firelight playing on her skin.

"You're not disappointed that I'm not blonde?"

"Hush!" he commanded in a mock stern voice. "I wouldn't change one color of you."

She turned to look up at him, then began to unbutton

his shirt. His chest was smooth and hard with muscle, lightly covered with hair. His stomach was strong and flat. Nicole felt her own muscles tighten at the sight of his beautiful body. His lean hardness was such a contrast to her own softness. She enjoyed his body. She enjoyed watching him walk, the way his muscles played beneath his skin as he worked to control an unruly horse. She liked to watch him throw hundred-pound bags of grain onto a wagon. She shivered as she pressed her mouth to the warm brown skin that covered the ridges of his stomach.

Clay was watching her, saw the range of emotions cross her expressive eyes. When at last they turned to the smoky brown of sheer lust, he felt chills run up his spine. The woman fired him in a way no other ever had. No longer did he care for the words of love, but he wanted her. He nearly tore his clothes from his body, pulling off the long, tight boots faster than he ever had before.

No longer were his kisses sweet and gentle, but as he took her ear in his mouth he threatened to tear it from her head. His lips, tongue, and teeth ran down her neck, across her shoulder, then back again to her breast.

Nicole arched under his touch. His tongue on her breast sent little sparks of fire through her veins. His mouth traveled down her stomach, making it contract under the sweet torment of his kisses. She buried her hands in the thick richness of his hair, dragging his mouth back to her own.

"Clay," she whispered before his mouth on hers stopped her words.

He moved his body on top of hers, and she smiled, her eyes closed, as she felt the weight of him. He was hers, thoroughly and completely hers.

When he entered her, it was, as always, a surprise to her, a shock of delight as she reexperienced his maleness. He filled her completely until she thought she would die from ecstasy.

They moved together, slowly at first, until Nicole felt she could bear the slowness no longer. Her hands caressed the round, hard smoothness of his back and buttocks, feeling the muscles work, feeling the power that lay just under his hot skin.

When they came together, Nicole could feel the contractions in her body from her waist to her toes. When Clay rolled off her and gathered her close to him, her legs throbbed. She smiled and snuggled against him, kissing his shoulder, tasting the salt of his sweat.

They fell asleep together.

Chapter 13

WHEN NICOLE FIRST AWOKE, SHE THOUGHT SHE
would do anything to
They moved
are

WHEN NICOLE FIRST AWOKE, SHE THOUGHT SHE WAS
back in the cave with Clay. But the sun across the bed,
shining through Ellen's lacy curtains, soon reminded
her where she was. The place beside her was empty,
but the pillow still bore an indentation from Clay's
head.

She stretched luxuriously, the sheet falling away
from her nude body. After they'd made love in the cave
last night, they'd slept for hours. When they awoke, the
moon had risen, the fire was out, and they were both
cold. They had quickly bundled into their damp clothes
and run for the sloop. Clay sailed it slowly down the
river to the Backes's house.

Once inside the house, Clay had raided the kitchen
and returned to Nicole with a large basket of fruit,
cheese, bread, and wine. He laughed as Nicole became
amorous after only half a glass of wine. They made love
again amid the food, kissing and eating, teasing and
laughing, until they fell asleep again in each other's
arms.

Nicole moved and pulled a piece of apple out from
under her right hip. She smiled at it before setting it on
the bedside table. She knew Ellen's sheets would be
stained for life after their antics of last night. But how
did one apologize for that? Could she say she'd poured
wine into the small of Clay's back and then sipped it
out, unfortunately spilling some when he grew impatient and turned over before she could drink it all? No,
that wasn't something you could tell your hostess.

She threw back the covers, then rubbed her bare

arms. There was the first nip of fall in the air. In the wardrobe hung a velvet dress of just the color of the wine she and Clay had shared last night. Quickly, she put it on, buttoning the tiny pearl buttons to her neck. It was long-sleeved, high-necked, fitting tightly across her breasts and then falling away in a gathered skirt to the floor. It was a simple, elegant gown, and it was warm, just what she would need for today's coolness.

She went to the mirror to arrange her hair. She wanted to look especially nice today. Clay had said that at the noon dinner he'd announce their plans for a second marriage and invite the people to his house for a Christmas wedding. Nicole had been able to persuade him to wait and prepare a party for the event. Ellen's guests would begin leaving this afternoon, and he wanted to make the announcement before they left.

Nicole got lost only once before she found the garden door that led to the lawn where the tables had been newly set up. Several people milled about the tables, talking slowly and eating quietly. Everyone seemed to be tired and ready for the long party to end. Nicole looked forward to returning to Arundel Hall—as its mistress.

She saw Bianca sitting alone at a little table under an elm tree. She felt a twinge of conscience at the sight. In a way, it didn't seem fair that the Englishwoman had come such a long way, expecting to be married, only to discover her fiancé was already married. Hesitantly, Nicole took a step forward. Then Bianca looked up, over a plate of food, at her. Bianca's eyes were filled with the fires of hatred. Her look was lethal if not fatal.

Nicole's hand flew to her throat, and she backed away. Suddenly, she felt like a hypocrite. Of course, she could afford to offer Bianca sympathy, since she—Nicole—had won. Winners can always afford to be gracious. She turned toward the tables and picked up a plate, but her appetite was gone.

"Excuse me, Mrs. Armstrong," said a man who towered over her.

Nicole looked up from the food she was pushing around on her plate. "Yes?"

She saw a tall, strong young man, but his eyes bothered her. They were little and close together, and now they glittered wildly.

"Your husband asked if you'd meet him at the sloop."

Nicole rose instantly and walked around the table toward the man.

He chuckled. "I like an obedient woman. Clay sure knows how to train his."

Nicole started to make a retort to his statement, but she stopped herself. She knew any answer she made would not give him the setdown he deserved. "I thought Mr. Armstrong was at the horse races," she said, purposely using the formal title. She followed him across the lawn toward the river.

"Not many men let their women know where they are *all* the time," he smirked, eying her up and down, his little eyes lingering on her breasts.

Nicole stopped where she was. "I think I'll return to the house. Would you please tell my husband that I'll meet him there?" She turned on her heel and started back toward the house.

She hadn't taken two steps before the man's hand clamped hard on her upper arm.

"Listen to me, you little Frenchy," he said, his lips drawn back in a snarl. "I know all about you. I been told about your lyin', foreign ways. I know what you done to my cousin."

Nicole stopped struggling and stared at him. "Cousin? Release me or I'll scream."

"You do, and that husband of yours won't live till mornin'."

"Clay! What have you done with him? Where is he? You hurt him, and I'll . . . I'll—"

"What?" he said avidly. "You sure are hot for him, ain't you? I told Pa you were little better than a bitch in heat. I seen the way you flaunt yourself around him. No good woman'd do that."

"What do you want?" Nicole said, her eyes large.

He smiled at her. "It ain't what I want so much as what I'm gonna take. Now, are you listenin'?"

She nodded silently, her stomach rolling.

"You're gonna walk with me to that wharf where my family's boat's tied. It ain't fine like you're used to, but it's good enough for a woman like you. Then you're gonna get on the boat real quiet and we're gonna take a little trip."

"To Clay?"

"Why, sure, honey. I told you he was gonna be all right if you just did what I said."

Nicole nodded, and the man's hand moved to her elbow, but the grip was just as hard as before. All she could think of was that Clay was in some kind of danger and she must help him.

He led her to the far end of the wharf where two other men waited in an old, patched sloop. One was an older man, skinny and dirty, with a Bible under his arm. "There she is!" he said loudly. "A Jezebel, a fallen, sinful woman."

Nicole glared at the man, then started to speak, but the man who'd held her arm gave her a sharp push. She landed hard against the young boy.

"I told you to keep quiet," growled the man who shoved her. "Take care of her, Isaac, and see she don't make any noise."

Nicole looked up at the boy, who put his hands on her shoulders. His touch was gentle. His features were softer, less harsh than the other two men's. She lurched forward as the sloop moved, and the boy steadied her. She turned to look back at the Backes's house. There, riding across the lawn, wearing a large white hat, was Clay. The horse he rode was crowned with a large wreath of flowers. He had obviously just won a race and was celebrating.

Nicole's mind clicked instantly. The men didn't have Clay, had never held him. She knew she was close enough to the house that a scream could be heard. She opened her mouth and filled her lungs, but she never made that scream because a large, hard fist slammed into her face. She slumped, unconscious, into Isaac's arms.

"You had no reason to do that, Abe!" Isaac said as he supported Nicole's limp body.

"Like hell I didn't. If you hadn't been staring at her with blind eyes, you'd have seen she was about to scream."

"There are other ways she could have been stopped," Isaac said. "You could have killed her!"

"No doubt you'd have used kisses to stop her," Abe sneered. "I'm sure she's used to those. Why don't you take her now? Me and Pa'll keep watch."

"You're talkin' sinful, boy!" Elijah Simmons said. "That woman is a harlot, a sinner, and we're takin' her to save her soul."

"Sure, Pa," Abe said as he winked at Isaac.

Isaac looked away from his brother and picked Nicole up in his arms. He ignored Abe's smirks. He held her as he sat on the deck, his back against the rail. He hadn't realized she was so tiny, more like a child than a full-grown woman.

He grimaced when Abe tossed him some rope and a dirty handkerchief and ordered him to tie her up. At least if he did it, he knew he wouldn't hurt her fine skin.

He'd wrestled with himself for the last day, ever since Abe had said they were going to kidnap pretty little

Mrs. Armstrong. Abe had told their father that Clay was really married to their cousin Bianca, but that the harlot Nicole had bewitched Clay until he'd deserted Bianca and openly lived with the French whore. That had been enough for Elijah. He was ready to stone the girl.

Isaac had been against the kidnapping from the beginning. He wasn't sure he believed everything Bianca said, even if she was his own cousin. She hadn't been exactly overjoyed to meet them that first day. But Abe kept ranting about the injustice that had been done when Nicole substituted herself for their cousin. He said they'd kidnap Nicole only long enough to get the marriage ended and allow Bianca time to marry Clay.

Now, holding Nicole across his lap, Isaac couldn't imagine her as a liar and a woman greedy for Clay's money. She seemed really to care for Clay. But Abe said that any woman who looked at a man like Nicole looked at Clay wasn't a good woman. Wives had to be good women, quiet and unphysical like their mother. Isaac was puzzled by Abe's words, because if he had a choice, he'd rather marry a woman like Nicole than one like his mother. Maybe he and Nicole were two of a kind, both of them bad.

"Isaac!" Abe commanded. "Stop your dreamin' and pay attention. She's comin' to, and I don't want her screamin'. Put that gag on her."

Isaac obeyed his brother, just as he'd done all his life.

Slowly, Nicole opened her eyes. Her jaw and head hurt horribly, and it took a moment for her eyes to clear. She tried to flex her jaw, but something held her, nearly strangled her.

"Be quiet," Isaac said. "You're safe with me." His voice was a whisper, meant only for her ears. "I'll take the gag off in a minute, when we get there. Close your eyes and rest."

"She awake yet, that daughter of Satan?" Elijah called back to his younger son.

Nicole looked up at the boy who held her. She didn't want to trust any of them, but she had no other choice. She watched as he slowly blinked his eyes at her. Understanding, she closed her own, blocking out the sunlight.

"No, Pa," Isaac called. "She's sleepin'."

"Wes," Clay said, a frown making a crease between his brows. "Have you seen Nicole?"

Wes looked away from the pretty redhead who fluttered her lashes at him. "You lost her already, Clay? I think I'm going to have to give you lessons in keeping your women," he teased. He stopped when he saw his friend's face. He set down his mug of ale and followed Clay away from the tables. "You're worried, aren't you? How long has it been since you've seen her?"

"This morning. I left her to sleep while I went to the races. Ellen said she saw Nicole come downstairs but hasn't seen her since. I asked some of the women, but none of them has seen her."

"Where's Bianca?"

"Eating," Clay said. "I checked her first. There's not much she could do anyway. Several women said Bianca hasn't left the tables all day."

"Could Nicole have gone for a walk, maybe just looking for some peace and quiet?"

Clay frowned harder. "At dinner we were to announce that we planned a second marriage at Christmas. We were going to invite everyone to a party."

"Dinner was over an hour ago," Wes murmured as he watched several of the guests walk toward the wharf. They were leaving to go home. "She wouldn't have missed that."

"No," Clay said flatly, "she wouldn't."

The men's eyes met. Both were remembering James's and Beth's deaths. If even an accomplished sailor like James could drown—

"Let's get Travis," Wes said.

Clay nodded once, then turned back to the remaining guests. The knot in his stomach was growing larger.

When the question of Nicole's safety was raised, the reaction of the guests was immediate. All chores were stopped and entertainment ceased. The women quickly organized a plan to comb the woods surrounding the plantation. The children ran from one dependency to another to see if Nicole could be found. The men went to the river.

"Can she swim?" Horace asked.

"Yes," Clay said, his eyes scanning the water, looking for a small, dark-haired body.

"Did you have a fight with her? Maybe she got a ride back to Arundel Hall."

Clay turned on Travis. "No! Goddamn it! We didn't have a fight. She wouldn't have left without telling me."

Travis put his hand on Clay's shoulder. "Maybe she's in the woods picking walnuts and forgot the time." His voice said he didn't believe that any more than Clay did. From what he'd seen of Clay's new wife, she was a sensible, considerate young woman. "Horace," he said quietly, "let's get the dogs."

Clay turned back toward the house. It was all he could do to keep his rage under control. He was angry at himself for leaving her alone for even a few minutes and angry at her for whatever had taken her from him. But the worst of his anger was helplessness. She could be ten feet away from him, or fifty miles, and he had no idea where to start looking.

No one noticed Bianca standing to one side, a full plate in her hand, smiling. Her work was done now, and she could go home. She was tired of hearing people ask who she was and why she lived with Clay.

The dogs were confused by so many scents from so many people. They seemed to find Nicole's scent everywhere, and they were probably right.

While Horace worked with the dogs, Clay began to question people. He talked individually to every man, woman, and child on the enormous plantation. But it was always the same—no one remembered seeing her that morning. One of the slaves said he had served her some scrambled eggs but he couldn't remember what she had done after that.

At night, the men carried torches into the woods. Four men took their sloops up and down the river, calling for Nicole. The far side of the river was searched, but there was no sign of her.

When morning came, the men began to straggle back to the house. They avoided Clay's hot look of misery.

"Clay!" a woman shouted, running toward him.

His head jerked up immediately to see Amy Evans waving her bonnet at him as she ran from the wharf.

"Is it true?" Amy asked. "Is your wife missing?"

"Do you know something?" Clay demanded. His eyes were sunken in his head, his face covered with unshaved whiskers.

Amy put her hand to her breast, her heart pounding from the run. "Last night, one of the men stopped at our house and asked if we'd seen your wife. Ben and I said we hadn't, but this morning at breakfast, Deborah, my oldest, said she'd seen Nicole with Abraham Simmons down by the wharf."

"When!" Clay said, grabbing the stout little woman by the shoulders.

"Yesterday morning. I sent Deborah back to the sloop to see if she could find our shawls because it was too cool without them. She said she saw Abe with his hand on Nicole's arm, leading her toward the river. She said she never liked Abe, she wanted to stay away from him, so she went to our sloop, got the shawls, and never looked back."

"Did she see Nicole get on the Simmons's boat?"

"No, nothing. They were blocked from sight by that big cypress tree, and Deborah wanted to get back to the races. She didn't think anything about it, didn't even remember it until this morning at breakfast when Ben and I were talking about your wife's disappearance."

Clay was staring at the woman. If Nicole had gotten onto the boat, then she was still alive. She hadn't been drowned as he'd begun to fear. And there could be a hundred reasons why she'd gone with Abe Simmons. All the man had to do was say someone needed her, and she'd never look back.

Clay's hands tightened on Amy's strong shoulders. Then he bent and gave her a resounding kiss on the mouth. "Thank you," he breathed, his eyes once again regaining color.

"Any time, Clay," Amy said, laughing.

Clay released her and turned around. His friends and neighbors were standing quietly by. None of them had had a wink of sleep all night.

"Let's go," Travis said as he slapped Clay on the shoulder. "Elijah's wife is probably having another baby, and Abe grabbed the first woman he saw."

Clay and Travis looked at each other for a long moment. Neither of them believed his words. Elijah was crazy and far from harmless. Abe was a sullen, high-tempered young man who openly resented the wealth of the planters around him.

Clay turned away when someone touched his arm. Janie stood there, a full basket of food held out to him. "Take this," she said quietly. For the first time since Clay had known her, her cheeks were no longer pink. Her whole face was gray with worry.

Clay took the basket from her and caressed her hand firmly. Then he looked back at Travis and at Wes, who stood beside his brother. He nodded once, and the three men walked quickly toward Clay's sloop. Wes ran to his sloop first, and when he joined Clay and his brother, he carried a brace of pistols. The men were grimly silent as they cast off and started downriver toward the Simmons's farm.

All day long, Nicole wavered between sleep and unconsciousness. When she was awake, the trees passing above her seemed unreal, patterns of shade and sunlight. Isaac had placed her carefully on a pile of rags and old feed bags. The slow drifting of the boat and the dull ache of her jaw made her calm, unworried about the bindings on her ankles and wrists, the gag across her mouth.

The river system of Virginia was extensive. Abe sailed the little sloop in and out of tributaries that linked one major river to another. There were some waterways that were so narrow that the two men had to use oars to propel themselves between the enclosing trees.

"Abe, where are you going?" Isaac asked.

Abe smiled secretly. He had no intention of informing his brother of his destination. He'd found the little island years ago, and it'd always stayed in the back of his mind that someday it would be useful. Soon after they'd gotten the woman on board, Abe had let his father off at their farm. He knew that soon the men would be there to search for the woman, and old Elijah would hold them off. Elijah would never lie about the fact that he'd taken the woman, but it would be hours before anyone would make any sense out of his rantings. Abe smiled at his own cleverness. Now all he had to do was control the boy. He glanced back at the woman, tied helplessly, quietly lying on the heap of rags. He smiled and wet his lips.

At sundown, Abe guided the boat toward shore.

Isaac stood up and frowned. It had been an hour since they'd seen a light from a house. For some time, the water had been little more than stagnant green slime. The air was fetid and hostile. "Let's get out of here," Isaac said, looking about him. "Nobody could live in this stench."

"Exactly what I have planned. Jump down there and get that rowboat. Do it!" Abe commanded as Isaac started to speak.

Isaac was too used to obeying his older brother. He didn't like the slimy water, and even as he watched, a long snake slithered across its surface. He jumped over one side of the sloop, felt the greenish brown mud suck at his feet up to his ankles. He waded through it, the foamy slime attaching itself to his knees, and untied the little rowboat. He hopped inside and used the oars to guide the rowboat to the side of the sloop.

Abe stood on deck holding Nicole in his arms. He handed her down to his little brother, then lowered himself into the rowboat. "Put her in the bottom and grab the oars," he commanded. "We've still got a long way to go."

Isaac did as he was told, resting Nicole against one of his legs. He didn't like the look of fear in her eyes, and he wanted to reassure her.

Abe snorted as he looked at his brother. "Don't get any ideas about her, boy. She knows who she belongs to."

Isaac looked away, remembering Nicole with Clay. He had no idea his brother meant differently.

It wasn't easy maneuvering through the thick water. Several times Isaac had to stop and free his oars from whatever piece of unseen filth held them. It was growing dark, and the overhanging trees completely blocked what little light there was. Isaac looked up, and it seemed to him that the trees were dipping toward them, trying to devour him.

"Abe, I don't like this place. We can't leave her here. Why don't we take her back to the farm?"

"Because she'd be found there, that's why. And I don't believe I mentioned leaving her here. There! Pull into shore there."

Isaac used his oars as poles to push the little rowboat to shore. Abe jumped out and searched beside a tree for a few moments before he found a lantern. He grunted in satisfaction that it was where he left it. He lit it quickly. "Come on, follow me," he said as he left Isaac to pick up Nicole.

"Just a few minutes and I'll take off the ropes," Isaac whispered as he held Nicole in his arms.

She nodded wearily, her head against his shoulder.

Abe held the lantern high and revealed a short, stout door that looked to be set in nothing but darkness. "I found this place a long time ago," he said proudly as he unfastened the latch.

It was a small, one-room, stone cabin. Inside it was bare except for the dirt and leaves on the floor.

Isaac put Nicole down, standing her on her unsteady feet, then took the gag off her mouth. She gasped as tears came to her eyes in gratefulness. He untied the ropes from her wrists. As he knelt to untie the bindings from her feet, Abe shouted at him.

"What the hell are you doing? I didn't tell you to untie her!"

Isaac glared at his brother in the darkness. "What can she do? Can't you see she's so tired now she can hardly stand up? Is there anything to eat around here? And what about some water?"

"There's an old well out back."

Isaac looked around in disgust. "What is this place? Why would anyone want to build something here?"

"It's my guess this wasn't always swamp. The river changed course and cut this part off. There's wild pigs around here, plenty of rabbits, and a couple of apple trees by the shore. Now stop askin' questions and get some water. I left a tin bucket here last time."

Reluctantly, Isaac went out into the blackness.

Nicole leaned against the stone wall. Her wrists and ankles ached, and she still didn't have enough feeling in them to move them. She was only vaguely aware when Abe came to stand beside her.

"Tired, are you?" he said quietly as his big hand caressed the side of her neck. "You're gonna be even more tired tomorrow after I get through with you. You ain't ever been loved like I'm gonna love you."

"No," she whispered, and took a step to the side, away from him. Her numb feet refused to work, and she fell forward onto her hands and knees.

"What did you do to her?" Isaac demanded from the doorway. He bent and lifted Nicole.

"My God, boy!" Abe said in a half laugh. "Somebody'd think you were in love with her, the way you act. What is she to you anyway? You heard the story. She's little better'n a whore."

"Are you all right?" Isaac asked, his hands on Nicole's shoulders.

"Yes," she murmured.

Isaac moved away from her, then gave her a drink from a tin cup. She drank greedily. "That's enough," he said. "Let's sit down and get some rest." He put his arm around Nicole's shoulders and led her to the far wall.

"You are younger'n I thought," Abe said with distaste. He started to say more but he stopped.

Isaac sat on the floor, then pulled Nicole down beside

him. "Don't be afraid," he said when she stiffened. "I won't hurt you."

She was too weary, too cold, too numb to care about propriety. When she sat beside Isaac, he pulled her head to his shoulder, and they both were instantly asleep.

"Isaac!" Abe called, pushing his little brother on the shoulder. "Wake up!" His eyes were on Nicole. It angered him that the bitch gave so much to his little brother. Isaac wasn't even a man yet, barely fifteen, and he'd never had a woman. Yet he sure acted like he knew about women, the way he handled that Nicole. Abe watched her, had watched her for the last hour as the daylight slowly entered the little cabin. Her black hair had come unpinned, and the dampness made little curls cling to her face. Her thick lashes curved across her cheek. And that mouth! It was about to drive him wild. It made him sick to see the way Isaac's arm was so possessive around the woman, his hand resting just under her velvet-clad breast.

"Isaac!" Abe called again. "You plannin' to sleep all day?"

Slowly, Isaac came awake. His arm tightened around Nicole, and he smiled down at her.

"Come on, get up," Abe said in disgust. "You got to go to the sloop and get the supplies."

Isaac nodded. He didn't question his brother about why he should make the trip instead of Abe. Isaac had always obeyed his brother. "Are you all right?" he asked Nicole.

She nodded mutely. "Why have I been brought here? Are you asking Clay for a ransom?"

"Go get the food," Abe commanded when Isaac started to speak. "I'll answer her questions. Go on!" he commanded when Isaac seemed to hesitate.

Abe stood in the doorway and watched his young brother walk down the path.

216

As soon as she was alone with him, Nicole knew she should be afraid of Abe. Yesterday, her mind hadn't been working clearly, but today she sensed the danger she was in. Isaac was a sweet and innocent boy, but there was nothing sweet or innocent about Abe. She stood up quietly.

Abe whirled on her. "Now we're alone," he said quietly. "You thought you were too good to have anything to do with me, didn't you? I seen the way you hung on Isaac, the way you let him touch you and hold you." He took a step toward her. "You one of those women what only likes young meat? You only like little boys?"

Nicole stood straight, her spine rigid, refusing to let this awful man see her fear. Her grandfather's voice came to her: "The Courtalains carry the blood of kings." Her eyes darted toward the door. Maybe she could get past him to the outside.

Abe chuckled deep in his throat. "There's no way to get out past me. You might as well just lay back and enjoy it. And don't expect Isaac to come rescue you either. He'll be gone for hours."

Nicole moved slowly along the wall. Whatever happened, she wouldn't give in to him easily.

Before she'd taken one good step, a long arm shot out and grabbed a handful of her hair. Slowly, very slowly, he wound the thick mass around his hand and drew her to him.

"Clean," he whispered. "I bet that's the cleanest hair I ever smelt. Some men don't like black hair, but I do." He chuckled. "I guess you're real lucky that I do."

"I don't think you'll get as much ransom if you harm me," she said, his face close to hers. His little eyes were almost black as he stared at her, and he smelled of old sweat and rotten teeth.

"You're a cool one," he said, grinning. "How come you ain't cryin' and beggin'?"

She gave him a cold look, refusing to allow her fear to show. Her grandfather had faced an angry mob. What was one dirty, evil-minded man compared to that?

He held her by the hair close to him. He ran his other hand over her shoulder, down her arm, his thumb caressing the curve of her breast. "Your value don't depend on what I do to you. As long as I keep you alive, I can have my fun with you."

"What do you mean?" Nicole thought maybe she could keep him talking.

"Never mind. I ain't interested in explainin' myself to you." His hand moved to the curve of her hip. "That's a real pretty dress, but it's gettin' in my way. Take it off!"

"No," she said quietly.

He pulled her hair until her neck threatened to break.

Her eyes teared from the pain, but still she would not undress herself. She would not play the whore for any man.

He released her abruptly, then laughed. "You are the haughtiest bitch I ever did meet." He went to the doorway and picked up the ropes Isaac had left on the floor. "Since you won't do it yourself, maybe I'll just have to help you. You know, I ain't ever seen a woman without a stitch of clothes on."

"No," Nicole whispered, and backed away, her hands vainly trying to hold on to the stone wall behind her.

Abe laughed as he lunged at her and grabbed her by one shoulder. She tried to twist away, but she couldn't as his thick fingers bit into her flesh. He forced her to her knees. Nicole moved forward and sank her teeth into the muscle just above his knee. The next moment, she was sent sprawling across the room.

"Damn you!" Abe swore. "You'll pay for that."

He grabbed her ankle and tied one end of a rope around it. The rough hemp cut into her already sore flesh. She kicked at him, but he held her easily. He grabbed her arms and tied the wrists together. There was an iron hook embedded in the stone wall where game had once been hung. Abe lifted Nicole by the rope around her wrists and tied her to it. Her feet barely touched the floor.

She gasped at the pain of her extended arms. He tied her feet together, then lashed the rope to another hook. She was helpless, tied tightly to the wall.

Abe stood back and admired his handiwork. "You don't look like such a fine lady now," he said, rubbing his leg where she'd bitten him. He took a long knife from his pocket.

Nicole's eyes widened at the sight.

"Now you look like you're gainin' the proper respect for a man. One thing my pa knows for sure is how to treat a woman. All them women at the Backes's house make me sick. Their husbands let 'em talk, give 'em money to bet on the horses. You'd think they were men, the way they acted. Some of 'em think they're better'n men. Last summer I asked one of those girls to marry me, and you know what she did? She laughed at me. I was payin' her a great honor, and she laughed at me! Just like you! You fit in right well with them. You're so pretty, married to a rich man, you couldn't even give me the time of day."

The pain in Nicole's arms was too much to allow her much room to think. Vaguely, she was aware of Abe's rantings. Maybe she had been guilty of ignoring him, of snubbing him. "Please release me," she whispered. "Clay will pay you whatever you want."

"Clay!" he sneered. "How can he give me what I want? Can he give me a lifetime away from a crazy father? Can he make a real lady agree to marry me? No! But he can give me a few hours' pleasure with his lady."

He moved closer to her, the knife upraised. His eyes sparkled with threat. He slipped the knife under the first button of the bodice of her gown. She drew her breath in sharply as the cold steel touched her skin. The button popped off and flew across the little room.

One by one, he cut the buttons off, then he slashed the satin sash that held the dress under her breast. He put his hand to her and gently parted the wine-colored velvet. He caressed her right breast through her thin chemise.

"Nice," he whispered. "Real nice." He used the tip of the blade to cut the chemise away neatly.

Her breasts lay bare before him. Nicole closed her eyes, tears squeezing out at the corners.

Abe stepped back to admire her. "You don't look much like a lady now," he smiled. "You look just like them women in Boston. They liked me. They begged me to come back to them." Suddenly, his mouth turned hard. "Let's see the rest of you."

He inserted the knife at the top of the long skirt and very slowly slashed the velvet to the hem. It hung open, exposing the nearly transparent chemise beneath.

"Lace," Abe whispered as he lifted the hem of the chemise. "My ma always wanted a piece of real lace so she could make a collar for her Sunday dress. And here you're wearin' lace on your underclothes." With a swift, violent motion, he jerked the chemise away.

He stared at her nude body, the round hips, the small waist, and her breasts lifted high by her uplifted arms. He ran his hand up one thigh. "So this is what ladies look like under all their silks and velvets. No wonder Clay and Travis and them others let 'em backtalk."

"Abe!" Isaac called. "You inside? One of the oars broke and—" He stopped as he entered the cabin doorway. What he saw nearly made him ill. Nicole was tied to the wall, her arms stretched far over her head. Abe's body blocked Isaac's view, but the boy could see the pieces of Nicole's dress, the shreds of her chemise hanging to the floor. Isaac's boyish face turned from confusion to anger to rage.

"You said she wouldn't be hurt," he said through clenched teeth. "I trusted you."

Abe turned on his little brother. "And I told you to go back to the sloop. I gave you an order, and I expected it to be obeyed." He still held his knife, now aimed at Isaac.

"So you could use her, is that why you wanted me out of the way? Were you planning to use her like you did the little Samuels girl? Her parents had to send her away after that. She was scared to go to sleep at night, scared you'd come for her. Only she wouldn't say who you were, but I knew."

"So what?" Abe said. "You make her sound like she was a child. She was engaged to one of the Peterson boys. She was givin' it to him, so why not to me?"

"You!" Isaac choked. "No woman would ever want you. I've seen 'em try to be nice to you, but you only wanted the ones you had to take." He grabbed the bucket at his feet and threw it at Abe's head. "I'm sick of watchin' you use women! I've had enough! You let her go!"

Abe easily dodged the flying bucket. He grinned maliciously. "Remember the last time you defied me, boy?" he said, circling, crouched over, the knife passing from one hand to the other.

Isaac glanced at Nicole when Abe moved away. He wasn't excited by the woman's helpless position. It repulsed him. He looked back at Abe. "I remember that I was twelve the last time," he said quietly.

"So the boy thinks he's become a man," Abe laughed.

"Yes, I have."

Isaac lunged so fast that Abe didn't really see his little brother move. He was used to a controllable, awkward child. He hadn't seen his brother grow up.

When Abe first felt his brother's fist in his face, he was astonished. He slammed back against the stone wall, the breath nearly leaving him. When he eased himself up, his rage matched Isaac's. No longer did he think he was fighting his own brother.

"Look out!" Nicole screamed at Isaac as Abe lunged forward. The knife blade sank into Isaac's thigh, and Abe pulled it up, making a deep, long slash.

Isaac gasped and jerked away from the knife. The cut was too deep to bleed much yet. He grabbed Abe's wrist, forcing his older brother down. The knife fell to the floor and, like a cat, Isaac grabbed it. Abe's arm swung out as he tried to take the knife, and he felt it cut into his shoulder.

He jumped back to the safety of the wall by the door, his hand over the cut in his shoulder. Blood was beginning to ooze between his fingers. "You want her for yourself, is that it?" he said through clenched teeth. "You can have her!" He turned quickly and slipped through the open doorway. He slammed the door shut, and Nicole and Isaac could hear the bolt being shot home.

Isaac stumbled toward the door and made one weak effort to throw his weight against it. His leg was beginning to bleed, and he was going into shock.

"Isaac!" Nicole called as she saw his eyes begin to close as he leaned his back against the door. "Cut me loose, and I'll help you. Isaac!" she called again when he didn't seem to hear her.

In a blur of pain, Isaac stumbled toward her and lifted his arm toward the ropes binding her hands.

"Cut it, Isaac," she encouraged when he seemed

about to forget where he was and what he needed to do.

He used the last of his strength to saw at the ropes, which were, thankfully, half rotten. When the rope fell away, Isaac collapsed to the dirt floor of the cabin and Nicole fell forward onto her hands and knees. Quickly, she untied her ankles.

Abe's bloody knife was on the floor. Quickly, she cut away her chemise, tore it into strips, then cut away Isaac's trousers to expose his wound. It was deep but clean. She bound it tightly to stop the bleeding. Isaac seemed to be in shock, not saying anything, not moving. When she finished with his leg, she gave him a little water to drink, but he wouldn't take it.

Suddenly, she was so very tired. She sat down, leaned against the stone wall, and pulled Isaac's head into her lap. The contact seemed to soothe him. She stroked his dark hair away from his forehead, then put her head against the wall. They were locked inside a stout stone cabin. They had no food or other supplies. They were on a desolate island where no one could find them, yet Nicole suddenly felt safer than she had in the last twenty-four hours. She slept.

Chapter 14

THE SIMMONS FARM WAS LOCATED ON A BACKWATER piece of land twelve miles upriver from the Armstrong plantation. It was worthless land, rocky and unfertile. The house was little more than a shack, small, filthy, the roof needing patching. The yard of hard-packed earth was filled with chickens, dogs, a litter of pigs, and several half-dressed children.

Travis tied the sloop to the rotting wharf while Clay jumped ashore and walked toward the house, the other men behind him. The children looked up from their chores to stare with sullen, uncurious eyes. Even as young as they were, they were beaten. They'd lived a life of constant hard work with a father who told them they were doomed to the fires of eternal damnation.

Clay ignored the children as he bellowed, "Elijah Simmons!"

The skinny old man appeared from inside the house. "What d'you want?" he asked, his little eyes sleepy, as if he'd just been awakened. He turned to one of the children, a little girl of no more than four. In her lap was a chicken, and she was wearily plucking the feathers from it. "You, girl!" Elijah said. "You better not leave any pinfeathers on that bird. You do, and I'll take you to the woodshed."

Clayton looked with disgust at the old man. He slept while his children labored. "I want to talk to you."

As the dirty old man began to wake up, his little eyes narrowed to hardly more than slits. "So! The heathen has come to seek his salvation. You'll need forgiveness for your whoring ways."

224

Clay grabbed the man's shirt front, lifting him so that his feet barely touched the ground. "I don't need any of your preaching! Do you know where my wife is?"

"Your wife?" the man spat. "Scarlet women are not made into wives. She's a daughter of Satan and should be taken from the earth."

Clay's fist smashed into the man's long, bony face. He slammed against the doorjamb and slid downward slowly.

"Clay!" Travis said, his hand on his friend's arm. "You aren't going to get anything out of him. He's crazy." Travis turned to the children. "Where's your mother?"

The children looked up from the chickens and beans they were working with and shrugged. They were so beaten, so defeated, that not even seeing their father hit interested them.

"I'm here," said a soft voice from behind the men. Mrs. Simmons was even thinner than her husband. Her eyes were sunken, her cheeks hollow.

"We heard that my wife was seen getting into a boat with your son. She's been missing for nearly two days now."

Mrs. Simmons nodded tiredly as if the news was no shock to her. "I ain't seen her or nobody who's a stranger." She put her hand behind her lower back to ease the pain. She looked to be six months pregnant. She didn't deny the idea that her son could have had something to do with Nicole's disappearance.

"Where's Abe?" Wesley asked.

Mrs. Simmons shrugged. Her eyes darted toward her husband, who was regaining consciousness. She looked as if she wanted to escape before he was fully awake. "Abe ain't been home for days."

"You don't know where he went? Does he know?" Clay asked, nodding toward Elijah.

"Abe don't tell anybody much. He and Isaac took

the sloop and went off. Sometimes they're gone for days."

"You don't know where?" Clay asked desperately.

Travis grabbed Clay's arm. "She doesn't know anything, and I doubt if the old man does either. Abe wouldn't have let them know what he planned. I think the best thing we can do is send out a search party. We can send people to the houses up and down the river and ask if they've seen anything."

Clay nodded silently. He knew that was the sensible thing to do, but it would take so much time. He tried to block out the vision of Abe and Nicole. Abe was a man warped by many years of living under Elijah's stern, insane rule. He turned away and headed back to the sloop. His rage at his sense of frustration was horrible! He wanted to destroy and maim, anything but this slow talking, talking, talking.

Wes walked behind Clay and his brother as they returned to the sloop. He stopped when a handful of pebbles hit his back.

"Psst! Over here."

Wes looked toward the shrubs by the river and could barely see the outline of a small figure. He walked toward it, and a young girl stepped out. She was a pretty little thing with big green eyes. Although she was cleaner than the other Simmons children, she was dressed in a ragged, thin cotton dress. "Did you want me?"

She stared at him in wonder. "You're one of them rich men, ain't ya? One of them what lives in a big house on the river?"

Wes knew he was rich compared to this child. He nodded once.

She looked around her to make sure no one else was near. "I know somethin' about where Abe's gone," she whispered.

226

Instantly, Wes bent to one knee. "What?" he demanded.

"My ma has a cousin, a lady cousin. That's hard to believe, ain't it? This cousin come to Virginia, and Abe said she was gonna give us some money. He and Pa and Isaac went to a party, a real party," she breathed. "I never been to a party."

"What did Abe say?" Wes asked impatiently.

"He came home, and I heard him tell Isaac they were gonna take some lady away and hide her. Then Mama's cousin would give them some of Mr. Armstrong's cows."

"Clay's?" Wes asked, puzzled. "Where did they take the lady? Who is your mother's cousin?"

"Abe only said he knew where he was takin' the lady, and he wouldn't even tell Isaac."

"Who is the cousin?"

"I don't remember her name. Abe said she was really Mr. Armstrong's wife, that the little one was a liar and wanted to take what should have been Abe's."

"Bianca," Wes said in wonder. He'd always felt she was at the bottom of all this; now he was sure. Wes stared at the child, then grinned at her. "Honey, if you were older, I think I'd kiss you for this. Here." He reached into his pocket and withdrew a twenty-dollar gold piece. "My mother gave it to me. It's yours now."

He pressed the gold into the child's hand.

She held onto it tightly and gaped at him. No one had ever given her anything except curses and beatings. To her, Wesley, so clean and smelling so good, was like an angel come to earth. Her voice was very quiet. "When I grow up, will you marry me?"

Wesley grinned broadly. "I just might." He stood up. Then, on impulse, he kissed her cheek heartily. "Come see me when you grow up." He turned away quickly and went toward the sloop where Clay and Travis waited impatiently. The news that Bianca was involved and had some information about Nicole's whereabouts sent all memory of the little girl from his mind.

But not so the child. She stood silently, watching the departing sloop. All her thirteen years she'd been isolated with her family. She'd never known there was anything outside her father's meanness, her mother's hardship. No one had ever been kind to her, no one had ever kissed her before. She touched her cheek where Wes had kissed her, then turned away. She had to find a hiding place for the gold piece.

Bianca saw Clay running from the wharf to the house, and she smiled to herself. She knew he would find out she was involved in Nicole's disappearance, and she was ready for him. She sipped on the last of the chocolate, finished the last apple turnover, then delicately wiped her mouth.

She was in the upstairs bedroom, and she smiled as she looked around it. It had changed greatly in the last two months. It wasn't so plain anymore. There was pink tulle everywhere, and the finials on the bed had been gilded. The mantel was covered with little porcelain figures. She sighed. It wasn't nearly complete, but she was working on it.

Clay burst into the room, his heavy boots clanging on the hardwood floors. Bianca winced at his crudeness and made a mental note to order more carpets.

"Where is she?" Clay demanded, his voice flat and hard.

"I take it I am supposed to know what that means." Bianca rubbed her plump upper arms and thought of the winter furs she'd order.

Clay took one long stride toward her, his eyes narrowed.

Bianca gave him a look of warning. "You touch me, and you'll never find her."

Clay backed away.

"How disgusting!" Bianca sneered. "The mere hint of danger to that lying little slut, and it makes you quiver."

"If you value your life, you'll tell me where she is."

"If you value *her* life, you'll keep your distance from me."

Clay gritted his teeth. "What do you want? I'll give you half of everything I own."

"Half? I thought she'd be worth more."

"All of it, then. I'll sign the entire plantation over to you."

Bianca smiled and walked to the window to straighten a curtain. She fingered the pink silk. "I don't know what I've done to make everyone think I'm stupid. I'm not unintelligent at all. If you signed this place over to me, then took your dear French whore away, what would happen to me?"

Clay clenched his fists to his sides. It was all he could do to keep from strangling her, but he would do nothing to endanger Nicole.

"I'll tell you what would happen to me," Bianca continued. "Within one year, this place would be bankrupt. You Americans are a disgusting lot. Your servants think they are as good as their masters. They would never obey me. Then, after I am bankrupt, what happens? Maybe you'd return and buy the place back for a song. You'd have everything you wanted, and I'd have nothing."

"Then what else can I give you?" Clay sneered.

"I wonder how much you really love my maid?"

Clay was silent, staring at her. He wondered how he could ever have thought she looked like Beth.

"You say you'll readily give me your property, but will you give me anything else in order to save her? Let me explain. I guess you know that I have cousins in America. Not exactly the type one would introduce in public, but useful—oh, yes, very useful. The man Abe was agreeable to anything I suggested."

"Where has he taken her?"

Bianca sneered at him. "Do you think I'm going to tell you so easily? After all you've done to me? You've humiliated me, used me. I've been here for months, waiting and waiting, while you flaunted that bitch in front of the whole world. Now it's my turn to keep *you* waiting.

"Now, where was I? My dear cousins, of course. In exchange for a few farm animals, they agreed to do whatever I wanted, including, I'm sure, murder."

Clay took a step backward. Murder had not entered his mind.

Bianca smiled at his reaction. "I believe you're beginning to understand. Now, let me tell you what I want. I want to be mistress of this plantation. I want you to run it, and I want to enjoy its benefits. When I appear in society, I want to do so as a respectable married woman, not as some unneeded appendage as I was at the Backes's party. I want the servants to obey me."

She turned away from him for a moment; then, when she looked back, her voice was quiet. "Are you familiar with the Revolution in France? Everyone reminds me of my former maid's relatives in France. They were, I believe, mostly beheaded. The mob is still angry in France, still looking for aristocrats to take to their guillotine."

She paused. "This time Abe only took her to an island buried in the Virginia waterways, but next time she'll be put on a ship back to France." She smiled. "And don't think that getting rid of Abe will rid you of the threat. He has relatives everywhere, all of whom would be glad to help me in any way I want. And if anything happens to me, including so much as a hangnail caused by you, I've left money to ensure that Nicole is returned to France."

Clay felt as if someone had kicked him in the stomach. He took a step backward and collapsed into a chair. The guillotine! The story of Nicole's grandfather, his head on a pike, was vivid. The way she had clung to him, terrified of all that had happened to her, whirled in his head. He couldn't risk the possibility of her returning to that horror.

His chin shot up. He'd keep her safe, always watch over her, never let her out of his sight. Then he knew how hopeless an idea that was. At the Backes's, she'd only been away from him for two hours. She would have to live like a prisoner. And one moment's lost vigilance, and . . . what? Death? Terror worse than what she'd already known? He couldn't do anything that would subject her to that possibility.

He tried to reason with Bianca. "I can give you enough money so that you'll have a good dowry. You can get an English husband if you have a dowry."

Bianca snorted. "You certainly don't understand women, do you? I would return to England in dishonor. All the men would say you had paid me rather than marry me. I'm sure I'd get a husband, but he'd only laugh at me, ridicule me. I want more out of life than that."

Clay stood up, knocking over the chair. "What would you get if you married me? You know I couldn't do more than hate you. Would you want that?"

"Any woman would rather be hated than laughed at. At least hate carries an amount of healthy respect with it. Actually, I think we'd make an admirable couple. I could run your house, be your hostess. I could give magnificent parties. I would be the perfect wife. And you, on the other hand, would never be troubled by a jealous wife. As long as you ran the plantation satisfactorily, you would be completely free to pursue whatever you wish, including women." She shuddered. "As long as you kept away from me."

"I assure you, you needn't fear that I'd ever touch you."

She smiled. "If that was meant as an insult, it wasn't taken as such. I have no desire to be touched by you or any other man."

"What about Nicole?"

"Of course, we now go back to her. If you marry me, she will be unharmed. She may even stay at the mill, and you can visit her for your . . . ah, more earthly pleasures. I'm sure the two of you will enjoy your rutting."

"What guarantees do I have that after we're married one of your cousins won't pop up in the middle of the night?"

Bianca looked thoughtful for a moment. "I'm not sure you do have a guarantee. Perhaps it will hold you to your bargain if you're never quite sure what will happen to her."

Clay stood still. No guarantee. His beloved's life depended on the whims of a greedy, selfish bitch. But what choice did he have? He could defy Bianca's demands and remain married to Nicole, but he'd live his life terrified that he would find her dead. Did he love her so selfishly that he'd risk her life for a few months of pleasure? After all, it wasn't his life that was in danger, but hers. Briefly, he thought of asking Nicole for her opinion, but he knew she'd risk anything to stay with him. Was his love so much weaker that he couldn't make sacrifices for her?

"Do you know where she is?"

"I have a map," Bianca smiled, as if she knew she'd won. "I want your agreement to my terms before I give it to you."

Clay swallowed over the lump in his throat. "The marriage cannot be annulled without the testimony of the doctor who witnessed the wedding. Very little can be done until he returns from England."

Bianca nodded. "I must agree to that. When he arrives, I expect the marriage to be annulled and ours to take place. If it is delayed at all, then Nicole will disappear. Is that clear?"

Clay sneered at her. "You've made yourself more than clear. I want the map."

Bianca walked across the room to one of the porcelain figures on the bow-front cabinet, picked it up, and pulled a little roll of paper from the inside. "It's crude," she said, "but I believe it's legible." She smiled. "Dear Abe has been on the island with her for two days and a night, and it'll be another night before you reach her. He said he planned to enjoy her. I'm sure he's had plenty of time by now. Of course, she was quite used before she ever went with Abe. By the way, have you asked yourself why she went so readily with him? Why didn't she scream? The wharf is only a short distance from where there were at least twenty people."

Clay took a step toward her, then stopped. If he so much as touched her, he'd kill her. He didn't think his conscience would hurt him much, but he knew she'd carry out her threats even from death. He turned on his heel, the map clutched tightly in his hand, and left the room.

Bianca stood at the window and watched him walk toward the wharf. A feeling of triumph surged through her body. She'd show them! She'd show them all! Her father had laughed at her when she'd packed to go to America. He'd said that Clay wouldn't be too upset when he found himself married to a lovely little filly like Nicole. He'd thought the story of the mistaken marriage was so good that he'd told at least twenty people before Bianca left England. No telling how many he'd told by now.

Bianca clenched her jaw hard. She knew what they were all saying. They said Bianca was just like her mother. Her mother had taken to her bed anything that was male. As a little girl, listening to the sounds from her mother's bedroom, Bianca had vowed never to allow a man to soil her, to put his rough, greedy hands on her fine white body.

When Bianca'd said she was going to America, her father accused her of being like that woman, said she was hot for the crude American, just the type of man her dead mother liked. How could Bianca return to England after having spent months in Clay's house? She'd have no wedding ring but a great deal of money, just the way her mother used to return from her many week-long trips. Even thousands of miles away, she could almost hear the snickers and see the smirks about what she'd done to earn the money.

No! She stamped her foot. She would own the Armstrong plantation no matter what she had to do. Then, she smiled, she'd invite her father to visit her. She'd show him her wealth, her husband, their separate bedrooms. She'd prove to him that she wasn't like her mother. Yes, she smiled. She'd show them!

"Did she tell you?" Wes asked as soon as Clay reached the sloop.

He held out the map. "She told me." His voice was dead.

"That bitch!" Wes said violently. "You ought to be horsewhipped for ever bringing her to America in the first place. And to think that you almost married her! When we get back and Nicole is safe again, I hope you throw that fat slut into the hold of a ship and get rid of her as fast as possible."

Clay stood silently, his dark eyes staring out at the river. He didn't answer Wesley's tirade; there was little he could say. Could he tell his friends he probably would marry Bianca after all?

"Clay?" Travis asked quietly, his voice full of concern. "Are you all right? You don't think your wife has been harmed, do you?"

Clay turned, and Travis frowned at the bleakness of his friend's face. "How should a man feel when he's just sold his soul to the devil?" he asked quietly.

Isaac cleaned the pan of the last of the rabbit and baked apples. He put the pan down and rested against the stone wall of the cabin, his legs stretched stiffly out on the grass. His thigh, tightly bound with strips of Nicole's petticoat, throbbed. As he closed his eyes and let the sun beat down on him, he smiled into the warmth. The air around the little island smelled bad, the water was alive with poisonous snakes, they had little or no hope of rescue, but Isaac had no desire to leave the place. In the last two days, he'd eaten better than he ever had at home, even though Nicole had only one pan to cook in. He'd been able to rest, something else that was new to his life.

He smiled more broadly as he heard the familiar swish of Nicole's velvet skirt. He opened his eyes and waved at her. She'd taken the lace off her petticoat and tied little bows down the front of her dress to hold it together where Abe had slashed it. Isaac was amazed at her. All his life, he'd thought the women who lived in the big houses were useless, but Nicole had shown no hysterics after the knife fight with Abe. She'd knelt and bound Isaac's wound to stop the bleeding, then calmly gone to sleep.

In the morning, the door was revealed to have hinges of heavy leather. Nicole used Isaac's pocket knife and sawed at the leather, while Isaac leaned against the door to keep it from falling. It had taken all their strength to open the door enough to slip through. Afterward, Isaac rested while Nicole made a snare from a piece of cord trim on her petticoat and caught a rabbit. Isaac was astonished that she knew how to do something of that nature. Nicole laughed and said her grandfather had taught her how to make a snare.

"Are you feeling better?" Nicole asked, smiling down at him. Her hair hung down her back to her waist, thick and rich.

"Yes. 'Cept maybe I'm lonesome. Could you talk to me?"

Nicole smiled and sat down beside him.

"Why ain't you afraid?" Isaac asked. "I think most women would be scared to death of this place."

Nicole thought for a moment. "I think emotions are relative. There have been times when I've been very, very frightened. In comparison, this place seems almost safe. We have food and water, the weather isn't too cold yet, and when your leg is better, we'll get off the island."

"You're sure of that? Have you looked into the water lately?"

She smiled. "Snakes do not scare me. Only people can truly hurt you."

Isaac felt a strong stab of guilt. She hadn't asked a single question about why he and Abe had abducted her. She could have, and probably should have, let him bleed to death.

"You're staring at me oddly," Nicole said.

"What's going to happen when we do get back to civilization?"

Nicole felt a surge of joy shoot through her. Clay, she thought. She would leave the mill in someone else's hands and return to Clay's house. She'd be there with him and the twins, as they were once, except now Bianca would have no power to come between them.

Her thoughts returned to Isaac. "I don't guess you want to return to your home. Maybe you'd like to work for me at the mill. I'm sure we could use another man."

Isaac's face changed from one color to another. "How can you offer me a job after what I've done to you?" he whispered.

"You saved my life."

"But I brought you here! You would never have been in this situation if it hadn't been for me."

"That's not true, and you know it," she said. "If you'd refused to go with Abe, he would have taken someone else or come alone. Then what would have happened to me?" She put her hand on his arm. "I owe you a lot. The least I can do is offer you a job."

He stared at her silently for several minutes. "You're a lady, a *real* lady. I think my life is going to be better since meeting you."

She laughed, and he watched the sunlight play on her hair. "And you, kind sir, would do well in any court in the world. Your gallantry is excessive."

He grinned back at her, happier than he ever had been in his life.

Suddenly, Nicole jumped. "What was that?"

Isaac sat still and listened. "Get me the knife," he whispered. "And you hide. Slip into the scum at the edge of the water. No one will ever find you there. Whatever you do, don't come out until it's safe."

Nicole gave him her sweetest smile. She had no intention of abandoning him, wounded as he was, to the mercies of whoever approached so quietly. And she certainly had no intention of burying herself in the scum of the water. She handed Isaac the knife. Then, when she went to help him stand, he pushed her away.

"Go!" he commanded.

Nicole slipped behind the willow trees at the edge of the island, then slowly made her way toward the quiet footsteps. She saw Travis first, his broad, thick form unmistakable. Instantly, her eyes blurred with tears. Hastily, she wiped them away and watched Travis as he walked away from her.

She felt Clay's presence behind her rather than heard him. She whirled about, her hair flying. She stood as still as if she were made of stone.

Silently, he opened his arms to her.

She leaped into them, burying her face in his neck, her body pressed hard against his. She felt his face against her cheek, and she knew his eyes were also wet.

Still holding her aloft, he turned her chin so she looked at him. He studied her face, devouring it. "You're well?" he whispered.

She nodded, her eyes on his. There was something wrong, deeply wrong. She sensed it.

He clutched her close again. "I thought I was going to go crazy," he said. "I couldn't bear it again."

"You won't have to," she smiled, relaxing against his body, enjoying the warmth and strength of him. "My own naiveté got me into this. I won't be so careless again."

"Next time you won't be given a choice," he said fiercely.

"Clay, what do you mean by next time?" She tried to push away from him.

He pushed her head to one side and began to kiss her. As soon as his lips touched hers, Nicole stopped thinking. It had been so very long since they'd been together.

"Ahem!"

Clay's head came up to stare at Travis and Wesley.

"I see you found her," Wes said, grinning. "We hated to interrupt you, but this is a filthy place, and we'd like to leave."

Clay nodded, his face serious, his dark brows drawn down over his eyes.

"What about him?" Travis said, his voice heavy with

disgust. He pointed to an unconscious Isaac sprawled in the mud. The bandages around his leg were reddening with blood. There was a swelling lump on his jaw where he'd obviously been hit.

"Isaac!" Nicole gasped and pushed out of Clay's arms. She was at the boy's side immediately. "How could you?" she glared up at Travis. "He saved my life. Didn't you wonder how he got such a cut on his leg? If I were his prisoner, I could have run away from him."

Travis stared down at Nicole in amusement. "I don't guess I stopped to think at all. I came around a corner of the shack, and he came at me with a knife." His eyes twinkled. "I guess I should have stepped back and considered the situation."

"I'm sorry," Nicole said. "I think my nerves are a bit raw." She quickly started to untie the bloody bandages from Isaac's leg. "Clay, give me your shirt. I need some more bandages."

When Nicole turned, her hand out to take the shirt, she looked up at three bare-chested men, each handing her a shirt. "Thank you," she whispered, blinking back tears. It was going to be good to get home again.

Chapter 15

NICOLE PAUSED, HER NEEDLE IN HER HAND, AS SHE glanced toward the window for the hundredth time. There was no need to try to keep from crying because her tears had all been used. It had been nearly two months since she'd seen Clay. During the first month, she'd been bewildered, confused, stunned. Then, for weeks, she'd cried. Now she felt numb, as if part of her body had been removed and she was adjusting to it.

After Clay had taken her from the island, he'd returned her to the mill. All during the long journey down the river to the Armstrong plantation, Clay had held her tightly, at times preventing her from breathing properly. But she didn't care. His arms about her were what she wanted.

When they had reached the wharf, Clay told Travis to tie the sloop first to the mill wharf. Nicole had been puzzled because she assumed she would go to the house with him. After clutching her to him almost in desperation, he had released her abruptly and jumped back into the boat, not looking back as Travis sailed the boat toward Clay's wharf.

For days, Nicole had watched for Clay. When he didn't come, she'd made excuses for him. She knew Bianca still lived in his house with him. Perhaps it was taking longer for him to get her on a ship to England.

When a month had passed and there was still no word, the tears started. Alternately, she had cursed him, forgiven him, understood him, cursed him again. Had he been lying to her when he said he loved her?

Was Bianca's power over him stronger than he had thought? She was too angry at him to think rationally.

"Nicole," Janie said quietly—there were a lot of whispers in the house now. "Why don't you take the twins and go cut some evergreens? It looks like it's going to snow. Wes will be here later, and we can decorate the house for Christmas."

Slowly, Nicole rose, but she didn't feel much in the spirit for Christmas.

"You will not tear out the east wall of my house," Clay said in a deadly serious voice.

Bianca sneered at him in disgust. "This house is too small! In England, it wouldn't be better than a gate-keeper's cottage."

"Then may I suggest you return to England?"

"I won't stand for your insults, do you hear me? Have you forgotten my cousins?"

"Since there isn't a moment when you don't mention them, I don't believe I could forget them. Now, I have work to do. Get out of here!" He glared at her over the ledger, watched as she put her nose in the air and stormed out of the office.

When she was gone, Clay poured himself a drink. He'd had about all he could take of Bianca. She was probably the laziest human he'd ever encountered. She was constantly angry because the servants refused to obey her. At first, Clay had made halfhearted attempts to force them into obedience, but soon he gave up. Why should he make them as miserable as he was?

He left the office and went to the stables to get his horse. Two months he'd spent with that bitch! Every day, he tried to think of the nobility of his gesture, how he was probably saving Nicole's life by his martyrdom. But self-inflicted pain can only go so far. Now that he'd had more time to think, he saw a way out of Bianca's plans. He and Nicole could leave Virginia. They could plan a time when they wouldn't be missed for a few days and then go west. There was new land opening all the way to the Mississippi River. He'd like to see that river.

Bianca was right about one thing. She'd be bankrupt in less than a year. He could arrange for Travis to buy back the plantation after Bianca ran it into the red. Travis and Wes could force Bianca off the land. Just so long as Nicole was safely out of the fat bitch's reach.

Clay sat on his horse just at the edge of the river. There was smoke coming from Nicole's chimney. At first, he'd stayed away from her because the sight of her caused him too much pain. Quite often in the last months, he'd stood on a hill and watched the activity across the water. He had longed to go to her and talk to her, but he couldn't until he had a plan. Now he did.

Big, fat snowflakes were beginning to fall, and as Clay watched, he heard the sound of hammering. He could see one lone figure on top of the mill, hammering loose wooden shakes down more securely.

With a smile, Clay dismounted from his horse, slapping the sleek black rump of the horse and watching as it made its way toward the stables. Then, he went to the rowboat and rowed himself across the river.

He picked up a hammer from the toolbox at the base of the ladder leaning against the mill and climbed to the roof. Wesley looked up in surprise, grinned, and silently held out a handful of nails. Clay quickly arranged the heads in one direction and began hammering, feeding the nails with his left hand as quickly as a machine. The physical labor felt good after the quarrel with Bianca.

It was nearly dark when the two men climbed down the ladder, both sweaty and tired. But it was a good tired, from labor shared with a friend.

They went inside the mill, where it was warm and a

tub of water waited for them. The snow was coming down more heavily.

"We certainly haven't seen you in a while," Wes said, his voice heavy with criticism.

Clay didn't answer as he removed his shirt and began to wash.

"Janie said Nicole cried herself to sleep every night for weeks," Wes continued. "Maybe that doesn't matter to you. After all, you do have that overblown copy of Beth to keep you warm."

Clay stared at him. "You're making judgments about things you know nothing of."

"Then maybe you should explain it to me."

Clay dried himself slowly. "We've known each other all our lives. Have I ever done anything to cause this much hostility?"

"Not until now! Damn it, Clay, she's a beautiful woman. She's kind, sweet "

"You don't have to tell me!" Clay interrupted. "Do you think I *want* to stay away from her? Has it ever occurred to you that there are circumstances beyond my control?"

Wes stood quietly for a moment. He'd been wrong not to trust his friend. He put his hand on Clay's shoulder. "Why don't you come inside? Nicole promised to make doughnuts, and the twins will be glad to see you."

"You seem rather free with Nicole's hospitality," Clay said coldly.

Wes grinned. "That's the Clay I know. If you don't take care of her, someone has to."

Clay turned and left the mill, heading toward the house. He'd not been inside the house since Nicole had moved there. Even as he stood just inside the door, the warmth of the place hit him. It was more than the physical warmth from the enormous fireplace, but something intangible, felt inside rather than against the skin.

The winter sun was coming through the sparkling clear windows. There was very little furniture, and Clay recognized most of it as the castoffs he'd sent some time ago. The dishes in the cabinet next to the fireplace were chipped and mismatched. There were very few cooking utensils.

Yet, in spite of the plainness, at that moment Clay would have traded his beautiful house for this simple dwelling. Janie bent over an iron pot of bubbling oil, turning doughnuts as they rose to the surface. The twins hovered over her, oblivious to the men standing behind them.

"Mandy," Janie said, "if you try to eat them while they're so hot, you're going to get burned, and you know it."

Mandy giggled as she grabbed a fresh doughnut and bit into it. Her eyes teared when she burned her mouth, but she wouldn't show Janie that she was in pain.

"You are as stubborn as your uncle," Janie said in disgust.

Clay chuckled, and Janie whirled to face him. "You'd better be careful when you talk about someone. They just might be listening."

Before Janie could reply, the twins screeched, "Uncle Clay!" and leaped into his arms. Clay grabbed one child under each arm and swung them around. When he lifted them, they put their arms around his neck. "Why didn't you come before? Do you want to see my new puppy? You want a doughnut? They're good but very hot."

Clay laughed and hugged them to him. "Did you miss me?"

"Yes, very much. Nicole said we had to wait until you came to see us, that we couldn't go see you."

"Is that fat lady still there?"

"Alex!" Nicole said from the staircase. "You are to remember your manners." She walked slowly toward Clay, her heart pounding in her throat. She was appalled that his presence could upset her so much. Since he'd been able to abandon her so lightly, obviously she meant very little to him. She worked at keeping her anger under control. "Won't you have a seat?" she asked formally.

"Yeah, Clay," Wes grinned. "Have a seat. Janie, you think those doughnuts are cool enough now?"

"Just about." She set the plate on the big table. "Where have you been, you ungrateful, wretched—" she hissed under her breath, unable to think of a word strong enough for him. "If you mistreat her again, you'll answer to me."

Clay smiled at her, then grabbed her rough, raw hand and kissed it. "You're magnificent as a protector, Janie. If I didn't know you, I'd almost be frightened."

"Maybe you should be," she snapped, but her eyes were twinkling.

Nicole had her back to them as she calmly poured out noggins of eggnog. With shaking hands, she set a mug before Clay.

His eyes never left hers as he lifted the cup. "Eggnog," he said. "I've never had that except at Christmas."

"It *is* Christmas!" the twins laughed.

Clay looked around him and noticed for the first time the evergreens and holly across the mantelpiece. He hadn't realized it was Christmastime. The last months of hell, spent near Bianca's nagging tongue, were fading into the distance.

"Nicole is going to make a turkey tomorrow, and Mr. Wesley and Mr. Travis are going to be here," the twins said.

Clay looked at Wes. "Think there'll be room for another guest?"

The men exchanged looks. "That would be up to Nicole."

Clay looked at his wife for a long moment, waiting for her answer.

Nicole felt her anger coming to the surface. He was using her! He spent days in bed with her, told her he loved her, then suddenly he dropped her on her doorstep like so much baggage. Now he comes sauntering into her house after months of silence, and what does he want? He expects her to kiss his feet in welcome. She stiffened her back and turned away from him. "Of course, you and Bianca are welcome. I'm sure she would enjoy the festivities as much as anyone."

Wesley smothered a laugh as he watched the frown crease Clay's brow.

"Bianca can't—" Clay began.

"I insist!" Nicole said narrowly. "May I say that one isn't welcome without the other?"

Suddenly, the atmosphere of the house was more than Clay could bear. They didn't realize the picture they presented. Wes leaned back in a chair smoking on a pipe he'd taken from the mantel. The twins happily stuffed themselves with doughnuts. The mention of Bianca's name made him remember the misery of his own household.

He rose. "Nicole, could I speak to you?" he asked quietly.

"No," she said firmly. "Not yet."

He nodded and left the warmth of the house.

Bianca was waiting for him when he entered Arundel Hall. "So! You couldn't stay away from her, could you?"

He brushed past her, not answering her.

"That man who runs the stables came to me and asked where you were. He was worried that you'd been hurt since your horse came back alone. They're always worried about you—and about her! No one on this place cares anything about me."

Clay turned and sneered at her. "You care enough about yourself to make up for everyone. Did you realize that tomorrow is Christmas Day?"

"Of course! I told the servants I wanted a special meal to be prepared. They, I am sure, will ignore me and, as usual, you won't do anything about it."

"A meal! That's your main interest, isn't it?" Suddenly, he lunged at her, grabbed her dress by the neckline. "You're going to get your wish. Tomorrow we're going to go to Nicole's for dinner." Maybe if Nicole saw them together, she'd realize how miserable he was. And he wanted to spend the day with Nicole, so badly that he was willing to subject them all to Bianca's vile personality. Perhaps she'd just eat and remain quiet.

She tried to jerk away from him but couldn't. His closeness made her stomach turn. "I will not go!" she breathed.

"Then I'll give orders that no food will enter this house all day."

Her eyes widened in horror. "You wouldn't."

He pushed her away from him until she slammed into the wall, hard. "You make me sick. You will go even if I have to carry you." He looked her up and down. "If I can. God, but it's going to be good to get rid of you." He stopped, appalled at what he'd said. He turned away, went into the library, and slammed the door behind him.

Bianca stood quietly for a moment, staring at the door. What did he mean, get rid of her?

She turned away and slowly went up the stairs. Nothing was going as she had planned. Abe had visited her soon after she'd given the map to Clay. He'd been bleeding from the cut in his arm, and Bianca had nearly become ill. The dreadful man demanded money from her so he could get out of Virginia, away from Clay's revenge. Bianca had had to pry open a box in the library to get him some pieces of silver.

She'd told him he had to stay near because she might need him again. He'd just laughed at her as he tied a piece of cloth around his arm, saying Bianca'd caused him to lose his family and his inheritance. Then he'd said something very rude about what she could do with her future needs.

Now, Bianca knew there was no one else. She told Clay she had other relatives, but that was a hollow threat. If he did throw her on a ship, no one would take Nicole as she had threatened. Nothing would happen. Bianca would be thrown aside, and no one, absolutely no one, would care.

She closed the door to her bedroom and looked out the window into the dark garden. The new snow was making it beautiful. Would she have to give it up? For a while she had felt safe, but now she was beginning to worry again.

She had to do something—and quickly. She had to get rid of Nicole before the French bitch took everything. Abe was gone, so she couldn't carry out her threat to send Nicole back to France. But, of course, Clay didn't know that—yet. Bianca had no doubt that he would sooner or later find out.

She clutched at the curtain, crushing the pink silk. The way the two of them rutted, it's a wonder Nicole wasn't pregnant by now. After seeing Clay with the twins, Bianca guessed that if Nicole were going to have a baby, his baby, no power on earth would make him leave her.

Suddenly, Bianca dropped the curtain, smoothed the fabric lovingly. What if someone else were going to have Clay's baby? Wouldn't little Miss Frenchy have her nose put out of joint? And what if Clay thought Nicole were bedding someone else? She probably would, Bianca thought. She's so hot for a man, she probably slept with Isaac on the island. Or Wesley!

Bianca smiled and caressed her stomach. Thinking always made her hungry. She started toward the door. She had a lot of thinking to do, and she'd need her nourishment.

"Merry Christmas!" Travis bellowed as Clay and Bianca entered Nicole's little house. Bianca wore a sullen, hostile look. She ignored Travis and looked at the food piled high on the big table in the center of the room. She wrenched her arm free from Clay's grasp and went toward the table.

"You choosin' that over Nicole?" Travis drawled.

"Mind your own business," Clay said sharply and walked away, Travis's laugh sounding behind him.

Janie handed Clay a small cup of liquor. He drank it quickly, needing its warmth and strength. He gasped when he finished. The stuff was delicious. "What is this?"

"Bourbon," Travis answered. "It's from the new land of Kentucky. Some peddler brought some in last week."

Clay held out his cup to Janie again.

"Go easy on it. It's strong stuff."

"But it's Christmas!" Clay said with false joviality. "It's time to eat, drink, and be merry." He raised his cup in salute to Bianca, who was slowly circling the table, nibbling little bits and pieces of food from all the dishes.

Everyone quieted as Nicole entered the room. She wore a gown of sapphire blue velvet, off the shoulders, with deep décolletage and thin embroidered blue ribbons around the high waist. Her long dark hair was down, perfectly arranged in fat curls, braided and entwined with dark blue ribbons studded with hundreds of seed pearls.

Clay could only stand and gaze at her longingly as her eyes avoided him. Knowing that she had a right to be angry didn't make the pain any less.

Wes stepped forward and offered his arm to Nicole. "Just seeing a sight like you is enough of a Christmas gift for me. Don't you agree, Clay?"

Bianca spoke as Clay stared mutely. "Is that some of the fabric that was meant for me?" she asked sweetly. "Some that you and Janie took without permission?"

"Clay!" Travis said, "You'd better do something with that woman before I do it."

"Be my guest," Clay said calmly, then poured himself more bourbon.

"Please," Nicole said, still avoiding Clay's eyes. "Let's have some eggnog. I must get the twins. They're in the mill admiring the new puppies. I won't be a minute."

Clay set his empty cup down and walked to the door with her, where he took her cape from the wooden peg by the door.

"I don't want you near me," she said under her breath. "Please stay here."

Clay ignored her as he opened the door and followed her outside. Putting her chin in the air, she walked ahead of him, trying to pretend he wasn't there.

"It's a pretty little nose, but if you don't lower it you're going to stumble."

She stopped in her tracks and whirled on him. "It's a joke to you, isn't it? Something that is life and death to me is only a cause for amusement to you. This time, you're not going to talk your way out of my anger. I've been hurt and humiliated too many times."

Her eyes were enormous and blazing in the starlight as she looked up at him, her mouth drawn tightly until her lower lip nearly disappeared. All that was left was her full, sensual upper lip. He ached to kiss it. "I've never meant to hurt you," he said quietly. "And certainly not to humiliate you."

"Then, out of ignorance, you've done a fine job, a superior job! You called me a whore five minutes after I met you. You allowed me to run your home, yet discarded me as soon as your dear Bianca appeared."

"Stop it!" he commanded, grabbing her shoulders harshly. "I know our relationship hasn't been an ordinary one, but—"

"Ordinary!" she said sarcastically. "I'm not even sure it's been a relationship. I think I *am* a whore. You snap your fingers, and I come running."

"I wish that were true." His voice was heavy with amusement.

Uttering what was obviously a French oath, she snarled at him and kicked his shin very hard.

He released her as he bent to rub his shin. Limping, he hurried after her and grabbed her arm. "You're going to listen to me!"

"Like I did when you told me about Beth? Or like the time you asked me to remarry you? Am I supposed to be naive enough to believe you again? Then, when I'm vulnerable and fall into your arms, will you again tire of me and return to your dear Bianca? There's only so much a woman will do for the man she loves."

"Nicole," Clay said, holding her firmly by one arm and caressing the other one with his hand, "I know you've been hurt. I've been hurt, too."

"Poor dear," she smiled. "You have to make do with only two women in your bed."

His jaw hardened. "You know what Bianca's like. I get closer than a foot, and she turns green."

Nicole's eyes widened; her voice was high. "You want sympathy from me?"

He fastened his hands on her shoulders. "I want your

trust. I want your love. Could you stop hating me for a minute and just consider that there's a reason why I haven't seen you? Is that too much to ask after what we've been through? Maybe I have done some things to make you distrust me, but I love you. Doesn't that mean anything to you?"

"Why?" she whispered, blinking back her tears. "You just left me with no word, just dropped me as if you were through with me. On the island, all I thought about was getting home, the two of us together at Arundel Hall."

He pulled her close to him, felt her tears wetting his shirt. "Didn't Isaac mention his cousin?"

The time on the island was a blur in her mind.

"I wanted to explain then and there, but I couldn't. I was so frightened that I couldn't even speak to you about it."

She tried to raise her head, but he pushed it back down. "Frightened? But I was safe. Abe was gone. You weren't afraid of Isaac, were you?"

"Bianca is Isaac's cousin. They're one of the reasons she came to America. She guaranteed Abe a bull and some heifers if he'd take you away until she could get the marriage annulled. One of old Elijah's daughters told Wes about the plan."

"And Bianca told you where I was?"

He pulled her even closer. "For a price. She told me that if I didn't marry her, she'd have one of her many relatives return you to France." He could feel Nicole shiver against him; the thought was as horrible to her as it was to him.

"Why didn't you tell me? Why did you just leave me so abruptly?"

"Because you would have marched up to the house and defied Bianca. You would have dared her to try to send you back."

"It's what should have been done."

"No, I can't risk losing you," he said as he stroked her hair.

She pulled away from him. "Why do you tell me this now? Why aren't you still cowering behind Bianca's ample skirts?"

Shaking his head, he chuckled. "I talked to Isaac since he began working for you. He said the reason you went with Abe so quietly was because you thought I was in trouble. Was I supposed to do less, knowing that your life could be in danger?"

"Let's go back inside and tell Bianca."

"No!" It was a command. "I will not risk you, do you understand? All she has to do is arrange for your capture again. No! I won't risk it."

"So, do you propose that we spend the rest of our lives meeting at Christmas just so Bianca can have what she wants?" Nicole asked angrily.

He ran his finger along her upper lip. "You have a sharp tongue. I prefer it when you use it for something besides lashing me."

"Maybe you need to be lashed. You certainly seem afraid of Bianca."

"Damn you! I've been very patient, but I've had enough of your insults. I'm not afraid of Bianca. It's taken all my control to keep from killing the bitch. But I knew that if I hurt her, I'd hurt you."

"Isaac said Abe left Virginia. Are you sure there are any more relatives? Bianca could be lying."

"Wes went back to the girl who'd helped him before. She said that Bianca was related to her mother, and her mother had hundreds of relatives."

"But surely not many of them would do what Bianca wanted."

"People would do anything for money," he said in disgust. "And Bianca has all of the Armstrong plantation at her disposal."

Nicole put her arms around his chest, clung to him.

"Clay, what are we going to do? We have to risk it. Maybe she's bluffing."

"Possibly, but I can't be certain. It's taken me months, but I've come up with a plan. We'll go west. We'll change our names and leave Virginia."

"Leave Virginia?" she asked, pulling away again. "But your home is here. Who will run the plantation?"

"Bianca, I guess," he said flatly. "I offered to give her the whole place, but she said she wanted a husband to run it."

"*My* husband!" Nicole said fiercely.

"Yes, yours always. Listen, we've been out here too long. Can you meet me tomorrow by the cave? Can you find it all right?"

"Yes," she said hesitantly.

"You don't trust me, do you?"

"I don't know, Clay. Every time I believe in you, in us together, something dreadful happens. I can't stand anything else. You can't imagine how horrible the last months have been for me. Not knowing, wondering, always confused."

"I should have told you. I know that now. I just needed time to think." He paused. "At least you haven't had to spend time with Bianca. Do you know that woman wants to tear away part of my house and add a wing? If it was left to her, she'd make it into a monstrosity like that place of Horace's and Ellen's."

"If you leave her, she'll be able to do what she likes to the house."

It was a while before Clay answered. "I know. Let's get the twins and go back." He released her and took her hand in his.

All through the long, uncomfortable dinner, Nicole's thoughts whirled. It wasn't just Bianca she was fighting but Arundel Hall also. She knew how much Clay loved his home, how he talked about the place almost with reverence. Even when he'd seemingly neglected the house for the fields, he'd been aware that Nicole had given the house the attention he felt it deserved. She always felt that was what had prompted his first marriage proposal, when he'd said he'd remain married to her if Bianca didn't arrive.

Nicole picked at her food, vaguely listening to Travis's plans to visit England in the spring. Clay was right, she didn't trust him. Too many times, she'd held her heart out to him and he'd rejected it. Even remembering the time he'd gotten her drunk and made her admit she loved him made her blush. Later, he'd invited her to his house, and when Bianca arrived he was no longer aware of Nicole's presence. He'd made love to her at the Backes's house but deserted her soon afterward. Of course, he always had marvelous reasons. First, there was the story of Beth, and now Bianca's treachery. She believed him—the stories were too bizarre to be lies—but now he said he was going to leave Virginia—and Bianca—so they could be together. He said he hated Bianca, yet he'd lived with her for months.

She stabbed at a piece of turkey. She had to believe him! Of course, he hated Bianca and loved her. There were logical reasons why Bianca lived with him and she didn't. But at the moment, she couldn't remember a single one of them.

"I think the turkey's already dead," Wes said at her side.

"Oh," she said in puzzlement, then tried to smile. "I'm afraid I'm not very good company."

Travis grinned at her. "Any woman who looks like you doesn't need to do or say anything. Someday, I'm going to find a pretty little girl and keep her inside a glass jar. I'll only let her out when I want her."

"Probably about three times a night would be my guess," Wesley said as he helped himself to more candied yams.

"I will not stand for this kind of talk!" Bianca said

255

stiffly. "You Colonials must remember that a lady is present."

"The way I been raised, ladies don't live with men they're not married to," Travis said flatly.

Bianca's face turned red with anger as she stood up quickly, knocking over her chair and upsetting the table. "I will not be insulted! I am the one who will own Arundel Hall, and when I do—" She stopped, then let out a scream as Mandy, staring up at the big woman, her plate in her hand, let slide a great wad of cranberry sauce onto Bianca's skirt.

"You did that on purpose!" Bianca screamed, and drew back her hand to strike the child.

Everyone was on their feet to stop her. But Bianca stopped herself as she gasped, her eyes tearing; then she jumped backward from the table, holding out her foot. There, resting against her thick ankle, was a large, very hot plum pudding.

"Get it off me!" she screamed, kicking her foot.

Nicole was the one who tossed her a towel, but no one bent to help her wipe away the sticky mess. Travis pulled Alex out from under the table. "I think his fingers are burned, Janie."

"Such a waste," Wes said sadly, watching Bianca trying to balance herself as she made swipes at her foot with the towel. Her stomach was so large that she could hardly reach her ankle.

"Not a waste at all," Janie said. "In fact, I don't believe I've ever enjoyed any dessert as much."

"Clayton Armstrong!" Bianca screeched. "How dare you stand there and let them insult me like this!"

Everyone turned toward Clay. No one had noticed that all through dinner he'd been drinking heavily of the bourbon. Now, his eyes were glazed and he looked with disinterest at Bianca's gyrations.

"Clay," Nicole said quietly, "I think you'd better take Bianca . . . home."

Clay rose slowly, seeming oblivious to everyone around him as he grabbed Bianca's arm and pulled her toward the door, ignoring her screams that the pudding was still burning her. He pulled her outside as she grabbed her cape, and he took a jug of the bourbon. The cold, snow-filled air threatened to freeze the wet, sticky mass to Bianca's ankle.

Bianca followed Clay reluctantly, stumbling in the dark behind him. Her dress was ruined; she could feel the cold cranberry juice against her thighs, and her ankle hurt from the burn and the cold. Tears blurred her eyes so that she could hardly see where she was going. Once again, Clay had humiliated her. He had done nothing else since she'd arrived in America.

At the wharf, Clay grunted as he lifted Bianca and set her inside the rowboat. "You put on any more weight and we'll sink," he said, his voice slightly slurred.

She'd had all the insults she was going to take, she thought as she stiffened. "You seemed to like this new drink," she said sweetly, nodding at the stoneware jug in the bottom of the rowboat.

"It makes me forget for a while. Anything that can do that, I like."

Bianca smiled into the darkness. When they landed across the river, she took the hand he offered and stepped onto shore, following him quickly back to the house. By the time they reached the garden door, she was trembling because she knew what she must do, even though the idea came close to making her sick to her stomach.

Clay set the jug on the hall table and stepped back outside.

Bianca muttered, "Peasant!" lifting her skirts and running up the stairs to her room, ignoring the pain of her ankle and her wildly beating heart as she flung open a drawer and withdrew a small bottle of laudanum. The

257

bourbon combined with the sleeping drug would make Clay unaware of anything that happened to him. She just had time to add a few drops to the liquor she poured into a glass. The stuff smelled vile!

Clay lifted one eyebrow at her when she offered him the glass. But he was already too drunk to question her actions. He lifted the glass in a mock salute to her, then downed the fiery liquid in one gulp. Setting the glass on the table, he lifted the jug to his lips.

Bianca merely smiled at his crudeness and watched him mount the stairs. When she heard the door to his bedroom open and each of his boots fall to the floor, she knew it was time.

The hall was dark, and Bianca stood alone, listening. The idea repulsed her; she hated a man's touch as much as her mother had loved it, but as she took one last look around the hall, she knew that if she didn't climb into bed with Clay, she'd lose all of this. She grabbed the bottle of laudanum and went up the stairs.

Inside her own room, her hands were trembling as she undressed and slipped into a pale pink silk nightgown, crying a little as she drank some of the laudanum. At least, the drug would help dull her senses.

Moonlight flooded Clay's room, and Bianca saw him sprawled across the bed. He wore nothing, and the silver light on his bronze skin made him look as if he were made of gold, but Bianca saw nothing beautiful in the sight of the naked man. The laudanum made her feel as if she were in a dream.

Slowly, she slipped in beside Clay on the bed, dreading the idea of having to make advances toward him. She didn't know if she could.

Clay needed no encouragement. He'd been dreaming of Nicole, and now the touch of a woman's silk gown, the smell of perfumed hair, made him react. "Nicole," he whispered as he pulled Bianca close to him.

But even in his drunken, drugged state, Clay knew this was not the woman he loved. Reaching out to touch her, he encountered a handful of lumpy fat and, with a muffled grunt, turned away to relapse into his dream of Nicole.

Bianca, rigid, breath held, waited for his animal lust to take over. When he merely grunted and turned away, it was some moments before she realized he was not going to touch her. Cursing vilely, she told his sleeping form what she thought of his lack of masculinity. If the plantation weren't so important to her, she'd give this caricature of a man to Nicole, and she was welcome to him.

But now there had to be something done. In the morning, Clay had to believe he'd deflowered Bianca, or her plan would never work. The laudanum she'd taken was a hindrance to her as she rose and stumbled down the stairs, but she could have been even more drugged and she'd still have been able to find her destination—the kitchen.

On the big table was a roast beef marinating in herbs, and Bianca half filled an earthenware mug with beef blood. Grabbing six leftover rolls from a cabinet to reward herself for her cleverness, she started back to the house.

Upstairs again, the rolls eaten, the laudanum making her eyes too heavy to hold open, she slipped in beside Clay and doused herself with blood, hiding the mug well under the bed. Cursing him again for making her go through this ordeal, she fell asleep beside him.

Chapter 16

THE EARLY MORNING SUN BEAT DOWN ON THE LIGHTLY crusted snow and flashed back into Clay's red eyes. The pain in his eyes went directly to his head where everything vile that had ever been created seemed to exist. His body seemed to weigh a thousand pounds, and each movement was an ordeal, even as he picked up another handful of snow and pressed it to his dry, swollen tongue.

Worse than his raging headache and his churning stomach was the memory of this morning. He woke beside Bianca. At first, he'd been able to do nothing but stare because his body hurt too much to be able to think.

Opening her eyes quickly, Bianca'd gasped when she saw him. She sat up, pulling the sheet to her neck. "You animal!" she said through clenched teeth. "You dirty, filthy animal!"

As she told him that he'd dragged her to his bed and raped her, Clay couldn't speak.

When she'd finished, he laughed because he didn't believe he could ever have gotten that drunk.

But when Bianca'd stepped from the bed, there'd been blood on the sheets, blood on her nightgown. Before Clay could reply, Bianca had begun telling him that she was a lady, that she wouldn't be treated like his whore, that if she had a child Clay would have to marry her.

Clay hadn't bothered to reply as he'd stepped from the bed and begun to dress quickly. He'd wanted to be as far away from Bianca as possible.

Now, sitting in the clearing he had built with James and Beth, he kept remembering things. Maybe he'd been so drunk that he had made love to Bianca. This morning, he couldn't remember anything after he'd left Nicole's.

Nicole was the one who worried him. What if Bianca did become pregnant? He pushed the thought out of his mind.

"Clay?" Nicole called. "Are you here?"

Smiling, he stood up to greet her as she came into the clearing.

"You didn't say what time. Oh, Clay! You look awful! Do your eyes feel as bad as they look?"

"Worse," he said hoarsely as he held out his arms to her.

Nicole got within two feet of him, then stopped, her eyes blinking rapidly. "You smell as bad as you look."

He grimaced. "Didn't I hear that love was blind?"

"Even blind people can smell. Sit down and rest or build a fire in the cave. I brought some food with me. You didn't eat much last night."

He groaned. "Don't mention last night."

It was an hour later, when they'd eaten breakfast and the little cave was warm, that Nicole was ready to talk as she leaned against the stone wall of the cave, a blanket across her legs. She wasn't yet ready to sit easily in Clay's arms. "I didn't sleep much last night," she began. "All night, I kept thinking about what you'd told me about Bianca and her relatives. I want to believe you . . . but it's difficult. All I can see is that I am your wife, yet she lives with you. It's almost as if you want both of us."

"Do you really believe that?"

"I try not to. But I know Beth had a strong hold over you. Maybe you don't realize how close you are to your home. Last night you talked of just walking away and leaving this place. Yet at one time you were willing to

kidnap a woman merely because she looked like someone who belonged here."

"You mean more to me than the plantation."

"Do I?" she asked. Her eyes were wide, dark, liquid.
"I hope I do," she whispered. "I hope I mean that
much to you."

"But you doubt me," he said flatly. Through his
mind was going the vision of Bianca in his bed, Bianca's
virgin blood on the sheets. Was Nicole right not to trust
him? Turning to the little niche that held the unicorn set
in glass, he stood and held it in his hands. "We made
vows on this," he said. "I know we were children and
had a lot to learn about life, but we never broke the
vows."

"Sometimes innocent pledges are the most sincere,"
she smiled.

Clay held the glass in his hand. "I love you, Nicole,
and I vow that I will love you until the day I die."

Nicole stood before him and put her hand over his.
There was something that bothered her. Beth, James,
and Clay had touched the little unicorn, then Beth had
had it sealed in glass so no one else could ever touch it.
It was a silly thing, really, but Nicole couldn't help
remembering Beth's portrait, so very like Bianca. A
swift thought ran across her mind. When would she be
worthy to touch what Beth had touched?

"Yes, Clay, I love you," she whispered. "I always
have, and I always will."

Carefully, he set the glass unicorn back into the wall,
unaware of Nicole's frown. He turned and pulled her
close to him. "We can go west in the spring. There are
always wagon trains being organized. We'll leave at
different times so no one will know we've gone together."

Clay went on, but Nicole wasn't listening. Spring was
months away. Spring was the time when the earth came

alive again, when the crops were to be planted. Would Clay be able to walk away, to leave all the people who depended on him?

"You're shivering," he said quietly. "Are you cold?"

"I think I'm frightened," she said honestly.

"There's no reason to be afraid. We've been through the worst of it now."

"Have we, Clay?"

"Hush!" he commanded, and lowered his mouth to hers.

It had been a long time since they'd been together, not since the party at the Backes's. Whatever sensible reasons Nicole had for her fears, they fled when Clay kissed her. Her arms went around his neck and pulled his face closer to hers as his hand turned her head and slanted her mouth so that her lips parted. He was hungry for her, starved for the sweet nectar of her that would wash away the filth of the night with Bianca—a night confused with visions of Beth, a pink silk gown, and flecks of blood on a white sheet.

"Clay!" Nicole gasped. "What's wrong?"

"Nothing. Just too much to drink last night. Don't go away," he whispered as he pulled her tightly against him. "I need you so much. You are warm and alive, and I am so haunted by people." He kissed her neck. "Make me forget."

"Yes," she whispered. "Yes."

Clay pulled her down with him to the floor of the cave on top of a quilt. It was warm and sweet-smelling inside the little room. Nicole wanted him urgently, but Clay wanted to take his time. Slowly, he unbuttoned the front of her soft wool dress and put his hand inside, cupping her breast, his thumb teasing the soft crest.

"How I've missed you!" he whispered, his mouth following his hand.

Nicole arched beside him, her mind a whirl of

flashing colors. As she fumbled with the buttons of his vest, she was unable to remember what she was doing, since his mouth and hands seemed to make her incapable of performing even a simple task.

Smiling at her ineptitude, Clay pulled back. Her eyes were closed, her lashes a thick, lush curve against her cheek. As he caressed her cheek, ran his finger along her lips, his reverie changed from sweetness to passion. His hands quickly unfastened the buttons of his vest, his shirt, boots, and trousers following.

Nicole lay on her back, her head propped on her arm, watching the firelight in the little cave play deliciously with the skin over his muscles, dancing from one indentation to a mound of strength. She ran her finger up his back.

He turned, nude, all golden skin and bronze.

"You're beautiful," she whispered, and he smiled at her before he kissed her again, his hand easily slipping her dress from her shoulders, running over her smooth, firm body, exploring it slowly, as if it weren't very familiar to him. When he pulled her on top of him, she lifted her hips and guided him into their lovemaking.

"Clay!" she gasped as he moved her hips, slowly at first, building rapidly until she clung to him, her hands clutching at him hungrily. She collapsed on top of him, weak, throbbing, satiated.

"Let me get this straight, lady," the burly young man said, spitting a thick stream of tobacco juice near her feet. "You want me to give you a baby? Not give you one of mine what's already born but to plant one in you?"

Bianca stood rigid, her gaze level. It had taken very few questions to find Oliver Hawthorne, a man who was willing to do something for a price and keep his mouth shut. Her first thought had been to pay him to return Nicole to France, but the Hawthornes didn't have the reputation of dishonesty that the Simmons did.

After the failed attempt to get Clay to impregnate her, she realized something had to be done or all her future dreams would collapse. It wouldn't be long before Clay realized she had no power over him. She must get herself with child, no matter what she had to do!

"Yes, Mr. Hawthorne. I want to have a child. I've investigated your family, and you seem to be especially prolific."

"Investigated, huh?" He smiled at the woman, appraising her. He didn't mind her plumpness, since he liked big women with strong backs, eager, energetic women in bed, but he did mind her look of never having worked in her life. "I reckon you mean that the Hawthornes can make babies even when they can't get their tobacco to grow."

She nodded curtly. The less she had to talk to the man, the better she liked it. "This is, of course, to be kept confidential. In public, I will not acknowledge that I have ever met you, and I expect the same treatment."

Oliver's eyes twinkled. He was a short, heavyset man with a broken front tooth, and he had a feeling the whole situation was a dream and he was going to wake up very soon. Here was a woman offering to pay him for giving her a tumble, or as many as it took to impregnate her. It made him feel like a horse put out to stud, and he rather liked the idea. "Sure, lady, whatever you say. I'll act like I never saw you or the kid before, though I warn you that my six kids all look like me."

It would serve Clay right to claim a child as his when it obviously looked like another man, she thought. The child would be short and sturdy, so unlike Clay's tall, slim grace. "That's all right," she said, the dimple appearing in her left cheek. "Can you meet me tomorrow at three o'clock behind the tannery on the Armstrong plantation?"

"Armstrong, huh? Clay havin' trouble makin' his own babies?"

Bianca stiffened. "I don't plan to answer any questions, and I'd prefer you don't ask them."

"Sure," Oliver said, then looked around them cautiously. They were on a road four miles from the Armstrong plantation, a place she'd chosen in her message to him. As he reached out and touched her arm, she jumped backward as if she'd been burned.

"Don't touch me!" she said through clenched teeth.

Frowning in puzzlement, he watched her turn and angrily walk down the road toward the driver who waited for her around a bend. She was an odd one, he thought. She didn't want him to touch her, yet she wanted him to make her pregnant. She sneered at him as if he repulsed her, but she wanted to meet him in the afternoon to make love. In broad daylight! The thought of that made Oliver's skin glow, and he reached inside his trousers to readjust himself more comfortably. He wasn't one to look a gift horse in the mouth. Maybe more of those la-de-da ladies would need him to make up for their weak men. Maybe Oliver could make a living at this, and to hell with tobacco.

He straightened his shoulders and began to walk home.

For the next month, Nicole felt she was content, if not happy. Clay and she met often in the clearing beside the river. They were joyous meetings, full of love and plans for the trek west. They were like children, talking of what they'd take, how many bedrooms their house would have, how many children they'd have, the names they'd give them. They spoke of when they'd tell the twins and Janie of their plans, for of course they would go with them.

One evening in late February, the sky darkened menacingly and lightning threatened to split the little house in half.

"Why are you so jumpy?" Janie asked. "It's just a storm comin' up."

Nicole put her knitting into the basket on the floor, since it was no use trying to continue. Every storm took her back to that night when her grandfather was taken.

"Are you upset because you can't meet Clay?"

Astonishment showed on Nicole's face.

Janie chuckled. "You don't have to tell me what's been going on. I can read your face. I always figured you'd tell me when you were ready."

Nicole sat on the floor before the fire. "You're so good and patient with me."

"You're the one who's patient," Janie sniffed. "There isn't another woman alive who'd put up with what Clayton is giving you."

"There are reasons—" Nicole began.

"Men always have reasons when it comes to women." She stopped suddenly. "I shouldn't be saying these things. There's more to this than I know, I'm sure. Maybe there's a reason Clay is meeting his wife like some city woman."

Eyes twinkling, Nicole smiled. "City woman, is it? Maybe, someday, when I'm living with him and see him every day, I'll look back fondly at this time when I was so adored."

"You don't believe that any more than I do. You should be in Arundel Hall now, supervising the place, instead of that fat—"

As a sharp slash of lightning cut off her words, Nicole gave a little scream of fright and clutched at her heart.

"Nicole!" Janie said, jumping up, her mending falling to the floor. "Something is wrong." Putting her arm

267

around Nicole's shoulders, she led her back to her chair. "I want you to sit down and relax. I'll make us some tea, and yours is going to have some brandy in it."

Nicole sat down, but she didn't relax. The branches of a tree slapped against the roof, and the wind whistled in through the windows, blowing the curtains. The night outside was black and, to Nicole, horrible-looking.

"Here," Janie said, thrusting a steaming cup of tea into her hands. "Drink this, and then you're going to bed."

Trying to calm herself as she drank the tea, she could feel the brandy warming her, but her nerves were too on edge to relax.

At the first pounding on the door, she jumped so high that half the tea spilled down the front of her dress.

"That has to be Clay," Janie smiled, grabbing a towel. "He knows about you and storms, and he's come to sit with you. Now, dry yourself and put on a pretty smile for him."

With shaking hands, Nicole patted at the tea-stained wool and tried to smile as she anticipated Clay's appearance.

As Janie threw open the front door, a welcome and a lecture for Clay were already taking form. She was going to let him know what she thought of his neglect of his wife.

But the man standing there wasn't Clay. He was a short man, slightly built, with thin blond hair that straggled over the collar of his green velvet coat. About his throat was a white silk scarf that was tied so it covered the lower edge of his chin. He had small eyes, a knife blade of a nose, and a small, thick-lipped mouth.

"Is this the house of Nicole Courtalain?" he asked, his head tilted backward, as if he were trying to look down on Janie, which was impossible since she was several inches taller.

His voice was so thickly accented that Janie had difficulty understanding what sounded to her like, "Ees thees thee ouse of—" The name was one Janie had never heard before.

"Woman!" the small man commanded. "Have you no tongue or no brains?"

"Janie," Nicole said quietly, "I am Nicole Courtalain Armstrong."

Obviously appraising her, he spoke less angrily. *"Oui.* You are her daughter." He turned on his heel and walked back into the night.

"Who is he?" Janie demanded. "I couldn't even understand him. Is he a friend of yours?"

"I never saw him before. Janie! There's a woman with him."

The two women rushed out into the night. Nicole put her arm around one side of the woman, the man on the other side, as Janie grabbed a suitcase from the ground and followed them.

Inside the house, they led the woman to a chair before the fire, and Janie poured tea and brandy while Nicole went to a chest to get a quilt. It was when Janie had the tea ready and handed it to the exhausted woman that she had time to get a good look at her. It was like looking at an older version of Nicole. The woman's skin was unlined, clear, and perfect, her mouth exactly like Nicole's, a combination of innocence and sexuality. The eyes, though like Nicole's, were vacant, lifeless.

"There now," Nicole said, tucking the quilt around the woman's legs before she glanced up and saw the odd look on Janie's face. Nicole looked up at the woman from where she was kneeling on the floor, her hands still on the quilt. As she looked at the familiar features, her eyes filled with tears, then slowly, softly, they ran down her cheeks. "Mama," she whispered. "Mama." She bent forward and buried her face in the woman's lap.

Janie saw that the older woman made no response to Nicole's gesture or words.

"I had hoped—" the man beside her said. "I had hoped that seeing her daughter again would bring her back."

The man's words made Janie understand the woman's vacant eyes; they were the eyes of someone who wanted to see nothing more in life.

"Can we get her to bed?" the man asked.

"Yes, of course," Janie said firmly, kneeling beside her friend. "Nicole, your mother is very tired. Let's take her upstairs and put her to bed."

Silently, Nicole rose. Tears made her face damp, and her eyes never left her mother's face. Half in a daze, she helped her mother upstairs, helped Janie undress her, unaware that her mother never spoke.

Downstairs, Janie made more tea and brandy, then sliced ham and cheese for sandwiches for the young man.

"I thought both my parents were killed," Nicole said quietly.

The man ate quickly, obviously very hungry. "Your father was. I saw him guillotined." He seemed oblivious to Nicole's wince of pain. "My father and I went to see the guillotining, as almost everyone else did. It was the only sport left in Paris, and it helped to make up for the fact that we had no bread. But my father is—how do you say?—a romantic. Every day, he'd come home to his cobbler's shop and talk to my mother and me about the waste of all the beautiful women. He said it was a shame to see the lovely heads roll into the basket."

"Could you tell the story with less detail?" Janie said, her hand on Nicole's shoulder.

The man held up a ceramic pot of mustard. "Dijon. It is good to see French things in this barbarian country."

"Who are you? How did you rescue my mother?" Nicole asked softly.

He bit into a piece of cheese liberally spread with mustard, then smiled. "I am your stepfather, little daughter. Your mother and I are married." He stood and took her hand. "I am Gerard Gautier, now one of the magnificent Courtalains."

"Courtalain? I thought that was Nicole's maiden name."

"It is," Gerard said, returning to his seat at the table. "It is one of the oldest, richest, most powerful families in Europe. You should have seen the old man, my wife's father. I saw him once when I was a child. He was as big as a mountain and, it was said, as strong. I've heard he could make the king tremble from his wrath."

"The most common of people made the king tremble," Nicole said bitterly. "Please tell me how you met my mother."

Gerard gave Janie a disdainful look. "As I was saying, my father and I went to see the guillotinings. Adele, your mother, walked out behind your father. She was so beautiful, so regal. She wore a dress of pure white, and with her black hair she looked like an angel. The whole crowd stopped talking when she walked past. Everyone could see that her husband was so proud of her. Their hands were tied behind them, and they could not touch, but their eyes met, and several people sniffed because the two handsome people obviously loved each other. My father nudged me and said that he could not stand to see such a magnificent creature put to death. I tried to stop him, but—" Gerard shrugged. "My father does what he wants."

"How did he save her?" Nicole urged. "How did he get her through the mob?"

"I do not know. Every day, the crowd has a different flavor. Sometimes they cry as the heads roll; sometimes they laugh or cheer. It depends on the weather, I guess. That day, they were romantic, like my father. I watched as he pushed his way through them, then grabbed Adele's bindings about her wrists and pulled her into the crowd."

"What about the guards?"

"The crowd liked what my father was doing, and they protected him. They closed around him like water. When the guards tried to follow, the people tripped them and gave them false directions." He stopped and smiled, finishing the last of a large glass of wine. "I was standing on top of a wall where I could see everything. It was such a sight! The people yelled every direction imaginable to the guards, yet all the while my father and Adele were walking quietly back to our shop."

"You saved her," Nicole whispered, looking down at her hands in her lap. "How can I ever thank you?"

"You can take care of us," he said quickly. "We have come a long way."

"Anything," Nicole answered. "What is mine is yours. You must be tired and want to rest."

"Wait a minute!" Janie said. "There's more to this story. What happened to Nicole's mother after your father rescued her? Why did you leave France? How did you find out Nicole was here?"

"Who is this woman?" Gerard demanded. "I do not like servants who treat me like this. My wife is the Duchess de Levroux."

"The Revolution killed all titles," Nicole said. "In America, everyone is equal, and Janie is my friend."

"A pity," he said, his eyes scanning the simple room, yawning hugely before he stood. "I am quite tired. Is there a suitable bedroom in this place?"

"I don't know about suitable, but there's places to

sleep," Janie said with hostility. "The attic has the twins and us three women. The mill has some spare beds."

"The twins?" Carefully noting the fine quality of the deep gray wool of her gown, he caught Nicole's eyes. "Of what age?"

"Six."

"They are not yours?"

"I care for them."

He smiled. "Good. I believe I must make do with your mill. I would not like to be awakened by children."

As Nicole started toward her cape by the door, Janie stopped her. "You go to your mother and see that she's all right. I'll take care of him."

Smiling gratefully, she bid Gerard goodnight and went upstairs to where her mother lay peacefully sleeping. The storm had subsided outside, and gentle flakes of snow were silently falling. As Nicole held her mother's warm hand in hers and watched her, she was flooded with memories—her mother lifting her and swinging her about just before she left for a court ball, her mother reading to her, pushing her in a swing. When Nicole was eight years old, Adele had had identical dresses made for them. The king said that someday the two of them would be twins, for Adele would never grow older.

"Nicole," Janie said when she returned. "You are not going to sit there all night. Your mother needs rest."

"I won't disturb her."

"And you won't help her either. If you don't sleep tonight, you'll be too tired tomorrow to be of any use to her."

Even though she knew Janie was right, Nicole sighed because she was afraid that if she closed her eyes her mother would disappear. Reluctantly, she stood and kissed her mother before turning away to get undressed.

An hour before sunrise, everyone in the little house was awakened by hideous screams—screams of absolute terror. As the twins shot out of their beds and ran to Janie, Nicole ran to her mother's side.

"Mama, it's me, Nicole. Nicole! Your daughter. Mama, be still, you're safe."

The woman's wild-eyed terror showed she obviously did not understand Nicole's words. Even though Nicole spoke in French, the words had no effect; Adele was still afraid, still screaming, screaming as if her whole body were being torn apart.

The twins put their hands over their ears and hid in the folds of Janie's flannel nightgown.

"Get Mr. Gautier," Nicole shouted, holding her mother's flailing hands as she fought her daughter.

"I am here," he said from the head of the stairs. "I thought she might wake like this. Adele!" he said sharply. Then, when she didn't respond, he slapped her hard across the cheek. The screams stopped at once, and she blinked a few times, then collapsed, sobbing, into Gerard's arms. He held her for a moment before quickly putting her down on the bed.

"She'll sleep for about three hours now," he said, rising before turning back toward the stairs.

"Mr. Gautier!" Nicole said. "Please, there must be something we can do. We can't go off and just leave her."

He turned and smiled at Nicole. "There is nothing anyone can do. Your mother is totally insane." Shrugging as if the matter meant very little to him, he went down the stairs.

Pausing only long enough to grab her bedrobe from its peg, Nicole raced down the stairs after him. "You can't just say something like that and leave," she said.

274

"My mother has been through some horrible experiences. Surely, after she rests and is once again sure of her surroundings, she will recover."

"Perhaps."

Janie entered the room, the twins close behind her. By silent agreement, the discussion was postponed until everyone had eaten and the twins were out of the house.

As Janie cleared the dishes away, Nicole turned to Gerard. "Please tell me what happened to my mother after your father rescued her."

"She never recovered," he said simply. "Everyone thought she was so brave when she was walking to her death, but the truth was she had long ago lost touch with reality. They had kept her in prison for a long time, and she'd seen one after another of her friends taken away to be executed. After a while, I guess her mind refused to accept that the same fate awaited her."

"But when she was safe," Nicole said, "didn't that reassure her?"

Gerard looked with interest at his fingernails. "My father should not have rescued her. There was much danger in keeping one of the aristocracy in our house. The day he took her, the crowd was for him, but later someone could turn us in to the citizens' committee. It was very dangerous for all of us. My mother began to cry every night in fear. Adele's screams woke the neighbors. They kept quiet about the woman we hid, but we wondered how long it would be before they asked for the reward offered for the duchess."

Sipping on the coffee Janie had given him, he studied Nicole for a few moments. She was especially lovely in the morning light, her skin dewy from her night's sleep, her eyes luminous as she listened to the story, and he rather liked the way she looked at him, expectantly, with great interest.

He continued, "When we heard that the duke had

been killed, I went to the mill where he'd hidden. I wanted to know if there was anyone else left in the family. The miller's wife was very angry because her husband had been murdered with the duke. It took me a long while to get her to tell me about Adele's daughter and that you'd gone to England. At home, when my parents heard the story of the miller, they were very frightened. We knew we had to get Adele out of our house."

Nicole rose and went to the fire. "You had little choice. You could either turn her over to the committee or get her out of the country, under another name, of course."

Gerard smiled at her quick understanding. "And what better disguise than the truth? We were quietly married, then went abroad on our honeymoon. In England, I found Mr. Maleson, who told me you had worked for his daughter and both of you had gone to America.

"Maleson was a strange man," he said. "He told me the strangest tale, which I did not half understand. He said you were married to his daughter's husband. How can that be? Is a man allowed to have two wives in this country?"

Janie gave a derisive snort before Nicole could answer. "Clayton Armstrong makes his own laws in this part of the country."

"Armstrong? Yes, that is the name Maleson said. He is your husband, then? Why is he not here? Is he away on business?"

"Business!" Janie said. "I wish he were. Clay lives across the river in a big, beautiful house with a fat, greedy snob, while his wife lives apart from him in a miller's shack."

"Janie!" Nicole snapped. "You've said quite enough."

"The problem is, you've said too little. Anything Clay tells you, you just bow down and say, 'Yes, Clay. Please, Clay. Whatever you want, Clay.'"

"Janie! I will not listen to any more of this. We have a guest, in case you've forgotten."

"I haven't forgotten anything!" she snapped as she turned toward the fire, her back to Nicole and Gerard. Every time she thought of Clay and the way he treated Nicole, she got angry. She didn't know if she was angry at Clay for the way he behaved or at Nicole for so calmly accepting the treatment. Janie felt Clay didn't deserve Nicole, that she should end the marriage and look at other men. But every time Janie said this, Nicole refused to listen, saying she trusted Clay as well as loved him.

The thoughts of everyone stopped as the screams began again, echoing through the little house, the sheer horror of them raising chills on Janie and Nicole.

Slowly, tiredly, Gerard rose. "It's the new place that frightens her. Once she gets used to it, the screams will be less frequent." He went toward the stairs.

"Do you think she will recognize me?" Nicole asked.

"Who can tell? For a while, she had lucid days, but now she is always frightened." He shrugged before disappearing into the attic, and moments later the screams quieted.

Cautiously, Nicole went into the attic. Gerard sat on the edge of the bed, one arm thrown carelessly across Adele's shoulders as she clung to him, looking about her wildly. Her eyes opened wide in alarm when she saw Nicole, but she didn't resume her screaming.

"Mother," Nicole said quietly, slowly. "I am Nicole, your daughter. Remember the time Father brought me a pet rabbit? Remember how it got out of its cage, and no one could find it? We looked through every wing of the chateau, but we couldn't find it."

Adele's eyes seemed to become calmer as she stared at Nicole.

Taking her mother's hand in her own, she continued. "Do you remember what you did, Mother? To play a joke on Father, you released three female rabbits in the chateau. Remember the nest of baby rabbits Father found with his hunting boots? You laughed so hard. But then Father laughed when more rabbits were found inside the chest with your wedding gown. And remember Grandfather? He said you were both children playing games."

"He organized a hunt," Adele whispered, her voice hoarse from a throat raw with screaming.

"Yes," Nicole whispered, tears blurring her vision. "The king was visiting that week, and he and Grandfather and fifteen of their men dressed as if they were going to war and set out to find all the rabbits. Do you remember what happened then?"

"We were soldiers," Adele said.

"Yes, you dressed me in my cousin's clothes. Then you and some of the court ladies dressed in the soldiers' costumes. Remember the queen's old aunt? She looked so funny in men's trousers."

"Yes," Adele whispered, caught up in the story. "We had fish for supper."

"Yes," Nicole smiled. "The ladies caught all the rabbits and let them loose on the grounds, and to punish the men for being such bad soldiers, you only allowed fish to be served for supper. Oh! Remember the salmon pâté?"

Beginning to return the smile, Adele answered, "The chef shaped it into rabbits, hundreds of little rabbits."

With tears on her cheeks, Nicole waited.

"Nicole!" Adele said sharply. "Whatever are you doing in that awful gown? A lady must never wear wool. It is too confining, too concealing. If a gentleman wants wool, he should be a shepherd. Now, go and find

278

something in silk, something made by butterflies, not by those nasty old sheep."

"Yes, Mama," said the obedient daughter calmly, kissing her mother's cheek. "Are you hungry? Would you like a tray brought to you?"

Adele leaned against the wall behind the mattress set on the floor, seeming to be unaware of Gerard, who dropped his arm from around her. "Send something light. And use the blue and white Limoges china for today. After I eat, I will rest, then send the chef so we can plan menus for next week. The queen will be here, and I want to plan something very special. Oh, yes, if those Italian actors arrive, tell them I will speak to them later. And the gardener! I must talk to him about the roses. It is so much to do, and I am so tired. Nicole, do you think you could help me today?"

"Of course, Mama. You rest, and I will personally bring you something to eat. I will speak to the gardener myself."

"You calm her," Gerard said, following Nicole down the stairs. "I haven't seen her so relaxed in a long time."

Her mind reeling, Nicole went across the room calmly. Her mother still believed she lived in a time when she had fine servants who had nothing to do except help her dress. Nicole had been young enough to adjust to a harsh, cruel world where she wasn't pampered, but she doubted if her mother could do so.

Slowly, Nicole took a small skillet from the wall, then began breaking eggs for an omelet. Clay, she thought, wiping tears away with the back of her hand, how can I go away with you now? Her mother was here, and she needed her. Janie needed her, the twins needed her, Isaac was her responsibility, and now Gerard and Adele also needed her. What right did she have to feel sorry for herself? She should be grateful that she wasn't alone in the world.

A sharp sound from the attic signaled that Adele was impatient that her meal was taking so long. Suddenly, the front door burst open, the cold air rushing in.

"Excuse me, Nicole," Isaac said. "I didn't know you had company, but there's a man here with some new bolting cloth. He needs you to look at it."

"I'll be there as soon as possible."

"He said he's in a hurry, since it looks like a big snow's comin'. He wants to get to the Backes's before it hits."

The tapping from the attic became more insistent. "Nicole!" Adele called loudly. "Where is my maid? Where is my breakfast?"

Quickly, Nicole loaded the food on a tray and hurried past Isaac up the stairs to her mother.

Adele looked at the plain wicker tray, the brown-glazed earthenware, the hot omelet oozing cheese for only a second before she picked up a piece of toasted bread between her thumb and forefinger. "What is this? Bread? Peasants' bread? I must have croissant!"

Before Nicole could say a word, Adele had smashed the bread into the omelet.

"The chef has insulted me! Send this back, and tell him that if he values his job he will not serve this swill to me again." She picked up the pot of tea and poured it over the contents, the hot tea running through the wicker and onto the bedcovers.

Looking at the mess her mother was creating, Nicole began to feel very tired. The covers would have to be washed—by hand. The breakfast would have to be recooked, and she'd have to persuade her mother to eat it, somehow without making her start screaming again. And Isaac needed her at the mill.

She carried the dripping tray downstairs.

"Nicole!" Janie nearly knocked Isaac down as she ran into the room. "The twins have disappeared. They told Luke they were going to run away because a crazy lady had come to live with them."

"Well, why didn't Luke stop them?" Nicole slammed the tray on the table. Already, Adele was tapping on the floor.

"He said he thought it was a joke, that no crazy lady lived here."

Nicole raised her hands in helplessness. "Isaac, get the other men, and let's start searching. It's too cold for them to be outside alone." She turned to Gerard. "Would you prepare my mother something to eat?"

He lifted one eyebrow at her. "I'm afraid I do not do women's work."

Janie gasped. "Listen, you!"

"Janie!" Nicole snapped. "The twins are more important now. I'll take her some bread and cheese. She'll have to make do with that. I'll join the search as soon as possible. Please," she added when she saw Janie glaring at Gerard. "I need help now. Please don't add to my problems."

Janie and Isaac left the house as Nicole began tossing bread and cheese into a basket. Adele's tapping was urgent now, and Nicole was unaware of the way Gerard watched her as he leaned nonchalantly against a wall cabinet.

Nicole felt guilty about the way she had fairly tossed the food into her mother's lap, and she could see the hurt in Adele's eyes. Leaving her mother added to her guilt feelings, but the twins must be found. Even as she ran out the door and started calling the twins, she saw the two wayward children running across the yard toward her.

Chapter 17

GLANCING AT THE CLOCK ON THE CABINET BY THE door, Nicole moved slowly from the fireplace to the kitchen table. She must remember to punch down the brioche dough in ten minutes. The twins were playing quietly in the far corner of the room, Alex with several carved wooden animals and Mandy with a wax-faced doll that was supposed to be a farmer's wife.

"Nicole," Alex asked, "can we go outside after we eat?"

She sighed. "I hope so, if the snow stops falling. Maybe you can get Isaac to help you build a snowman."

The twins grinned at each other as they returned to their play.

The door opened, and the rush of cold air threatened to extinguish the fire. "This is the coldest March I have ever seen," Janie said as she held her hands out to the fire. "I don't think spring will ever come."

"Nor do I," Nicole whispered. She balled her hand into a fist and punched it viciously into the rising dough. Spring! she thought. The time when she and Clay were to go away together. Janie said that this winter had been the wettest and coldest she had ever seen in Virginia. Because of the snow, they had all been housebound—four adults and two children caught together in the small house. In the month since Gerard and Adele had arrived, Nicole had seen Clay only once. Yet even then he had looked distracted, worried about something.

"Good morning," Gerard said as he came down the stairs. Immediately after his arrival, the sleeping arrangements had changed. He and Adele now slept in the twins' bed upstairs, while the children slept on mattresses set up each night on the first floor. Janie and Nicole slept upstairs, a curtain separating them from the married couple.

"Morning!" Janie snorted. "It's nearly noon."

Gerard, as usual, ignored her. They had come to dislike each other with a great intensity. "Nicole," he said in a pleading voice, "do you think you could do something about the noise so early in the morning?"

She was too tired from cooking and cleaning and taking care of so many people to make any answer.

"And also, the cuffs on my lavender jacket are soiled. I do hope you can clean them," he continued, holding his arms out and studying the clothes he wore. His blue jacket reached to his knees, tight about the waist, fastened with heavy black braid, and flaring broadly over his slim hips that were covered in breeches buttoned at his knee, above silk hose leading to thin, flexible pumps. A vest of yellow satin, embroidered with bright blue stars, covered a white silk shirt fastened with a green cravat. He'd been appalled when he discovered that Nicole didn't know that a green cravat meant he was French nobility. "It's a small way in which we can separate ourselves from the commoners," he said.

The tapping on the ceiling made Nicole look up from her bread. Adele was awake earlier than usual.

"I'll go to her," Janie said.

Nicole smiled. "You know she's not used to you yet."

"Is she going to start screaming again?" Alex asked anxiously.

"Can we go outside?" Mandy asked.

"No and no," Nicole answered. "You can go out later." She grabbed a small tray, poured a glass of sweet apple cider, and carried it up to her mother.

"Good morning, dear," Adele said. "You aren't

looking well at all this morning. Aren't you feeling well?" Adele spoke French, as she always did. Although Nicole had tried to get her to speak English, a language she spoke quite well, Adele refused.

"I'm just a little tired is all."

Adele's eyes twinkled. "That German count kept you dancing for too long last night, didn't he?"

It was no use to try to reason or explain, so Nicole merely nodded. If her mother came back to reality for even a short time, she began to scream, and drugs had to be used to make her stop. Sometimes, she wavered between hysteria and a fanciful calmness. During a calm stage, she spoke of murder and death, of her time in prison, of her friends who walked out the door and never returned. Nicole hated those times the most, since she remembered too many of the people her mother said had been executed. She remembered sweet, frivolous women who had never known anything except luxury and comfort all their lives. Every time she thought of those women walking toward their deaths, she could hardly keep from crying.

A voice from downstairs drew her attention. Wesley! she thought with a surge of joy, grateful that her mother was leaning back against the pillows of the bed and closing her eyes. Adele rarely got out of bed, but she sometimes demanded hours of attention.

As always, feeling a little guilty, Nicole left her mother and went down to greet her guest. She hadn't seen Wes since that awful Christmas dinner more than three months ago.

He was deep in discussion with Janie, and Nicole could tell she was explaining about Gerard and Adele. "Wesley," she said, "it's so good to see you again."

There was a big smile on his face as he turned, but it faded instantly. "Good God, Nicole! You look awful! You look like you've lost twenty pounds and haven't slept in a year."

"That's about the truth," Janie said irritably.

As Wes looked from Janie to Nicole, he saw that neither woman looked good. The roses were gone from Janie's cheeks. Behind the women was a little blond man standing over the twins, watching the children with a slight curl of distaste on his thick lips.

"Alex and Mandy, do you think you can get some boots and heavy coats on? And Nicole, I want you and Janie to dress warmly, too. We're going for a walk."

"Wes," Nicole began, "I really can't. I have bread rising and my mother—" She stopped. "Yes, I would like to go for a walk."

Nicole ran upstairs to get her new cloak, the one Clay had had made for her because she had won the bet on the horses at the Backes's party. The deep maroon camlet, a mixture of mohair and silk, shimmered from the long, lush nap as she swirled the heavy cape around before fastening it about her shoulders. The hood hanging down her back showed the deep, rich, black mink that lined the entire cape.

The outside air felt good and clean with the snow still falling, the flakes often landing on her lashes. The dark mink framed her face as she drew the hood up.

"What's been going on?" Wes asked as he drew Nicole aside once they were outside, watching Janie, the twins, and Isaac engaging in a halfhearted snowball fight. "I thought everything would be fine between you and Clay after the Backes's party and after we got you off the island."

"It will be," she said confidently. "It will just take time."

"I have no doubt Bianca is at the bottom of this."

"Please, I'd rather not talk about it. How have you and Travis been?"

"Lonely. We're getting sick of each other's company. Travis is going to England in the spring to look for a wife."

"To England? But there are several beautiful young women right around here."

Wesley shrugged. "That's what I told him, but I think you spoiled him. Personally, I'm going to wait for you. If Clay doesn't wise up soon, I'm going to try to steal you away from him."

"Don't say that, please," she whispered. "I think maybe I'm superstitious."

"Nicole, something is wrong, isn't it?"

Tears came to her eyes. "I'm just so tired and . . . I haven't seen Clay in weeks. I don't know what he's doing. I have this awful fear that he's fallen in love with Bianca and doesn't want to tell me."

Smiling, Wes put his arms around her, pulling her close. "You have too much to do, too much responsibility. The last thing you should have to worry about is Clay's love. How can you think he's in love with a bitch like Bianca? If she's in his house and you're here, then it's for a damned good reason." He paused. "Your safety, maybe, since I can't think of anything else that would keep Clay away from you."

Sniffling, she nodded against him. "Did he tell you?"

"Some of it, but not much. Come on, let's go help them build a snowman, or better yet, let's challenge them to a snowman duel."

"Yes," she smiled, drawing away from him. She wiped her eyes with her knuckle. "You'll think I'm no older than the twins."

He kissed her forehead as he smiled. "Some child! Come on, let's go before they use up all the snow."

A voice crying from the direction of the river stopped them. "Hello! Is anyone home?"

Wesley and Nicole turned and walked toward the wharf.

An older man, heavyset, with a fresh scar across his left cheek, was walking toward them. He wore the dress of a sailor, a knapsack thrown over his shoulder.

"Mrs. Armstrong?" he said as he came to stand before her. "Don't you remember me? I'm Dr. Donaldson from the *Prince Nelson.*"

He did seem vaguely familiar, but she couldn't remember exactly where she'd seen him before.

Several lines showed at the corners of his eyes as he smiled. "The circumstances were, I admit, not the best when we met, but I see things have turned out well." He held out his hand to Wesley. "You must be Clayton Armstrong."

"No," Wes said as he took the man's hand. "I'm a neighbor, Wesley Stanford."

"Oh, I see. Well, then, maybe I am needed. I hoped things had changed, I mean with this young lady being so kind and pretty."

"The doctor on the ship!" Nicole gasped. "At the marriage!"

"Yes." He grinned. "As soon as I got to England, a message reached me that I was to return to Virginia at once since I was the only witness who would testify that it was a forced marriage. I came as soon as I could and got directions to the mill. It was confusing about where the Armstrong plantation was and who lived at the mill. I took my chances and came here first."

"I am so glad you did. Are you hungry? I could scramble some eggs and there's ham and bacon and a pot of beans."

"You don't have to ask me twice."

Later, when the three of them were seated at the table, the doctor told them of the captain of the *Prince Nelson* and his first mate, Frank. Both men had been drowned on their return trip to England.

"I refused to sail with them again after what they'd done to you. I guess I should have tried to stop them but I knew they'd just get another witness, and besides, I knew the annulment laws too. I knew I'd be the witness you needed if you did want that annulment."

"Then why did you go back to England so fast?" Wes asked.

The doctor grinned. "I didn't exactly have a choice. We were all in a tavern celebrating our safe arrival. The next thing I knew, I woke aboard ship with a splitting headache. It was three days before I could even remember my name."

A loud tapping coming from the ceiling interrupted his talk and made Nicole jump. "My mother! I forgot her breakfast. Please excuse me." With deftness, Nicole poached an egg and carefully set it atop a day-old slice of brioche, next to an apple tart on a separate plate and a steaming cup of café au lait. She hurried up the stairs with it.

"Sit with me for a while," Adele said. "It's very lonely here."

"There is a guest below, but later I'll come and we can talk."

"Is he a man? Is your guest a man?"

"Yes."

Adele sighed. "I hope he's not one of those awful Russian princes."

"No, he's an American."

"An American! How extraordinary. There are so few of them who are gentlemen. Whatever you do, don't let him use strong language in front of you. And notice how he walks. You can always tell a gentleman by his posture. If your father wore rags, he'd still look like a gentleman!"

"Yes, Mama," Nicole said dutifully before going down the stairs. Her life seemed very remote from judging whether a man was a gentleman or not.

"Wesley was telling me that Mr. Armstrong lives across the river. The marriage didn't work out, then?" the doctor asked.

"It hasn't been easy, but I still have hope." She was trying to smile.

But she didn't realize how much her face told of what she thought, or that there were sunken circles of tiredness under her eyes, almost hiding the fact that they were alive with hope—and desperation.

Dr. Donaldson frowned. "Have you been eating well, young lady? Getting enough sleep?"

Wes spoke before she could answer. "Nicole adopts people the way some people adopt stray cats. Recently, she took on two more to care for. She has Clay's niece and nephew, who shouldn't be her responsibility, and now she has her mother, who demands queenly service, and her mother's husband, who thinks he's the king of France."

Nicole laughed. "You make it sound as if my life is a great burden. The truth is, Doctor, I love the people around me. I wouldn't give up one of them."

"I never thought you should," Wes answered. "You should just be living in the house across the river, and Maggie should be doing the cooking, not you."

Taking the pipe out of his pocket, the doctor leaned back in his chair. Things hadn't gone very well for the little French lady, he thought. The young man, Wes, was right when he said she deserved better than to be worked to death. He'd planned to travel north, to Boston, right away, but now he decided he'd stay in Virginia for the next few months. He hated the way she'd been forced into a marriage she didn't want, had always felt somehow responsible. Now he knew he must stay close by in case she did need help.

Nicole threw the hood back from her head and let the breeze touch her face. She moved the oars of the little rowboat into and out of the water. The snow was still on the ground. There were no buds on the trees, but something indefinable said that spring was in the air. It was two weeks since the doctor had first visited her. She smiled when she thought of how he'd said he'd be near if she needed him. How could she ever need him? She wanted so badly to tell him, to tell them all, that she and Clay would be leaving Virginia quite soon.

She'd been planning for months. The twins and Janie would, of course, go with her and Clay. She hated leaving her mother, but Gerard would be there, and later, when they had a house, Adele could come and live with them. Isaac could run the mill, and as long as he supported Gerard and Adele, the remaining profits could be his. When Adele joined Nicole in the west, Isaac could have the mill and run it with Luke's help.

Oh, yes, it was all going to work out perfectly.

Yesterday, Clay had sent her a note asking her to meet him in the clearing this morning. Last night, she'd hardly been able to sleep. She kept dreaming of this meeting with Clay when all their plans would begin to come alive.

She took a deep breath of the clean, cold air, then caught a whiff of smoke. Clay was already at the cave. She threw the rope of the rowboat onto the bushes that led to the clearing, then stepped ashore and tied it.

She ran down the little path. As in part of her dream, Clay stood there, waiting for her, his arms outstretched. She leaped the last few steps and flung herself at him. He was so tall, so strong, and his chest was so hard. He held her very close, so close she couldn't breathe. But she had no desire to breathe. All she wanted was to melt into him, become part of him. She wanted to forget herself, to exist only with him.

He lifted her chin so that she faced him. His eyes were hungry, dark, ravenous. Nicole felt a surge of fire sear through her body. This is what she'd missed! She strained upward to clutch at his mouth with her teeth. She gave a low sound that was half growl, half laugh.

Clay's tongue touched the corner of her mouth, just in the tiny hollow.

Nicole's knees grew weak.

Clay laughed against her throat, then picked her up in his arms and carried her inside the velvet darkness of the cave.

There was a frenzy of movement. They were two people starved for each other, desperate, eager, greedy, demanding, as the fire burned along their skin and cried angrily to be released. Their clothes were discarded in seconds, flung about the cave with total disregard.

They didn't speak as they came together. They allowed their skin to do their talking. They were fierce with each other. Nicole arched against Clay, and lightning flashed in her head. As she felt the throbbing sensations run through her, she smiled and began to relax.

"Clay," she whispered, "I've missed you so much."

He held her tightly to him, his breath soft and warm against her ear. "I love you. I love you so very much." His voice sounded sad.

She pushed away from him, then snuggled against him so that her head rested in the hollow of his shoulder. "Today is the first morning I've been able to believe it's nearly spring. It seems I've waited forever for spring."

Clay leaned over her and got her cape. He spread it over them, the mink against their skin.

Nicole smiled deliciously and rubbed her thigh over Clay's. The moment was perfect—held in her lover's arms, alone, their bodies sated, caressed by the luscious mink.

"How is your mother?" Clay asked.

"She doesn't scream as much as she did. I'm glad because it frightens the twins terribly."

"Nicole, I've told you that you should send the twins back to me. There's no room for them with you."

"Please let them stay."

He hugged her closer. "You know I wouldn't take

them away from you. It's just that you have too many people and too much to do."

She kissed his shoulder. "You're kind to worry, but they're really no problem. Now, if you wanted to take Janie and Gerard, I might consider your proposal."

"Is Janie giving you problems?"

"No, not really. She and Gerard hate each other, and they constantly pick at each other. I just get tired of listening, that's all."

"If Janie hates someone, it's usually for a good reason. You haven't said much about your stepfather."

"My stepfather." Nicole smiled. "It's odd to think of Gerard as being a replacement for my father."

"Tell me about your life. I feel so removed from you."

She smiled again, feeling his love all around her. "Gerard is infatuated with being part of the French aristocracy. It seems so humorous when you realize there are hundreds of people in France wanting to be part of the common people."

"From what I hear, his being in your house isn't exactly humorous. You know that if you need any-thing—"

She put her fingertips over his lips. "You're all I need. Sometimes, when it gets very noisy and everyone seems to be pulling at me, I stop and think about you. This morning when I woke, I was terribly excited about the warmth in the air. Do you think the weather is the same in the west as it is here? And do you really know how to build a house? When do you think we can leave? I've been wanting to pack for a long time, but I didn't feel it was time yet to tell Janie."

She stopped when he didn't make any response. She rose on one elbow to look at him. "Clay, is everything all right?"

"Perfectly," he said flatly. "At least, it will be."

"What do you mean? Something is wrong. I can tell."

"No, nothing serious anyway. Nothing is going to upset our plans to leave."

She frowned at him. "Clay, I know you, and I know you have a problem. You haven't mentioned Bianca, yet I pour out all my troubles to you."

He smiled slightly at her. "You wouldn't know how to pour out your troubles. You are so kind, so loving, so forgiving, that half the time you don't even see how people use you."

"Use me?" she laughed. "No one uses me."

"I do, the twins do, your mother, her husband, even Janie. We all impose on you."

"You make me sound like a saint. I have many things I want out of life, but I'm practical. I know that I must wait to get what I want."

"And what do you want?" he asked quietly.

"You. I want you and my own home and the twins. And maybe some other children—your children."

"You'll have it! I swear it! It's all going to be yours."

She stared at him for a long while. "I want to know what is wrong. It has to do with Bianca, doesn't it? Has she found out about our plans? If she's threatening you again, I won't stand for it this time. My patience is nearly gone."

Clay put his arm around her firmly and pulled her head to his shoulder. "I want you to listen to me, to all of the story before you say a word." He took a deep breath. "First of all, I want to tell you that it will make no difference to our plans."

"It?"

She tried to lift her head to look at him, but he stopped her.

"Just listen to me, then I'll answer questions." He paused, staring at the ceiling of the cave. It had been three weeks since Bianca had told him she was pregnant. At first, he'd laughed at her, saying that she lied. She'd merely stood there and smiled at him, so self-satisfied. She'd been the one to have the doctor come to her and examine her. Since then, Clay had lived in hell. He couldn't believe the news. It had taken a long time to decide that Nicole meant more to him than the child Bianca carried.

"Bianca is pregnant," he said quietly. When Nicole didn't react, he went on. "The doctor came and confirmed it. I've thought about it for a long time, and I've decided to go ahead with our plans to leave Virginia. We'll make our home in a new place, together."

Still, Nicole did not say a word. She lay on his shoulder as calmly as if he'd said nothing.

"Nicole? Did you hear me?"

"Yes," she said quite evenly.

He loosened his arm so that he could move back from her, see her face.

Without looking at his eyes, she sat up, then turned her back to him and slowly pulled her chemise over her head.

"Nicole, I wish you'd say something. I wouldn't have told you at all except Bianca's already told half the county. I didn't want you to hear it from someone else. I thought I should tell you."

She didn't say a word as she slipped her dress over her head, rolled one woolen stocking on, then the other.

"Nicole!" Clay demanded, then grabbed her shoulders to turn her to look at him. He gasped at what he saw there. Her brown eyes, usually so warm and loving, were cold and hard.

"I don't believe you want me to say anything."

He pulled her to him, but her body was rigid against him. "Please talk to me. Let's get this thing out in the open and discuss it. Once we clear the air, we'll be able to make plans."

She stared at him, half smiling. "Make plans? Plans to go away and leave an innocent child with no one to care for it except Bianca? Don't you know she'll make a magnificent mother?"

"What the hell do I care about her motherhood skills? You're what I want, you and you alone."

She lifted her hands and pushed his away. "Not once have you said that the child couldn't be yours."

He stared at her, his eyes never blinking. He'd expected this, and he planned to be honest. "I was drunk, and it was only the one night. She put herself in my bed."

She gave him a cold smile. "I guess I'm supposed to forgive what's done under the influence of alcohol. After all, look at all that's happened to me because of it. I was drunk the first time you made love to me."

"Nicole." He leaned toward her.

She jumped backward. "Don't touch me," she said under her breath. "Don't ever touch me again."

He grabbed her shoulder, hard. "You're my wife, and I have a right to touch you."

She pulled back her hand and slapped him as hard as she could. "Your wife! How dare you say that to me? When have I ever been anything but your whore? You use me when you need me to get rid of your physical desires. Isn't Bianca enough for you? Are you the type of man who needs more than one woman for his lust?"

Her handprint stood out vividly on his skin. "You know that isn't true. You know I've always been honest with you."

"Know? What do I know about you? I know your body, I know you have power over me, both mentally and physically. I know you can get me to do what you want; you can make me believe the most outrageous stories."

"Listen to me, believe me. I love you. We'll go away together."

She threw back her head and laughed. "You are the one who doesn't know me. I admit I haven't shown much pride while I was around you. Actually, I've done little more than flop on my back when you enter a room, or on my knees, or astride you. I don't even ask what your pleasure is; I just obey."

"Stop it! This isn't you!"

"It isn't? Who is the real Nicole? Everyone thinks she is an earth mother, nurturing everyone, taking the responsibility of everyone's problems, asking so little from others. It's not like that! Nicole Courtalain is a woman, a full-fledged woman, with all the greeds and passions of other women. Bianca's so much smarter than I am. She sees what she wants, and she goes after it. She doesn't sit at home and wait patiently for a message from some man to meet her for a morning romp. She knows that isn't the way to get what she wants."

"Nicole," Clay said, "please calm down. You're saying things you don't mean."

"No," she smiled. "I think that for once I'm saying things I do mean. I've been in America for all these months, and I've spent all of that time waiting. I waited for you to tell me you loved me, then I waited for you to make up your mind between Bianca and me. I think how utterly stupid I've been, how simple-minded and starry-eyed. Like a child, I trusted you."

She gave a snort of laughter. "Did you know that Abe tore my clothes off and tied me to a wall? I was so stupid that all I could think of was that he'd soil me for you. Can you imagine that? You were probably in bed with Bianca while stupid little me was worrying about keeping myself clean for you."

"I've had about enough. You've said too much already."

"My, my! The demanding Clayton Armstrong has had too much. Too much of which one of us? Curvy Bianca or skinny little Nicole?"

"Stop and listen to me. I told you it doesn't make any difference to me. We'll go away just as we planned."

She glared at him, her upper lip curled into a snarl. "But it makes a difference to me! Do you think I want to spend my life with a man who could so easily abandon his own child? What if we did go west and had a child? If you saw some sweet young thing, maybe you'd run off with her and leave *our* child."

Her words stung him, and he drew back. "How can you believe that?"

"How can I not? What have you ever done to make me believe any differently? I was a fool, and for some reason, maybe your broad shoulders or some such nonsense, I fell in love with you. You, being a man, used my schoolgirl lust to full advantage."

"Do you really believe that?" he asked quietly.

"What else can I believe? I have done nothing but wait. Every minute I have waited—waited to start living. Well, no more!" She jammed her shoes on, stood up, and started toward the mouth of the little cave.

Clay quickly pulled his pants on and went after her. "You can't leave like this," he said, grabbing her arm. "I have to make you understand."

"But I do understand. You've made your choice. I guess it was a test of who got pregnant first. The Courtalains have never been fertile. Too bad, perhaps I would have won the race. Would I have the big house then? The servants?" She paused. "The baby?"

"Nicole."

She looked down at his hand on her arm. "Release me," she said coldly.

"Not until you see reason."

"You mean I'm to stay until you sweet-talk me back

into your arms, don't you? It's over. It is dead, flat over between us."

"You can't mean that."

Her voice was very quiet. "Two weeks ago the doctor from the ship I came to America on came to see me."

Clay's eyes widened.

"Yes, your witness that you so urgently wanted at one time. He said he'd help me to get an annulment."

"No," Clay breathed, "I don't want—"

"It's past time for what you want. You've had everything, or should I say everyone, you wanted. Now it's my turn. I'm going to stop waiting and start living."

"What are you talking about?"

"First an annulment, then I plan to enlarge my business. There's no reason why I shouldn't make use of this beautiful land of opportunity."

A log fell in the little fireplace, and the glass that held the unicorn caught Nicole's eye. She gave a dry, cold laugh. "I should have known what you were like when we made those childish vows. I wasn't pure enough to touch the unicorn itself, was I? Only your dear, dead Beth was good enough for that."

She pushed past him and went outside into the cool morning. Very calmly, she went to the rowboat and began to row herself back to the mill wharf. Her grandfather had told her never to look back. It wasn't easy to keep her mind from crying out for Clay. She conjured a picture of Bianca, content and pregnant, her hands resting on the mound that was Clay's child. She glanced at her own flat stomach and was thankful that she had no child.

By the time she reached the wharf, she was feeling better. She stood and looked up at the little house. It was going to be her permanent home for a while, and she thought of it as such. She would need more room, a parlor downstairs, and two more bedrooms upstairs. Immediately, she realized that she had no money.

There was good, flat farmland adjoining the mill, and she vaguely remembered Janie mentioning that it was for sale. She had no money for land.

Then she remembered her clothes. They were certainly worth something. Why, the sable muff alone . . . How she'd like to throw everything into Clay's face! She'd like to have the clothes delivered to him, dumped in his hallway. But that bit of show would cost her too much. At the Backes's, several women had admired her clothes. Suddenly, she thought with regret of the mink-lined cape she'd left on the floor of the cave. But she could never go back there—never!

Plans were whirling in her head as she entered the single room of the little house. Janie was bent over the fire, her face red from the heat. Gerard lounged in a chair, insolently smashing a doughnut into a plate. The twins were in a corner, giggling behind a book.

Janie looked up. "Something's happened."

"No," Nicole said. "At least nothing new." She studied Gerard. "Gerard, I've just come to the conclusion that you would make an excellent salesman."

His eyebrows came up. "People of my class—" he began.

Nicole cut him off as she grabbed the plate out from under his fork. "This is America, not France. If you eat, you work."

He gave her a sullen look. "What is there to sell? I know nothing about grain."

"The grain sells itself. I want you to persuade some lovely young women that they will be even lovelier in silks and sables."

"Sables?" Janie asked. "Nicole, what are you talking about?"

Nicole gave her a look that stopped her from speaking. "Come upstairs with me while I show you the clothes." She turned to the twins. "And you two are going to get lessons."

"But Nicole," Janie interrupted, "you don't have time. The mill dresser is already here."

"Not me," she said firmly. "Upstairs is a highly educated woman, and she will be only too happy to tutor the children."

"Adele?" Gerard scoffed. "You won't even be able to make her understand what you want, much less get her to do it."

"We don't like the screaming lady," Alex said, holding Mandy's hand and stepping back.

"Enough!" Nicole said loudly. "I've had enough of these complaints. Janie and I are not running a free hotel any longer. Gerard, you are going to help me get some money for some land. Mother is going to take care of the children, and the twins are going to get an education. From now on, we're a family, not an aristocracy with a couple of servants." She turned and went up the stairs.

Janie grinned up at her. "I don't know what's happened to her, but I like it!"

"If she thinks I'm going to—" Gerard began.

Janie waved a hot, sticky spoon in front of his face. "You either work or we ship you back to France, and you can get your head cut off or make shoes like your father. You got that?"

"You can't treat me like this!"

"I can, and I will. If you don't get up those stairs like Nicole said, I may use my fist on that ugly little face of yours."

Gerard started to speak, but he stopped as he stared at Janie's fist in his face. She was a large, strong woman. He stepped back from her. "We aren't finished yet." He muttered several curses in French as he followed Nicole up the stairs.

Janie turned to the twins, gave them a warning look, clapped her hands smartly, and sent them scurrying up the stairs.

Chapter 18

IT WAS WESLEY WHO SAILED NICOLE UPRIVER TO where Dr. Donaldson was staying and then took them all to the judge's house. Wes didn't say much when Nicole told him she wanted her marriage to Clay annulled. In fact, no one said very much, and it seemed to Nicole that everyone believed it was inevitable. She was the last one to have any faith in Clay.

It was surprising how little time it took to end a marriage. Nicole worried that since so many people had seen her with Clay and since the marriage had been consummated, it would make a difference. She found out that they could even have had children and, because of the force used during the ceremony, still have had the marriage annulled.

The judge had known both Clay and Wesley all their lives. He'd met Nicole at the Backes's party. He hated to dissolve the marriage, to declare it had never existed, but he couldn't dispute the doctor's testimony. Besides, he'd heard the gossip about the woman Clay lived with. He made a mental note to visit Clay very soon and tell him what he thought of his immoral behavior. The judge looked at the pretty little French-woman with sympathy. She didn't deserve what Clay had put her through.

He declared the marriage annulled.

"Nicole?" Wes asked when they left the judge's house. "Are you all right?"

"Of course," she said flatly. "Why shouldn't I be? If you wanted to buy some land, where would you go first?"

"To the owners, I guess. Why?"

"Do you know Mr. Irwin Rogers?"

"Sure. He lives about a mile down the road."

"Could you take me there and introduce me?" she asked.

"Nicole, what's this all about?"

"I want to buy the farmland next to the mill. I thought I'd put in a crop of barley this spring."

"Barley? But Clay can give you—" He stopped at Nicole's look.

"I am no longer related to Clayton Armstrong, nor do I have anything to do with him. I will make my own way in the world."

She started walking down the road, but Wes grabbed her arm. "I can't believe it's really over between you and Clay."

"I think it's been over for a long time, but I was too blind to see it," she said quietly.

"Nicole," Wes began, staring down at her. The sunlight on her face made her eyes sparkle. He studied her mouth, the upper lip so fascinating. "Why don't you marry me? You've never even seen my house. It's enormous. You could have all the people you take care of live there, and we wouldn't even see them. Travis and I have more money than we know what to do with, and you wouldn't have to work."

She stared at him a moment, then smiled. "Wesley, you are very sweet. You don't want to marry me." She turned away from him.

"Yes, I do! You'd make a perfect wife. You could run the whole plantation, and everyone likes you."

"Stop!" she laughed. "You're making me feel very old." She stood on tiptoe and kissed the corner of his mouth. "I thank you for your offer, but I have no desire to leave one marriage and go directly into another one." She narrowed her eyes at him. "And if you dare look relieved, I will never speak to you again."

He lifted her hand and kissed it, rubbing her fingers between his. "I may cry, but I certainly won't look relieved."

She laughed and pulled her hand away. "I need friends more than a lover right now. If you really want to help me, maybe you could get Mr. Rogers to give me a good price on the land."

Wesley watched her for a moment. His marriage proposal had been a spur-of-the-moment thing, but now he thought how pleasant it would be to be married to someone like Nicole. She would have surprised him if she'd accepted him, but he wished she had.

He grinned at her. "Old man Rogers is going to be so pleased to sell that land, he's going to practically give it to you."

"No violence," Nicole laughed.

"Maybe a broken toe or two, but that's all."

"Well . . . if it's just toes."

They laughed together and went down the road toward Mr. Rogers's house.

They did get a good price for the land. Nicole had very little cash from the clothes Gerard had sold, but Mr. Rogers allowed her to pay off the land slowly over the years. She also agreed to grind the grain from his farm for free for three years.

"He didn't exactly give us the land," Wes said when they left. "His grain ground free for three years!"

Nicole's eyes sparkled. "But wait until he gets his bill for the fourth year!"

After they left Mr. Rogers's house, they went to the printer's office, where Nicole had handbills printed advertising her mill's rates for grinding.

"Nicole!" Wes said as he heard her tell the printer the new rates. "How do you expect to make any money? That's a third less than Horace charges."

She smiled. "Competition and quantity. Would you bring your grain to me or to Horace?"

The printer laughed. "I think she's got you there, Wes. I'm going to tell my brother-in-law about this, and you can be sure he'll come to you."

Wesley looked at Nicole with new respect. "I had no idea there was a brain behind that pretty face."

She was serious. "I don't think there has been. Or, at least, it's been clouded with childish ideas of love and romance."

Wesley frowned as she left the printer's. He had the feeling she was hurt more than she'd admit. Damn Clay! he thought. He had no right to use Nicole the way he did.

At home again, Gerard was the one who gave Nicole trouble. The little man backed away from her in disgust.

"It was disgusting enough to have to sell ladies' dresses." He stopped and smoothed his hair. It was cut in the Brutus style, fashionably shaggy and unkempt. It lay close to his head, limp, without body or curl. "Of course, the women were pleased to meet me. They were not like the people in this house. They liked the stories of my family, the magnificent Courtalains."

"Since when has Nicole's family become yours?" Janie snapped.

"See!" Gerard shouted. "I am unappreciated."

"Both of you, stop it," Nicole said. "I'm tired of hearing you bicker. Gerard, you have proved yourself a perfect salesman. The women love your accent and your charming manners."

He preened under her compliments.

"If you want, you may give the handbills to the farmers' wives. In fact, that may be a good idea."

"Handbills are not silks," he muttered.

"But food is food," Janie said. "And if you want any, you'll work like the rest of us."

Gerard took a step toward Janie, his upper lip curled into a sneer, but Nicole put her hand on his forearm and stopped him. He looked from her hand to her face, then back again. He covered her hand with his. "For you, I would do anything."

Nicole, as politcly as possible, moved away from him. "Isaac will row you up and down the river to the houses."

Gerard smiled at her as if they were lovers, then quietly left the house.

"I don't trust him," Janie said.

Nicole waved her hand. "He's harmless. He just wants us to treat him royally is all. He'll soon learn."

"You're too generous. Just take my advice and stay well away from him."

Spring came quickly to the Virginia countryside, and with it came the ripening of the early crops. It wasn't long before the enormous grindstones in the mill were again turning after the long winter break. Nicole's handbills worked, and farmers came from miles around to bring their grain to the mill.

Nicole never allowed herself a minute to relax. She hired another man to help in the fields that were seeded with barley and wheat. Gerard reluctantly helped at the mill, but he made it clear that he considered the Americans beneath him. Nicole kept reminding him that her grandfather the duke had worked in a grain mill for two years.

No one seemed to consider the idea of the twins returning to Clay, and Nicole knew it was a sign of his trust in her. Once a week, Isaac rowed the children across the river to visit their uncle.

"He looks bad," Isaac said once after he returned.

Nicole didn't bother to ask whom he meant. In spite of all her work, Clay was never far from her mind.

"He drinks too much. I never knew him to drink so much before."

Nicole turned away. She should feel glad he was so miserable, since he certainly deserved it. But somehow she wasn't glad. She left Isaac and went to the vegetable garden. Maybe a few hours of hoeing would keep her mind off Clay.

An hour later, Nicole leaned against a tree and wiped her forearm across her face. She was hot and sweaty from the vigorous hoeing.

"Here, I brought you something," Gerard said as he handed her a glass of cool lemonade.

She nodded her gratitude and gulped all of the liquid.

Gerard brushed a piece of grass from the sleeve of her cotton dress. "You shouldn't be out here in the sun. It will ruin that beautiful complexion of yours." He ran his hand down her arm.

Nicole was too tired to move away from him. They stood in a deeply shaded place, out of sight of the house and mill.

"I'm glad we have this time alone," he said, moving closer to her. "It's strange that we live in the same house, yet we rarely have a chance to be alone, to have a private conversation."

Nicole didn't want to offend him, but neither did she want to encourage him. She stepped away. "You could talk to me at any time, I hope you know that."

He moved near her again, his hand running up and down her arm, caressing it. "You're the only one here who understands me." He spoke in French, moving his face closer to hers. "We're from the same country, the same people. No one else knows what France is like now. We're drawn closer together by our common bond."

"I consider myself an American now." She answered him in English.

"How can you? You are French as I am French. We are of the great Courtalains. Think how we could continue the line."

Nicole's back straightened as she glared at him. "How dare you!" she gasped. "Do you forget my

306

mother? You are married to her, yet you proposition me like some scullery maid."

"How can I forget her when her screams nearly drive me mad? Do you think there is a minute that I'm not aware that I am bound to her? What can she give me? Can she give me children? I am a man, a healthy man, and I deserve children." He grabbed her, pulled her close to him. "You are the only one. In all of this heathen country, you are the only one worthy to be the mother of my children. You are a Courtalain! Our children's blood would flow with the blue of kings."

It took Nicole a second to comprehend what he was saying. She felt her stomach turn over when she did understand. There were no words to express her feelings. She slapped him hard.

Gerard released her immediately and put his hand over his cheek. "You will pay for this," he whispered. "You will be sorry you ever treated me like one of these filthy Americans. I will make you know who I am."

Nicole turned away and went back to the garden. Janie had been right about Gerard after all. She vowed to stay away from the little Frenchman as much as possible.

Two weeks later, Wes brought the news that Clayton had married Bianca.

She braced herself against the impact of the news.

"I tried to reason with him," Wes said. "But you know how stubborn Clay is. He's never stopped loving you. When he heard about the annulment, he stayed drunk for four days. One of his men found him by the side of the swamp in the south pasture."

"I assume he sobered up for his wedding," she said coldly.

"He said he did it for the child. Goddamn him! I can't understand how he could stomach going to bed with that cow."

He caught Nicole's arm as she turned away. "I'm sorry I said that. I didn't mean to hurt you."

"How could you hurt me? Mr. Armstrong means nothing to me."

Wes stood quietly and watched her go. He could strangle Clay for what he'd done to that beautiful young woman.

Arundel Hall was filthy. It hadn't been cleaned in months. Bianca sat quietly at the dining table, eating ice cream and sugar cookies. Her enormous belly stuck out in front of her so far she looked as if she were about to deliver the child at any moment.

Clay came into the house, stopping at the dining room door. His clothes were muddy, his shirt torn. There were circles under his eyes, and his hair was plastered to his head from sweat. "What a lovely sight to come home to," he said loudly. "My wife. Soon to be mother of my child."

Bianca ignored him but continued slowly to eat the delicious, cold, rich ice cream.

"Eating for two, my dear?" he asked. When he got no response, he went upstairs. Dirty clothes were slung everywhere. He pulled open a drawer and saw that it was empty. No longer were there clean, mended shirts waiting for him.

He cursed and slammed the drawer, then went out of the house, walking quickly toward the river. He spent very little time at home now. His days he spent in the fields; his evenings he sat alone in the library and drank until he thought he could sleep. Even then, he rarely did.

At the river, he stripped off his clothes and dove into the water. After his bath, he stretched out on the grassy shore and fell asleep.

When he woke, it was night, and for a moment he didn't know where he was. In a dazed, half-awake, half-asleep mood, he walked back to the house.

He heard the moaning as soon as he entered the house. Quickly, he shook himself out of the sleep. Bianca lay curled at the foot of the stairs, her hand holding her stomach.

He knelt beside her. "What is it? Did you fall?"

She rolled her eyes at him. "Help me," she gasped. "The baby."

Clay didn't touch her but ran from the house to get the plantation midwife. Within minutes he was back, the woman following him. Bianca lay just as he'd left her. He lit a lantern as the woman bent over Bianca.

She ran her hands over Bianca's still form, and when she held them up to the light they were bloody. "Can you get her upstairs?"

Clay set the lantern down and lifted Bianca. The veins in his neck stood out as he strained to get her heavy form up the stairs. He laid her gently on the bed.

"Go get Maggie," the midwife said. "I'll need help for this one."

Clay sat in his library, drinking steadily while Maggie and the midwife tended to Bianca.

Maggie quietly opened the door. "She lost the baby," she said quietly.

Clay looked at her in amazement. Then he smiled. "Lost the baby, did she?"

"Clay," Maggie said. She didn't like the look in his eye. "I wish you'd stop drinking."

He poured another glass of bourbon. "Aren't you supposed to comfort me? Shouldn't you tell me there will be other children?"

"There won't be," the midwife said from the door. "She's a heavy woman, and when she went down those stairs, she went hard. There's a lot of damage inside her, especially to her female workin's. I'm not sure she's gonna live."

Clay drained the bourbon and refilled the glass. "She'll live. I have no doubt of that. People like Bianca don't die easily."

"Clayton!" Maggie commanded. "You're taking this too hard." She went to him and put her hand on his. "Please stop drinking. You won't be fit for a day's work tomorrow if you don't."

"Work," he said, and smiled. "Why should I work? What for? For my darling wife? For the son she just lost?" He drank some more bourbon, then began to laugh. It was an ugly laugh.

"Clay," Maggie said.

"Get out of here! Can't a man be alone once in a while?"

Slowly, the women left the room.

When the sun came up, Clay was still drinking, still waiting for the forgetfulness the drink would bring.

In the fields, the hands started their day's work. It was unusual not to see Clay watching them. Toward afternoon, they began to slow down. It was nice not to have the boss looking over their shoulders. By the fourth day, when Clay still did not come to the fields, some of the men didn't bother to go to work at all.

Chapter 19

IT WAS AUGUST OF 1796, ONE YEAR LATER.

Nicole stood on top of the hill and looked down at her property. Putting her hands at the small of her back, she massaged her tired muscles. It helped to ease the pain if she could see what had caused her fatigue. The hot August sun blazed down on the tall tobacco plants. The cotton would soon be bursting its pods. The golden wheat, almost ripe, waved gently in the breeze. The sound of the millstones, grinding evenly and steadily, floated up to her. One of the twins yelled, and Nicole smiled at Janie's sharp reprimand.

It had been well over a year since her marriage had been annulled. She realized that she marked all time from that hour in the judge's office. Since that fateful day, she'd done little besides work. Every morning, she was up before daylight, seeing to the mill, to the crops that were planted and harvested. The first time she'd taken her crops to market, the men had laughed, thinking they'd be able to get her produce for a low price. But Nicole wouldn't allow herself to be cheated; she drove a hard bargain. When she left the market, she was smiling, while the male buyers were frowning and shaking their heads. Wesley walked beside her and laughed.

This year, she'd enlarged her land holdings. She'd used all her crop money from last year and bought more land. She now owned one hundred twenty-five acres of land on the high side of the river. It had good drainage, fertile soil. She had a little trouble with erosion, but she and Isaac had spent some of the winter months laying stone fields. They'd also cleared the new land. It had been hard, cold work, but they'd done it. Then, early this spring, they'd set out tobacco plants, then seeded the other fields. There was a kitchen garden, a milk cow, and chickens by the house.

The house itself had not changed. Every penny had gone into improving the land. Adele and Gerard had one side of the attic, Janie and Nicole the other. The twins slept on pallets downstairs. It was a crowded existence, but they'd all learned to get along. Janie and Gerard rarely spoke to each other, each pretending the other didn't exist. Adele still lived in a dream world of prerevolutionary France. Nicole had been able to persuade her mother that the twins were her grandchildren and that Adele must personally help educate them. For days she'd be an excellent tutor. She'd spice the children's lessons with fascinating tales of her life at Court. She told about when she was a child, about the odd habits of the king and queen of France. At least, the habits sounded strange to the children. Once Adele told the story of how the queen had her clothes brought to her every day in wicker baskets lined with new green taffeta. The taffeta was never reused and was given to the servants. The twins had dressed themselves in green leaves and pretended they were Adele's servants. She was delighted.

Yet, sometimes, some little thing would set Adele off, and her fragile peacefulness would be shattered. Once, Mandy tied a red ribbon about her neck and Adele saw the child. It reminded her of her friends' executions, and she screamed for hours. The twins were no longer frightened of Adele's screams. They merely shrugged and went away or ran for Nicole to go to her mother. After a few days, in which Adele cringed in fear talking of murder and death, she'd return to her fantasy world. Never was she aware of the present, that she was in America, that France was far away. She knew only Nicole and the twins, tolerated Janie, and looked at Gerard as if he didn't exist. She was never allowed to meet strangers, who frightened her horribly.

Gerard seemed to be content that his wife had no idea who he was. Once she saw Nicole, Adele seemed to forget all the time she'd spent in jail and the time at Gerard's parents' house. To Nicole, she spoke of her husband and her father as if they were still alive, as if they would come home at any moment.

Gerard stood away from the rest of the people in Nicole's house. He made himself an outsider. He had not been the same since the day Nicole had slapped him. He would go away for days at a time and return in the middle of the night, giving no explanation of where he went. When he was at home, he often sat by the fire and watched Nicole, stared at her until she dropped stitches in her knitting or stuck a needle in her finger. He never said anything more about marrying Nicole, but sometimes she wished he would. At odd times, when she caught him staring at her, she wished he'd confront her and they could have a good argument. But she felt foolish every time she thought of it. He wasn't doing anything wrong when he watched her.

Whatever was said of Gerard, he pulled his weight at the mill. His hand-kissing manners and his thick, rich accent brought as much business as Nicole's low prices. An extraordinary number of young women came with their fathers to have their grain ground. Gerard treated them all like French aristocrats, young or old, fat or thin, ugly or pretty. The women simpered and giggled as he took their arms and led them around the mill. He never took them out of sight of their fathers.

Only once did Nicole have a glimpse of Gerard's thoughts. A particularly plain young woman was rolling her eyes in delight as Gerard kissed her palm and murmured in French over it. By a trick of the wind,

313

Nicole happened to hear what he said. Although he was smiling, he was calling the woman a piece of pig's offal. Nicole shuddered and walked away; she didn't want to hear any more.

She straightened her back and looked across the river. She hadn't seen Clay since he'd told her Bianca was pregnant. In a way, it seemed ages ago, yet at the same time it seemed like minutes. There wasn't a night she didn't think of him, long for him. Her body betrayed her often, and many times she wanted to ask him to meet her in the clearing. She didn't care about her pride or her higher ideals. She only wanted him, strong and hot against her skin.

She shook her head to clear her vision. It was better not to dwell on the past or to remind herself of what was not. She had a good life now, with people she loved around her. She had no right to be lonely or thankless.

She stared at the Armstrong plantation. Even from this distance, she could see that it wasn't being cared for. Last year's crops had been allowed to die in the fields. It had hurt her to see it, but there was nothing she could do. Isaac had kept her informed of what was happening. Most of the paid servants had left long ago. The indentures of some servants had been sold, along with nearly all of the slaves. Only a handful of people remained.

This spring, some of the bottomland had been planted, but that was all. The upper fields lay bare, with only rotting stems in them. Isaac said Clay didn't care and Bianca was selling anything she could find to pay for her clothes and the constant redecorating of the house. Isaac said the only person on the plantation who had any work to do was the cook.

"Not much to look at, is it?"

She whirled to see Isaac standing beside her. He was looking across the river. In the months since the kidnapping, Isaac and she had become very close.

There was a bond between them forged by shared tragedy. The people who worked for her she had always felt belonged to Clay, even Janie to an extent. It was only Isaac with whom she felt this special bond. And Isaac often looked at Nicole as if he'd die for her.

"He could make it if these crops are good, and so far the weather has been perfect," she said.

"I can't see Clay getting up the strength even to harvest the tobacco, much less take it to market."

"That's absurd. No one is a harder worker than Clayton Armstrong."

"Was," Isaac said. "I know he used to be, but now all he works at is lifting a bottle to his mouth. And what if he did work? That wife of his has spent more than four plantations could afford. Every time I take the twins over there, there's a bill collector hounding Clay. If he lets this crop rot in the fields, he'll lose everything. The law will put the place up for auction."

Nicole turned away. She didn't want to hear any more. "I think there's some paperwork I need to do. Did the Morrisons bring that extra barley you asked for?"

"This morning," he said, following her. He took a deep breath and wished again, for the thousandth time, that she'd relax a little, if not for her own sake, then for his. He wished Wesley would visit, but Travis had gone to England and Wes had his own plantation to run. No one else could get Nicole to stop working even for minutes.

Gerard leaned against a tree and watched Isaac follow Nicole back to the mill. He often wondered what went on between those two. They spent many hours together. In the last year, Gerard had met hundreds of people, and most of them had been willing to tell him anything he wanted to know. He knew Nicole was a passionate woman. He'd heard from a hundred people how she'd acted at the Backes's party. She'd acted like that, like a common street woman, in front of all those people, yet she'd slapped him when he touched her.

There wasn't a day when he didn't remember the way she'd slapped him, the way she'd looked at him as if he were something from under a rock. He knew why she'd refused him. She thought she was better than him. After all, she was one of the Courtalains, whose history was intertwined with French kings and queens. And who was he? A cobbler's son. He thought she'd accept him when she found out he was related to her, but she hadn't. To her, he was a cobbler's son, and no matter what he did, he'd never change in her eyes.

Gerard thought of what he'd had to do in the last year. She'd made him prostitute himself for those crude American women. They were coarse things, uneducated, and could speak only the flat American language. He loved to watch their eyes as he said hideous things to them in French. They were too stupid to know what he said.

Then, at night, Nicole teased him, played with him until he was past endurance. Only a curtain separated his room from hers. He'd lie in bed in the darkness, Adele snoring beside him, and listen to her undress. He knew the different sound of each garment. He knew when she stood nude, in that instant before she slipped her nightgown over her head. He imagined her golden body, imagined opening his arms and her sliding into them. Then he'd show her! He'd make her regret ever having slapped him.

He moved away from the tree. Someday he'd make her regret thinking she was better than him. He imagined everything he'd do to her. He'd make her crawl and beg. Yes! She was a passionate woman, but he'd never touch her unless she came to him on her knees. He'd show her that a cobbler's son was as good as any of her snobbish French relatives.

He moved through the trees and away from the mill. The place made him sick. All of them together, laughing and talking—about him, no doubt. Once he'd overheard two men talking about "the little Frenchy." He'd grabbed a rock then but had thought better of it. There were other ways to repay them, ways that wouldn't hurt either of them. Later that fall, both men had lost tobacco barns full of their crops. One of the men had gone bankrupt.

Gerard smiled in remembrance. As he walked along the ridge, a movement across the river caught his eye. It was someone, a large woman on horseback. He stopped and stared for a moment. Over the last year, he'd seen less and less activity over there. He'd never been particularly curious about Nicole's relationship with Armstrong. He knew she'd once been married to him and had acted like his whore at the Backes's party. So many times, Gerard had imagined Nicole acting that way with him. When she'd gotten the annulment so soon after he arrived, Gerard had been pleased. He knew she was telling him who she wanted. It had thrilled him, thinking she'd gotten the annulment so she could marry Gerard. He'd waited a while, then let her know that she'd be welcome in his bed.

He clamped his teeth together in memory. She was a tease, making promises one moment, then acting as if he'd insulted her the next.

As he watched, the woman across the river raised her whip and slapped the horse smartly on the rump. The horse jumped, then lowered its head and gave a violent shudder. The woman went flying through the air and landed on her backside in a storm of dust and pebbles.

Gerard hesitated for a second, then began to run toward the wharf. He had no idea of his intentions, but he knew he must get to the woman.

"Are you hurt?" he asked when he reached her.

Bianca sat quietly on the ground, her whole body

317

aching from the fall and from being on that cursed horse. She took a piece of dirt from her mouth and looked at it in disgust. She gave a jump of surprise when she saw Gerard. It had been so long since she'd seen a gentleman, and she recognized the French fashions immediately. He wore a green cloth coat with velvet collar and cuffs. His shirt was of white silk, the cravat tied to hide the point of his chin. His slim legs were encased in tan breeches, with six pearl buttons at the knee. His silk stockings were green and yellow striped.

She sighed heavily. It was so good to see a man in something besides buckskin and leather. It was also good to see a slim, gentlemanly form instead of the build of a field hand.

"May I help you?" Gerard repeated when the woman did not answer. He understood her look. He'd seen it often in America. The women were hungry for culture and refinement.

He stared down at her as he held out his hand for her. She was a large woman, a very large woman. Her low-cut red satin dress revealed an enormous, heaving bosom. Her arms were large, stretching the sleeves of her dress. Her face had the look of something that had once been pretty but was now bloated and distorted out of shape. In spite of the dated style of the dress and the inappropriate fabric, he knew it was expensive.

"Please allow me to help you," he said in his lush accent. "I fear that you will ruin that exquisite complexion if you stay here in the sun."

Bianca blushed a rosy pink, then took the hand he offered.

Gerard braced himself as he helped pull her up. She was even larger when she was standing beside him. She was two inches taller than he and outweighed him by at least sixty pounds.

He didn't release her hand but gently pulled her with him to the shade of a tree. With a sweeping motion, he removed his coat and spread it on the grass for her. "Please," he said with a bow. "You must rest after such a fall. A delicate young lady such as yourself should be careful." He turned toward the river.

Bianca awkwardly eased herself onto the coat, then looked at Gerard as he walked away. "You aren't leaving me, are you?"

He looked at her over his shoulder, leaving her no doubt that he would not, could not, leave her now that he'd found her.

Gerard stopped at the river and withdrew his handkerchief. It was Adele's, the only one she owned, pure silk, trimmed in Brussels lace and monogrammed AC. Gerard had carefully removed the A and left the C since he was now a Courtalain.

He wet the handkerchief and took it back to Bianca. He knelt beside her. "There is a smudge on your cheek," he said quietly. When she didn't move, he said, "Allow me," took her chin in his hand, and carefully began to wipe away the dirt.

Bianca thought it was odd that she felt no revulsion at Gerard's touch. After all, he was a man. "You'll . . . get your handkerchief dirty," she stuttered.

He gave her a smile of great tolerance. "What is silk next to a beautiful woman's skin?"

"Beautiful?" She opened her eyes very wide. Their blueness was almost obscured by her fat cheeks. The dimple in her left cheek was no longer visible but lost in the doughy plumpness. "No one has called me beautiful in a long time."

"Strange," Gerard said. "I would think your husband—surely a lady of your beauty is married—would tell you that every day."

"My husband hates me," Bianca said flatly.

Gerard considered this for a moment. He could feel the woman's need for a friend, a need to talk. He shrugged. He had nothing else to do today, and besides, sometimes the things lonely women told him became useful. "And who is your husband?"

"Clayton Armstrong."

Gerard lifted one eyebrow. "The owner of this place?"

"All of it," Bianca sighed. "At least what is left of it. He refuses to work it just because he hates me. He says he refuses to kill himself just so I can buy a few trinkets."

"Trinkets?" he encouraged.

"I am certainly frugal enough. I buy nothing I don't need—a few simple clothes, a carriage, a few furnishings for the house, nothing a lady of my station doesn't need."

"It is a shame you have such a selfish husband."

Bianca stared across the river. "It's all *her* fault. If she hadn't thrown herself at my husband, none of this would have happened."

"But I thought Nicole was once married to Mr. Armstrong." Gerard made no pretense of not knowing whom she meant.

"She was, but I fixed her. She thought she could take away what was mine, what I worked so hard for, but she couldn't."

Gerard looked about him, to the tobacco fields to his left. "What exactly does Armstrong own?"

Bianca's eyes came alive. "He's rich, or could be if he'd only do some work. There's a very nice house, except it's too small."

"And Nicole gave all this up?" he asked, half to himself.

Bianca's anger made her cheeks flush. "She didn't give it up. We played a game, and I won. That's all."

320

She had Gerard's interest now. "I wish you'd tell me about this game. I'd certainly like to hear about it."

He sat and listened with rapt attention to Bianca's story. He was amazed at her cleverness. Here was someone he could understand. He laughed when she told how she bribed Abe to kidnap Nicole. He was almost in awe of her when she spoke of planting herself in Clay's bed.

Bianca had never had anyone in America listen to her before, and certainly no one who showed any interest. She'd always thought her manipulation of Clay and Nicole was extraordinarily clever, but no one else had shown any interest. When Gerard seemed so eager, she went on to tell him about paying Oliver Hawthorne to impregnate her. She shuddered at the memory, told how she had to drug herself to be able to stand the man's touch.

Gerard burst out laughing. "It wasn't even Armstrong's child! How marvelous! Nicole must have been insane when she found out her dear husband was sleeping with someone else, had even made a baby." On impulse, he grabbed Bianca's fat hand and kissed the taut skin. "It's too bad you lost the child. It would have served Armstrong right if the child looked like a neighbor instead of him."

"Yes," Bianca said dreamily. "I would have liked for him to look like a fool, like he's made me appear."

"You could never look like a fool. It's the people who do not appreciate you who are fools."

"Yes, oh yes," she whispered. "You do understand."

The two of them sat quietly for a moment. Bianca felt as if she'd found her first friend, someone who was interested in her. Everyone else seemed to be on Clay's or Nicole's side.

As for Gerard, he wasn't sure what to do with Bianca's revelations, but he knew that, somehow, they'd be useful. "Let me introduce myself. I am Gerard Gautier, of the Courtalain family."

"Courtalain!" Bianca gasped. "But that's Nicole's last name."

"We are . . . related, yes."

Bianca's eyes instantly filled with tears. "You've used me," she whispered desperately. "You listened to me, yet you're on *her* side!" She started to rise, but her bulk made her awkward, clumsy.

Gerard took her shoulders in his hands and forcefully pushed her back down. "Because I am related to her certainly does not make me on her side. Far from it. I am a guest in her house, and there is not a moment when she does not let me forget that I am her charity."

Bianca blinked rapidly to clear away the tears. "Then, you know she is not the pure little angel everyone seems to believe she is! She married *my* fiancé. She tried to take Arundel Hall and the plantation away from me. Yet everyone seems to think I am the one in the wrong. I only took what was mine."

"Yes," Gerard agreed. "But by everyone, I assume you mean the Americans. But, then, what can you expect from so crude a group of people?"

Bianca smiled. "They're an ignorant lot. No one could see the way Nicole was carrying on with that horrid Wesley Stanford."

"Or Isaac Simmons!" Gerard said in disgust. "She spends many, many hours a day with that piece of trash."

A bell sounded in the distance behind them. It called the plantation workers who were left to dinner.

"I must go," Bianca said. "Could we . . . meet again?"

Gerard used his frail strength to help her up, then put his jacket on. It was not an easy task. "You could not prevent me from seeing you again. May I say that, for the first time since I've been in America, I feel as if I've found a friend."

"Yes," Bianca said quietly. "I feel the same way."

He took her hand and kissed it caressingly. "Tomorrow, then?"

"At lunch, here. I'll bring a picnic."

He nodded quickly, then left her.

Chapter 20

BIANCA STARED AFTER GERARD FOR A MOMENT. HE was really a fine figure of a man—his ways were delicate, refined, so far removed from the hideous Americans. She turned toward the house and sighed at the long way she had to walk. The distance was Clayton's fault. She'd wanted someone to drive her about the plantation in a carriage, but Clay laughed at the idea and said he wasn't about to put in roads because she was too lazy to walk.

During the long, hot walk to the house, she thought of Gerard. Why couldn't she have married someone like him? Why had she gotten a mean, crude man like Clayton? She could have been happy with a man like Gerard. She repeated the name several times. Yes, life with him would be sweet. He'd never sneer at her or say mean, hurtful things.

Once inside the house, her euphoria vanished. The house was filthy beyond belief. It had not had a thorough cleaning in more than a year. Cobwebs hung from the ceiling. Clothes, papers, and dead flowers littered the table tops. The floors were scuffed and dirty. The rugs were so full of dust that just walking on them raised little clouds.

Bianca had tried to keep a staff, but Clay had always interfered with her discipline. He always backed the servants against her. After a few months, he'd refused to hire anyone to work in the house. He said Bianca's temper was too vile to force anyone to endure it. Bianca'd argued with him, told him he had no idea how servants should be treated, but he'd ignored her as he always did.

"Here's my dear—dare I say little?—wife now," Clay said. He lounged against the stairwell, just in front of the dining room doorway. His shirt had once been white, but now it was dirty and torn. It was open to the waist, only halfheartedly tucked into the wide leather belt at his waist. His tall boots were caked with mud. In his hand was a glass of bourbon, just as there always was nowadays.

"I thought the dinner bell would bring you back," he said lazily. He ran his hand across his unshaven jaw. "No matter what happens, the mere mention of food brings you running."

"You disgust me," she sneered, and went into the dining room. The big table was heaped with food. Maggie was one of the few servants who'd stayed with Clay over the past year. Bianca seated herself carefully and spread a linen napkin in her lap as she studied the food.

"Such hunger!" Clay said from the doorway. "If you were able to look at a man like that, you'd own him. But men don't interest you, do they? The only interests you have are food and yourself."

Bianca put three fried crullers on her plate. "You know nothing about me. It may interest you to know that some men find me quite attractive."

Clay snorted and took a deep drink of the bourbon. "No man could be that big a fool. At least, I hope I am the only one who's that stupid."

Bianca continued to eat, slowly and steadily. "Did you know your dear, lost Nicole was sleeping with Isaac Simmons?" She smiled at the look on his face. "She always was a slut. She used to meet you, even while you lived with me. Women like that can't live without a man, no matter what kind of man he is. I bet she slept with Abe as well. Maybe I was a matchmaker when I put them on the island together."

"I don't believe you," Clay said under his breath. "Isaac's a boy."

"What were you like at sixteen? Now that she's free of you, she can do whatever she wants with whomever she wants. I bet you taught her some of your dirty little bed tricks, and now she's teaching dear, innocent Isaac."

"Shut up!" Clay yelled, and threw his glass at her head. Either he was already too drunk to aim straight or she was becoming adept at dodging, because he missed her.

He slammed out of the house, making his way past the office and toward the stables. He rarely went into his office these days; there didn't seem to be any need. In the stables, he grabbed a jug of bourbon and headed toward the river.

He sat down slowly at the edge of the water and leaned back against a tree. From here he could see Nicole's planted fields. The house and mill were out of sight, and he was glad for that. Just seeing the health and productivity of her fields was more than enough. He wondered if she ever thought of him, even remembered him. She lived with that little Frenchman Maggie said most of the women in Virginia drooled over. He dismissed the idea of Isaac. Bianca's mind was sick.

Clay drank deeply of the bourbon. It took more and more of the liquid to make him forget. Sometimes, at night, he woke from a dream where his parents, Beth, and James all accused him of forgetting them, of destroying what was theirs. In the morning, he'd wake with new convictions, new hope, plans for the future. Then he'd see Bianca, the filthy house, the fallow fields. Across the river, the sound of laughter or the shout of one of the twins would reach him. Without thinking, he'd reach for the whiskey. The whiskey dulled his senses, made him forget, kept him from hearing or thinking.

He didn't pay any attention when the clouds covered the sun. The day progressed, and the clouds grew darker. They rumbled and rolled lazily but powerfully. In the distance, a sharp flash of lightning cut across the sky. The heat of the day vanished as the wind began to rise. It blew across the fields of wheat and barley. It blew across Clay, tugging at his loose shirt. But the whiskey kept him warm. Even when the first drops fell, he didn't move. The rain began in earnest. It pelted against Clay's hat, collected on the wide brim, then ran down his face. He didn't even notice the cold wetness as his shirt stuck to his skin. He just sat and drank.

Nicole looked out the window and sighed. It had been raining for two days, not letting up even for a minute. They'd had to stop the millstones because the river had risen so much that it was difficult to control the water coming over the shoot. Isaac had assured her that her crops were safe as long as the stone walls held, and it looked as if they would. The water was draining down the terraced field into the river. They were safe from the rain if they didn't have to worry about erosion.

She jumped when a loud pounding on the door began. "Wesley!" she said, glad to see him. "You're drenched. Come in!"

He pulled the oilcloth raincoat off and shook it. Janie took it from him and hung it up to dry.

"Why in the world did you come out in this?" Janie said. "Did you have any trouble with the river?"

"Plenty! Is there any coffee? I'm as cold as I am wet."

Nicole handed him a large mug of coffee, which he drank as he stood before the fire. Gerard sat in a corner of the room, silent, staring, uninvolved. Wes could hear the twins upstairs, probably with Nicole's mother, a woman he'd seen only once.

"Well, we're waiting," Janie demanded. "What brings you here?"

"Actually, I was on my way to Clay's. There's going to be a flood if this rain keeps up."

"A flood?" Nicole asked. "Will Clay be harmed?"

Janie gave her a sharp look. "More to the point, will *we* be all right?"

Wes was watching Nicole. "Clay's land's always been susceptible to floods, at least that bottom piece is. It flooded once before when we were kids. But, of course, Mr. Armstrong had his other fields planted then."

"I don't understand."

Wes knelt and, with a piece of kindling, he began to draw a diagram of Clay's land, Nicole's, and the river. Just below the mill, the river took a sharp bend toward Clay's land, causing the land to fall away sharply, creating a flood plain. On Nicole's side, the land was high, but Clay's was bottomland with rich, fertile soil, but it was also the basin that would catch the river's overflow.

Nicole looked up from the drawing. "Then, my land is draining into Clay's, helping the river to rise."

"I guess you could look at it like that, but I hardly think it's your fault if Clay loses his crops."

"Loses! All of them?"

Wes ran a poker through the ash map. "It's his own fault. He knows about the floods. Every year, it was taking a chance to plant there, but the land is especially rich. He's always protected himself by planting more crops on the higher ground. Clay's dad used to consider it luck when he harvested those fields."

Nicole stood. "But this year, the only crops he has are the ones in the bottomland."

Wes stood beside her. "He knew better. He knew what could happen."

"Isn't there something that could be done? Does he have to lose everything?"

Wes put his arm around her shoulders. "You can't control the rain. If you could get it to stop, then he'd be saved, but that's the only thing that would do it."

"I feel so helpless. I wish I could *do* something."

"Wesley," Janie said sharply, "I bet you're hungry. Why don't you have something to eat?"

He grinned at her. "I'd love something to eat. Tell me what's been going on here. You think maybe I could see the twins?"

Janie went to the foot of the stairs. "The Duke of Wesley is here to see their royal highnesses."

Wes looked at Nicole in disbelief. She rolled her eyes, shook her head, and sighed, then held up her hands in helplessness. Wes choked on his laughter. The twins came scampering down the stairs and launched themselves into his arms. He twirled them around, tossing them into the air as they screamed with laughter.

"You ought to get married, Wes," Janie said in a deadly serious voice as she gave a meaningful look at Nicole.

"I will, as soon as you agree to marry me," he laughed. "No! I can't. I remember, I'm already promised to one of Isaac's little sisters."

"It's a good thing," Janie sniffed. "You ask me to marry you, and I will. Now put down those young 'uns and come over here and eat."

Later, as Wes ate and answered the twins' questions, he noticed Nicole's face. He knew what was upsetting her. He reached across the table and squeezed her hand. "Everything will work out, you'll see. Travis and I will see he doesn't lose the plantation."

Nicole's head shot up. "What do you mean lose the plantation? Losing one year's crops shouldn't make him lose the whole place."

Wes and Janie exchanged looks. "Ordinarily, it shouldn't, but then men rarely lose their entire crops. Clay should have planted above the flood level."

"But even if he does lose the crops, surely he has enough cash reserve to survive. I can't believe the plantation could go under in just one year."

Wes pushed his plate away. The rain thundered down on the roof. "You might as well know the truth. Last year, Clay let his crops rot in the field, but because of his hard work in the years before and his father's and brother's work, financially, the place was solid. But Bianca—" He faltered, watching Nicole's eyes. She tried to keep them blank, but he could read them, could see how Bianca's name hurt her.

"Bianca," he continued, "has run up some extraordinary debts. I saw Clay about a month ago, and he said she'd been borrowing money, using the plantation as collateral, in order to send money to her father in England. It seems she's trying to get back what used to be her family's house."

Nicole stood, walked toward the fire, and idly twirled the poker in the ashes. She remembered the park outside Bianca's house, the one that had once been Maleson property. Bianca never ceased to talk about how she would someday get her family home back. "And Clay just let her use his land? That doesn't sound like Clay."

Wes waited a while before he answered. "I'm not sure it is Clay. He's changed, Nicole. He doesn't really care what happens to the place or to himself. He never moves without a glass of whiskey in his hand. When I tried to reason with him, he wouldn't listen. He just ignored me. In a way, that was worse than anything else. Clay's always had a temper, and he'll strike out before he thinks, but now—" He trailed off, not finishing the sentence.

"So Clay lost last year's crops and now this year's. Are you trying to tell me he's bankrupt?"

"No. Travis and I have talked to the creditors, and we're backing Clay. I told Clay he had to keep Bianca from spending any more, though."

She turned to face him. "And did you tell Clay you were going to stand behind his debts?"

"Of course. I didn't want him to worry."

"Men!" Nicole said fiercely, then said some things in French that made Gerard, who listened passively to everything, raise his eyebrows. "How would you like for Clay to tell you he knew you couldn't handle your own land, but not to worry, that he'd take care of you?"

"It wasn't like that! We're friends; we've always been friends."

"Friends *help* each other, they don't destroy each other."

"Nicole!" Wes warned, getting angry. "I've known Clay all my life, and—"

"And now you throw an anchor to a drowning man, that's what!"

Wes stood up, his face growing red, his hands clutching the table.

Janie interceded. "Stop it, you two! You're acting like children. Worse than children, since the twins never act like that."

Wes began to calm down. "I'm sorry. I didn't mean to get angry, but Nicole, you're accusing me of some awful things."

She turned back to the fire, the poker still in her hand. She'd redrawn the bend in the river that Wes had shown her. She stared at it as she spoke. "I didn't mean anything. It's just that Clay's so proud. He loves the plantation, and he'd rather give it up than lose it."

"That doesn't make any sense."

She shrugged. "I guess it doesn't. Maybe I'm having difficulty expressing myself. Wes, isn't there any way we could keep the river from flooding?"

"Pray, maybe. If the rain stopped, the water might recede."

"Why doesn't that land flood every year? Why is it such a sometime thing?"

"The course of the river is changing. Clay's grandfather told us when we were boys that, when he was a boy, there was no bottomland, but each year the river moved a little and left some more lowland."

"Here," she said, stepping back from the map in the ashes. "Show me what you mean."

He knelt over the hearth. "I guess the river's trying to bend itself. This curve used to be straighter, broader, but over the years it's changed."

She studied the map. "What you're saying is that the river is eating away my high ground and creating this low, flat land of Clay's."

Wes looked at her in surprise. "I don't think you have to worry about it. It'll take fifty years for the river to take much of your land."

She ignored his look. "What if we gave the river god what it wanted?"

"What are you talking about?" Wes snapped. He thought she was being selfish because she was worried about the river taking her land.

"Nicole—" Janie said. "I don't like that tone of voice."

Nicole took a piece of kindling. "What if my land were cut away here?" She drew a line from one curve of the river to the other. "What would happen?"

"The land is wet and steep, and it'd probably break away and fall into the river."

"And how would that affect the water level?"

His eyes widened as he began to understand what was going on in her mind. "Nicole, you can't do that.

That would take days of digging, and the land that would fall away is covered with your wheat."

"You didn't answer my question. Would it lower the water level?"

"It would give the river another place to go, to expand—maybe. How can anyone know?"

"I'm asking for an opinion, not an absolute answer."

"Yes, damn it! The river would probably love to swallow your land instead of Clay's. What does the goddamn water care?"

"I would appreciate it if you would watch your language in front of the children," Nicole said primly. "Now, we'll need shovels, and picks for the roots and rocks, and—"

Wes interrupted her. "Have you looked outside? That rain is coming down so hard it could kill, and you're talking about working in it."

"I know of no other way to dig a trench. Perhaps you could bring the ditch indoors for us where it is nice and warm."

"I can't let you do this," Wes said flatly. "Clay can make it without your sacrifice. Travis and I will lend him the money, and next year will be better."

Nicole gave him an icy stare. "Will it? Will next year be better? Look at what we've done to him. We've all abandoned him. He's a man who needs a family. He was happy when he had his parents, James, Beth, and the twins. Then, one by one, they all left him. For a while, I gave him my love, but then I took that away—along with the twins." She lifted her arm and pointed toward the direction of Arundel Hall. "Once that was a happy house, full of people he loved and who loved him. What does he have now? Even his own niece and nephew live with a stranger instead of with him. We've got to show him that we care."

"But Travis and I—"

"Money! You're like a husband who gives his wife

money instead of the attention and love she needs. Clay doesn't need money; he needs to know that someone cares. He's got to feel that he isn't alone in the world."

Wes stood and stared at her, as did Janie and the twins. Gerard lowered his lashes in a lazy way, but they didn't flicker.

"Are you guessing at the way Clay feels?" Wes asked quietly. "Or are you transferring your feelings to him? Is it you who is lonely and wants to feel someone cares?"

Nicole tried to smile. "I don't know. I don't have time to think of it right now. Every minute we waste, the river is rising and getting closer to Clay's tobacco."

Wes suddenly grabbed Nicole and hugged her. "If I ever find a woman who loves me half as much as you love Clay, I'm going to hold on to her and never let her go."

Nicole pushed away from him and wiped a tear from the corner of her eye. "I'd like to have a few secrets, please. And, besides, I have no doubt you'll be as ridiculous as Clay and I have been. Now!" she said sharply. "Let's organize this. You wouldn't happen to have some shovels, would you?"

Janie untied her apron, hung it on a peg by the door, and then grabbed Wes's slicker.

"Where are you going?" Wes asked.

"While the two of you sit there and talk, I'm going to *do* something. First of all, I'm going to borrow some clothes from Isaac. Running around in this rain in wet skirts is not my idea of getting something done. Then I'm going to get Clay."

"Clay!" Nicole and Wes said in unison.

"The two of you may think he's an invalid, but I know better. He can dig as well as anybody, and he's still got a few men left who work for him. I just wish there was time to get Travis here."

Nicole and Wes still sat staring at her.

"Are the two of you going to grow roots? Nicole, come with me to the mill. Wes, you go stake out where the trench'll have to be cut."

Wes grabbed Nicole's arm and propelled her to the door. "Let's go! There's work to be done!"

Chapter 21

JANIE WAS SHOCKED WHEN SHE SAW ARUNDEL HALL. There was a big leak in the porch roof, and the floor was flooded. The door to the house stood half open, and the Oriental runner was soaked along one edge. She stepped inside the house and tried to push the door shut. The constant humidity of the rain had made the door swell until it was impossible to close. She rolled the wet carpet away from the door, then gasped at the warped and ruined floor before the door. The oak would have to be replaced.

Angry, she looked about the wide hallway. The oppressive wetness made the dirt and refuse inside the house stink. She closed her eyes for a moment and apologized to Clay's mother. Then she stalked down the hall toward the library.

She pushed the door open without knocking. She saw at once that it was the only room that hadn't been changed, but neither had it been cleaned. She stood in the doorway for several minutes while her eyes adjusted to the dimness.

"I must have died and gone to heaven," came a low, slurred voice from a corner. "My beautiful Janie wearing men's pants. Do you think you'll set a fashion?"

Janie went to the desk and lit a lamp, then turned it up brightly. She gasped when she saw Clay. His eyes were red, his beard dirty and scraggly. She doubted if he'd washed in weeks.

"Janie, girl, would you hand me that jug from the desk? I've been meaning to get it myself, but I don't seem to have the energy."

Janie stared at him for a moment. "How long has it been since you've eaten?"

"Eaten? There is no food. Didn't you know that my darling wife eats all the food?" He tried to sit up, but it was an effort for him.

Janie went to help him. "You stink!"

"Thank you, my dear, that's the kindest thing anyone's said to me in a long time."

She helped him stand up. He was very unsteady on his feet. "I want you to come with me."

"Of course. I will follow you wherever you wish."

"We're going out into the rain first. Maybe it'll help sober you, or at least wash you. Then we're going to the kitchen."

"Oh, yes," Clay said. "The kitchen. My wife's favorite room. Poor Maggie works harder now than when she cooked for the whole plantation. Did you know they're all gone now?"

Janie supported Clay as they went to the side door. "I know I never saw a worse case of feeling sorry for yourself than yours."

The cold rain hit both of them with a driving, slashing force. Janie ducked her head to keep from being pounded, but Clay didn't seem to notice as it cut at him.

Inside the kitchen, Janie stirred the coals and stoked the fire. She quickly set a pot of coffee on the grate. The room was a shambles, so unlike the sparkling clean place it once was. It had the look of a place that was uncared for, unwanted.

Janie helped Clay to sit down, then went back into the rain to get Maggie. She knew she'd need help sobering Clay.

An hour later, Maggie and Janie had forced an extraordinary amount of black coffee into him, as well as half a dozen scrambled eggs. All the while, Maggie talked.

"It's not a happy place anymore," Maggie said. "That woman pokes her nose into everything. She wants us all to bow down and kiss her fat feet. We all laughed at her before Clay married her." She paused and gave Clay a harsh look. "But after that, there was no pleasin' her. Everybody who could leave did. After she started cutting food rations, even some of the slaves ran away. I think they knew Clay wouldn't go after them. And they were right."

Clay was beginning to sober up. "Janie doesn't want to hear about our problems. People in heaven don't want to know about hell."

"You chose hell!" Maggie started what was obviously a much practiced speech.

Janie put her hand on Maggie's arm to stop her. "Clay," she said quietly, "are you sober enough to listen to me?"

He looked up from the plate of eggs. His brown eyes were sunk deep into his skull. His mouth was a straight line, the corners deeply etched. He looked older than Janie remembered. "What is it you have to say?" he asked flatly.

"Are you aware of what the rain's doing to your crops?"

He frowned, then pushed his plate away. Janie pushed it back toward him. He obeyed her and began to eat again. "I may be drunk, but I'm afraid I haven't been able to block out everything that's happened to me. Maybe I should say, everything that I've caused. I'm well aware of what the rain's doing. Don't you think it's a fitting end? After all my wife," he snarled the word, "has done to get this plantation, it looks like we're both going to lose it."

"And you're willing to allow that?" Janie demanded. "The Clay I've always known would fight for what he wanted. I remember you and James fighting a fire for three days."

"Oh yes, James," Clay said quietly. "I cared then."

"*You* may not care about yourself," Janie said fiercely, "but other people do. Right now, Wesley and Nicole are out in the rain trying to slice off a few acres of Nicole's land to save yours. And all you do is sit here and wallow in your own selfish pride."

"Pride? I haven't had any pride since . . . since one morning in a cave."

"Stop it!" Janie shouted. "Stop thinking of yourself and listen to me. Didn't you hear a word I said? Wes told Nicole that your land would probably be flooded, and she figured out a way to save your crops."

"Save them?" Clay's head came up. "The only way is if the rain stopped, or maybe a dam could be built upriver."

"Or, if the river had someplace else to go besides your land—"

"What are you talking about?"

Maggie sat down beside Clay. "You said Nicole is going to save Clay's crops. How?"

Janie looked from one interested pair of eyes to the next. "You know the sharp bend in the river just below the mill?" She didn't wait for an answer. "Nicole figured out that if she dug a trench through there, the river just might take that course instead of flooding your bottomland where your tobacco is."

Clay leaned back in his chair and stared. He knew exactly what Janie meant. The excess river water needed an outlet, and one place was as good as another. It was a while before he spoke. "She'd lose several acres of her land if the river did take that course," he said at last.

"That's what Wes said." Janie poured all three of them more coffee. "He tried to talk her out of it, but she said—" She paused and looked at Clay. "She said you needed someone to believe in you, that you need to feel someone cares about you."

Clay stood up abruptly and walked to the kitchen window. It was raining so hard that he had only an impression of the outside beyond the window. Nicole, he thought. He'd been drunk for nearly a year just so he couldn't think or feel, yet it hadn't come close to working. There wasn't a minute, drunk or sober, when he hadn't thought of her, what could have been, what would have been if only he'd . . . The more he thought, the more he drank.

Janie was right, he did feel sorry for himself. All his life, he'd felt he was in control, but then his parents had been taken, then Beth and James. He thought he wanted Bianca, but Nicole had confused him. When he realized how much he loved her, it was too late. By then, he'd already hurt her so much that she'd never trust him again.

The rain whipped against the glass. Somewhere, out in that cold deluge, she worked for him. She sacrificed her land, her crops, the security of all the people who depended on her, for him. What had Janie said? To show him that someone cares.

He turned to Janie. "I have about six men left on the plantation. I'll get them and some shovels." He started toward the door. "They're going to need food. Empty the larders."

"Yes, sir!" Maggie grinned.

The two women stared at the door after Clay shut it behind him.

"That sweet little lady still loves him, doesn't she?" Maggie asked.

"She's never stopped for a minute, although I've sure tried to get her to stop. In my opinion, no man's good enough for her."

"What about that Frenchman who lives with her?" Maggie said hostilely.

"Maggie, you don't know what you're talking about."

"I got a few hours to listen," she said, and began to throw food into burlap bags. They'd return to the mill to cook. It was better to get the raw food wet than to try to transport it when it was hot.

Janie smiled. "Let's get busy. I have a year's worth of gossip to tell you."

The rain was coming down so hard, Clay could hardly see to get his men across the river. The water lapped over the edges of the shallow rowboats and threatened to swallow the men along with the land. Already the river had risen enough that it had eaten several rows of Clay's tobacco.

Once ashore, the men put their shovels over their shoulders and trudged up the hill, their heads down, letting the brims of their hats protect them somewhat from the rain. Once they arrived at the site where the others were digging, they lost no time in going to work. The Clayton who'd come to give them their orders was not a man they wanted to disobey.

Clay sank the shovel into the soggy earth. Now was not the time to let himself think he was helping Nicole in her sacrifice. Suddenly, it seemed important to him to save his crops. He wanted to harvest that tobacco as much as he'd ever wanted anything in his life.

He dug with more energy than he'd ever experienced before. He acted like a demon possessed. He concentrated so hard on moving shovelfuls of earth that he didn't at first feel the hand on his arm. When he came back to the present, he turned to look into Nicole's eyes.

It was a jolt seeing her again. In spite of the hard, driving rain, they might have been alone. They both wore broad-brimmed hats, the water running down across their faces.

"Here!" she yelled over the fury of the rain. "Coffee." She held up a mug, her hand covering the open top.

He took it and drained it without a word.

She took the empty mug and walked away from him.

He stood quietly for a moment and watched her trying to walk in the sucking mud. She seemed especially small in the man's clothing, the big boots. All around him, trampled in the mud, were stalks of nearly ripe wheat—her wheat.

He looked around him for the first time. There were fifteen men digging at the trench. He recognized Isaac and Wes at one end. To his left lay the land they were trying to cut away. The wheat bent under the pelting rain, but the hill's slope assured good drainage. Not far away was a low stone wall. Clay had watched Isaac and Nicole build those walls. Every time she'd lifted a stone, he'd drunk a little bit more. Now, all that labor was being pushed into the river, discarded as if it meant nothing. And all for him.

He stabbed the shovel into the earth again and began to dig harder.

What little light there was began to fade a few hours later. Nicole came to him once again and pantomimed that he was to stop and eat. Clay shook his head and kept digging.

Night came, and the men still dug. There was no way to have lanterns, so they dug half by instinct and half by their increased night vision. Wesley tried to keep the diggers inside the lines he'd set.

Toward morning, Wes came to Clay and motioned for him to follow. The diggers were very tired, their bodies cold and aching. The shoveling was bad enough, but combined with the viciousness of the rain, it pushed them past exhaustion.

Clay followed Wes to the end point where the trench was being cut. They were very close to being through. In another hour or so, they'd know if their labor had accomplished anything. It flashed through Clay's mind that the river did not have to take Nicole's sacrifice. It could stay where it was and ignore the canal.

Wes looked in question to Clay, asking his opinion on the formation of the mouth of the trench. The rain was too loud and hard for them to speak over it. Clay pointed at a cutaway in the bend of the river, and the two friends began to dig there, together.

The sky began to lighten with the dawn. The men could see what they had done and where they must go. Only six feet were needed to complete the deep ditch.

Wes and Clay exchanged looks over Nicole's head. She dug beside the men, never looking up. The men had the same thought. In minutes, they'd know if they would succeed or not.

Suddenly, the river answered their question. It was too greedy to wait for the removal of the six feet. The water rushed into the trench from both sides at once. The wet, soft ground fell away as if it were made of pastry dough. The diggers barely had time to jump back before they were swept away. Clay grabbed Nicole about the waist and swung her to the safe, higher ground.

All the diggers stood back and watched the river consume the wheat-planted earth. The land fell in thick, dark, rich sheets, falling into the water, then disappearing forever. The turbulent water rushed across the land like volcanic lava.

"Look!" Wes yelled above the noise.

Everyone looked across the river to where he pointed. They'd been so fascinated by the sight of the earth falling that they hadn't noticed Clay's fields. As the river moved to fill the gap left by Nicole's land, which it now carried downstream, the level lowered considerably. The last rows of tobacco that had once been buried now were seen again, flattened and ruined, but the rows above them were safe.

"Hooray!" Nicole shouted, the first to do so.

Suddenly, the tiredness left everyone. They'd worked all night to accomplish one thing and they'd done it. Jubilation replaced their weariness. They began waving their shovels about in the air. Isaac grabbed Luke's hand and they did a little impromptu jig in the mud.

"We did it!" Wes shouted over the steady rain. He grabbed Nicole and tossed her in the air. Then, he turned her and threw her to Clay as if she were a sack of grain.

Clay was grinning broadly. *"You* did it," he laughed as he caught Nicole in his arms. "You did it! My beautiful, brilliant wife!" He crushed her to him and kissed her, a deep, hungry kiss.

For a moment, Nicole forgot the time, the place, all that had happened. She kissed Clay with all the passion she felt. She felt like a starving woman, and he was the only food for her.

"Time enough for that later," Wes said as he slapped Clay on the shoulder. His eyes carried a warning. The men watched them in curiosity.

Nicole stared up at Clay, and she knew that tears mingled with the rain on her face.

Reluctantly, he set her down. He moved away from her quickly, as if she were fire and he would be burned, but his eyes held hers in fascination and question.

"Let's eat," Wes shouted. "I hope the women made enough food, because I could eat at least a wagon-load."

Nicole turned away from Clay. Her body felt more alive than it had in months. "Maggie's here, so you know there's bound to be more than enough."

Wes grinned, then put his arm around her shoulders, and they started toward the mill.

There was a table set up on sawhorses, and there was enough food for a hundred hungry people. There was bread, fresh from the oven, still hot and fragrant. Crocks of cool butter awaited them. There was terrapin ragout, poached sturgeon, oysters, crab, ham, turkey, beef, and duck. There were eight kinds of pie, twelve vegetables, four cakes, three wines, three kinds of beer, as well as milk and tea.

Nicole stayed away from Clay. She took her heaping plate and sat by herself in a shadow of the grinding stones. He'd called her his wife, and for a moment she felt as if she was. It seemed so long ago that she'd been his wife, yet for some reason she knew she never was his wife, really. Only those brief days at the Backes's house had she felt she belonged.

"Tired?"

She looked up at Clay. He'd removed his wet shirt, and a towel was hanging around his neck. He looked vulnerable and lonely. Nicole ached to take him in her arms, to soothe him.

"Do you mind if I sit with you?"

She shook her head silently. They were partially hidden from the others, private.

"You aren't eating much," he said quietly, nodding toward her full plate. "Maybe you need some exercise to work up an appetite." His eyes twinkled.

She tried to smile, but his nearness made her nervous.

He took a piece of ham from her plate and ate it. "Maggie and Janie outdid themselves."

"They had your food to work with. It was kind of you to be so generous."

His eyes darkened as he stared at her. "Are we really such strangers that we can't talk? I don't deserve what you've done for me today. No!" he said when she started to interrupt. "Let me finish. Janie said I've been wallowing in self-pity. I guess I have been. I think I've been feeling that I didn't deserve what had happened to me. Tonight, I've had a lot of time to think. I believe

I've come to realize that life is what you make it. You said once that I couldn't make up my mind. You were right. I wanted everything and thought it would be given to me if I asked for it. I think I was too weak to take any kind of hardship."

She put her hand on his arm. "You aren't a weak man."

"I don't think you know me, any more than I know myself. I've done some terrible things to you, yet this—" He couldn't finish. His voice was weak. "You've given me back hope, something I haven't seen for a long time."

He put his hand over hers. "I promise I'm not going to let you down again. I don't just mean the tobacco, but in my life, too."

He looked down at her hand, caressed her fingers with his. "I didn't think it was possible, but I love you more than I ever did."

There was a lump in her throat, and she couldn't speak.

He looked into her eyes. "There are no words to say what I feel for you or to thank you enough for what you've done." He stopped abruptly, as if he were choking. "Goodbye," he whispered.

He was gone before she could speak.

Clay walked quickly out of the mill, leaving his shirt behind, ignoring the people who called out to him. Once outside, he was hardly aware that the rain had slowed to a drizzle. In the early morning light, he could see how the land had changed. Where once Nicole's fields had sloped away to the river, they now fell down drastically. The river itself was calmer, like a great animal that had fed well and was now digesting its feast.

The wharf was intact, and Clay rowed himself across the much wider river to his own wharf. He walked slowly to the house. It was as if he were awakening after a year's sleep. He felt James beside him, appalled at what Clay'd done to the lovely, productive plantation.

He also saw the neglect of his house. He stepped across the puddle in the hardwood floor.

Bianca stood at the foot of the stairs. She wore a voluminous, high-waisted wrapper of pale blue silk. Under it was a pink satin gown. The collar, cuffs, and down the front and hem of the wrapper were covered with a very wide border of spiky, multicolored feathers.

"So! There you are! You've been out all night again."

"Did you miss me?" Clay asked sarcastically.

She gave him a look that answered his question. "Where is everyone, and why isn't breakfast on the table?"

"I thought perhaps your concern was for me, but instead it's for Maggie's handiwork."

"I want an answer! Where is breakfast?"

"Breakfast is now being served across the river at Nicole's mill."

"Her! That slut! So that's where you've been. I should have known you couldn't live without your disgusting, primitive needs. What did she use this time to entice you? Did she tell you something about me?"

Clay looked away in disgust and started up the stairs. "Your name was never brought up, thank God."

"At least she's learned that," Bianca said smugly. "She's smart enough to know that I see through her, see what she's really like. The rest of you are too blind to see what a greedy, conniving liar she is."

Clay turned on Bianca with a snarl. He leaped four steps at once to stand before her. He grabbed her by the neck of her gown and slammed her hard against the wall. "You piece of filth! You have no right even to speak her name. You've never done a fair or decent thing in your life for anyone, and you accuse her of being just like you. Last night, Nicole sacrificed several acres of her land to save mine. That's where I've been all night, digging right beside her and other people who know what kindness and generosity are."

He pushed Bianca against the wall again. "You've used me all you're going to. From now on, I'm going to run this place, not you."

Bianca had to work hard to breathe. His hands were cutting off her circulation. Her fat cheeks bulged with the pressure. "You can't go to her. I'm your wife," she gasped. "This place is mine."

"Wife!" he sneered. "For the things I've done, I think I almost deserve you." He released her and stepped back. "Look at yourself! You don't like yourself any more than anyone else likes you." He turned away and went up the stairs to his room, where he fell on the bed and was asleep instantly.

Bianca stood as still as a piece of marble after Clayton left. What did he mean, she didn't like herself? She came from an old and important English family. How could she not be proud of herself?

Her stomach rumbled, and she put her hand to it. Slowly, she left the house and went to the kitchen. She knew nothing about cooking, and the barrels of flour and other raw ingredients were confusing to her. She was hungry, very hungry, and she could find nothing to eat. Tears blurred her eyes as she left the kitchen and walked toward the garden.

At the end of the garden was a little pavilion, privately hidden under two enormous old magnolia trees. She sat down heavily on a cushion; then, when she realized it was soaking wet, she started to rise. But what was the use? Her beautiful gown was already ruined. The tears ran down her face as she plucked at the feathers on her gown.

"May I disturb you?" came a quiet, accented voice.

Bianca's head shot up. "Gerard!" she gasped as more tears came to her eyes.

"You've been crying," he said sympathetically. He started to sit beside her, then saw the cushions were wet. He tossed one over the railing, then used a handkerchief, not Adele's silk one, to wipe most of the water from the wooden seat. He sat down. "Please tell me what is wrong. You look as if you could use a friend."

Bianca buried her face in her hands. "A friend! I have no friends! Everyone in this horrible country hates me. This morning, he said that I didn't even like myself."

Gerard bent forward and touched Bianca's hair. It wasn't quite clean. "Don't you realize that he'd say anything to hurt you? He only wants Nicole. He'll do anything or say anything to get her. He wants to drive you away so he can have her."

Bianca looked at him, her little eyes red over her swollen cheeks. "He can't have her. He's married to me."

Gerard smiled as if she were a child. "How very innocent you are. You're so sweet and vulnerable, so unsophisticated. Did he tell you where he was last night?"

She waved her hand. "He said something about a flood and Nicole saving his land."

"Of course, she'd save his land. She plans for it to be hers someday. She made it seem that she was making a grand sacrifice, but actually she was creating more bottomland for the Armstrong plantation. And someday she plans for it to be hers again."

"But how? There were witnesses to my marriage to Clay. It can't be annulled."

Gerard patted her hand. "You are a true lady. You

can't even imagine the treachery of those two. You played some tricks on them, but they were only tricks, nothing that really hurt anyone. Even the kidnapping wasn't meant to hurt. But their plans aren't so innocent —or fair."

"What . . . do you mean? Divorce?"

Gerard was silent for a moment. "I only wish it were divorce. I think they're planning . . . murder."

Bianca gaped at him for a moment. At first, she had no idea whose murder he meant. The idea of Nicole falling off a cliff appealed to her. If Nicole were gone, her life would be a lot better. But she was puzzled about why Clay would contemplate murdering Nicole.

Very slowly did she become aware of what Gerard meant. "Me?" she whispered. "They want to kill me?"

Gerard held her hand tightly. "I'm afraid I am as naive as you are. It took me a long time to understand what was going on. I couldn't understand why Nicole would voluntarily dig away part of her land unless she had a motive that no one else saw. It finally came to me this morning. Those barbarians made so much noise in the mill that I couldn't sleep. I realized that if Nicole once again became mistress of the plantation, then the new land created by the changing of the river's course would be to her advantage."

"But . . . murder!" Bianca gasped. "Surely, you must be wrong."

"Has Armstrong ever tried to hurt you? Ever struck you?"

"This morning. He pushed me against a wall. I could hardly breathe."

"That's what I mean. He's a violent man. He's starting to lose control over himself. Someday soon, you'll find a tiny cord stretched across the stairs, and when you start down them, you'll fall."

"No!" Bianca gasped, her hand to her throat.

"Of course, Armstrong will be quite some distance from the house when it happens. Later, all he has to do is remove the string. Then, he can play the bereaved husband, while you, my dear, will lie cold in a coffin."

Bianca's eyes were wild, frightened. "I can't let that happen. I must prevent it."

"Yes, you must be very careful. For my sake as well as your own."

She sniffed. "For your sake?"

Gerard lifted her hand, held it between both of his. "You are going to think me a cad, a man too bold. No, I cannot tell you."

"Please," she begged. "You said we were friends. You can tell me what's on your mind."

He looked at the floor but saw it was too wet to kneel upon. His silk stockings would be ruined.

"I love you," he said desperately. "How can I expect you to believe me? We've only met once before, but since then I've thought of little else. You haunt me always. My every thought has contained you. Please, don't laugh at me."

Bianca stared at him in astonishment. Never had a man declared undying love for her. Clay, in England, had asked her to marry him, but he'd been reserved, removed, as if he were thinking of something else while he proposed. The way Gerard looked at her made her breath quicken. He really did love her, she could see that. Several times since that first meeting, she had thought of him, but only as someone gentle and understanding. Now she looked at him in a new light. She could love this man. Yes, she could love someone with such fine manners.

"I couldn't laugh at you," she said.

He smiled. "Then, could I hope that you could ever return even a small amount of my affection? I wouldn't ask for much, just that I could see you once in a while."

"Of course," Bianca said, still bewildered by his declarations.

He stood and straightened his cravat. "I must go now. I want you to promise me you will be very careful. If anything were to happen to you, even if one hair on your lovely head were damaged, my heart would break." He smiled at her, then saw something on the rail of the pavilion. "I nearly forgot. Would you accept this small token of my affection?" He handed her a five-pound box of French chocolates. The candy had been given to him by a farmer's daughter who'd bought one of Nicole's dresses.

Bianca nearly snatched the box from his hands. "I have not eaten," she muttered. "He would not let me eat this morning." She threw the ribbon on the floor, then pulled the lid off. She ate five pieces before Gerard could take a breath.

Bianca stopped, her mouth full, a drop of wet chocolate at the corner of her lips. "What will you think of me?"

"What could I think but to love you?" Gerard said when he'd recovered from his astonishment at the way she'd attacked the box of candy. "I don't believe you realize that I love you as you are. I do not demand or want changes. You are a woman, a full, beautiful woman. I want no thin, shapeless girl. I love you the way you are."

Bianca looked up at him with just the expression she'd had when she looked at the chocolates.

Gerard smiled. "Could we meet again? Perhaps three days from now, at noon. I will bring a picnic lunch."

"Oh, yes," she breathed. "I would love that."

He bent from the waist, took her hand, and kissed it. He noticed that her eyes kept straying to the chocolates. After he left her alone, he stood for a moment in the shadow of a tree and watched her devour the full five pounds of candy in a matter of minutes. He smiled to himself and went back to the mill.

Three days later, Gerard sat across from Bianca in a secluded area of the Armstrong plantation. Between them were the remains of a feast. It had taken Janie all morning to prepare such a meal. Gerard frowned as he remembered the way Janie had refused at first to obey his commands and pack the picnic. Nicole's interference had made her obey. He didn't like a woman overstepping his rule.

"He's trying to starve me," Bianca said, her mouth full of caramel cream and almond cookies. "This morning for breakfast, I was only allowed two poached eggs and three biscuits. And he canceled my orders for some new dresses. I don't know what he expects me to wear. These stupid Americans can't even sew properly. The dresses constantly tear at the seams."

Gerard watched with interest the massive quantity of food that Bianca was devouring so rapidly. He'd requested enough food for six people, yet now he wasn't sure if it was enough. "Tell me," he said quietly, "have you been careful lately? Have you watched for danger?"

His statement was enough to make Bianca put down her fork. She buried her face in her hands. "He hates me. Everywhere, I see signs of his hatred. Ever since the rains, he's changed. He won't let me eat. He's hired women to clean the house, yet when I give them orders, they won't listen to me. It's almost as if I weren't the mistress of the plantation."

Gerard unwrapped a tiny chocolate-coated cheesecake. He touched her arm and held it out to her. Her eyes were brilliant, shining through her tears as she grabbed the little cake. "If you and I owned the plantation, everything would be different."

"We? How could we own it?" She'd already eaten

the cake and watched as Gerard unwrapped another one.

"If Armstrong were dead, you would inherit the place."

"He is as disgustingly healthy as one of his mules. I thought maybe he'd drink himself to death, but he hasn't touched anything since the rains."

"How many people know that? It's common knowledge that he's been drinking heavily for a year or more. What if he had an . . . accident while he was drunk?"

Bianca leaned back and stared at the remaining food. There wasn't much left, and she hated to leave it, but she honestly could hold no more. "I told you, he doesn't drink anymore," she said absently.

Gerard gritted his teeth at her denseness. "Don't you think we could arrange one last time?"

Slowly, Bianca lifted her head and looked at him. "What do you mean?"

"Clayton Armstrong is an evil man. He brought you here under false pretenses. Then, when he got you to this horrible country, he used you, mistreated you."

"Yes," Bianca whispered. "Yes."

"There isn't any justice in the world that allows something like that to continue. You are his wife, yet he treats you like dirt. For God's sake, he won't even allow you to eat!"

Bianca caressed her enormous stomach. "You're right, but what can I do?"

"Get rid of him." He smiled at Bianca's gasp. "Yes, you know what I mean." He leaned over the dirty dishes and took her hand. "You have every right. You're so sweet that you don't even realize that it's your life or his. Do you think a man like Clayton Armstrong would stop at murder?"

She looked at him in fright.

"What else can he do? He wants Nicole, and yet he's married to you. Has he asked you for a divorce?"

She shook her head.

"He will. And will you give it to him?"

Again, she shook her head.

"Then he'll find other ways to rid himself of an unwanted wife."

"No," Bianca whispered. "I don't believe you." She tried to get up, but her size and all the food she'd eaten made her immobile.

Gerard rose and put out his hands to her, his legs braced against her weight. "Think about it," he said when she faced him. "It's a matter of survival. It's him or you."

She turned away from him. "I must go." Her mind was whirling with the awful thoughts Gerard had placed there. She walked very slowly back to the house. Before she entered, she checked the doorways to make sure no one was hiding behind them. As she laboriously climbed the stairs, she knelt to feel for wires that were meant to trip her.

It was a week later when Clay first mentioned divorce to her. She was very weak and tired from lack of food and rest. She hadn't had a full meal since the picnic with Gerard. Clay had given orders that Bianca was to be placed on a strict diet. She hadn't had much rest either, because she kept having dreams that Clay was standing over her with a knife, screaming that it was either him or her.

When he did speak of divorce, it was like a nightmare coming to life. She sat in the morning room. Clay had it restored to the way it was before Bianca had redecorated it. It was as if he were already trying to remove all traces of her.

"What do we have to offer each other?" Clay was saying. "I'm sure you care as little for me as I do for you."

Bianca stubbornly shook her head. "You just want *her*. You want to push me out into the cold so you can have her. The two of you planned this all along."

"That is the most absurd thing I've ever heard." Clay tried to control his temper. "You were the one who forced me to marry you." He narrowed his eyes at her. "You were the one who lied about having my child."

Bianca gasped and put her hand to the folds of flesh that covered her throat.

Clay turned away and walked toward the window. He'd learned about Oliver Hawthorne only recently. The man lost most of his meager crops in the rain, and two of his sons had died from typhoid. He came to blackmail Clay for money. After Clay told him Bianca had miscarried, he threw the man off the plantation.

"You hate me," Bianca whispered.

"No," Clay said quietly. "Not anymore. All I want is for us to be free of each other. I'll send you money. I'll see that you're comfortable."

"How can you do that? You think I'm stupid, but I know that nearly everything you make goes back into this place. It looks like you're rich because you own so much, but you're not. How can you support the plantation and send me money?"

He whirled on her, his eyes black with anger. "No, you're not stupid, just unbelievably selfish. Don't you realize how much I want to get rid of you? Can't you see the way you disgust me? I'd be willing to sell the plantation just so I'd no longer have to look at that fat thing you call a face." He opened his mouth to say more. Then he stopped and walked quickly out of the room.

Bianca sat on the sofa, unmoving, for a long time. She wouldn't allow herself to think of what Clay had said to her. Instead, she was thinking of Gerard. How nice it would be to live in Arundel Hall with him. She'd be the lady of the manor, planning menus, supervising meals, while he did whatever men do outside. In the evening, he'd come home, and they'd share a lovely meal. Then, he'd kiss her hand goodnight.

She looked about the room and remembered how she'd once had it. Now it was so bare and plain. Gerard wouldn't keep her from redecorating. No, Gerard loved her. As she was.

She rose slowly from the couch. She knew she must see him, see the man she loved. There were no choices open to her now. Gerard had been right. Clay meant to get rid of her in any way he could.

Chapter 22

"WHAT ARE YOU DOING HERE?" GERARD DEMANDED AS
he helped Bianca from the rowboat on Nicole's side of
the river. He looked around anxiously.

"I had to see you."

"Couldn't you have sent a message? I would have
come to you."

Bianca's eyes filled with tears. "Please don't be angry
with me. I couldn't bear any more anger."

Gerard considered her for a moment. "Come with
me. We must keep out of sight of the house."

She nodded and followed him. It was difficult walking. She had to stop twice to catch her breath.

When they were on top of a rise overlooking the
house, Gerard let her stop. "Now, tell me what's
happened." He listened carefully to Bianca's long,
emotional outburst. "So he knows the child you carried
wasn't his."

"Is that bad?"

Gerard gave her a look of disgust. "The courts frown
on adultery."

"Courts? What courts?"

"The courts that will grant him a divorce and will
take everything away from you."

Bianca slid with her back to a tree until she sat down.
"I've worked so hard for everything. He can't take it
away from me. He can't!"

Gerard knelt before her. "Do you really mean that?
There are ways to prevent him from stealing from
you."

She stared at him. "You mean murder?"

"Isn't he trying to kill you? How would you like to return to England a divorced woman? Everyone would say you couldn't hold a man. What would your father say?"

Bianca thought of all the times her father had laughed at her. He had said Clay wouldn't want her after he'd gotten a taste of Nicole. He'd never let her forget it if she returned in disgrace. "How?" she whispered. "When?"

Gerard sat back on his heels. There was an odd light in his eyes. "Soon. It must be very soon. We mustn't let him talk to anyone about his plans."

Suddenly, a movement caught Bianca's eyes. "Nicole!" she gasped, then put her hand over her mouth.

Gerard turned instantly. Adele stood behind him, half hidden by the trees. It had taken Nicole a long time to persuade her mother that it was safe to walk in the woods behind the house. This was only her third time out alone.

He took one long stride and grabbed his wife's arm. "What did you hear?" he said, as his hand cut into her flesh.

"Murder," she said, her eyes almost whirling in fear.

Gerard struck her hard across the cheek. "Yes! Murder! Yours! Do you understand me? You say one word about this, and I'll take Nicole and the twins to the guillotine. Would you like to see their heads roll into the basket?"

Adele's expression went past terror to something that only someone who's known great horror could comprehend.

He ran his finger across her throat. "Remember," he whispered, then pushed her away.

She fell to her knees, quickly picked herself up, and scampered back toward the house.

Gerard adjusted his cravat, then turned to Bianca.

She was standing with her back to the tree, her eyes frightened. "What in the world is wrong with you?" he snapped.

"I've never seen you like that," she whispered.

"What you mean is you've never seen a man protect the woman he loves." He continued when he saw her frown. "I had to ensure that she wouldn't tell what she'd heard."

"She will. Of course she will."

"No! Not after what I said. She's insane, didn't you know?"

"Who is she? She looks like Nicole."

He hesitated. "Her mother." He went on before she could ask more questions, "Meet me tomorrow at one o'clock where we had the picnic. We'll make plans there."

"You'll bring lunch?" she asked eagerly.

"Of course. Now you must go before someone sees you. I don't want us seen together . . . Yet," he added. He took her hand and directed her to the wharf.

When Nicole returned from the mill, Janie greeted her at the door with a solemn face. "Your mother's having a bad one. Nobody can calm her down."

A horrible scream threatened to shake the roof from the little house, and Nicole ran up the stairs.

"Mother!" Nicole said, and tried to put her arms around her mother. Adele's lovely face was distorted so badly it was almost unrecognizable.

"The babies!" Adele shrieked, flailing her arms about wildly. "The babies! Their heads! They'll murder them, kill them. Blood everywhere!"

"Mother, please. You are safe!" Nicole was speaking in French, as was Adele.

Janie stood at the head of the stairs. "She seemed to be upset about the twins. Is that what she's saying?"

Nicole struggled with her mother's arms. "I think so.

360

She's talking about the babies. Maybe she means one of my cousins."

"I don't think so. She came tearing into the house a few minutes ago and tried to hide the twins in the little closet under the stairs."

"I hope the children aren't upset."

Janie shrugged. "They're used to her. They crouched in the closet, then got out when I got her upstairs."

"He'll kill them!" Adele screamed. "I didn't know him. I never knew him. The fat lady will kill them, too."

"What's she saying now?" Janie asked.

"Just nonsense. Could you get some laudanum? I think the only way she'll calm down is if she sleeps."

When Janie was gone, Nicole continued to try to soothe her mother, but Adele was wild, frantic. She kept talking of murder and the guillotine and a fat woman. When Adele mentioned Clayton, she gained Nicole's full attention.

"What about Clay?" Nicole asked.

Adele's eyes were wild, her hair flying. "Clay! They will kill him, too. And my babies, all my babies. Everyone's babies. They killed the queen. They'll kill Clay."

"Who will kill Clay?"

"Them. The baby-killers!"

Janie stood at Nicole's shoulder. "She looks like she's trying to tell you something. It almost sounded as if she said Clay's name."

Nicole took the cup of tea from Janie. "Drink this, Mother. It will make you feel much better."

It didn't take long for the laudanum to take effect. Downstairs, Gerard was just entering the house.

"Gerard," Nicole said. "Did something happen today to upset Mother?"

He turned toward her slowly. "I haven't seen her. Is she having one of her fits again?"

"As if you'd care!" Janie said, passing Nicole on the stairs and going to the fireplace. "Considering that she's your wife, you'd think you'd have some feeling for her."

"I would certainly never share my feelings with such as you," Gerard retorted.

"Stop it, both of you!" Nicole commanded. "Neither of you is helping my mother."

Gerard waved his hand. "It's just one of her fits. You should be used to them by now."

Nicole moved to the table. "Somehow, this one was different. It was almost as if she were trying to tell me something."

Gerard looked at her from under lowered lashes. "What could she say that she hasn't said a hundred times? All she ever talks about is murder and death."

"True," Nicole said thoughtfully. "Only this time she mentioned Clay."

"Clay!" Janie said. "She's never met Clay before, has she?"

"Not to my knowledge. And she kept talking about a fat woman."

"There's no guessing who that is," Janie snorted.

"Of course," Gerard inserted with uncharacteristic enthusiasm. "She must have seen Clay and Bianca together, and since they are strangers, she was frightened. You know how strangers terrify her."

"I'm sure you're right," Nicole said. "But somehow it seemed more than that. She kept saying someone was trying to kill Clay."

"She's always saying someone is trying to murder someone else," Gerard said angrily.

"Maybe, but she's never confused the past and the present quite like this before."

Before Gerard could say a word, Janie stepped forward. "There's no use worrying about it now. In the morning, you can try to talk to your mother. Maybe after a good night's sleep, she'll be able to explain herself more clearly. Now, sit down and eat your supper."

The little house was dark and silent. Outside, the river flowed slowly, gently, now that it had come closer to straightening its course. It was especially warm for September, and the four people in the attic bedroom slept without covers.

Adele was restless. Even under the heavy dose of the sleeping drug, she still tossed and turned, her dreams puzzled and confused. She knew she had something to tell, but she had no idea how to go about it. The king and queen of France seemed to mingle with a farmer named Clayton, a man whose face she could not see. But she could see death, his death, everyone's death.

Gerard stubbed out the thin cigar he'd been smoking and silently stepped out of the bed. He stood and looked down at his wife. It had been many months since he'd taken her in his arms. In France, he'd felt honored to be married to one of the Courtalains, even one as old as Adele. But when he'd seen Nicole, his feeling for his wife had died. Nicole was a younger, more beautiful version of her mother.

Quietly, without so much as a creak of a floorboard, he went to Adele's side, then sat on the edge of the bed. He leaned across her for his pillow.

She opened her eyes for just a moment before the pillow came down over her face. She started to fight but then knew it was no use. This was what she'd waited for. All those years spent in prison, she'd waited each second for death. Finally, it was coming, and she was ready for it.

Gerard removed the pillow from Adele's face. In death, she was quite pretty, younger than he'd ever seen her look before. He stood, then walked across the room to the blanket partition that concealed Janie and Nicole's room.

He stared for a long time at Nicole, her body barely hidden under her thin nightgown. His hand ached to caress the curve of her hip.

"Soon," he whispered. "Soon."

He returned to his bed, stretched out beside the woman he'd just murdered, and slept. His only thought was that her tossings would no longer disturb him.

When Nicole discovered her mother's lifeless form the next morning, the house was empty. The twins and Janie had gone to pick apples, and Gerard, as usual, was off by himself.

She sat quietly on the edge of the bed, held her mother's cold hand in her own, and caressed the cheek so like her own. She turned and very slowly left the house.

She walked up to the ridge overlooking the mill and the house. She suddenly felt so alone, so isolated. For years, she'd thought her family was dead. Then the reappearance of her mother had given her some solidarity again. All she had left now was Clay.

She looked across the river to Arundel Hall, so perfect in the early morning sun. But she didn't have Clay, she thought. She must realize he was gone, as surely as her mother was now gone.

She sat down on the ground, her knees drawn up, and buried her face. She would never stop loving him or needing him. Now all she wanted was the comfort of his arms holding her, telling her that life would still go on after her mother's death. Even Adele's last words had been of Clay.

Her head shot up. A fat woman was going to kill Clay. Of course! Adele had somehow overheard Bianca planning Clay's death.

Nicole's mind whirled with possible explanations. Bianca could have met someone she had hired on the mill side of the river. If Clay were dead, Bianca would own the plantation.

Nicole stood and ran to the wharf. She rowed herself across the river in record time. Once on land again, she lifted her skirts and ran to the house.

"Clay!" she called as she ran from room to room. Even as she ran, even in her urgency, she was aware of the house. It seemed to welcome her with open arms. Beth's portrait had been replaced over the mantel in the dining room. She gave a quick look and thought she saw a look of concern in Beth's eye.

She went to the library last. The feel of Clayton's presence was overpowering. The desk was cluttered but clean, a place of constant work.

She knew exactly when he came to stand behind her, but she didn't turn. The strong smell of his sweat mingled with the leather in the room. She breathed deeply, then slowly turned to face him.

She had seen very little of him in the past year, only once for any length of time. The humble, quiet Clay who'd come to help them dig the trench was a stranger to her. But this man before her now was the man she'd fallen in love with. His linen shirt was open to the waist, and he was drenched in sweat, his hands and forearms tobacco-stained. The way he stood, feet wide apart, hands on hips, reminded her of the first time she'd seen him, through a spyglass.

"You've been crying," he said flatly.

His voice sent shivers up her spine, and she had no idea why she was there. She turned away from him, took one step toward the door.

"No!" It was a command she obeyed. "Look at me," he said quietly.

She turned slowly.

"What has happened?" His voice was full of concern.

Sharp tears mounted behind Nicole's eyes. "My mother . . . died. I must go home."

His eyes held hers for a long moment. "Don't you know that you *are* home?"

The tears were threatening to spill. She had no idea he still had so much control over her. She shook her head, her lips silently forming a no.

"Come here." His voice was quiet, but it was the sound of command.

Nicole refused to obey him. Somewhere, there was a seed of reason in her brain, and she knew she should not renew what had once been between them. But her feet were not so sensible. One of them picked itself up and took a step forward.

Clay merely stared at her, the current between their eyes nearly tangible. "Come," he said once again.

The tears broke, and her feet leaped toward him. He caught her in his arms, nearly crushing her. He carried her to the couch, where he cradled her in his arms.

"If you're going to cry, you should do it where you belong, on your man's shoulder."

He held her and caressed her hair while she cried, pouring out her grief at her mother's death. After a while, he began to ask questions. He wanted her to talk about her mother, about the good times. She told of Adele's relationship with the twins, how they were like three children together.

Suddenly, she sat upright and told him what had brought her to Arundel Hall.

"You came to warn me that you thought someone would try to kill me?"

"Not someone," she said. "Bianca. I think Mother meant to tell me that Bianca planned to kill you."

He thought for a moment. "What if she'd heard Isaac or one of the other men talking about Bianca? One of my men told me the other day that if he had a wife like mine, he'd probably kill her."

"That's awful," Nicole gasped.

Clay shrugged. "Adele could have heard a similar statement. It would probably have come out in the same gibberish."

"But, Clay—"

He put a finger to her lips and stopped her. "I am pleased that you still care enough to warn me, but Bianca is not a murderess. She has neither the brains nor the courage." His eyes went to her mouth, where he ran his fingertip along her upper lip. "I've missed your funny upside-down mouth."

She drew back from him, not easy to do considering she was sitting on his lap. "Nothing's changed."

He smiled at her. "True. Nothing's changed between us since I nearly raped you in the ship's cabin. We've loved each other since our first meeting, and it will never change."

"No, please," she begged. "It's over. Bianca—"

He raised one eyebrow. "I don't want to hear her name again. I've had a lot of time to think since the flood. I realized then that you still loved me. It wasn't Bianca who caused the problems between us; it was our own stubbornness. You knew I was afraid to lose the plantation, and I wasn't strong enough alone, and you didn't believe in me enough."

"Clay—" she began. She knew in her heart how right he was, but she didn't like to hear it.

"It's all right, love. We're going to start again. But this time, we're staying together. This time, no one will be able to part us."

She stared at him. They'd been through so much, and yet their love had lasted. She knew they would make it.

She leaned back on his shoulder, and his arms held her close. "It seems like I haven't been away."

He kissed the top of her head. "You have to get off my lap, or I'm going to throw you down on this couch and have my way with you."

She wanted to laugh and tease with him, but the pain from her mother's death was inside her too thoroughly.

"Come with me, sweet," he said quietly. "Let's go back to the mill and see to your mother. We have time later to make plans." He lifted her chin in his hand. "Do you trust me?"

"Yes," she said firmly. "I do."

He stood her on the floor, then stood beside her. Nicole's eyes widened at the bulge in his trousers. The room suddenly seemed very warm.

"Come on," he said hoarsely. "And stop looking at me like that."

He took her hand and led her out of the room.

Neither of them saw Bianca standing just inside the dining room door. She'd been outside when she saw Nicole running toward the house. She'd hurried after her, planning what she'd say to her about trespassing. Inside the house she'd heard Nicole running through it, slamming bedroom doors, acting as if she owned the place. Bianca had been in the morning room—Nicole moved too quickly for the larger woman to keep pace with her—when she saw Clay. She'd stood outside the door and listened while they talked.

She had been pleased to hear Gerard's wife was dead. They'd never spoken of the fact that he was already married, but Bianca knew the woman was old and couldn't live too much longer.

She'd frozen when Nicole said Bianca was planning to murder Clay. When she heard Clay say Bianca wasn't smart enough or courageous enough, she began to thaw. She changed from ice to fire in seconds. She knew now that she'd be able to carry out Gerard's plan. Clayton Armstrong deserved to die after what he'd said about her.

She left the house and went to find a child she could send with a message to Gerard. She knew there was little time left before Clay took steps to rid himself of her.

Nicole stood outside the mill and drank deeply from a gourd dipper. The cool, fresh well water was welcome after a hard morning inside. The autumn grains were fully ripe, and there wasn't a minute when they weren't busy.

At least, the work kept her mind off the plans she and Clay had. They'd buried Adele in Clay's family plot, next to his own mother. "So she'll always be near us," he said. Then, the two of them had gone to Bianca and discussed their futures. Clay said he was tired of secrets and wanted things in the open from now on. Bianca had been quiet, listening carefully to what Clay had to say. The offer he made her for lifetime support was very fair, and both Clay and Nicole knew it would place a great burden on both of them in future years. Clay sought Nicole's hand under the table. There was a strong sense of support between them now.

After the meeting, they hadn't spoken but had walked to the hidden clearing by the river. In spite of the fact that it had been well over a year since they'd made love, there was no urgency. They took their time, looking at each other, exploring, savoring. They were rediscovering each other.

There had been no long explanations, no rehashing of what idiots they'd been. There was no sense of something going to happen, only a deep joy that they were together again. They had felt as if they were one person, not two people who mistrusted, misjudged, and misunderstood each other.

"Nicole!"

Gerard's sharp voice brought Nicole out of her reverie and into the present. "Yes?"

"We've been looking everywhere for you. One of the twins fell up on the ridge. Janie wants you to come."

She threw the dipper down, lifted her skirts, and started running, with Gerard close behind her. The ridge was empty. "Where are they?"

Gerard stepped very close to her. "You'd do anything for them, wouldn't you? You give yourself to everyone except me."

Nicole stepped backward. "Where are the twins?"

"With the devil, for all I care. I wanted to get you up here alone. I want you to take a little journey with me."

"I have work to do. I—" She stopped when she saw the pistol in Gerard's hands.

"Now I have your attention. Or does any man who points something large and hard at you get that?"

Nicole curled her lip and cursed him in French.

Gerard smiled at her. "Quite colorful! Now, I want you to go with me—quietly."

"No."

"I thought perhaps you'd say that. Remember how you thought my dear wife overheard that Bianca was planning to murder Armstrong? For once in that crazy woman's life, she was right about something."

Nicole stared at him, her eyes wide, enormous. "You killed my mother," she whispered.

"Clever girl. Too clever. Now, if you ever wish to see your lover alive again, you will obey me." He waved the pistol. "Through there, and remember that his life depends on you."

Nicole walked through the woods, away from the mill, then down to the river where Gerard had a rowboat hidden. He delighted in the fact that Nicole had to row him across while he sat in the stern and gave her orders. He talked constantly of his cleverness, of how Nicole had enticed him and teased him since he arrived.

They landed at a far corner of the Armstrong plantation. There was a vacant tool shed there, half hidden under a tree, its door hanging off a broken hinge.

They had barely reached the door when Bianca came from the trees. "Where have you been? And what is she doing here?"

"Never mind that," Gerard snapped. "Did you do it?"

Her eyes, almost hidden by her grotesquely fat cheeks, were unnaturally bright. "He wouldn't go riding. He wouldn't do what he was supposed to. I fixed the saddle with the glass like you said, but he wouldn't go."

"What happened?" Gerard demanded.

Bianca had been holding her skirt together. Now she released it. There was a great deal of blood down the front. "I shot him," she said, as if she were surprised at the fact.

Nicole screamed and would have started running toward the house, but Gerard caught her by the arm. He hit her hard across the mouth, sending her sprawling inside the tool shed.

"Is he dead?" Gerard demanded.

"Oh, yes," Bianca said. She blinked at him, and her voice sounded strangely like a child's. She pulled her other hand from behind her skirt. "I brought the other pistol."

Gerard grabbed it from her hand, then pointed it at her. "Get in here."

Bianca frowned in puzzlement, then stepped inside the shed. "Why is Nicole here? Why is my maid here?" she asked simply.

"Bianca!" Nicole screamed. "Where is Clay?"

Bianca turned slowly and looked at Nicole as she stood pressed against the wall. "You!" she whispered. "You did this!" She half fell toward Nicole, her hands like claws.

Nicole was nearly suffocated when Bianca's great weight came crashing down on her.

"Get off her, you fat whore!" Gerard yelled. He

tossed one pistol onto the floor behind him, put the other into his belt, and began to pull Bianca off Nicole.

"I want to kill her!" Bianca sneered. "Let me kill her now!"

Gerard pulled his gun and pointed it at her. "It's you who'll be killed, not her," he said.

Bianca smiled. "You don't know what you're saying. It's me, remember? The woman you love."

"Love!" Gerard snorted. "What man could love you? I'd as soon mate with one of the sows!"

"Gerard!" Bianca pleaded. "You're upset."

"You stupid, vain pig! To think you believed that I, a Courtalain, could ever love such as you. You will be found dead, a suicide, grief-stricken over your husband's death, which was caused, no doubt, by robbers."

"No," Bianca whispered, her hands outstretched, palms upward.

"Oh, yes," he smiled, obviously enjoying himself. "The Armstrong estate will be left to those obnoxious twins, and since there are no other relatives, Nicole will be their guardian and I will be her husband."

"Hers!" Bianca gasped. "You said you hated her."

He laughed. "It was a game, remember? You and I played a game, and I won."

Nicole was beginning to think again. Maybe she could divert Gerard's attention until someone found them. "No one would believe Bianca would kill herself over Clay. It's common knowledge that she hates him."

Bianca turned to Nicole with a look of hate. Then their one and only look of understanding passed between them. "Yes, the field hands and the house servants know that we rarely even see each other."

"But, lately, people have been saying you're reconciled, that Armstrong's stopped drinking and become the perfect husband," Gerard said.

Bianca looked bewildered.

"Bianca is an English lady," Nicole said. "In England, she's one of the peerage, and there is no peerage in France anymore. She would make an admirable wife."

"She is nothing!" Gerard said. "Nothing! Everyone knows royalty will be reinstated in France. Then, I shall be married to a duke's granddaughter. The magnificent Courtalains will live again through me!"

"But—" Nicole began.

"Enough!" Gerard screamed. "You think I'm stupid, do you not? Do you think I can't see through your schemes to keep me talking?" He waved the gun toward Bianca. "I would not have her if she were the queen of England herself. She is fat, ugly, and unbelievably stupid."

Bianca flew at him, her hands going for his face. Gerard struggled for a moment under her suffocating weight.

The pistol went off, and slowly Bianca moved away from him, her hands clutching her stomach, blood beginning to seep through her fingers.

Nicole's eyes had long been on the pistol Gerard had carelessly tossed to the floor, but now Gerard and Bianca struggled between her and it. She looked around the empty shed until she saw a loose board in the wall. With superhuman strength, she wrenched it free.

Moments after the pistol went off, Nicole hit Gerard with the board. He staggered as Bianca crumbled to the floor.

"You have hurt me," he whispered in French, his fingers touching the blood at his temple. "You will pay for that with every moment of your life."

He advanced toward her as she backed against the wall.

Bianca, her blood quickly flowing from her, looked through hazy vision to see Gerard advancing on her enemy. A pistol lay at her fingertips. She used the last of her strength to raise it, aim it, and pull the trigger. She died before she saw that her aim had been true.

Nicole stood absolutely still as Gerard suddenly jerked still. He seemed to react before she heard the shot. His eyes showed surprise, puzzlement at what had happened to him. Then, very slowly, he fell to the floor, dead, his eyes still showing his wonder.

Nicole stepped away from him. Both of them lay on the floor. Gerard's outstretched hand had fallen across Bianca's, and as Nicole watched, some death reflex made Bianca's hand tighten on Gerard's. In death, she held him as she never could have in life.

Nicole turned and ran from the shed. She ran the distance to the house. She must find Clay!

There was blood on the library floor but no sign of him. Nicole knew her heart had stopped beating long ago.

Suddenly, she stopped and sat on the couch, her face buried in her hands. She needed time to think and calm herself if she was to find him. Someone could have found Clay and taken him away. No, if that were the case, the house would be alive with activity.

Where would he go?

She stood up, because she knew where he'd go—to the clearing.

There were tears in her eyes as she ran the mile or more to the cave. Her lungs hurt and her heart pounded, but she knew she wouldn't stop.

She was no sooner through the secret gate than she saw him. He looked almost comfortable, lying beside the water, one arm outstretched.

"Clay," she whispered, kneeling beside him.

He opened his eyes and smiled at her. "I was wrong about Bianca. She was courageous enough to try to kill me."

"Let me see," she said as she pulled his bloody shirt

away from his shoulder. It was a clean wound, but he was weak from loss of blood. She was giddy with relief. "You should have stayed at the house," she said as she tore a strip off her chemise and began to bind his wound.

He watched her. "How did you know?"

"We've time for that later," she said brusquely. "You need a doctor right now." She started to stand, but he caught her arm.

"Tell me!"

"Bianca and Gerard are dead."

He stared at her for a long moment. There would be time later for details. "Go to the cave and get the unicorn."

"Clay, there isn't time—"

"Go!"

Reluctantly, she went to the cave and brought back the little silver unicorn sealed in glass. Clay set it on the ground and then smashed the glass with a rock.

"Clay!" she protested.

He leaned back on the grass, with the unicorn free at last. "You once said I thought you weren't worthy to touch what Beth had touched. What you didn't understand was it was I who was unclean." He lifted himself on one elbow—he had little strength after smashing the glass—and dropped the unicorn down the front of her dress. He gave her a lopsided grin. "I'll retrieve it later."

She smiled, tears rolling down her cheeks. "I must get a doctor."

He caught her skirt. "You'll return to me?"

"Always." She shifted the bodice of her dress. "There's a little silver horn poking me, and someone must remove it."

He smiled, his eyes closed. "I volunteer."

She turned away toward the gate.